TEEN TITANS GO!™

TO THE PIZZA DOME

Sholly Fisch Merrill Hagan Amy Wolfram
Writers

Ben Bates Jorge Corona
Lea Hernandez Dario Brizuela Jeremy Lawson
Artists

Jeremy Lawson Ben Bates Lea Hernandez
Colorists

Wes Abbott
Letterer

Dan Hipp
Series and Collection Cover Artist

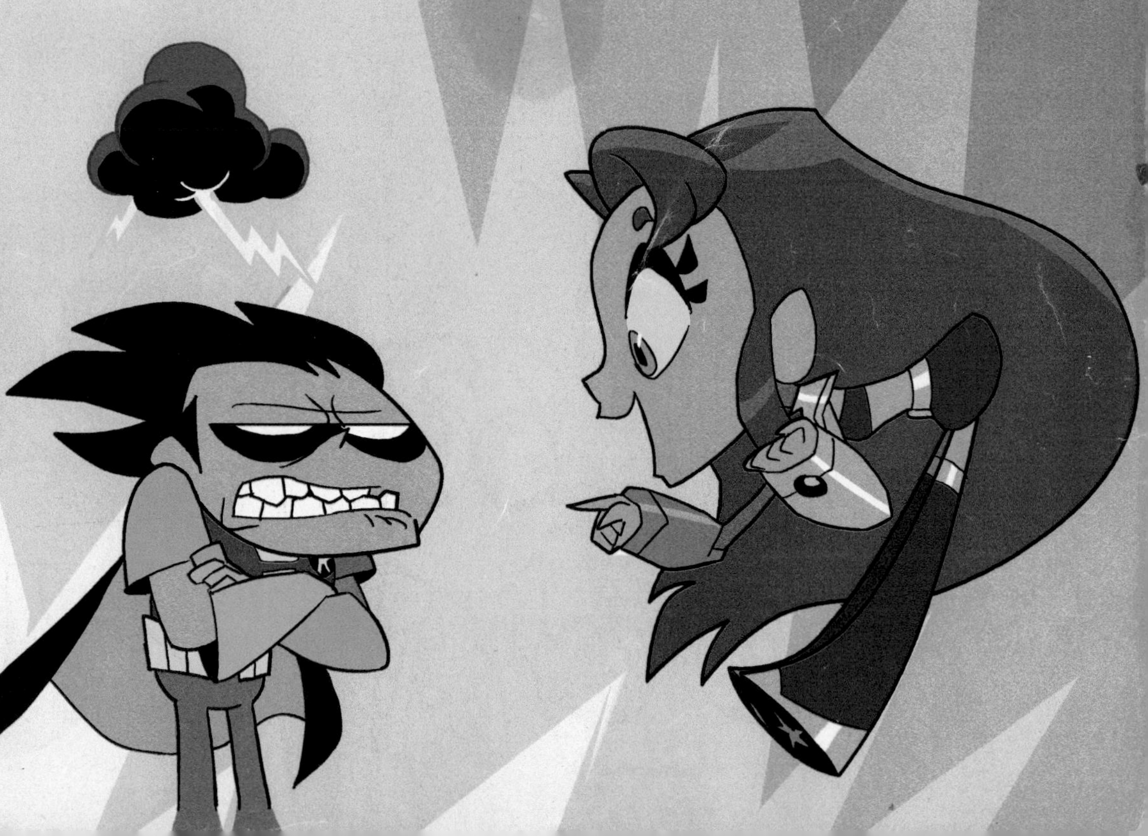

BRITTANY HOLZHERR Assistant Editor – Original Series   ALEX ANTONE Editor – Original Series
JEB WOODARD Group Editor – Collected Editions   LIZ ERICKSON Editor – Collected Edition
STEVE COOK Design Director – Books   SARABETH KETT Publication Design

BOB HARRAS Senior VP – Editor-in-Chief, DC Comics

DIANE NELSON President   DAN DIDIO and JIM LEE Co-Publishers   GEOFF JOHNS Chief Creative Officer
AMIT DESAI Senior VP – Marketing & Global Franchise Management   NAIRI GARDINER Senior VP – Finance
SAM ADES VP – Digital Marketing   BOBBIE CHASE VP – Talent Development
MARK CHIARELLO Senior VP – Art, Design & Collected Editions   JOHN CUNNINGHAM VP – Content Strategy
ANNE DEPIES VP – Strategy Planning & Reporting   DON FALLETTI VP – Manufacturing Operations
LAWRENCE GANEM VP – Editorial Administration & Talent Relations   ALISON GILL Senior VP – Manufacturing & Operations
HANK KANALZ Senior VP – Editorial Strategy & Administration   JAY KOGAN VP – Legal Affairs
DEREK MADDALENA Senior VP – Sales & Business Development   JACK MAHAN VP – Business Affairs
DAN MIRON VP – Sales Planning & Trade Development   NICK NAPOLITANO VP – Manufacturing Administration
CAROL ROEDER VP – Marketing   EDDIE SCANNELL VP – Mass Account & Digital Sales
COURTNEY SIMMONS Senior VP – Publicity & Communications
JIM (SKI) SOKOLOWSKI VP – Comic Book Specialty & Newsstand Sales
SANDY YI Senior VP – Global Franchise Management

TEEN TITANS GO! VOLUME 2: WELCOME TO THE PIZZA DOME

Published by DC Comics. Compilation and all new material Copyright © 2016 DC Comics. All Rights Reserved. Originally
published in single magazine form in TEEN TITANS GO! 7-12 and online as TEEN TITANS GO! Digital Chapters 13-24. Copyright
© 2014, 2015 DC Comics. All Rights Reserved. All characters, their distinctive likenesses and related elements featured in this
publication are trademarks of DC Comics. The stories, characters and incidents featured in this publication are entirely fictional.
DC Comics does not read or accept unsolicited submissions of ideas, stories or artwork.

DC Comics, 2900 West Alameda Ave., Burbank, CA 91505
Printed by RR Donnelley, Owensville, MO, USA. 6/10/16. First Printing.
ISBN: 978-1-4012-6730-8

Library of Congress Cataloging-in-Publication Data is available.

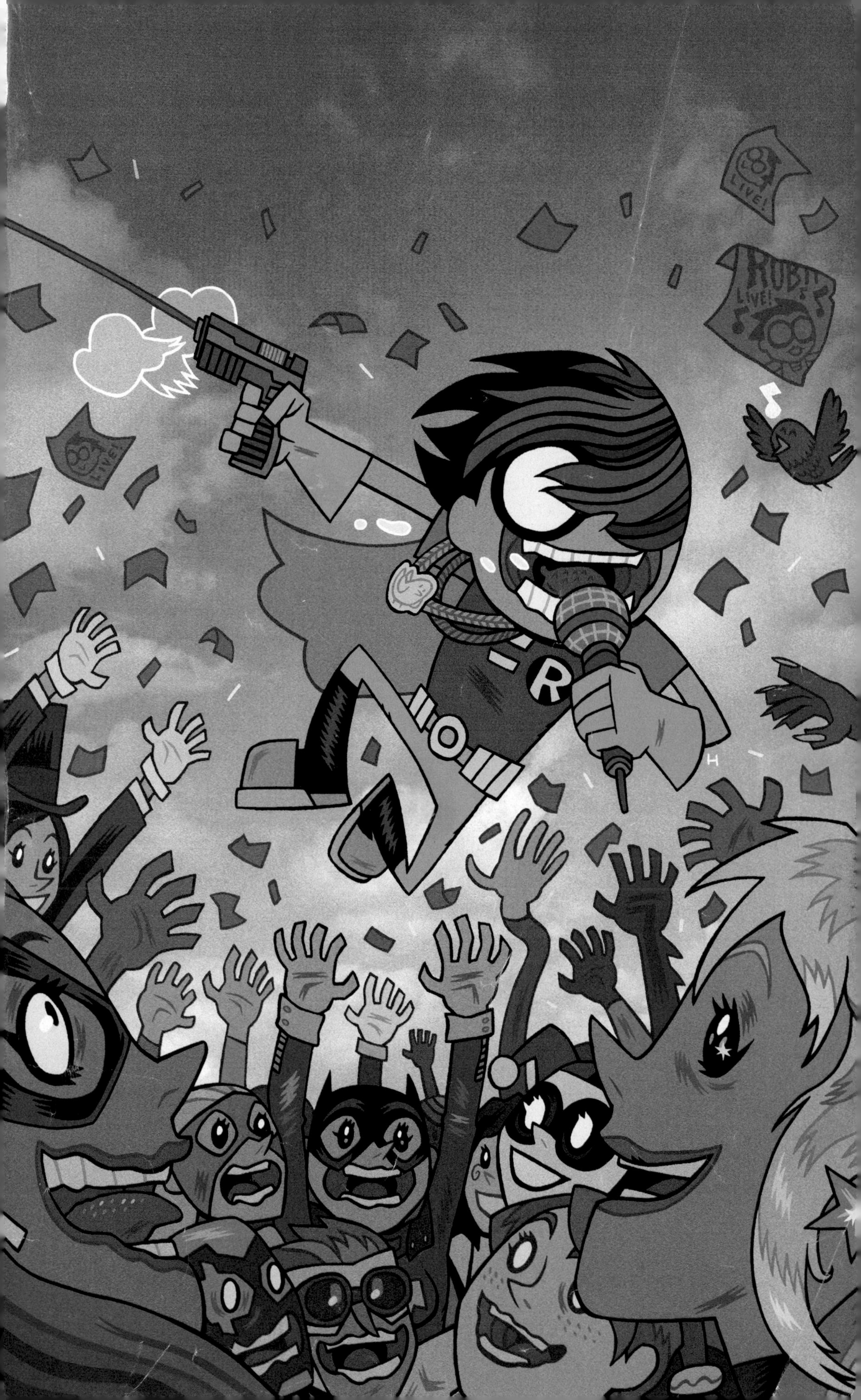
LIVE!
LIVE!
LIVE!

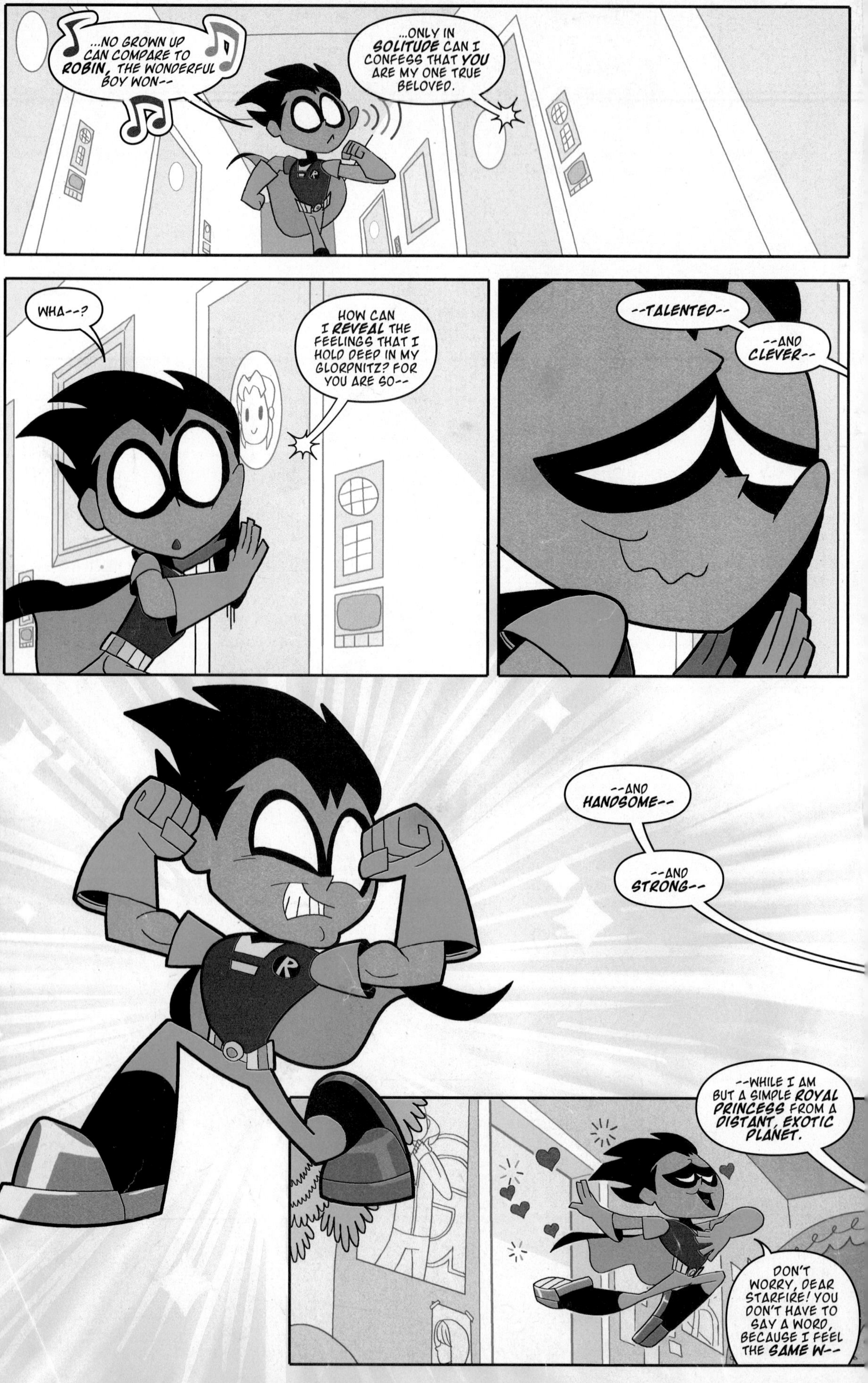
...NO GROWN UP CAN COMPARE TO ROBIN, THE WONDERFUL BOY WON--
...ONLY IN SOLITUDE CAN I CONFESS THAT YOU ARE MY ONE TRUE BELOVED.
WHA--?
HOW CAN I REVEAL THE FEELINGS THAT I HOLD DEEP IN MY GLORPNITZ? FOR YOU ARE SO--
--TALENTED--
--AND CLEVER--
--AND HANDSOME--
--AND STRONG--
--WHILE I AM BUT A SIMPLE ROYAL PRINCESS FROM A DISTANT, EXOTIC PLANET.
DON'T WORRY, DEAR STARFIRE! YOU DON'T HAVE TO SAY A WORD, BECAUSE I FEEL THE SAME W--

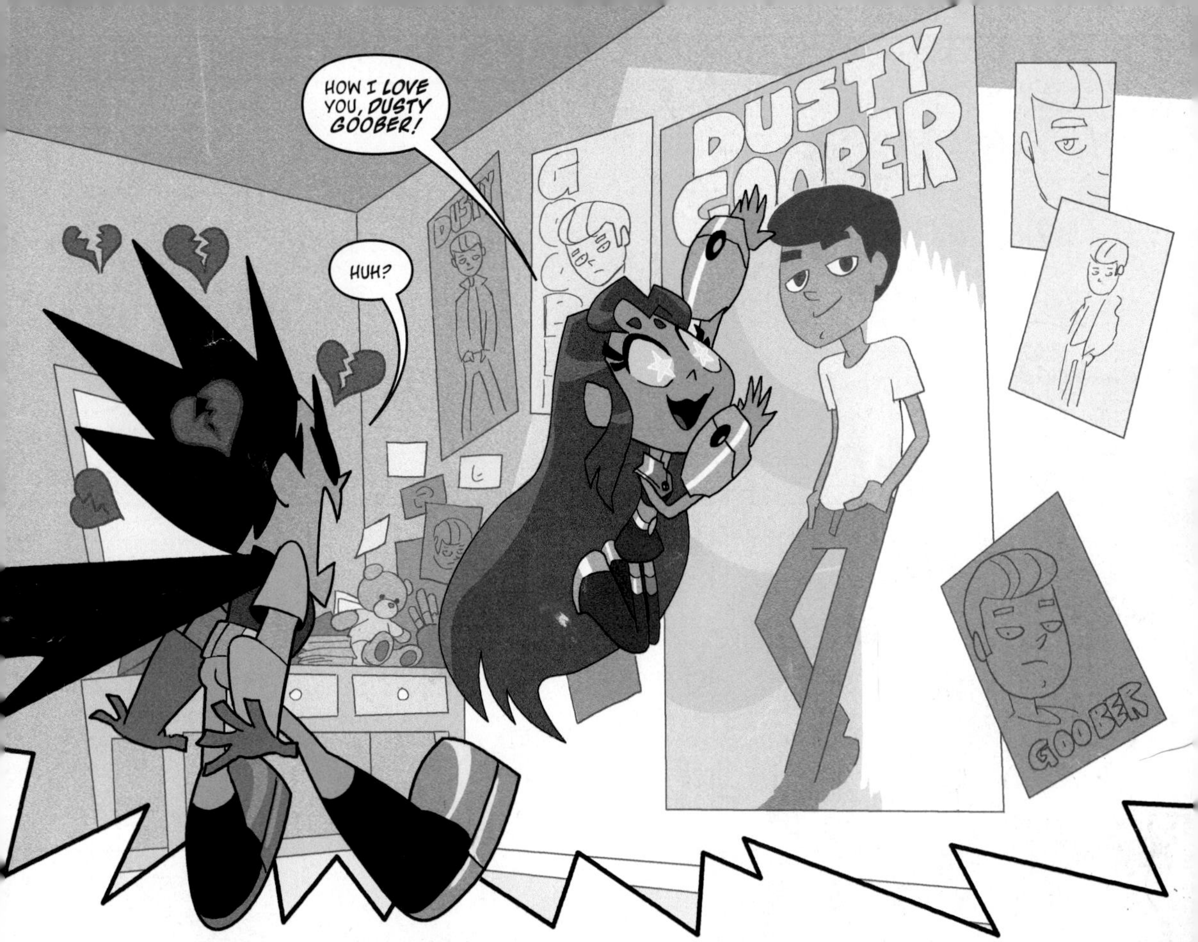
HOW I LOVE YOU, DUSTY GOOBER!
HUH?
DUSTY GOOBER
DUSTY
GOOBER

"STARSTRUCK"

WRITTEN BY SHOLLY FISCH
ART BY BEN BATES
LETTERS BY WES ABBOTT

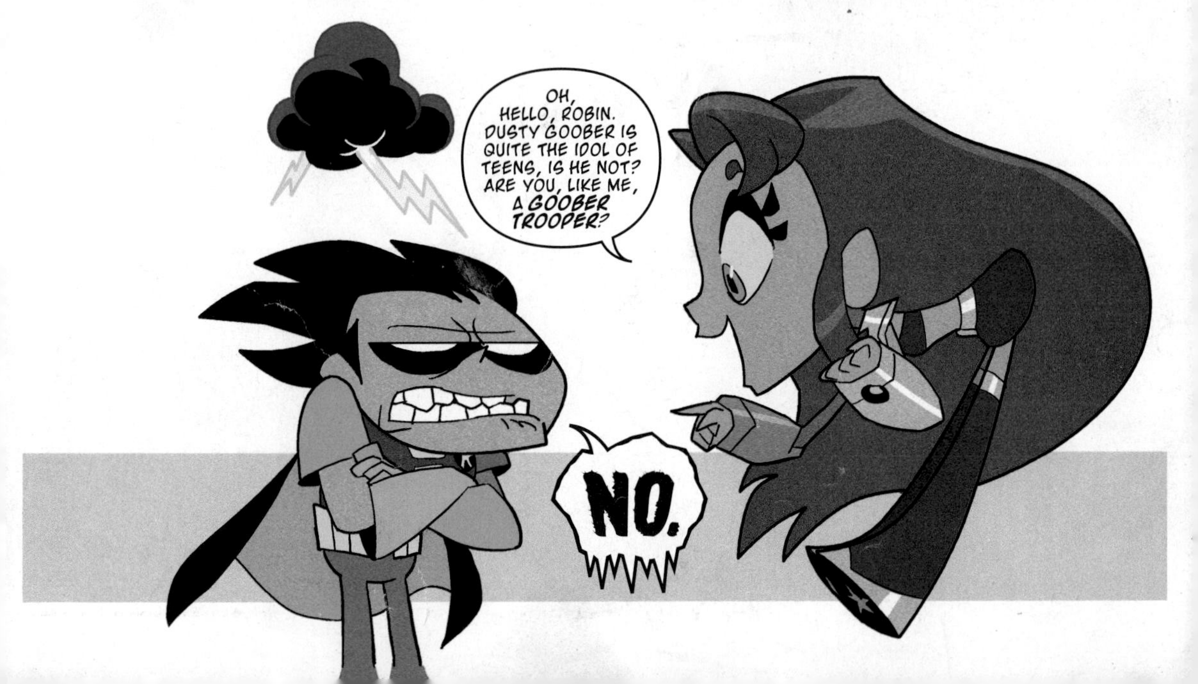
OH, HELLO, ROBIN. DUSTY GOOBER IS QUITE THE IDOL OF TEENS, IS HE NOT? ARE YOU, LIKE ME, A GOOBER TROOPER?
NO.

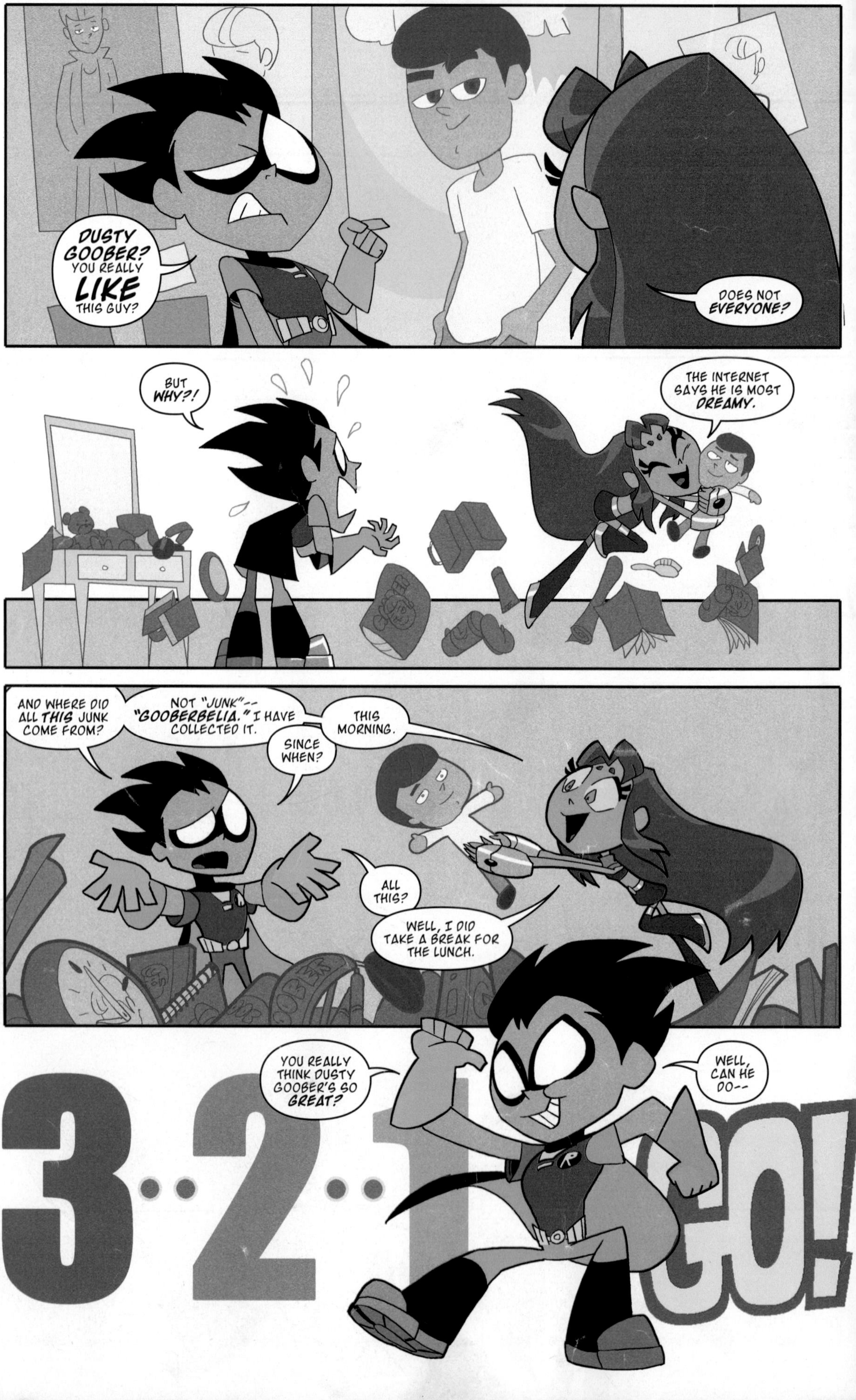
DUSTY GOOBER? YOU REALLY LIKE THIS GUY?
DOES NOT EVERYONE?
BUT WHY?!
THE INTERNET SAYS HE IS MOST DREAMY.
AND WHERE DID ALL THIS JUNK COME FROM?
NOT "JUNK"-- "GOOBERBELIA." I HAVE COLLECTED IT.
SINCE WHEN?
THIS MORNING.
ALL THIS?
WELL, I DID TAKE A BREAK FOR THE LUNCH.
YOU REALLY THINK DUSTY GOOBER'S SO GREAT?
WELL, CAN HE DO--
3..2..1 GO!

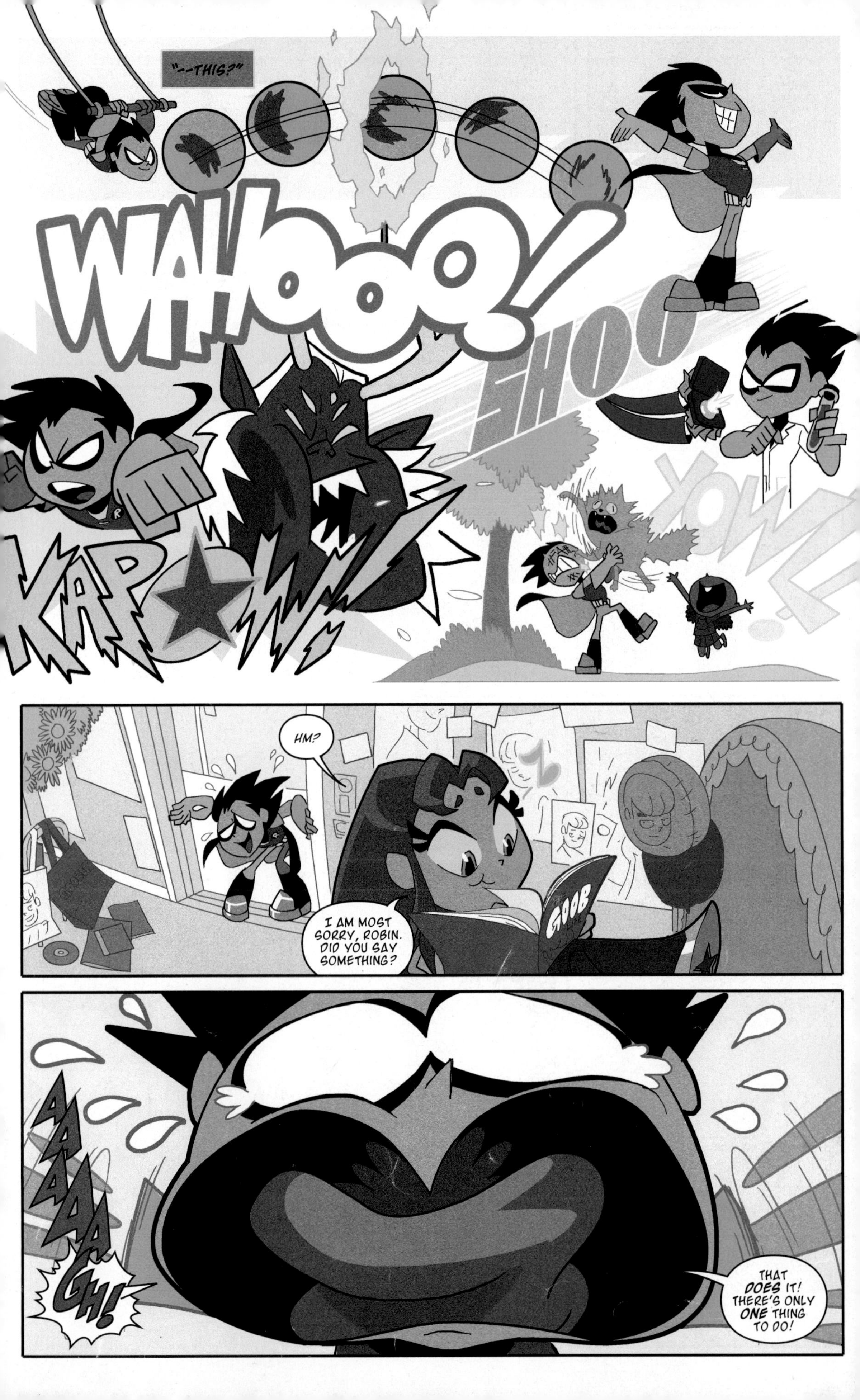
"--THIS?"
WAHOOO!
SHOO
KAPOW!
YOWL!
HM?
I AM MOST SORRY, ROBIN. DID YOU SAY SOMETHING?
GOOB
AAAAAGH!
THAT DOES IT! THERE'S ONLY ONE THING TO DO!

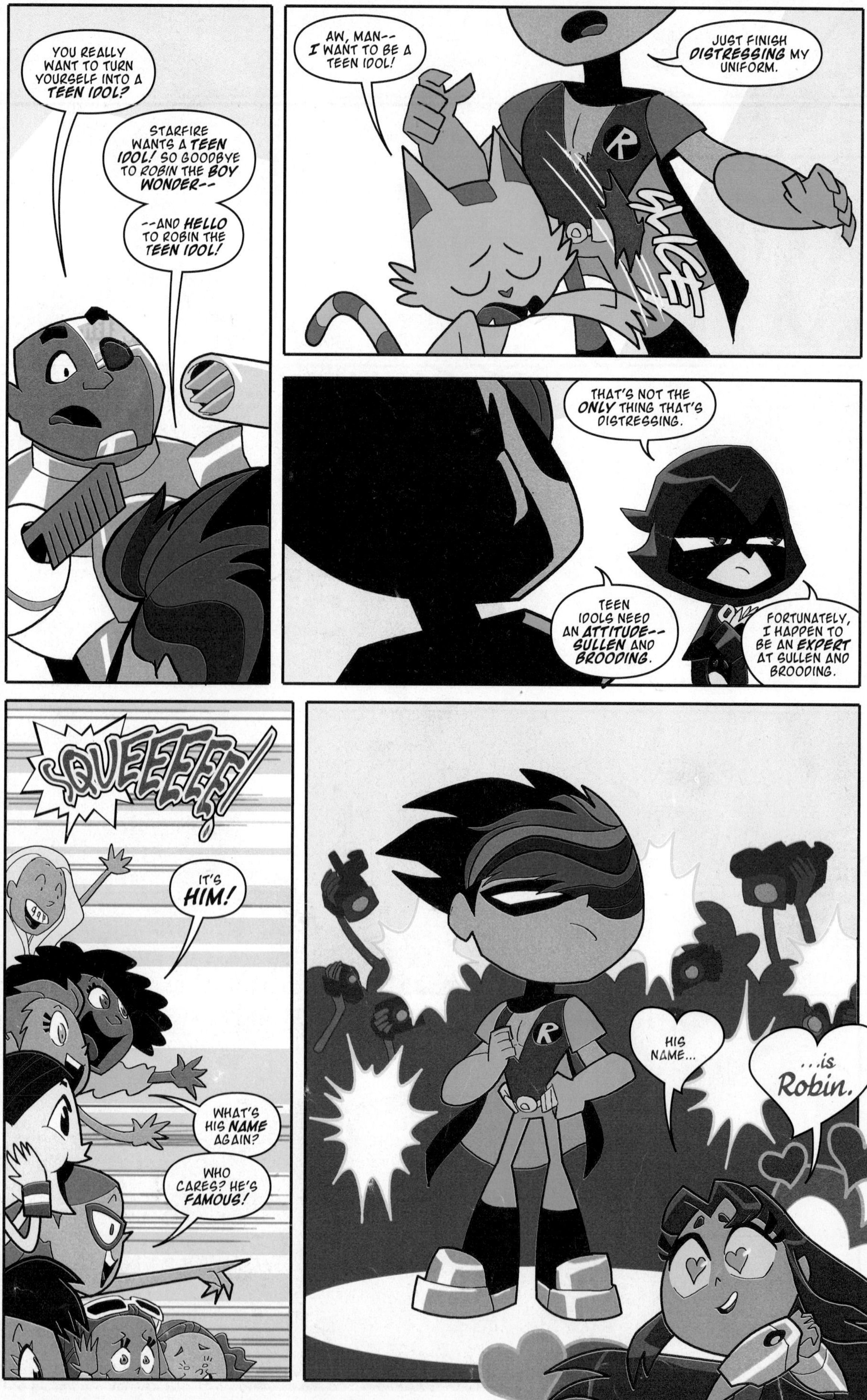
YOU REALLY WANT TO TURN YOURSELF INTO A TEEN IDOL?
STARFIRE WANTS A TEEN IDOL! SO GOODBYE TO ROBIN THE BOY WONDER--
--AND HELLO TO ROBIN THE TEEN IDOL!
AW, MAN-- I WANT TO BE A TEEN IDOL!
JUST FINISH DISTRESSING MY UNIFORM.
SLICE
THAT'S NOT THE ONLY THING THAT'S DISTRESSING.
TEEN IDOLS NEED AN ATTITUDE-- SULLEN AND BROODING.
FORTUNATELY, I HAPPEN TO BE AN EXPERT AT SULLEN AND BROODING.
SQUEEEEE!
IT'S HIM!
WHAT'S HIS NAME AGAIN?
WHO CARES? HE'S FAMOUS!
HIS NAME...
...is Robin.

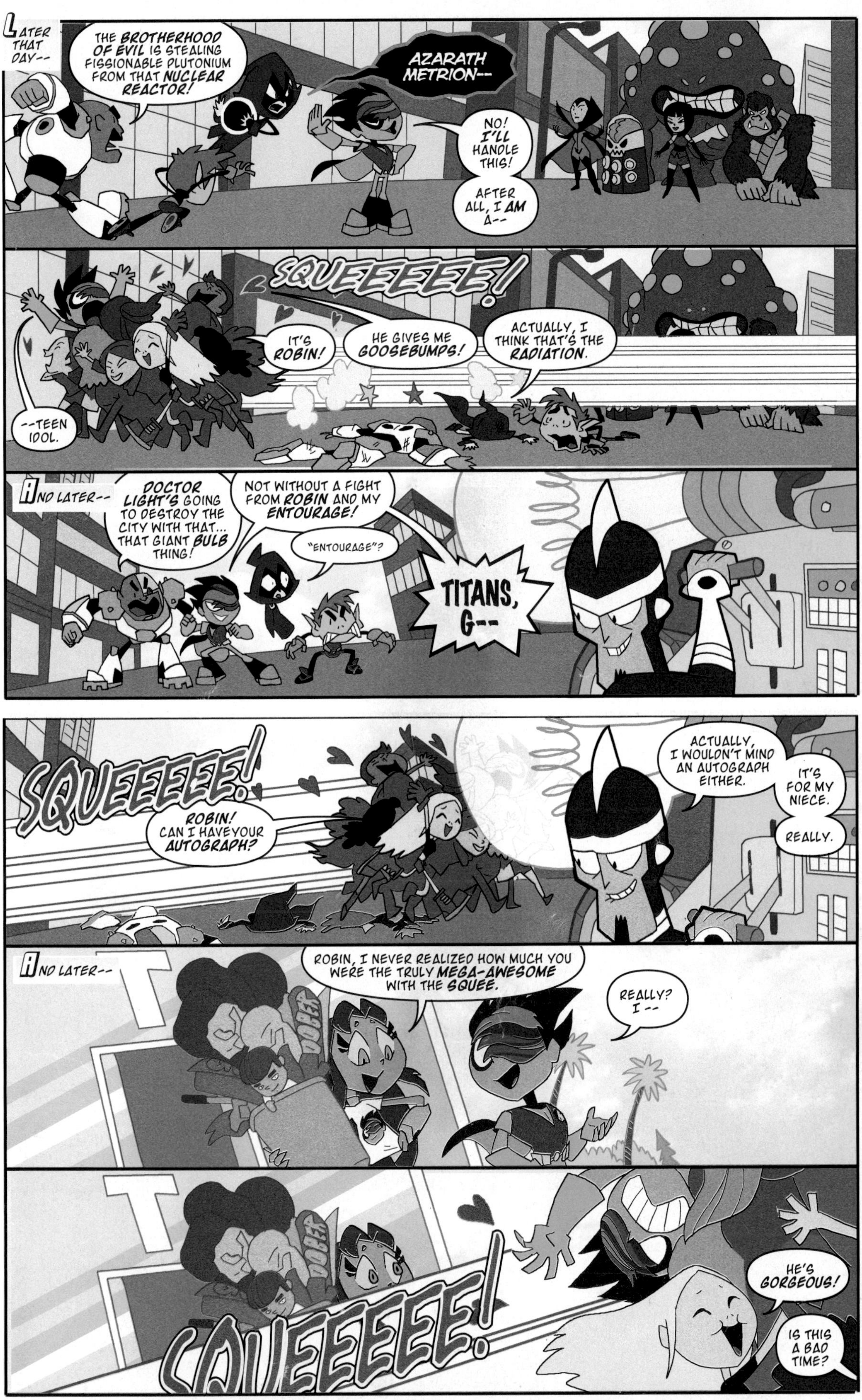

LATER THAT DAY--
THE BROTHERHOOD OF EVIL IS STEALING FISSIONABLE PLUTONIUM FROM THAT NUCLEAR REACTOR!
AZARATH METRION--
NO! I'LL HANDLE THIS!
AFTER ALL, I AM A--
--TEEN IDOL.
SQUEEEEEE!
IT'S ROBIN!
HE GIVES ME GOOSEBUMPS!
ACTUALLY, I THINK THAT'S THE RADIATION.
AND LATER--
DOCTOR LIGHT'S GOING TO DESTROY THE CITY WITH THAT... THAT GIANT BULB THING!
NOT WITHOUT A FIGHT FROM ROBIN AND MY ENTOURAGE!
"ENTOURAGE"?
TITANS, G--
SQUEEEEEE!
ROBIN! CAN I HAVEYOUR AUTOGRAPH?
ACTUALLY, I WOULDN'T MIND AN AUTOGRAPH EITHER.
IT'S FOR MY NIECE.
REALLY.
AND LATER--
ROBIN, I NEVER REALIZED HOW MUCH YOU WERE THE TRULY MEGA-AWESOME WITH THE SQUEE.
REALLY? I --
SQUEEEEEE!
HE'S GORGEOUS!
IS THIS A BAD TIME?

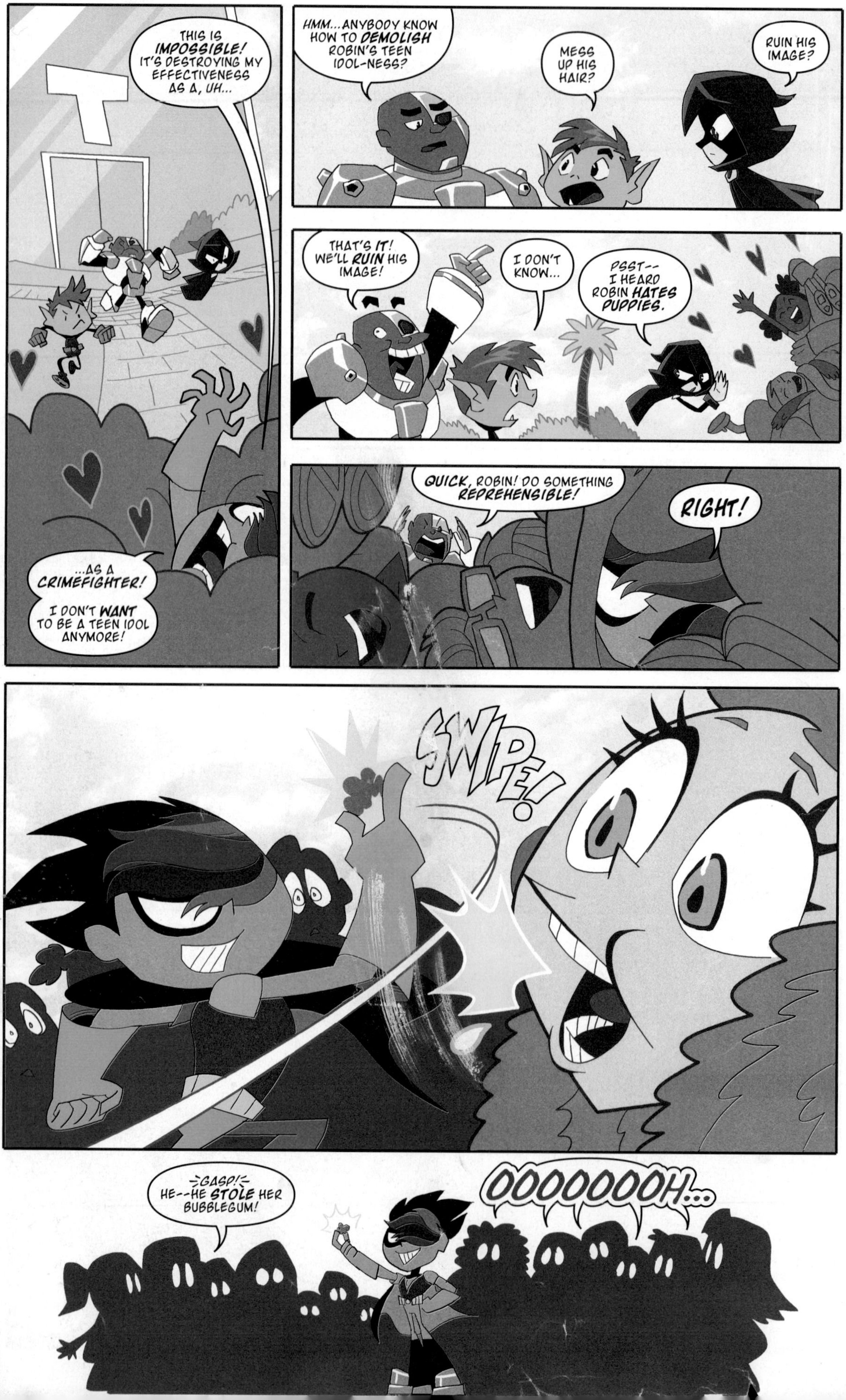

THIS IS IMPOSSIBLE! IT'S DESTROYING MY EFFECTIVENESS AS A, UH...
...AS A CRIMEFIGHTER!
I DON'T WANT TO BE A TEEN IDOL ANYMORE!
HMM... ANYBODY KNOW HOW TO DEMOLISH ROBIN'S TEEN IDOL-NESS?
MESS UP HIS HAIR?
RUIN HIS IMAGE?
THAT'S IT! WE'LL RUIN HIS IMAGE!
I DON'T KNOW...
PSST-- I HEARD ROBIN HATES PUPPIES.
QUICK, ROBIN! DO SOMETHING REPREHENSIBLE!
RIGHT!
SWIPE!
=GASP!= HE--HE STOLE HER BUBBLEGUM!
OOOOOOOOH...

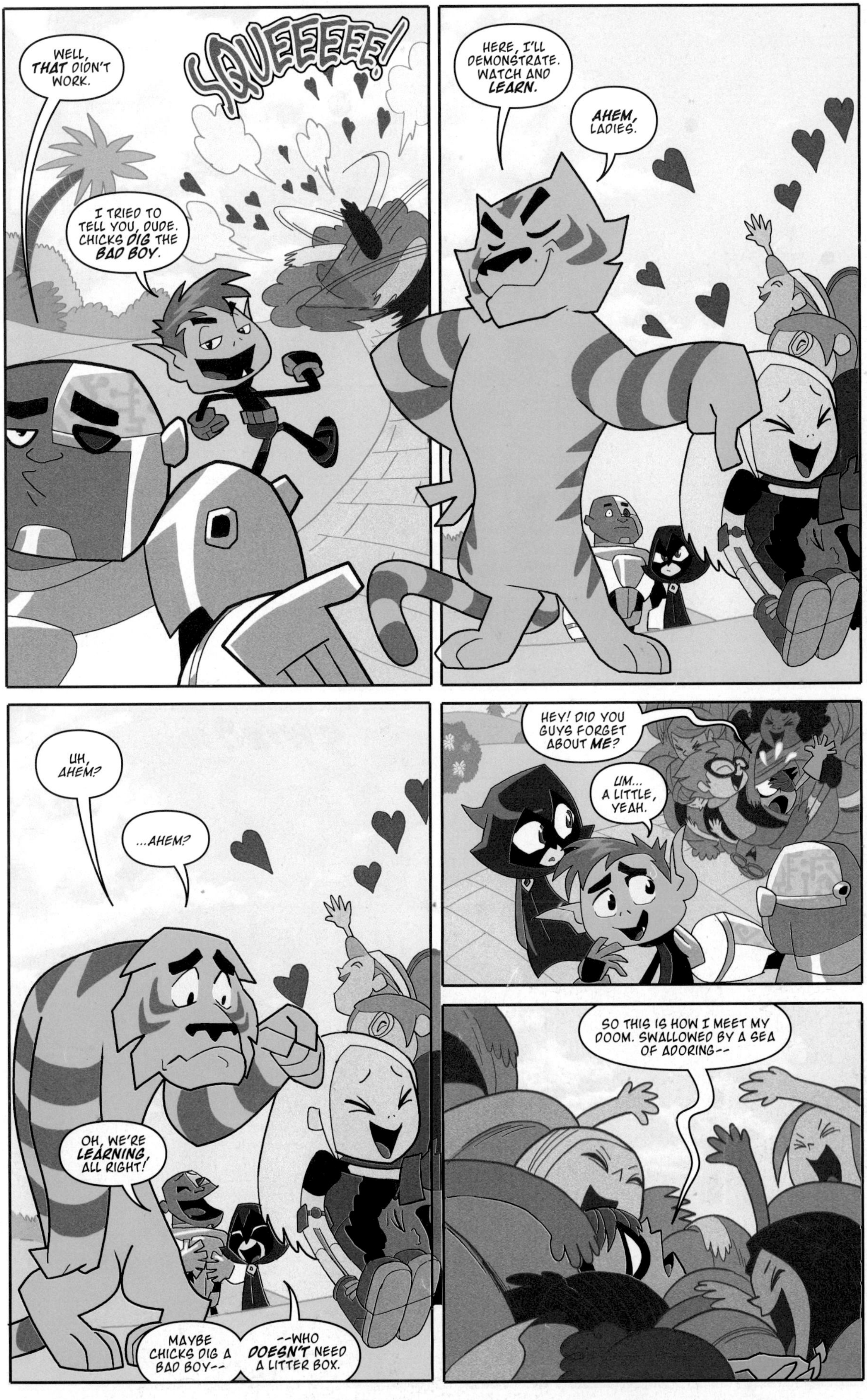
WELL, THAT DIDN'T WORK.
SQUEEEEEE!
I TRIED TO TELL YOU, DUDE. CHICKS DIG THE BAD BOY.
HERE, I'LL DEMONSTRATE. WATCH AND LEARN.
AHEM, LADIES.
UH, AHEM?
...AHEM?
OH, WE'RE LEARNING, ALL RIGHT!
MAYBE CHICKS DIG A BAD BOY--
--WHO DOESN'T NEED A LITTER BOX.
HEY! DID YOU GUYS FORGET ABOUT ME?
UM... A LITTLE, YEAH.
SO THIS IS HOW I MEET MY DOOM. SWALLOWED BY A SEA OF ADORING--

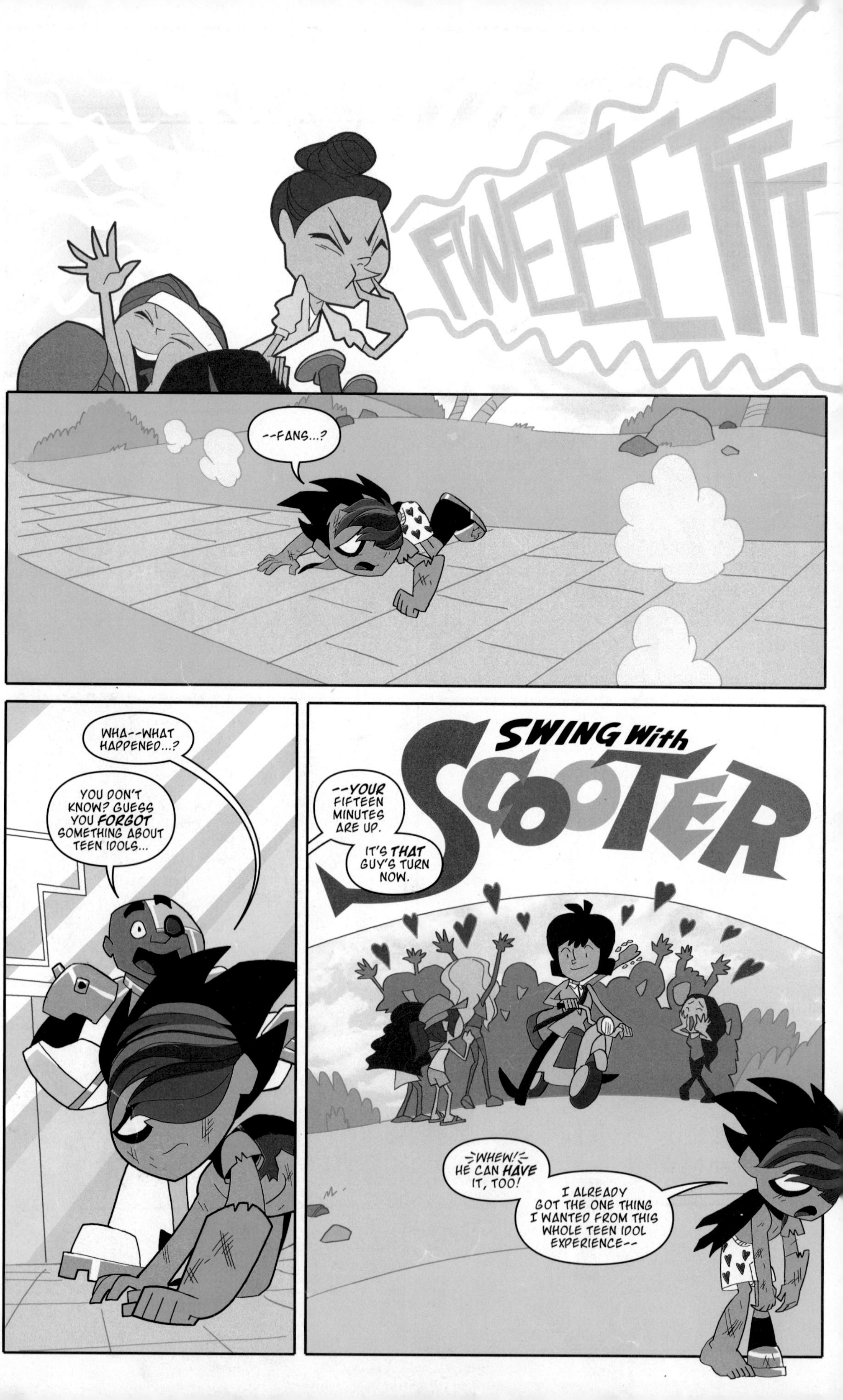
FWEEEETTT
--FANS...?
WHA--WHAT HAPPENED...?
YOU DON'T KNOW? GUESS YOU FORGOT SOMETHING ABOUT TEEN IDOLS...
SWING With SCOOTER
--YOUR FIFTEEN MINUTES ARE UP.
IT'S THAT GUY'S TURN NOW.
WHEW! HE CAN HAVE IT, TOO!
I ALREADY GOT THE ONE THING I WANTED FROM THIS WHOLE TEEN IDOL EXPERIENCE--

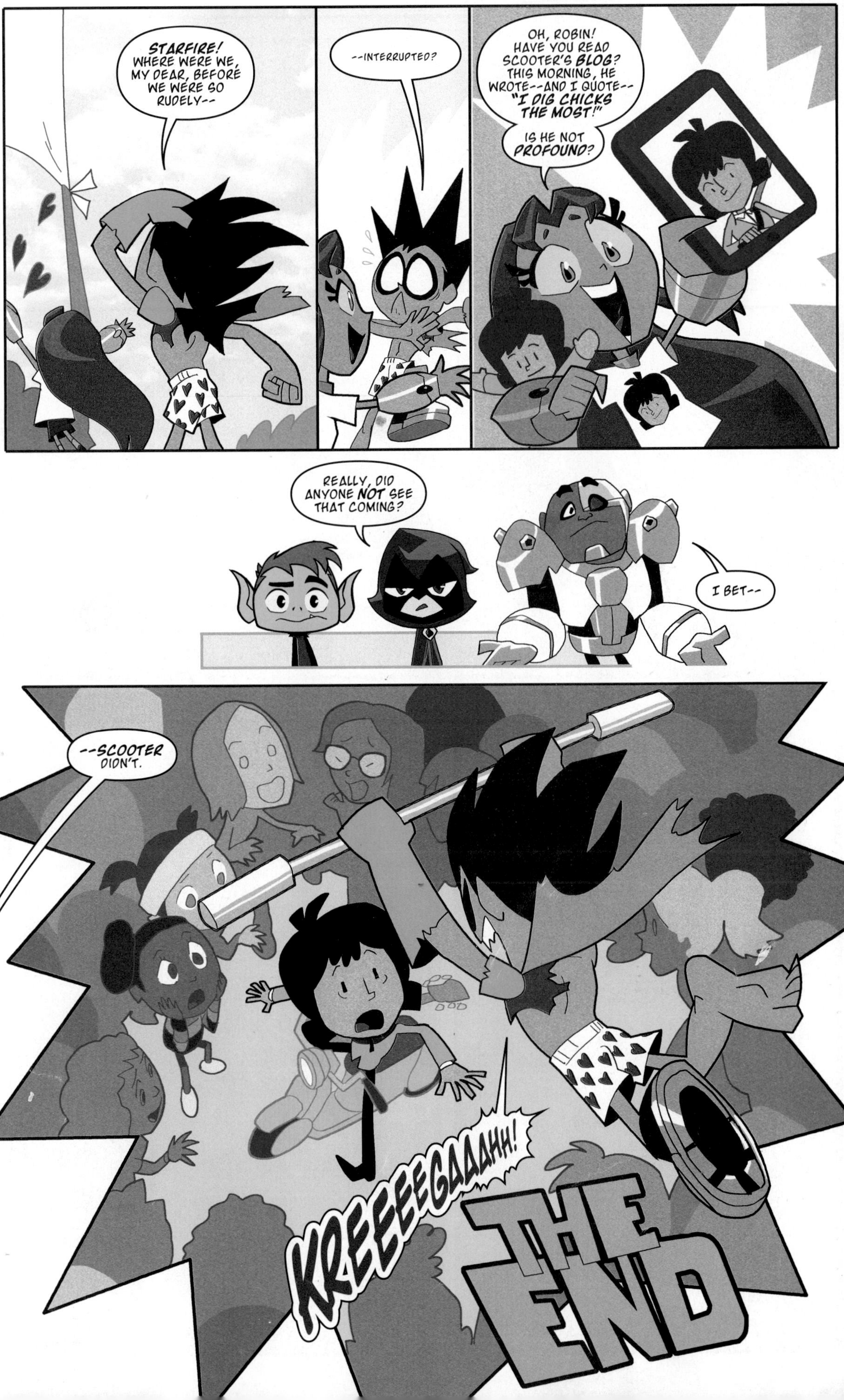
STARFIRE! WHERE WERE WE, MY DEAR, BEFORE WE WERE SO RUDELY--
--INTERRUPTED?
OH, ROBIN! HAVE YOU READ SCOOTER'S BLOG? THIS MORNING, HE WROTE--AND I QUOTE--"I DIG CHICKS THE MOST!"
IS HE NOT PROFOUND?
REALLY, DID ANYONE NOT SEE THAT COMING?
I BET--
--SCOOTER DIDN'T.
KREEEEEGAAAHH!
THE END

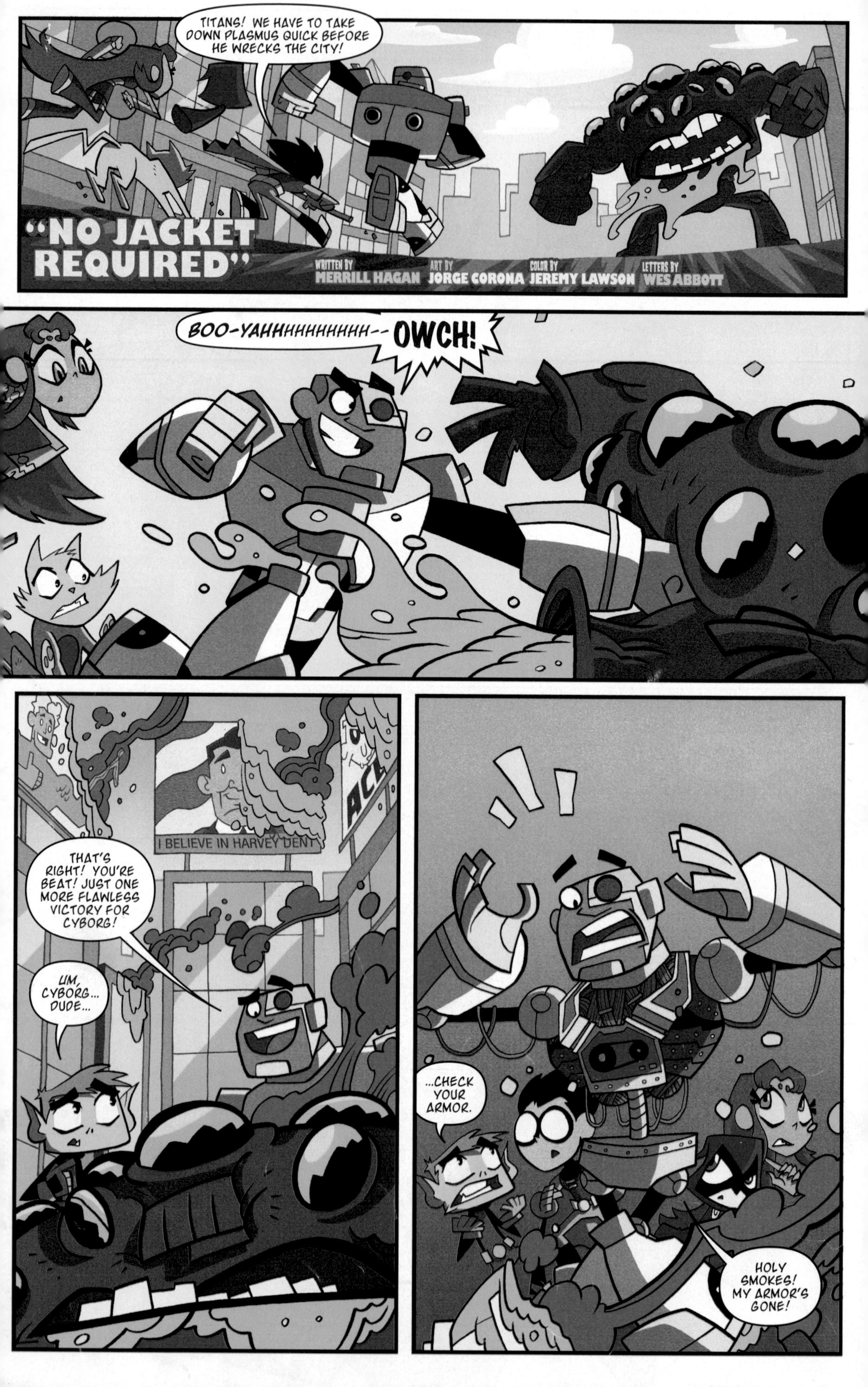
TITANS! WE HAVE TO TAKE DOWN PLASMUS QUICK BEFORE HE WRECKS THE CITY!
"NO JACKET REQUIRED"
WRITTEN BY MERRILL HAGAN
ART BY JORGE CORONA
COLOR BY JEREMY LAWSON
LETTERS BY WES ABBOTT
BOO-YAHHHHHHHHHH-- OWCH!
I BELIEVE IN HARVEY DENT
THAT'S RIGHT! YOU'RE BEAT! JUST ONE MORE FLAWLESS VICTORY FOR CYBORG!
UM, CYBORG... DUDE...
...CHECK YOUR ARMOR.
HOLY SMOKES! MY ARMOR'S GONE!

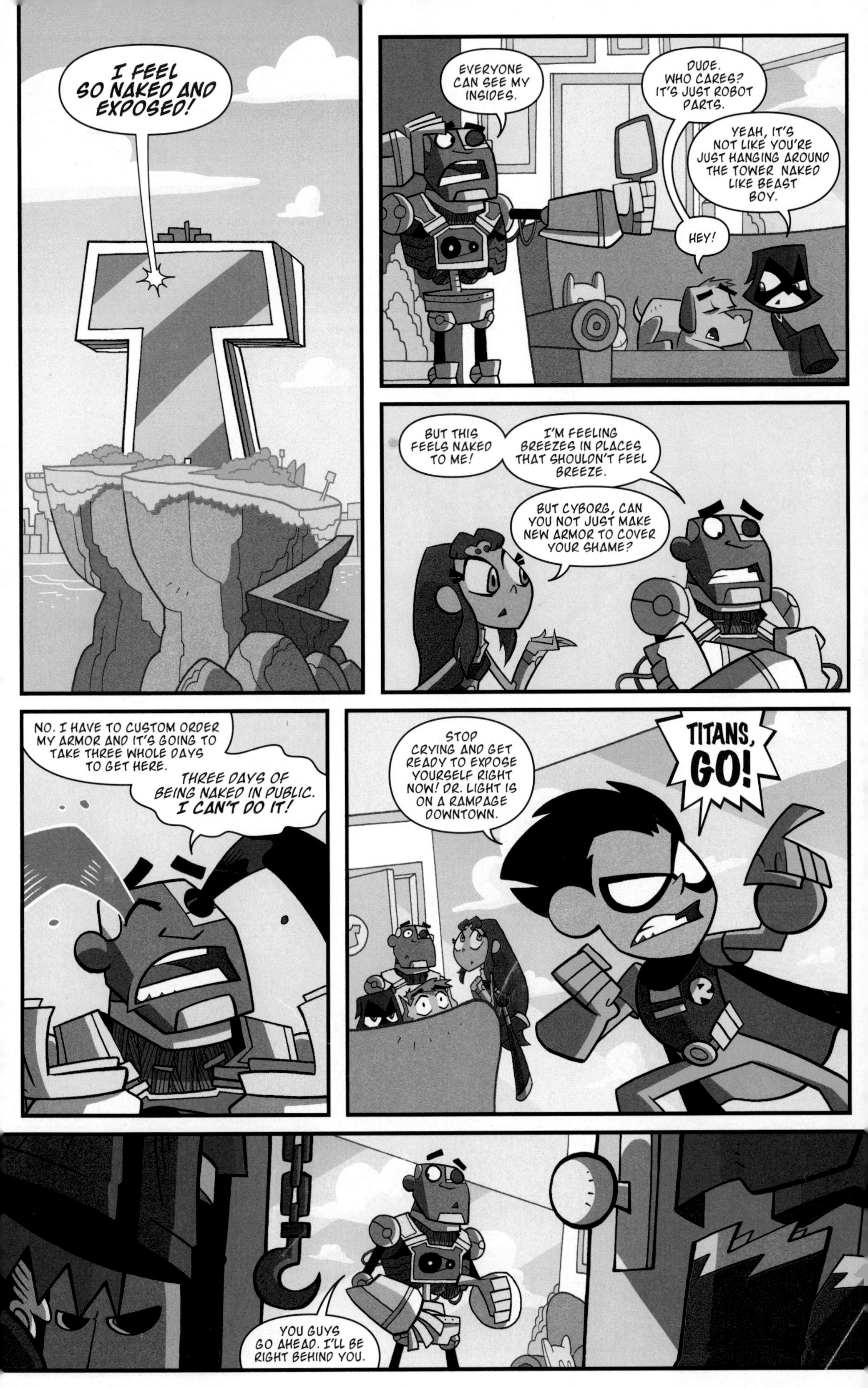
I FEEL SO NAKED AND EXPOSED!
EVERYONE CAN SEE MY INSIDES.
DUDE. WHO CARES? IT'S JUST ROBOT PARTS.
YEAH, IT'S NOT LIKE YOU'RE JUST HANGING AROUND THE TOWER NAKED LIKE BEAST BOY.
HEY!
BUT THIS FEELS NAKED TO ME!
I'M FEELING BREEZES IN PLACES THAT SHOULDN'T FEEL BREEZE.
BUT CYBORG, CAN YOU NOT JUST MAKE NEW ARMOR TO COVER YOUR SHAME?
NO. I HAVE TO CUSTOM ORDER MY ARMOR AND IT'S GOING TO TAKE THREE WHOLE DAYS TO GET HERE.
THREE DAYS OF BEING NAKED IN PUBLIC. I CAN'T DO IT!
STOP CRYING AND GET READY TO EXPOSE YOURSELF RIGHT NOW! DR. LIGHT IS ON A RAMPAGE DOWNTOWN.
TITANS, GO!
YOU GUYS GO AHEAD. I'LL BE RIGHT BEHIND YOU.

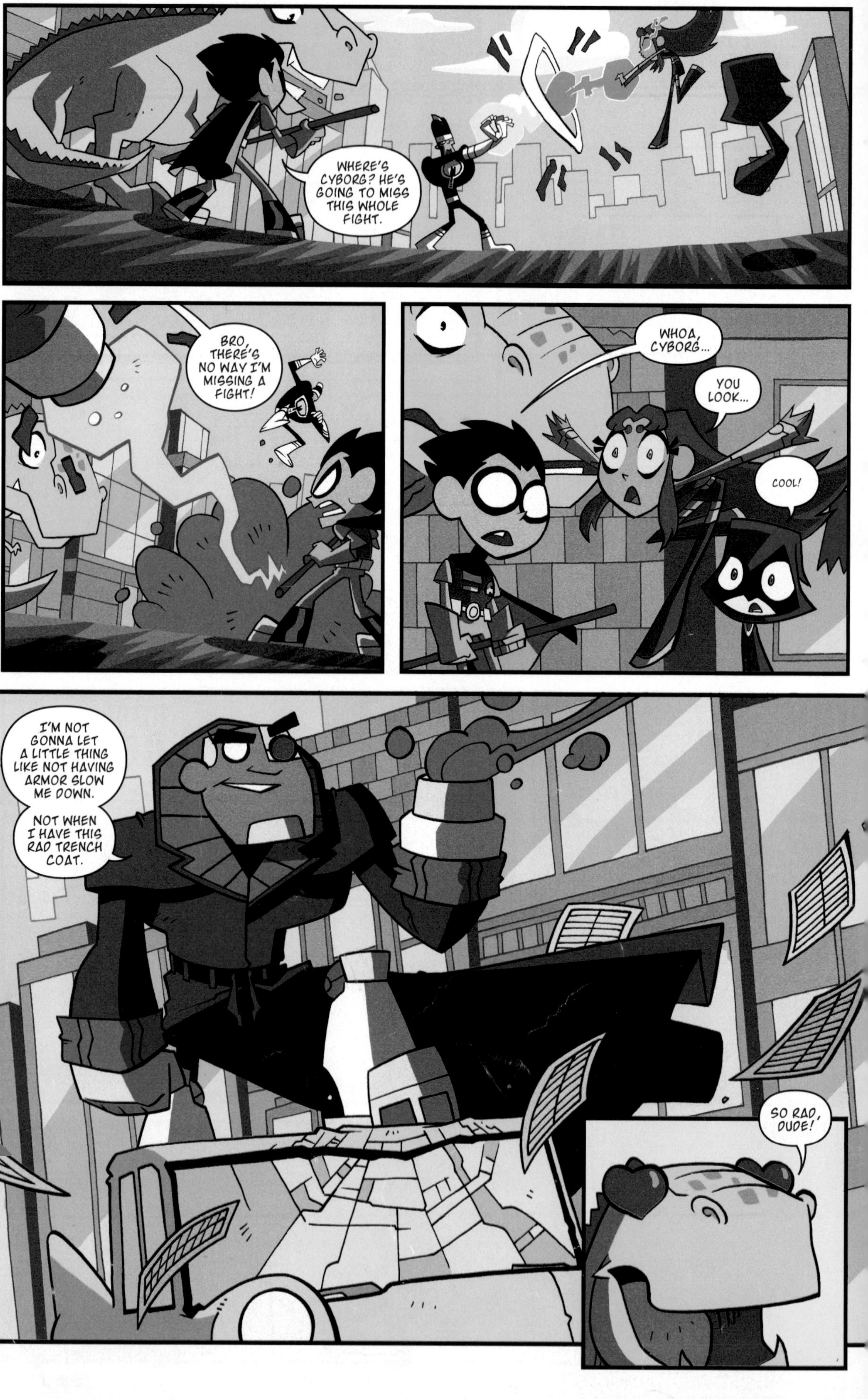
WHERE'S CYBORG? HE'S GOING TO MISS THIS WHOLE FIGHT.
BRO, THERE'S NO WAY I'M MISSING A FIGHT!
WHOA, CYBORG...
YOU LOOK...
COOL!
I'M NOT GONNA LET A LITTLE THING LIKE NOT HAVING ARMOR SLOW ME DOWN.
NOT WHEN I HAVE THIS RAD TRENCH COAT.
SO RAD, DUDE!

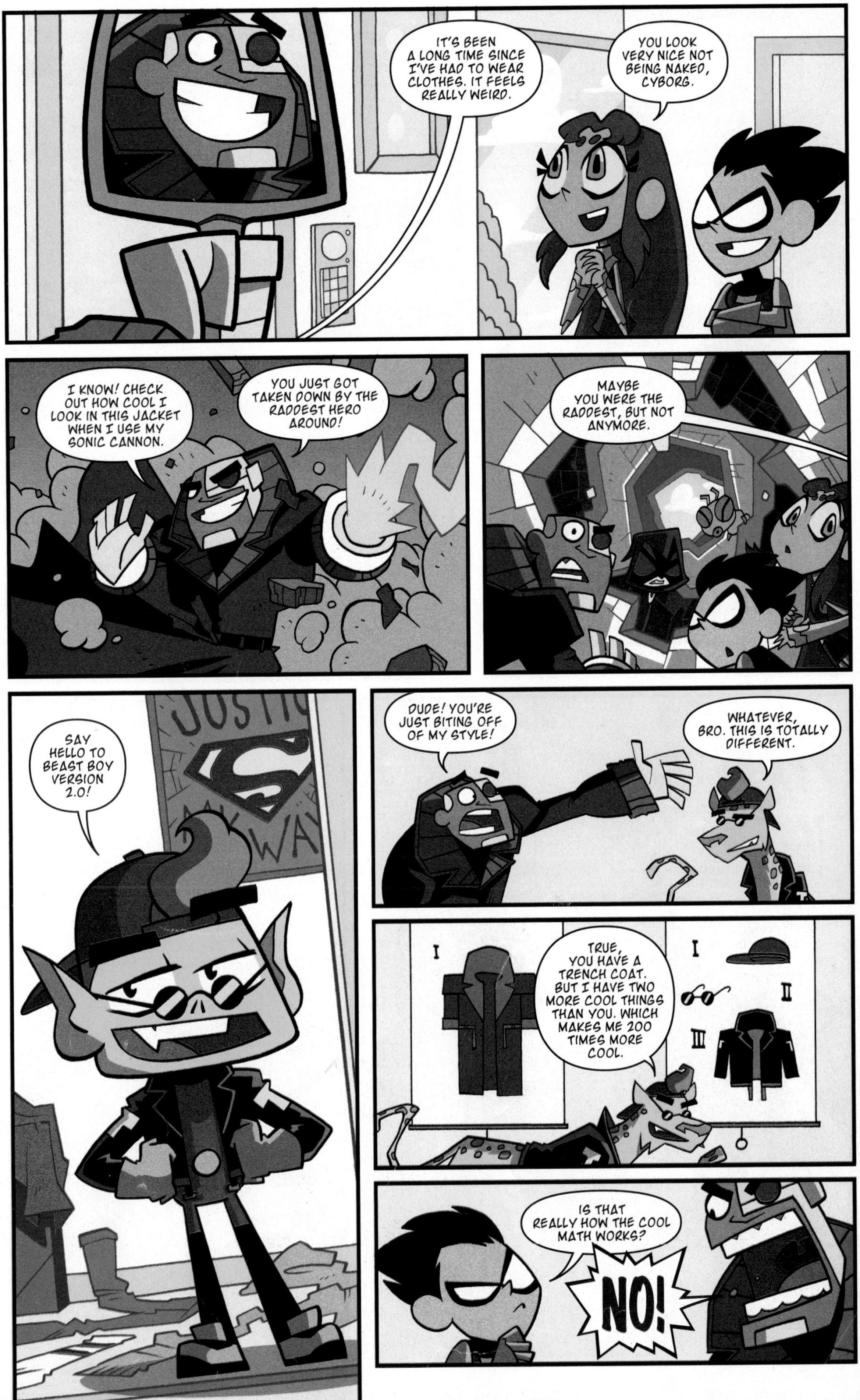
IT'S BEEN A LONG TIME SINCE I'VE HAD TO WEAR CLOTHES. IT FEELS REALLY WEIRD.
YOU LOOK VERY NICE NOT BEING NAKED, CYBORG.
I KNOW! CHECK OUT HOW COOL I LOOK IN THIS JACKET WHEN I USE MY SONIC CANNON.
YOU JUST GOT TAKEN DOWN BY THE RADDEST HERO AROUND!
MAYBE YOU WERE THE RADDEST, BUT NOT ANYMORE.
SAY HELLO TO BEAST BOY VERSION 2.0!
DUDE! YOU'RE JUST BITING OFF OF MY STYLE!
WHATEVER, BRO. THIS IS TOTALLY DIFFERENT.
TRUE, YOU HAVE A TRENCH COAT. BUT I HAVE TWO MORE COOL THINGS THAN YOU. WHICH MAKES ME 200 TIMES MORE COOL.
IS THAT REALLY HOW THE COOL MATH WORKS?
NO!

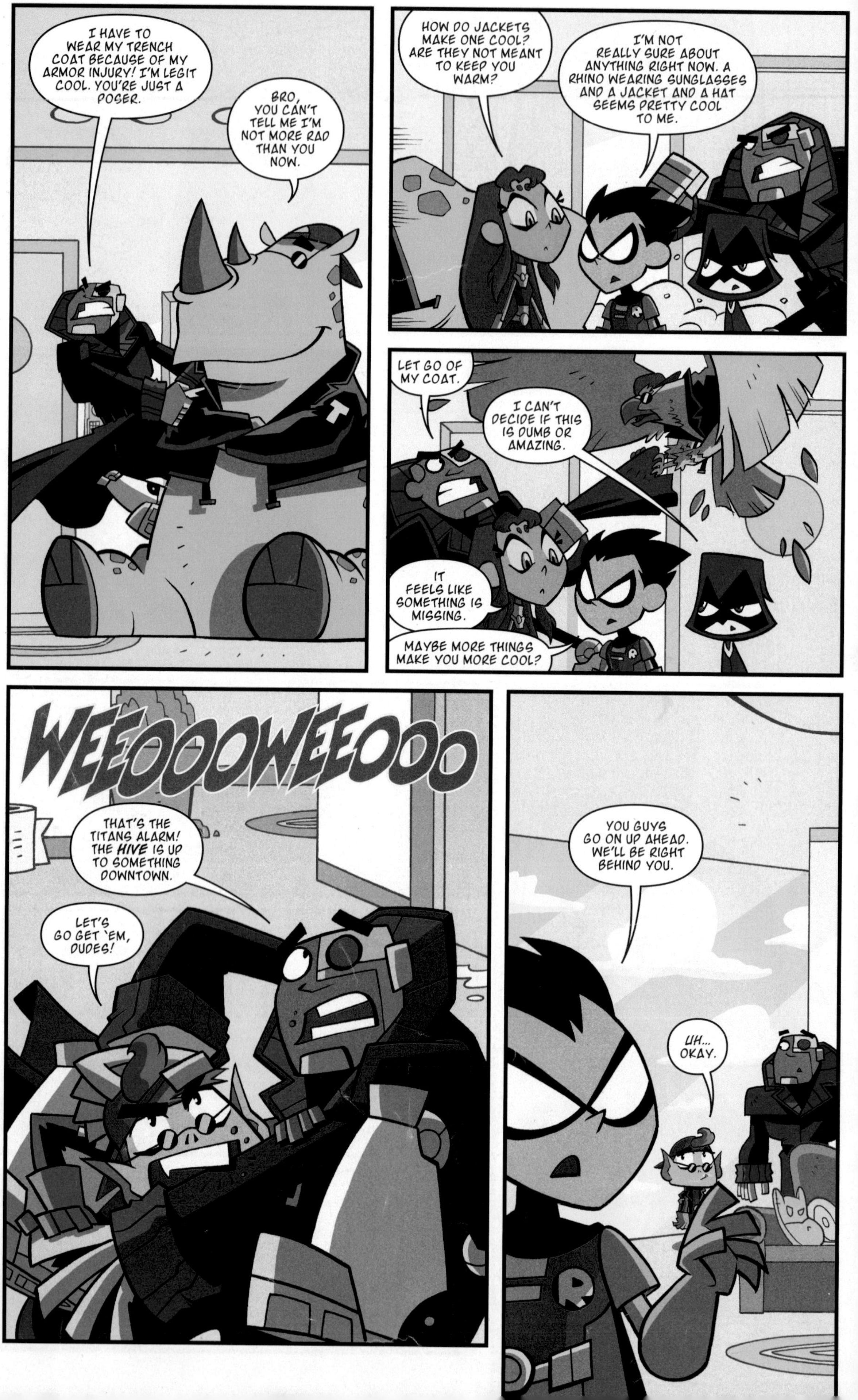
I HAVE TO WEAR MY TRENCH COAT BECAUSE OF MY ARMOR INJURY! I'M LEGIT COOL. YOU'RE JUST A POSER.
BRO, YOU CAN'T TELL ME I'M NOT MORE RAD THAN YOU NOW.
HOW DO JACKETS MAKE ONE COOL? ARE THEY NOT MEANT TO KEEP YOU WARM?
I'M NOT REALLY SURE ABOUT ANYTHING RIGHT NOW. A RHINO WEARING SUNGLASSES AND A JACKET AND A HAT SEEMS PRETTY COOL TO ME.
LET GO OF MY COAT.
I CAN'T DECIDE IF THIS IS DUMB OR AMAZING.
IT FEELS LIKE SOMETHING IS MISSING.
MAYBE MORE THINGS MAKE YOU MORE COOL?
WEEOOOWEEOOO
THAT'S THE TITANS ALARM! THE HIVE IS UP TO SOMETHING DOWNTOWN.
LET'S GO GET 'EM, DUDES!
YOU GUYS GO ON UP AHEAD. WE'LL BE RIGHT BEHIND YOU.
UH... OKAY.

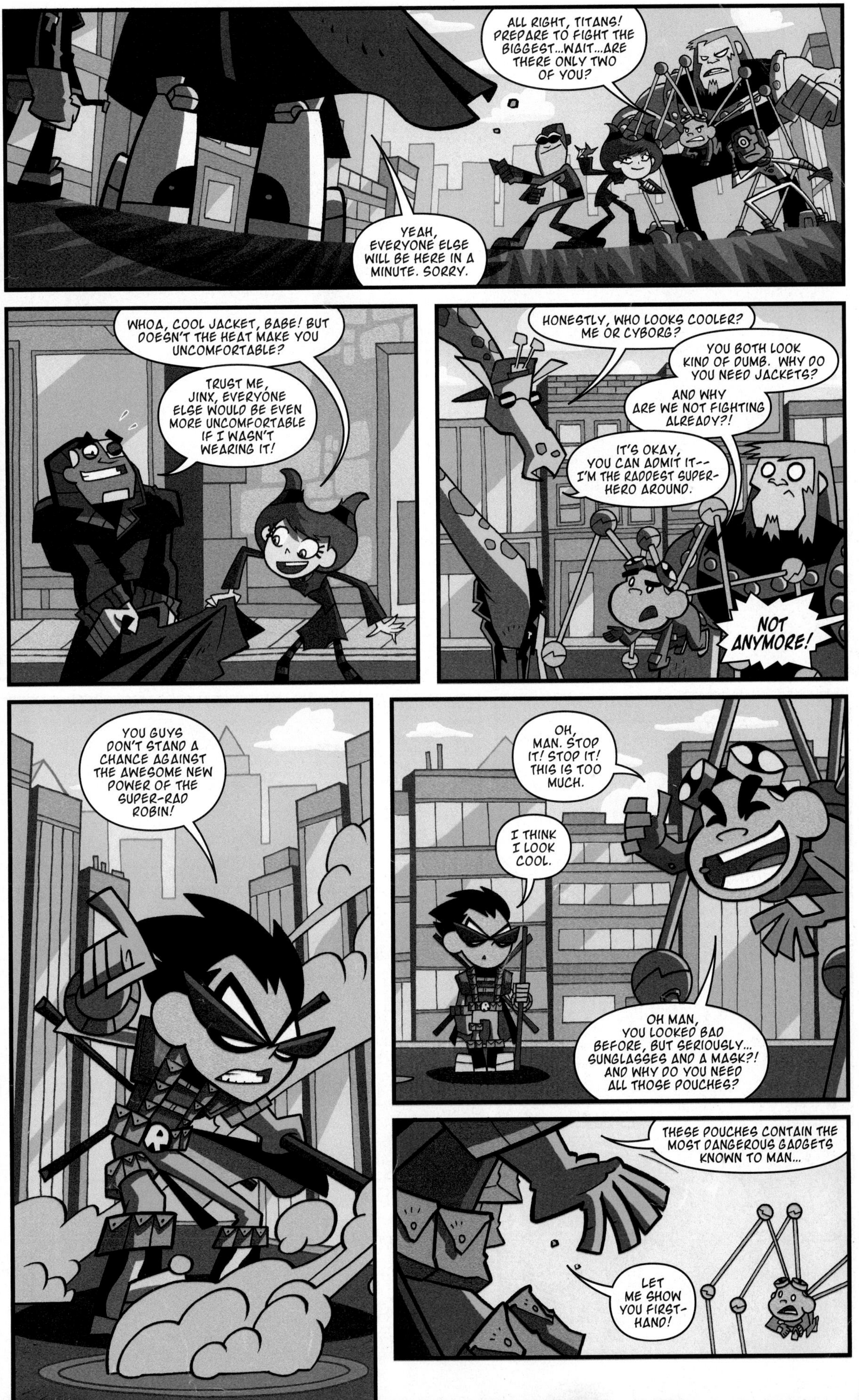
ALL RIGHT, TITANS! PREPARE TO FIGHT THE BIGGEST...WAIT...ARE THERE ONLY TWO OF YOU?
YEAH, EVERYONE ELSE WILL BE HERE IN A MINUTE. SORRY.
WHOA, COOL JACKET, BABE! BUT DOESN'T THE HEAT MAKE YOU UNCOMFORTABLE?
TRUST ME, JINX, EVERYONE ELSE WOULD BE EVEN MORE UNCOMFORTABLE IF I WASN'T WEARING IT!
HONESTLY, WHO LOOKS COOLER? ME OR CYBORG?
YOU BOTH LOOK KIND OF DUMB. WHY DO YOU NEED JACKETS?
AND WHY ARE WE NOT FIGHTING ALREADY?!
IT'S OKAY, YOU CAN ADMIT IT-- I'M THE RADDEST SUPER-HERO AROUND.
NOT ANYMORE!
YOU GUYS DON'T STAND A CHANCE AGAINST THE AWESOME NEW POWER OF THE SUPER-RAD ROBIN!
OH, MAN. STOP IT! STOP IT! THIS IS TOO MUCH.
I THINK I LOOK COOL.
OH MAN, YOU LOOKED BAD BEFORE, BUT SERIOUSLY... SUNGLASSES AND A MASK?! AND WHY DO YOU NEED ALL THOSE POUCHES?
THESE POUCHES CONTAIN THE MOST DANGEROUS GADGETS KNOWN TO MAN...
LET ME SHOW YOU FIRST-HAND!

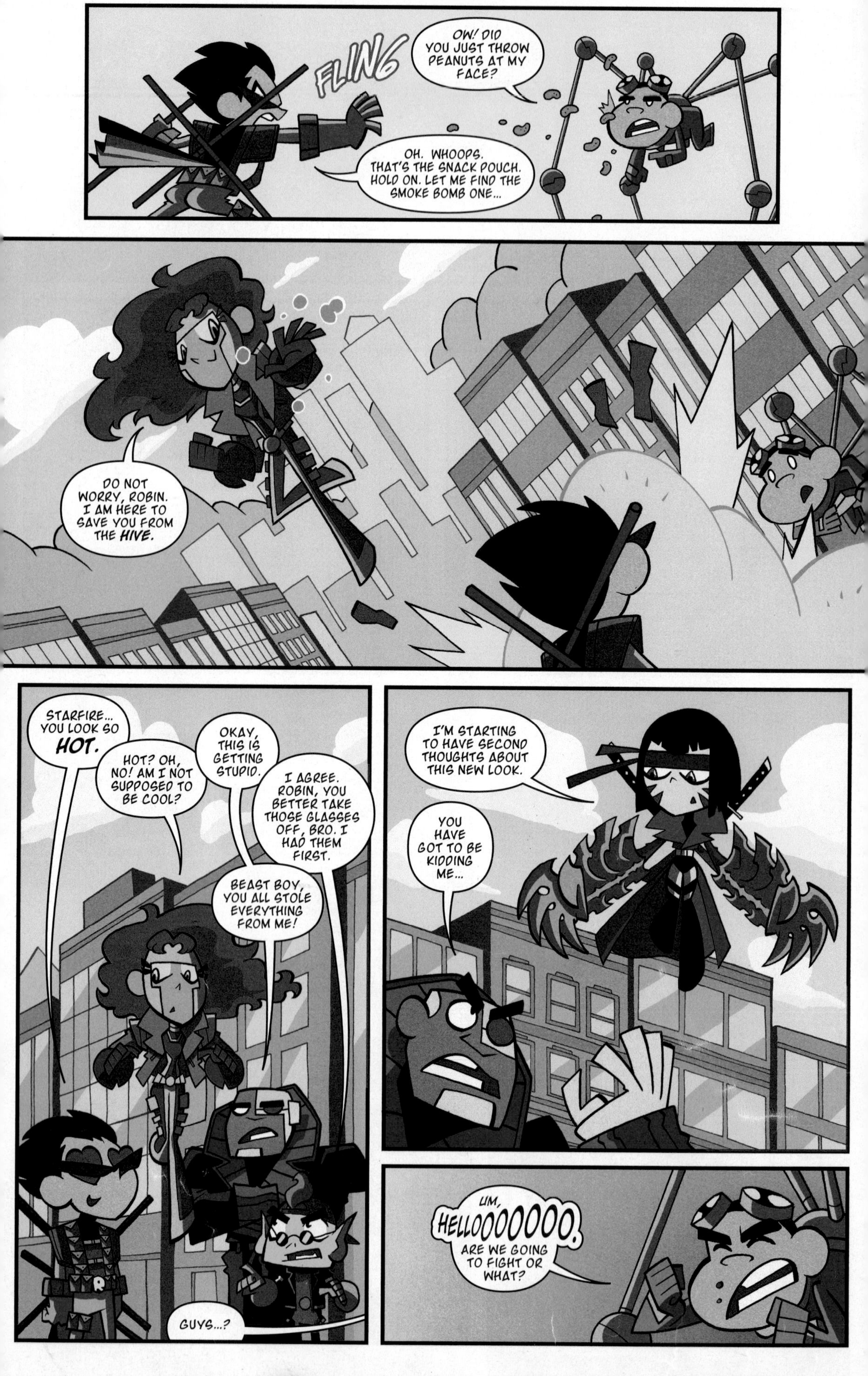
FLING
OW! DID YOU JUST THROW PEANUTS AT MY FACE?
OH. WHOOPS. THAT'S THE SNACK POUCH. HOLD ON. LET ME FIND THE SMOKE BOMB ONE...
DO NOT WORRY, ROBIN. I AM HERE TO SAVE YOU FROM THE HIVE.
STARFIRE... YOU LOOK SO HOT.
HOT? OH, NO! AM I NOT SUPPOSED TO BE COOL?
OKAY, THIS IS GETTING STUPID.
I AGREE. ROBIN, YOU BETTER TAKE THOSE GLASSES OFF, BRO. I HAD THEM FIRST.
BEAST BOY, YOU ALL STOLE EVERYTHING FROM ME!
GUYS...?
I'M STARTING TO HAVE SECOND THOUGHTS ABOUT THIS NEW LOOK.
YOU HAVE GOT TO BE KIDDING ME...
UM, HELLOOOOOOO. ARE WE GOING TO FIGHT OR WHAT?

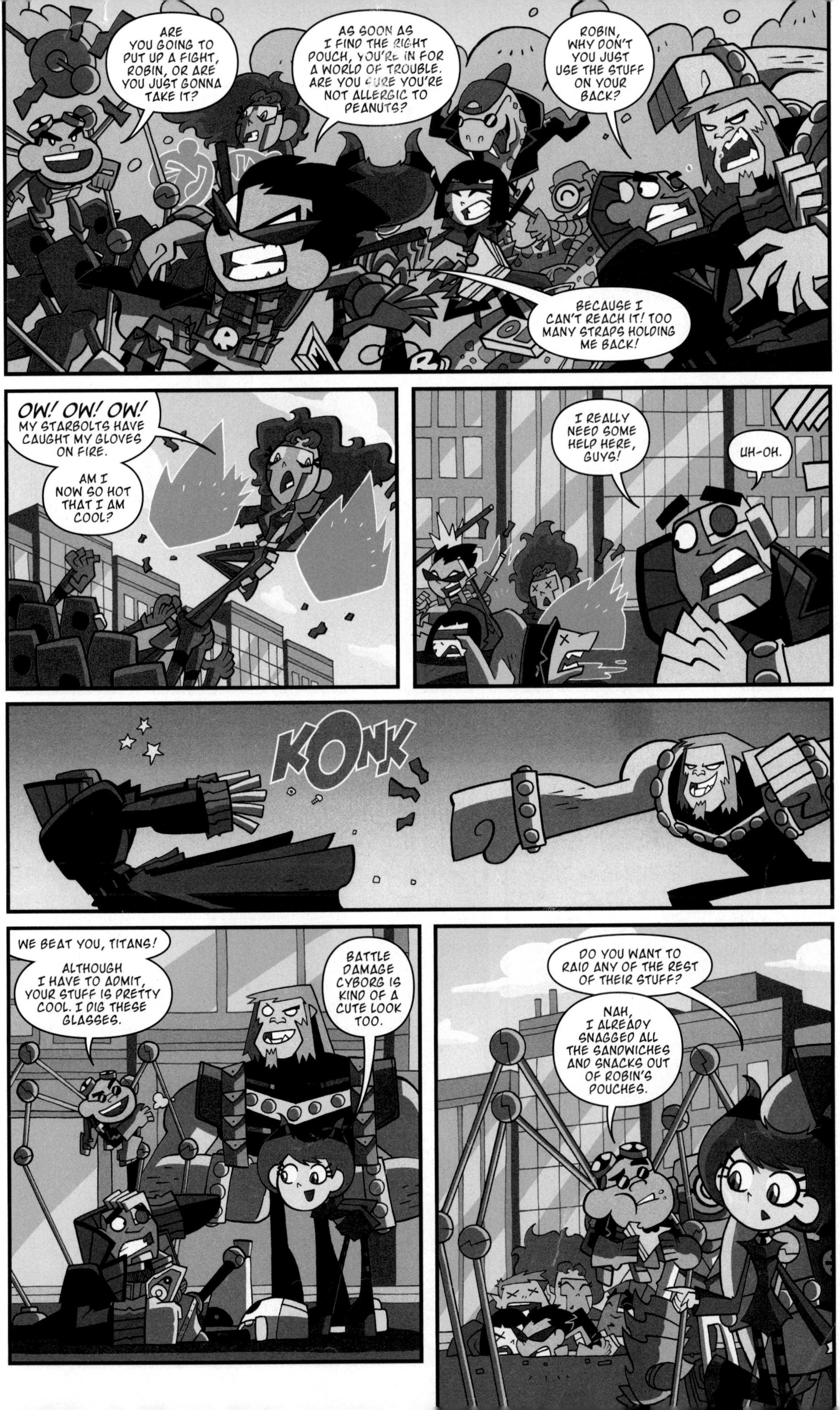
ARE YOU GOING TO PUT UP A FIGHT, ROBIN, OR ARE YOU JUST GONNA TAKE IT?
AS SOON AS I FIND THE RIGHT POUCH, YOU'RE IN FOR A WORLD OF TROUBLE. ARE YOU SURE YOU'RE NOT ALLERGIC TO PEANUTS?
ROBIN, WHY DON'T YOU JUST USE THE STUFF ON YOUR BACK?
BECAUSE I CAN'T REACH IT! TOO MANY STRAPS HOLDING ME BACK!
OW! OW! OW! MY STARBOLTS HAVE CAUGHT MY GLOVES ON FIRE.
AM I NOW SO HOT THAT I AM COOL?
I REALLY NEED SOME HELP HERE, GUYS!
UH-OH.
KONK
WE BEAT YOU, TITANS!
ALTHOUGH I HAVE TO ADMIT, YOUR STUFF IS PRETTY COOL. I DIG THESE GLASSES.
BATTLE DAMAGE CYBORG IS KIND OF A CUTE LOOK TOO.
DO YOU WANT TO RAID ANY OF THE REST OF THEIR STUFF?
NAH, I ALREADY SNAGGED ALL THE SANDWICHES AND SNACKS OUT OF ROBIN'S POUCHES.

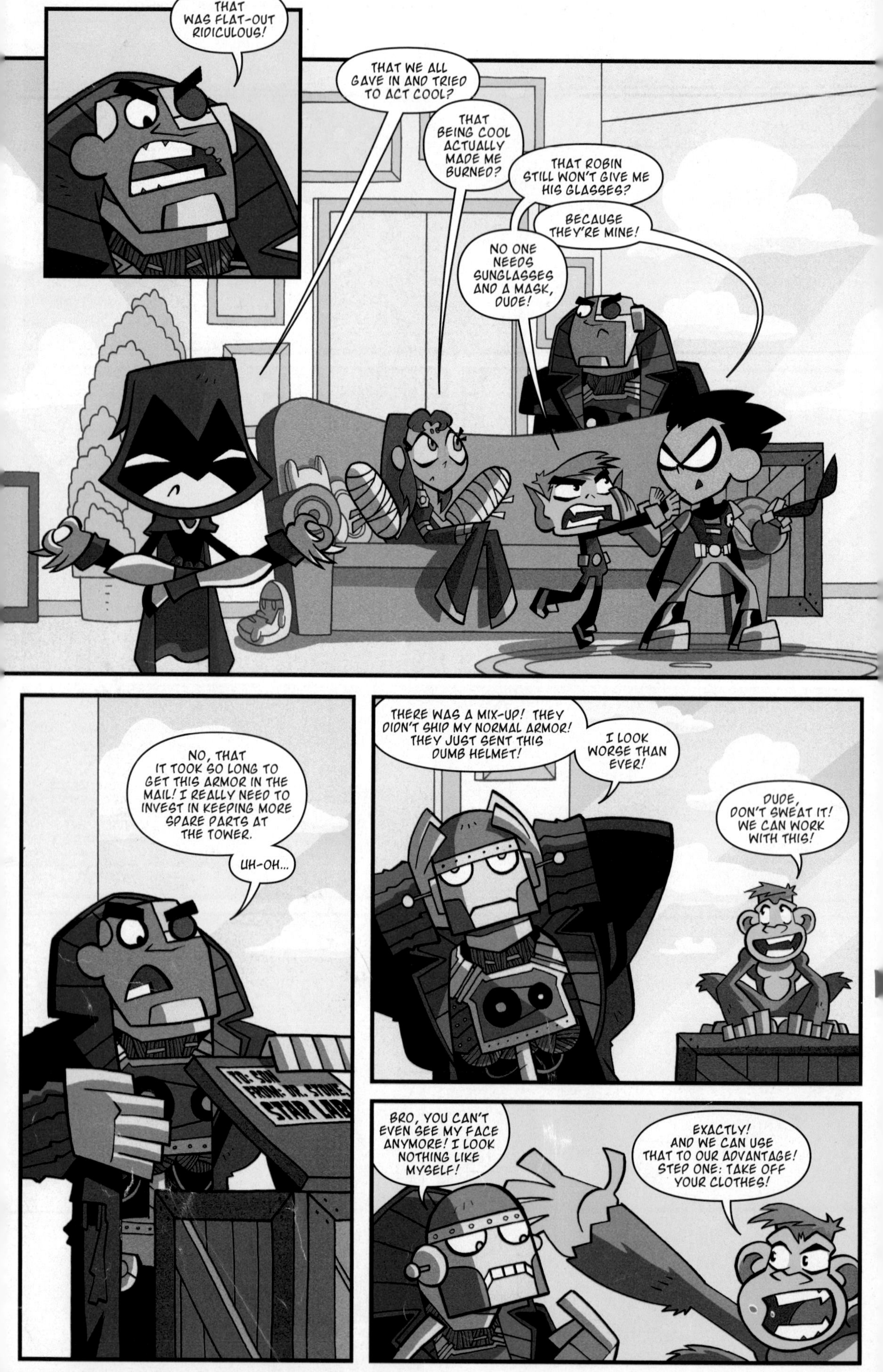
THAT WAS FLAT-OUT RIDICULOUS!
THAT WE ALL GAVE IN AND TRIED TO ACT COOL?
THAT BEING COOL ACTUALLY MADE ME BURNED?
THAT ROBIN STILL WON'T GIVE ME HIS GLASSES?
BECAUSE THEY'RE MINE!
NO ONE NEEDS SUNGLASSES AND A MASK, DUDE!
NO, THAT IT TOOK SO LONG TO GET THIS ARMOR IN THE MAIL! I REALLY NEED TO INVEST IN KEEPING MORE SPARE PARTS AT THE TOWER.
UH-OH...
TO: CY
FROM: DR. STONE, STAR LAB
THERE WAS A MIX-UP! THEY DIDN'T SHIP MY NORMAL ARMOR! THEY JUST SENT THIS DUMB HELMET!
I LOOK WORSE THAN EVER!
DUDE, DON'T SWEAT IT! WE CAN WORK WITH THIS!
BRO, YOU CAN'T EVEN SEE MY FACE ANYMORE! I LOOK NOTHING LIKE MYSELF!
EXACTLY! AND WE CAN USE THAT TO OUR ADVANTAGE! STEP ONE: TAKE OFF YOUR CLOTHES!

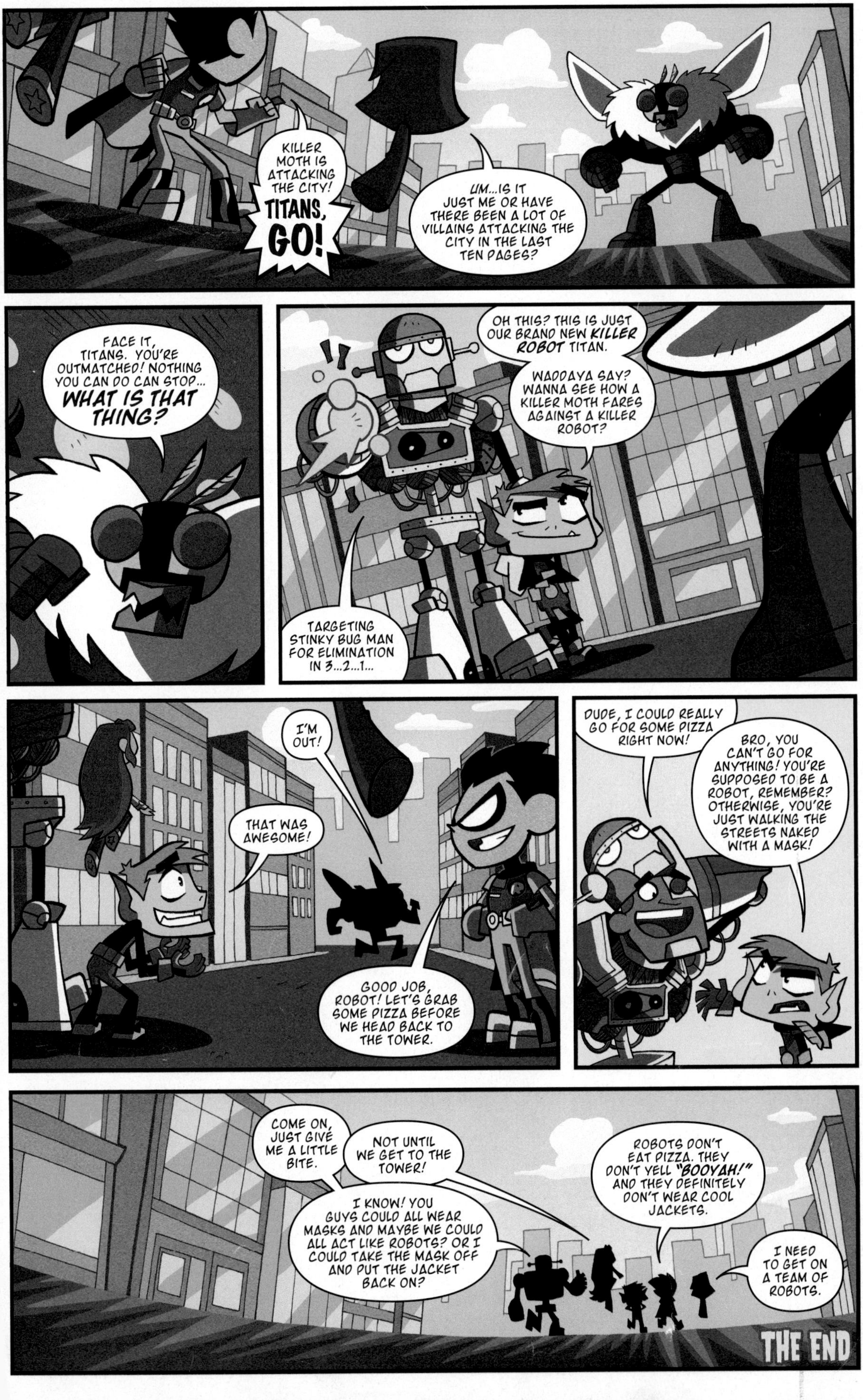
KILLER MOTH IS ATTACKING THE CITY! TITANS, GO!
UM...IS IT JUST ME OR HAVE THERE BEEN A LOT OF VILLAINS ATTACKING THE CITY IN THE LAST TEN PAGES?
FACE IT, TITANS. YOU'RE OUTMATCHED! NOTHING YOU CAN DO CAN STOP... WHAT IS THAT THING?
OH THIS? THIS IS JUST OUR BRAND NEW KILLER ROBOT TITAN.
WADDAYA SAY? WANNA SEE HOW A KILLER MOTH FARES AGAINST A KILLER ROBOT?
TARGETING STINKY BUG MAN FOR ELIMINATION IN 3...2...1...
I'M OUT!
THAT WAS AWESOME!
GOOD JOB, ROBOT! LET'S GRAB SOME PIZZA BEFORE WE HEAD BACK TO THE TOWER.
DUDE, I COULD REALLY GO FOR SOME PIZZA RIGHT NOW!
BRO, YOU CAN'T GO FOR ANYTHING! YOU'RE SUPPOSED TO BE A ROBOT, REMEMBER? OTHERWISE, YOU'RE JUST WALKING THE STREETS NAKED WITH A MASK!
COME ON, JUST GIVE ME A LITTLE BITE.
NOT UNTIL WE GET TO THE TOWER!
I KNOW! YOU GUYS COULD ALL WEAR MASKS AND MAYBE WE COULD ALL ACT LIKE ROBOTS? OR I COULD TAKE THE MASK OFF AND PUT THE JACKET BACK ON?
ROBOTS DON'T EAT PIZZA. THEY DON'T YELL "BOOYAH!" AND THEY DEFINITELY DON'T WEAR COOL JACKETS.
I NEED TO GET ON A TEAM OF ROBOTS.
THE END

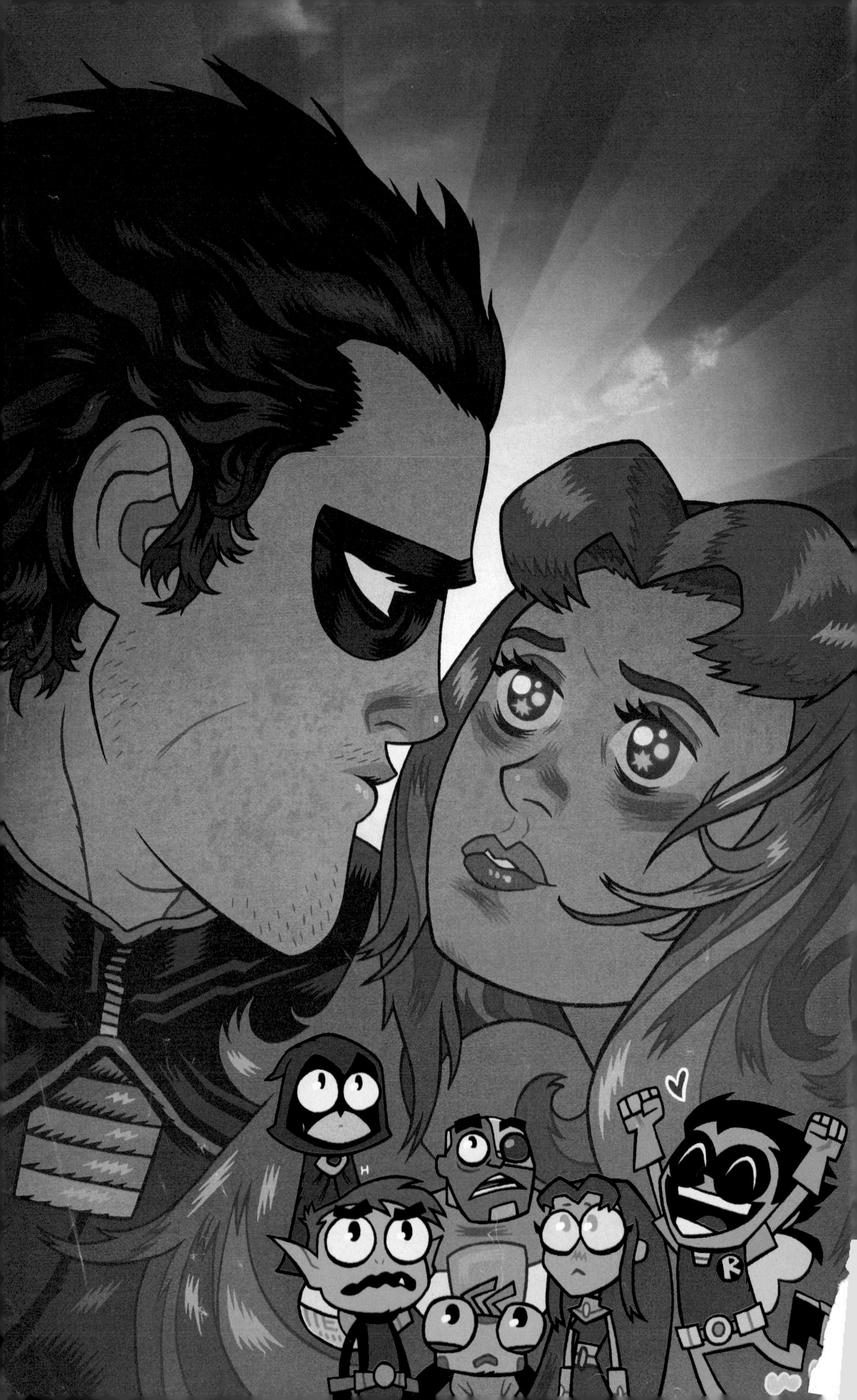

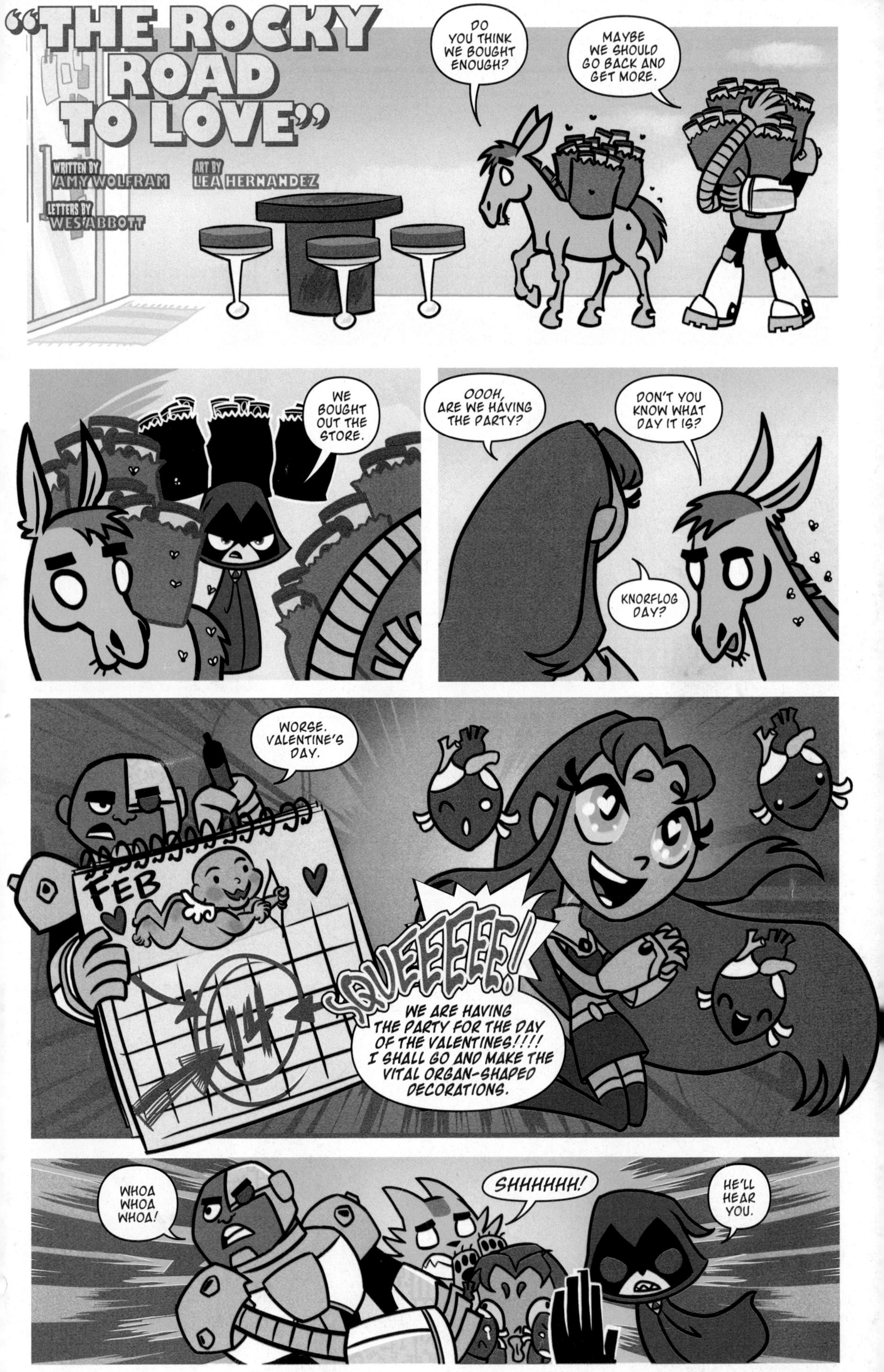

"THE ROCKY ROAD TO LOVE"
WRITTEN BY AMY WOLFRAM
ART BY LEA HERNANDEZ
LETTERS BY WES ABBOTT
DO YOU THINK WE BOUGHT ENOUGH?
MAYBE WE SHOULD GO BACK AND GET MORE.
WE BOUGHT OUT THE STORE.
OOOH, ARE WE HAVING THE PARTY?
DON'T YOU KNOW WHAT DAY IT IS?
KNORFLOG DAY?
WORSE. VALENTINE'S DAY.
FEB
14
SQUEEEEE!
WE ARE HAVING THE PARTY FOR THE DAY OF THE VALENTINES!!!! I SHALL GO AND MAKE THE VITAL ORGAN-SHAPED DECORATIONS.
WHOA WHOA WHOA!
SHHHHHH!
HE'LL HEAR YOU.

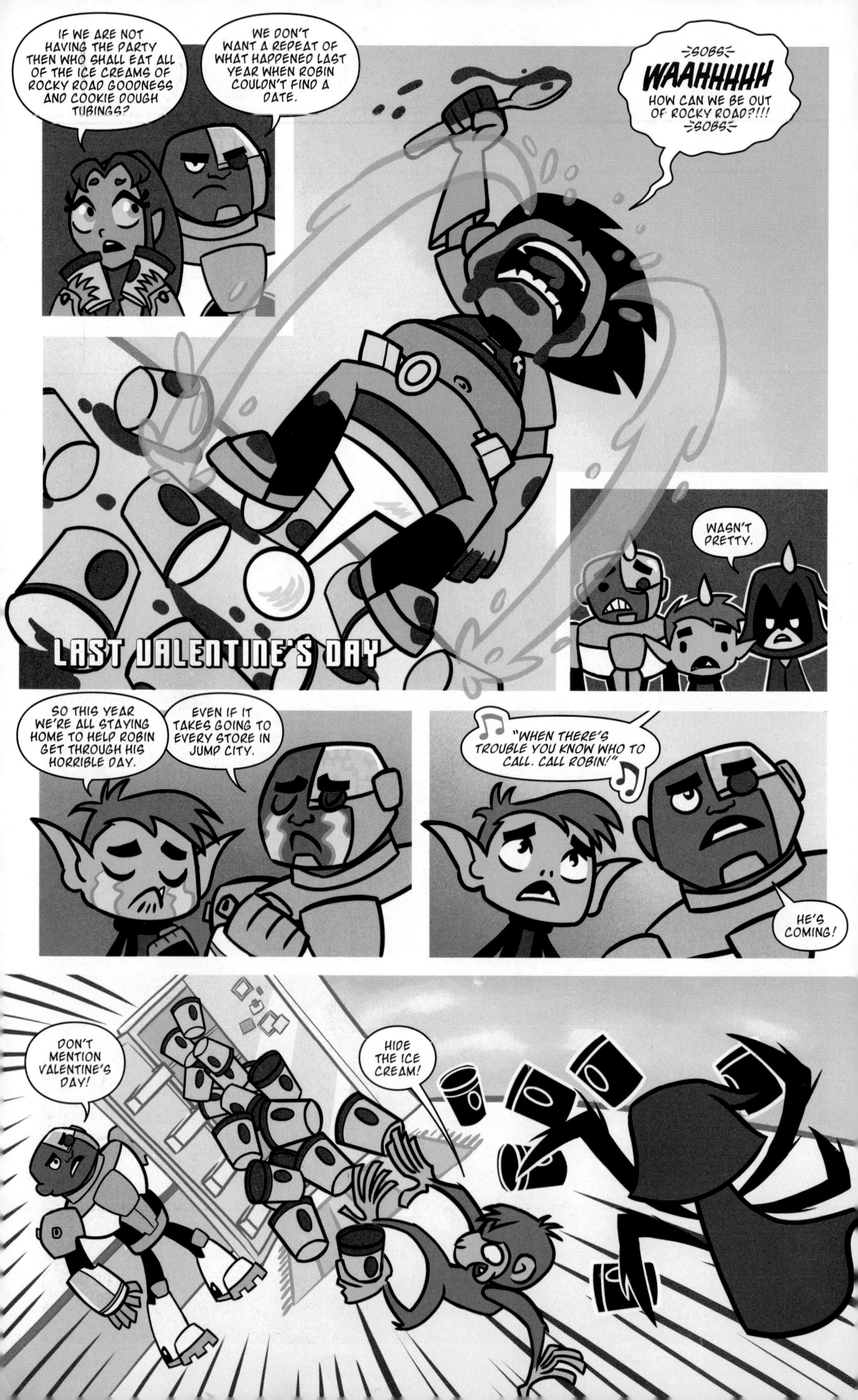
IF WE ARE NOT HAVING THE PARTY THEN WHO SHALL EAT ALL OF THE ICE CREAMS OF ROCKY ROAD GOODNESS AND COOKIE DOUGH TUBINGS?
WE DON'T WANT A REPEAT OF WHAT HAPPENED LAST YEAR WHEN ROBIN COULDN'T FIND A DATE.
-SOBS- WAAHHHHH HOW CAN WE BE OUT OF ROCKY ROAD?!!! -SOBS-
LAST VALENTINE'S DAY
WASN'T PRETTY.
SO THIS YEAR WE'RE ALL STAYING HOME TO HELP ROBIN GET THROUGH HIS HORRIBLE DAY.
EVEN IF IT TAKES GOING TO EVERY STORE IN JUMP CITY.
"WHEN THERE'S TROUBLE YOU KNOW WHO TO CALL. CALL ROBIN!"
HE'S COMING!
DON'T MENTION VALENTINE'S DAY!
HIDE THE ICE CREAM!

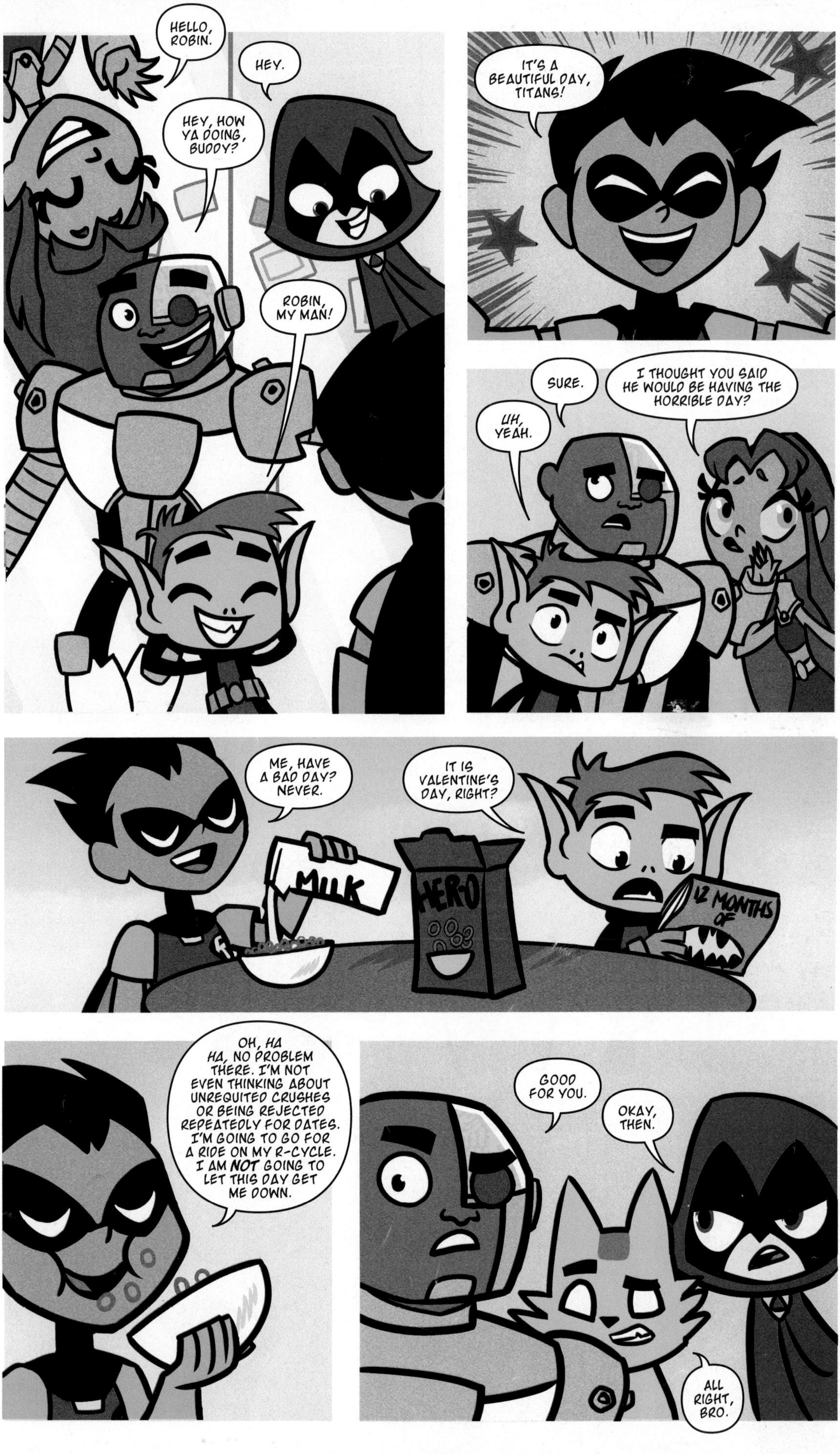
HELLO, ROBIN.
HEY.
HEY, HOW YA DOING, BUDDY?
ROBIN, MY MAN!
IT'S A BEAUTIFUL DAY, TITANS!
SURE.
I THOUGHT YOU SAID HE WOULD BE HAVING THE HORRIBLE DAY?
UH, YEAH.
ME, HAVE A BAD DAY? NEVER.
IT IS VALENTINE'S DAY, RIGHT?
MILK
HER-O
12 MONTHS OF
OH, HA HA, NO PROBLEM THERE. I'M NOT EVEN THINKING ABOUT UNREQUITED CRUSHES OR BEING REJECTED REPEATEDLY FOR DATES. I'M GOING TO GO FOR A RIDE ON MY R-CYCLE. I AM NOT GOING TO LET THIS DAY GET ME DOWN.
GOOD FOR YOU.
OKAY, THEN.
ALL RIGHT, BRO.

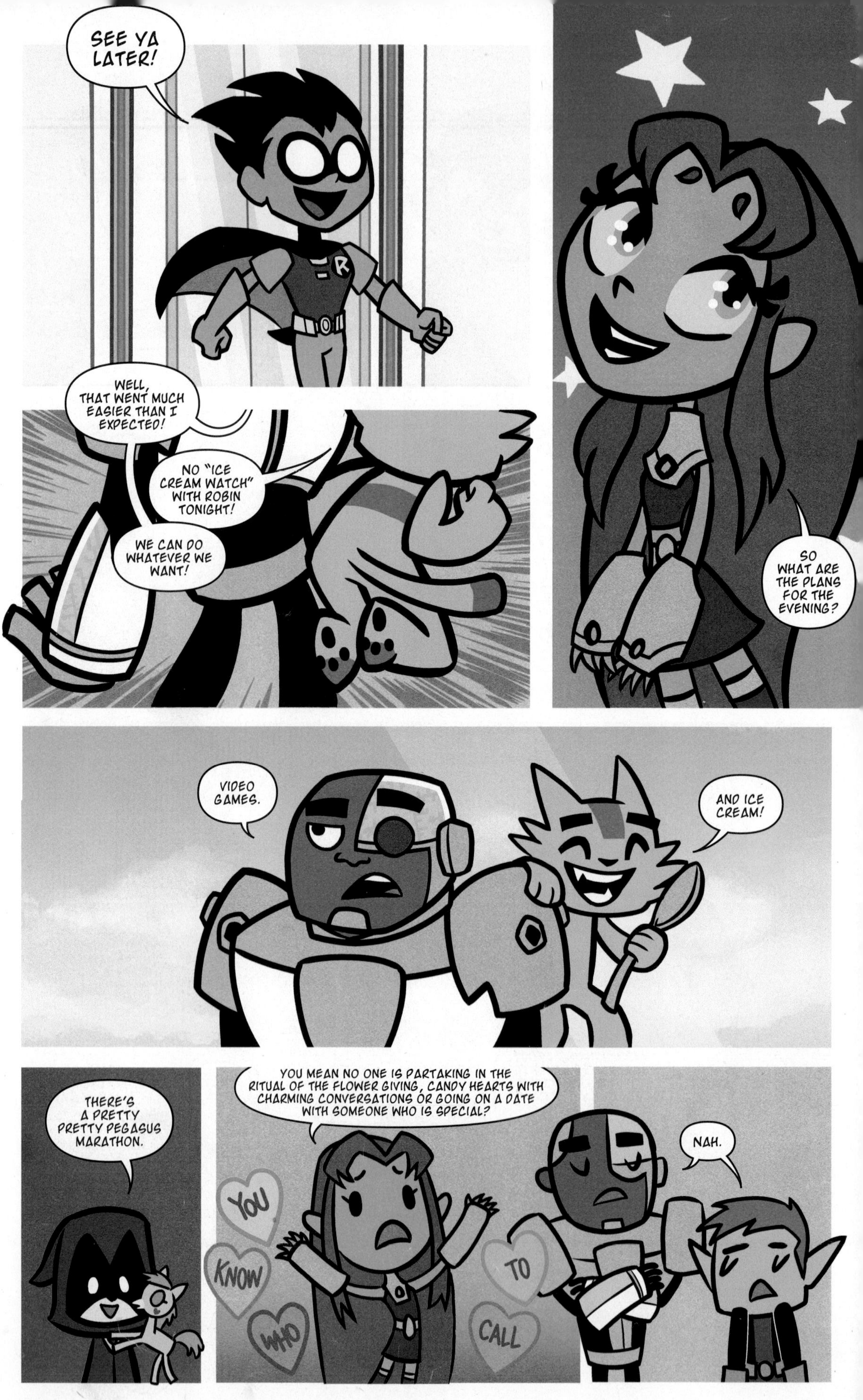
SEE YA LATER!
WELL, THAT WENT MUCH EASIER THAN I EXPECTED!
NO "ICE CREAM WATCH" WITH ROBIN TONIGHT!
WE CAN DO WHATEVER WE WANT!
SO WHAT ARE THE PLANS FOR THE EVENING?
VIDEO GAMES.
AND ICE CREAM!
THERE'S A PRETTY PRETTY PEGASUS MARATHON.
YOU MEAN NO ONE IS PARTAKING IN THE RITUAL OF THE FLOWER GIVING, CANDY HEARTS WITH CHARMING CONVERSATIONS OR GOING ON A DATE WITH SOMEONE WHO IS SPECIAL?
YOU
KNOW
WHO
TO
CALL
NAH.

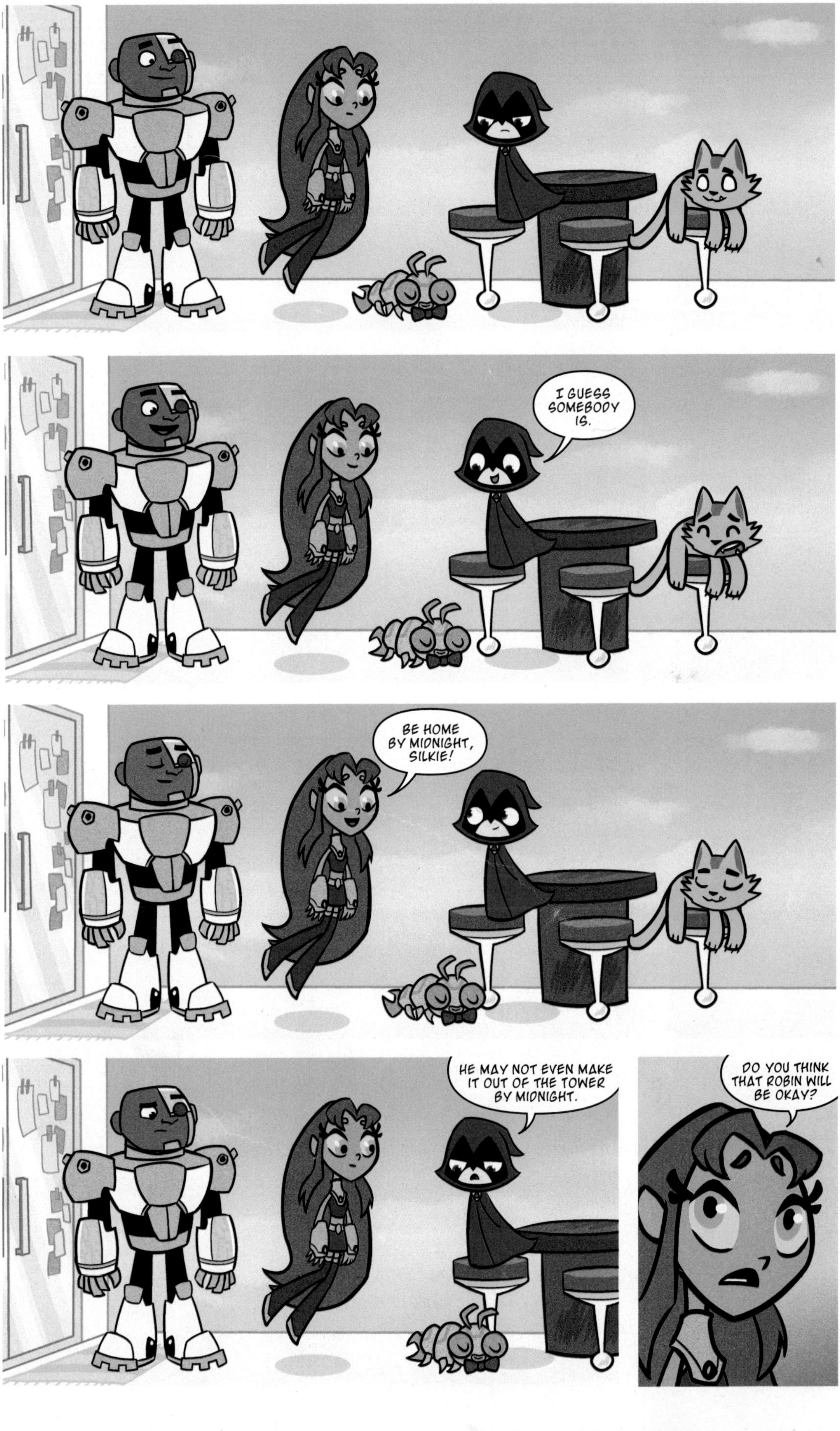
I GUESS SOMEBODY IS.
BE HOME BY MIDNIGHT, SILKIE!
HE MAY NOT EVEN MAKE IT OUT OF THE TOWER BY MIDNIGHT.
DO YOU THINK THAT ROBIN WILL BE OKAY?

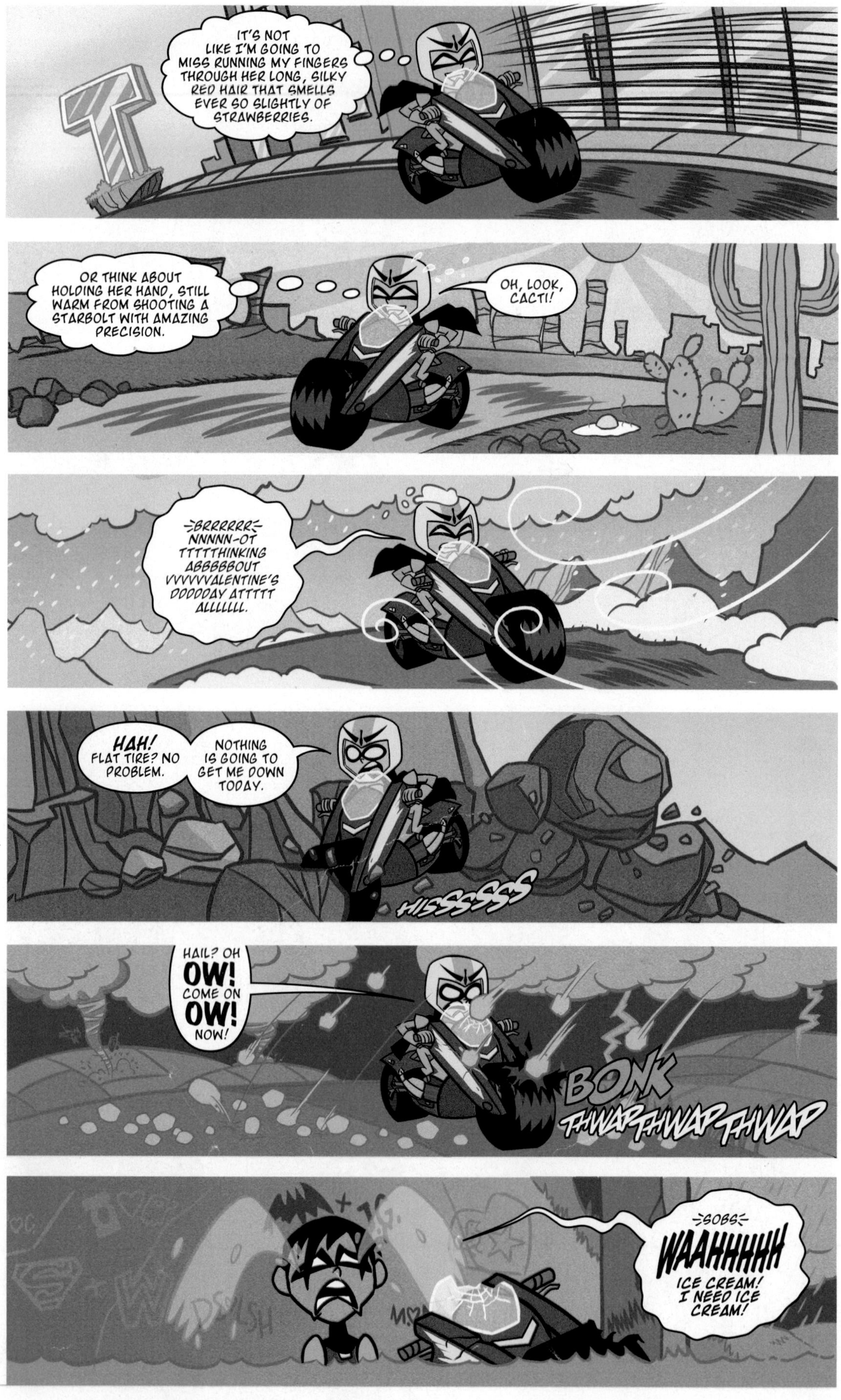
IT'S NOT LIKE I'M GOING TO MISS RUNNING MY FINGERS THROUGH HER LONG, SILKY RED HAIR THAT SMELLS EVER SO SLIGHTLY OF STRAWBERRIES.
OR THINK ABOUT HOLDING HER HAND, STILL WARM FROM SHOOTING A STARBOLT WITH AMAZING PRECISION.
OH, LOOK, CACTI!
~BRRRRRR~ NNNNN-OT TTTTTHINKING ABBBBBOUT VVVVVVALENTINE'S DDDDDAY ATTTTT ALLLLLLL.
HAH! FLAT TIRE? NO PROBLEM.
NOTHING IS GOING TO GET ME DOWN TODAY.
HISSSSSS
HAIL? OH OW! COME ON OW! NOW!
BONK
THWAP THWAP THWAP
~SOBS~
WAAHHHHH
ICE CREAM! I NEED ICE CREAM!

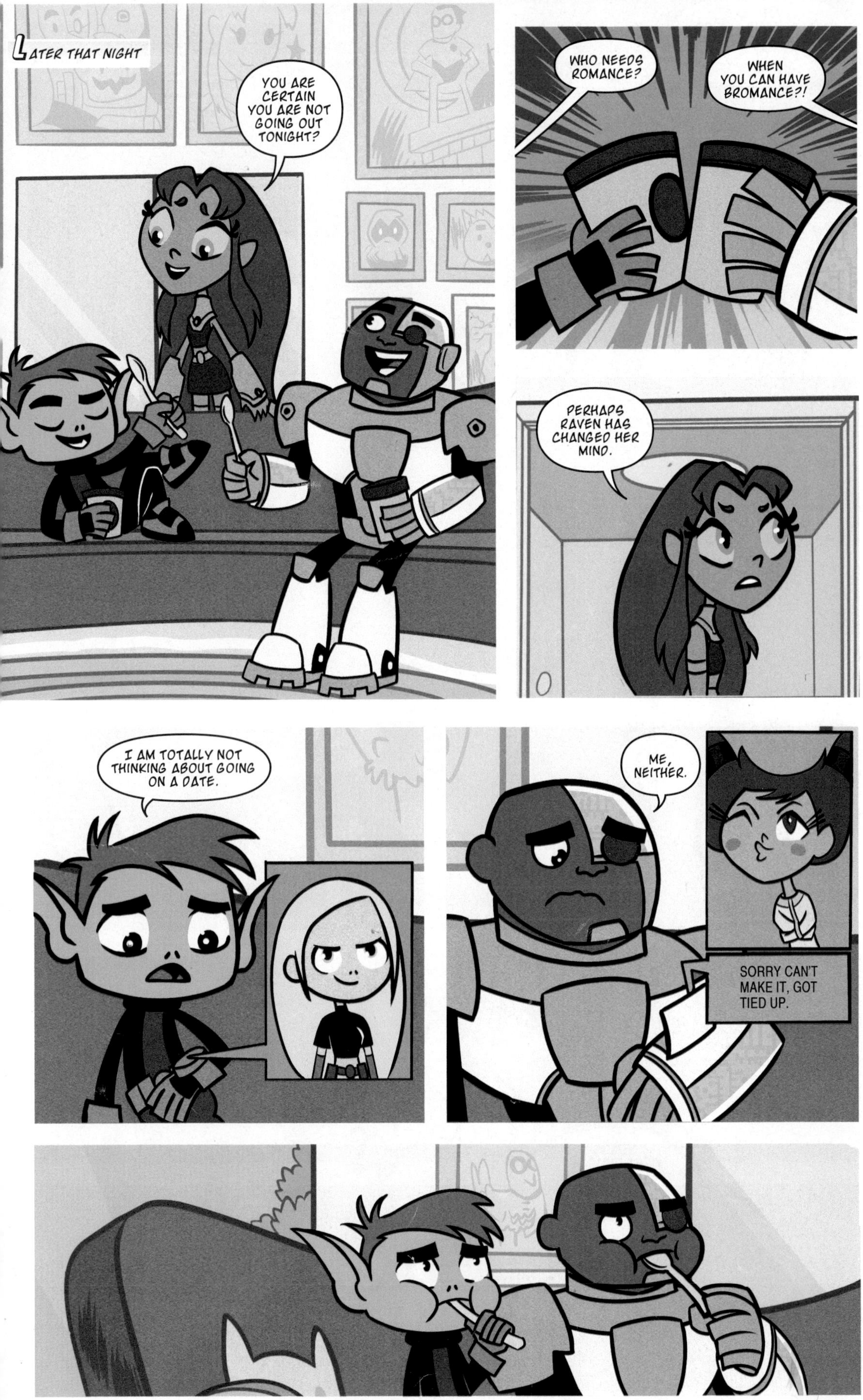

LATER THAT NIGHT
YOU ARE CERTAIN YOU ARE NOT GOING OUT TONIGHT?
WHO NEEDS ROMANCE?
WHEN YOU CAN HAVE BROMANCE?!
PERHAPS RAVEN HAS CHANGED HER MIND.
I AM TOTALLY NOT THINKING ABOUT GOING ON A DATE.
ME, NEITHER.
SORRY CAN'T MAKE IT, GOT TIED UP.

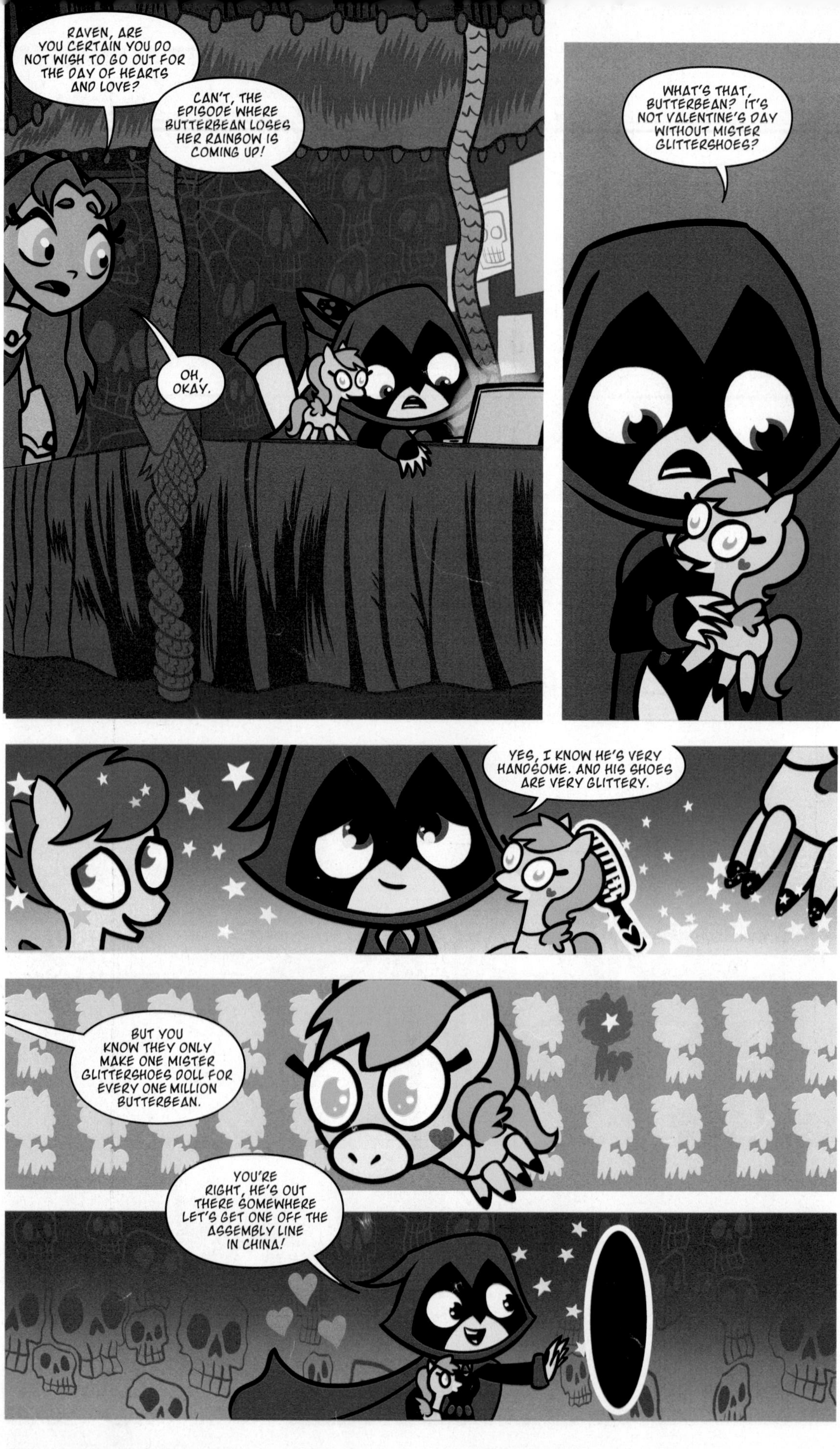
RAVEN, ARE YOU CERTAIN YOU DO NOT WISH TO GO OUT FOR THE DAY OF HEARTS AND LOVE?
CAN'T, THE EPISODE WHERE BUTTERBEAN LOSES HER RAINBOW IS COMING UP!
OH, OKAY.
WHAT'S THAT, BUTTERBEAN? IT'S NOT VALENTINE'S DAY WITHOUT MISTER GLITTERSHOES?
YES, I KNOW HE'S VERY HANDSOME. AND HIS SHOES ARE VERY GLITTERY.
BUT YOU KNOW THEY ONLY MAKE ONE MISTER GLITTERSHOES DOLL FOR EVERY ONE MILLION BUTTERBEAN.
YOU'RE RIGHT, HE'S OUT THERE SOMEWHERE LET'S GET ONE OFF THE ASSEMBLY LINE IN CHINA!

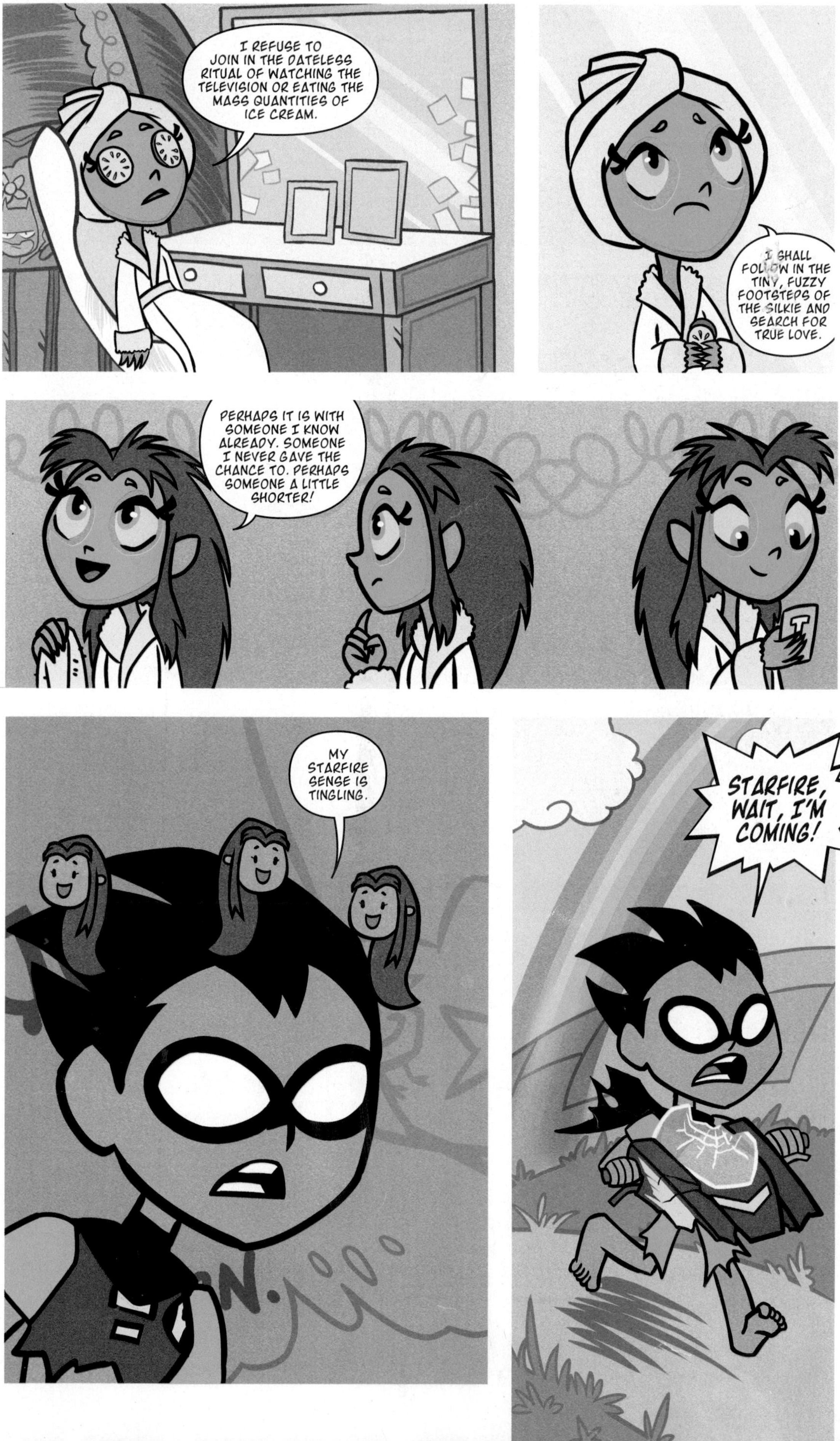
I REFUSE TO JOIN IN THE DATELESS RITUAL OF WATCHING THE TELEVISION OR EATING THE MASS QUANTITIES OF ICE CREAM.
I SHALL FOLLOW IN THE TINY, FUZZY FOOTSTEPS OF THE SILKIE AND SEARCH FOR TRUE LOVE.
PERHAPS IT IS WITH SOMEONE I KNOW ALREADY. SOMEONE I NEVER GAVE THE CHANCE TO. PERHAPS SOMEONE A LITTLE SHORTER!
MY STARFIRE SENSE IS TINGLING.
STARFIRE, WAIT, I'M COMING!

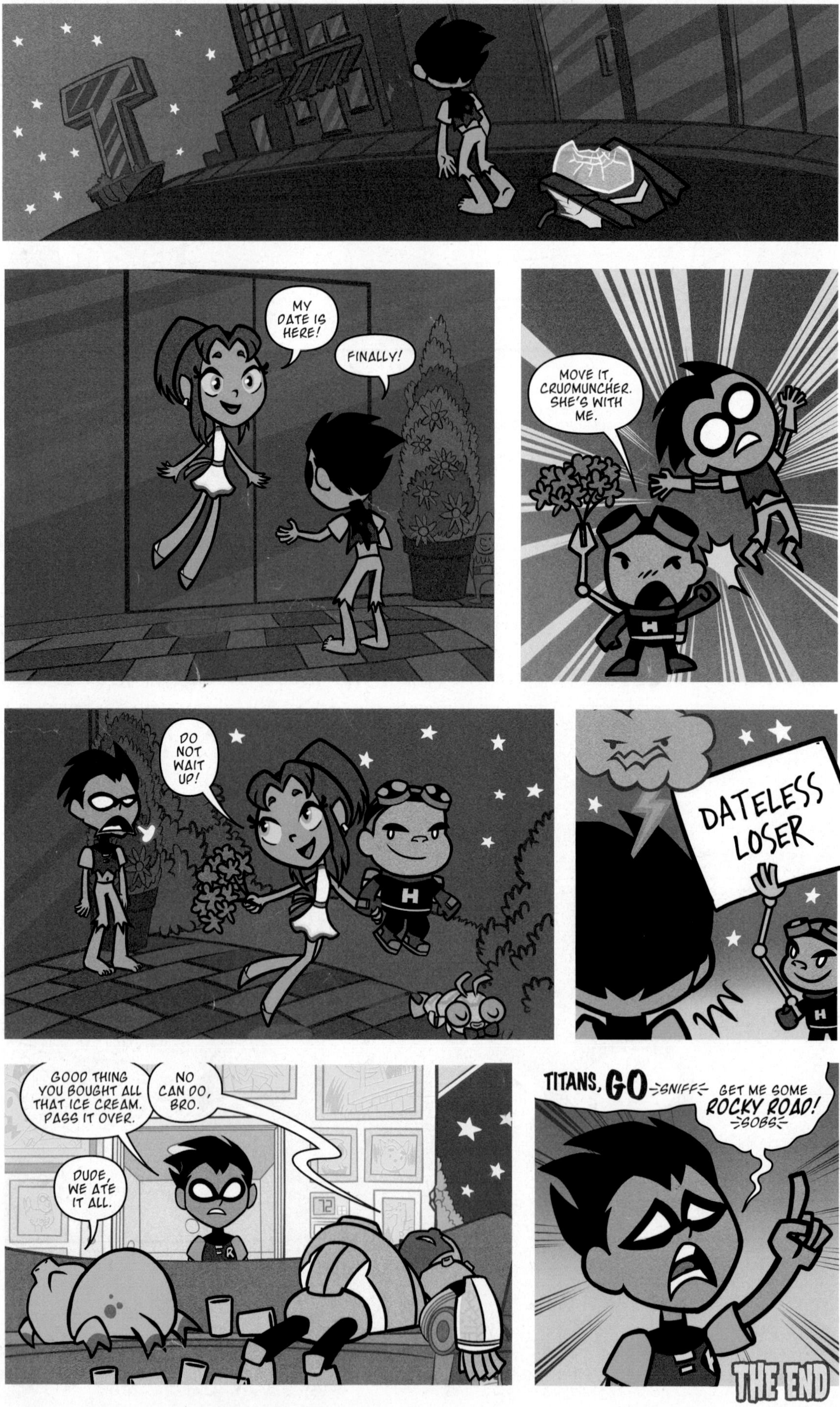
MY DATE IS HERE!
FINALLY!
MOVE IT, CRUDMUNCHER. SHE'S WITH ME.
DO NOT WAIT UP!
DATELESS LOSER
GOOD THING YOU BOUGHT ALL THAT ICE CREAM. PASS IT OVER.
NO CAN DO, BRO.
DUDE, WE ATE IT ALL.
TITANS, GO =SNIFF= GET ME SOME ROCKY ROAD! =SOBS=
THE END

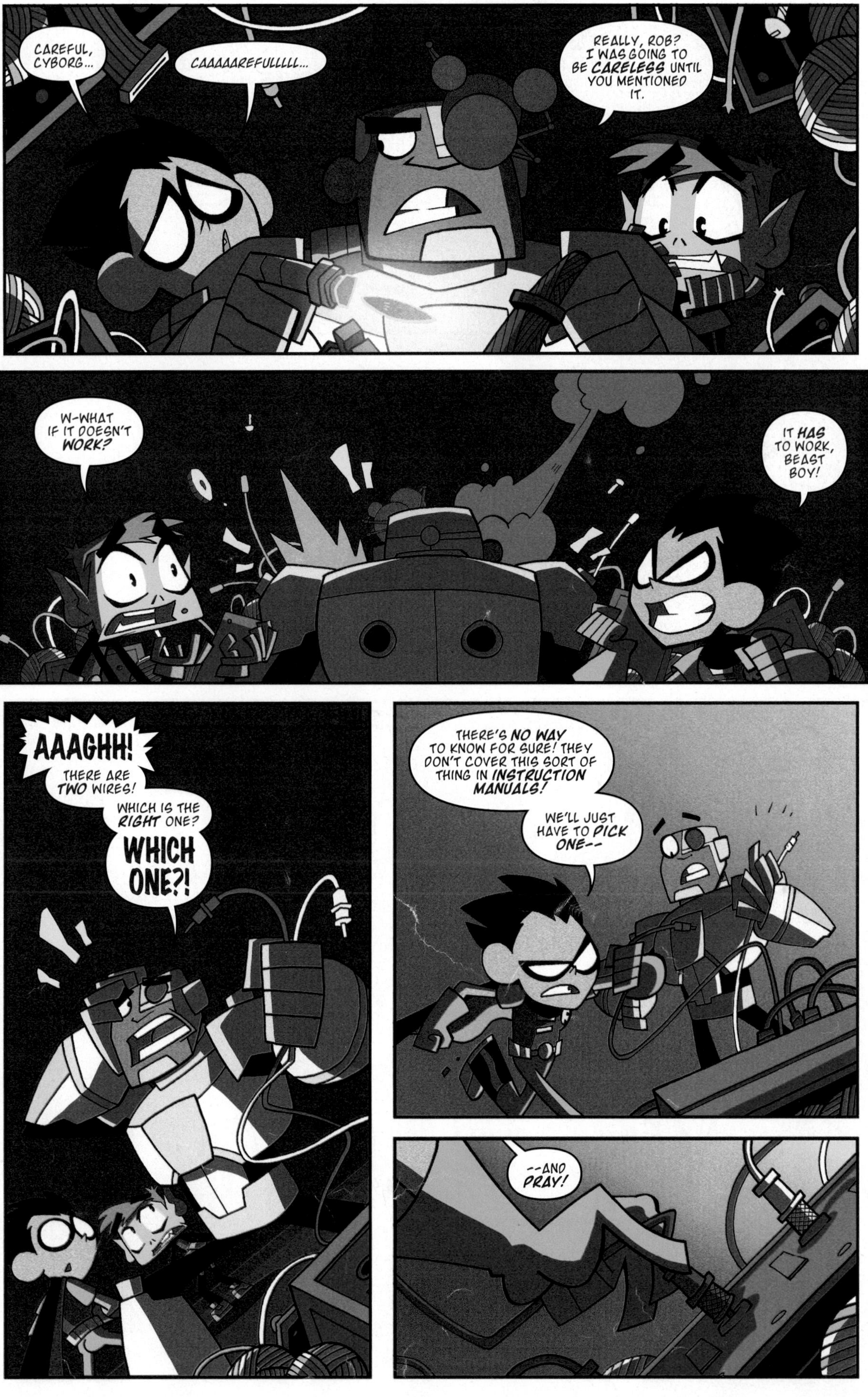
CAREFUL, CYBORG...
CAAAAAREFULLLLL...
REALLY, ROB? I WAS GOING TO BE CARELESS UNTIL YOU MENTIONED IT.
W-WHAT IF IT DOESN'T WORK?
IT HAS TO WORK, BEAST BOY!
AAAGHH!
THERE ARE TWO WIRES!
WHICH IS THE RIGHT ONE?
WHICH ONE?!
THERE'S NO WAY TO KNOW FOR SURE! THEY DON'T COVER THIS SORT OF THING IN INSTRUCTION MANUALS!
WE'LL JUST HAVE TO PICK ONE--
--AND PRAY!

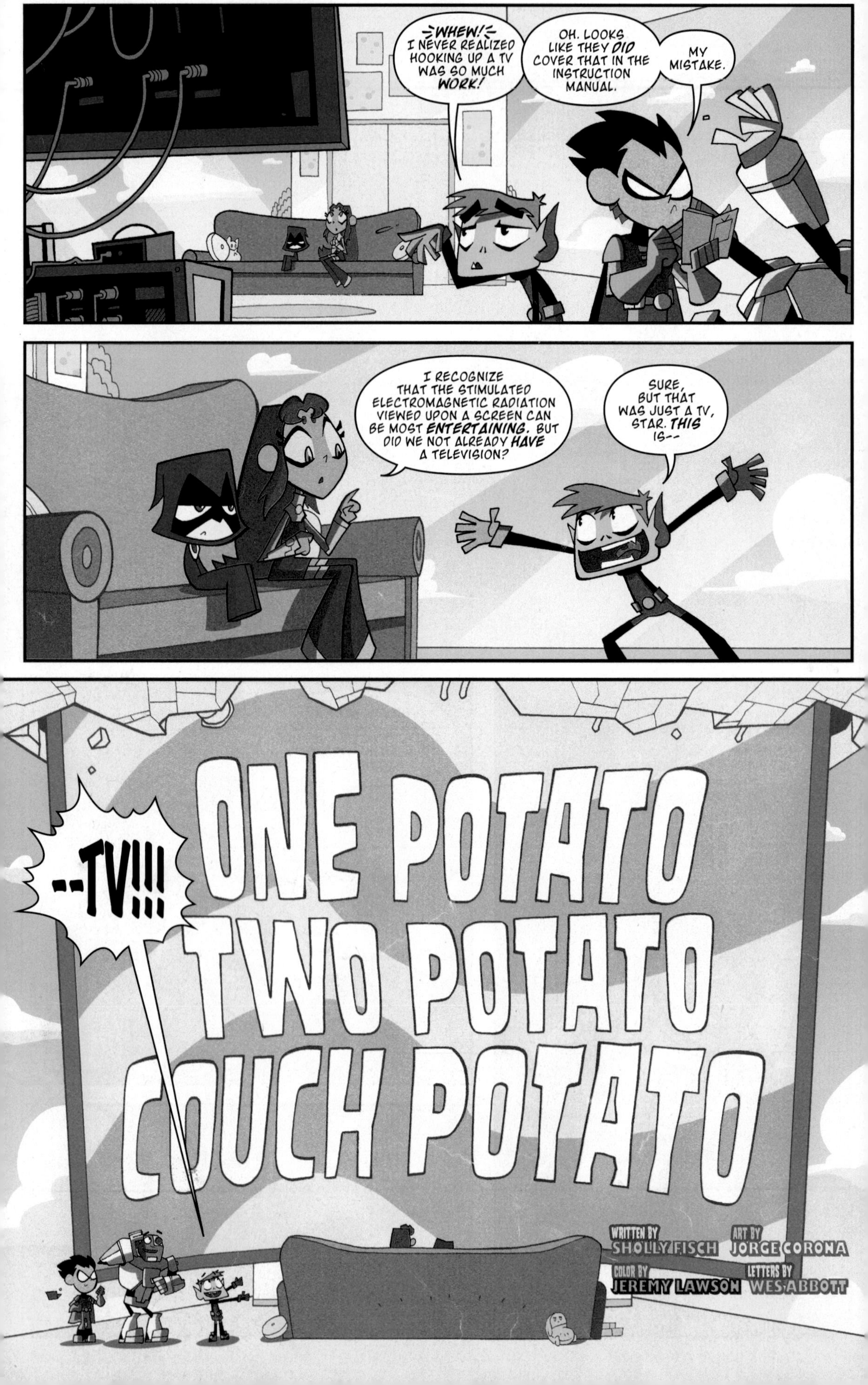

WHEW! I NEVER REALIZED HOOKING UP A TV WAS SO MUCH WORK!
OH. LOOKS LIKE THEY DID COVER THAT IN THE INSTRUCTION MANUAL.
MY MISTAKE.
I RECOGNIZE THAT THE STIMULATED ELECTROMAGNETIC RADIATION VIEWED UPON A SCREEN CAN BE MOST ENTERTAINING. BUT DID WE NOT ALREADY HAVE A TELEVISION?
SURE, BUT THAT WAS JUST A TV, STAR. THIS IS--
--TV!!!
ONE POTATO TWO POTATO COUCH POTATO
WRITTEN BY SHOLLY FISCH
ART BY JORGE CORONA
COLOR BY JEREMY LAWSON
LETTERS BY WES ABBOTT

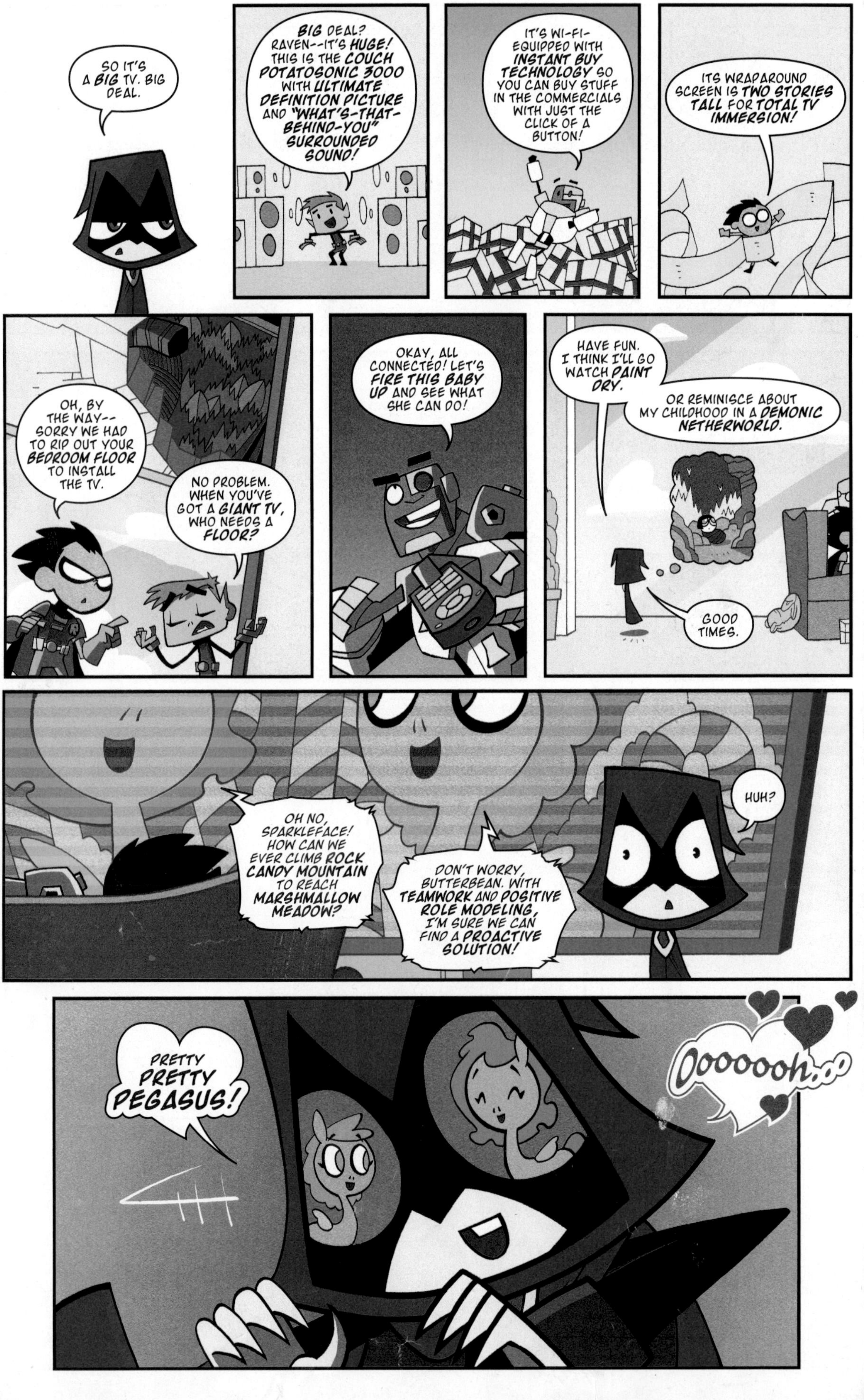
SO IT'S A BIG TV. BIG DEAL.
BIG DEAL? RAVEN--IT'S HUGE! THIS IS THE COUCH POTATOSONIC 3000 WITH ULTIMATE DEFINITION PICTURE AND "WHAT'S-THAT-BEHIND-YOU" SURROUNDED SOUND!
IT'S WI-FI-EQUIPPED WITH INSTANT BUY TECHNOLOGY SO YOU CAN BUY STUFF IN THE COMMERCIALS WITH JUST THE CLICK OF A BUTTON!
ITS WRAPAROUND SCREEN IS TWO STORIES TALL FOR TOTAL TV IMMERSION!
OH, BY THE WAY--SORRY WE HAD TO RIP OUT YOUR BEDROOM FLOOR TO INSTALL THE TV.
NO PROBLEM. WHEN YOU'VE GOT A GIANT TV, WHO NEEDS A FLOOR?
OKAY, ALL CONNECTED! LET'S FIRE THIS BABY UP AND SEE WHAT SHE CAN DO!
HAVE FUN. I THINK I'LL GO WATCH PAINT DRY.
OR REMINISCE ABOUT MY CHILDHOOD IN A DEMONIC NETHERWORLD.
GOOD TIMES.
OH NO, SPARKLEFACE! HOW CAN WE EVER CLIMB ROCK CANDY MOUNTAIN TO REACH MARSHMALLOW MEADOW?
DON'T WORRY, BUTTERBEAN. WITH TEAMWORK AND POSITIVE ROLE MODELING, I'M SURE WE CAN FIND A PROACTIVE SOLUTION!
HUH?
PRETTY PRETTY PEGASUS!
Ooooooh...

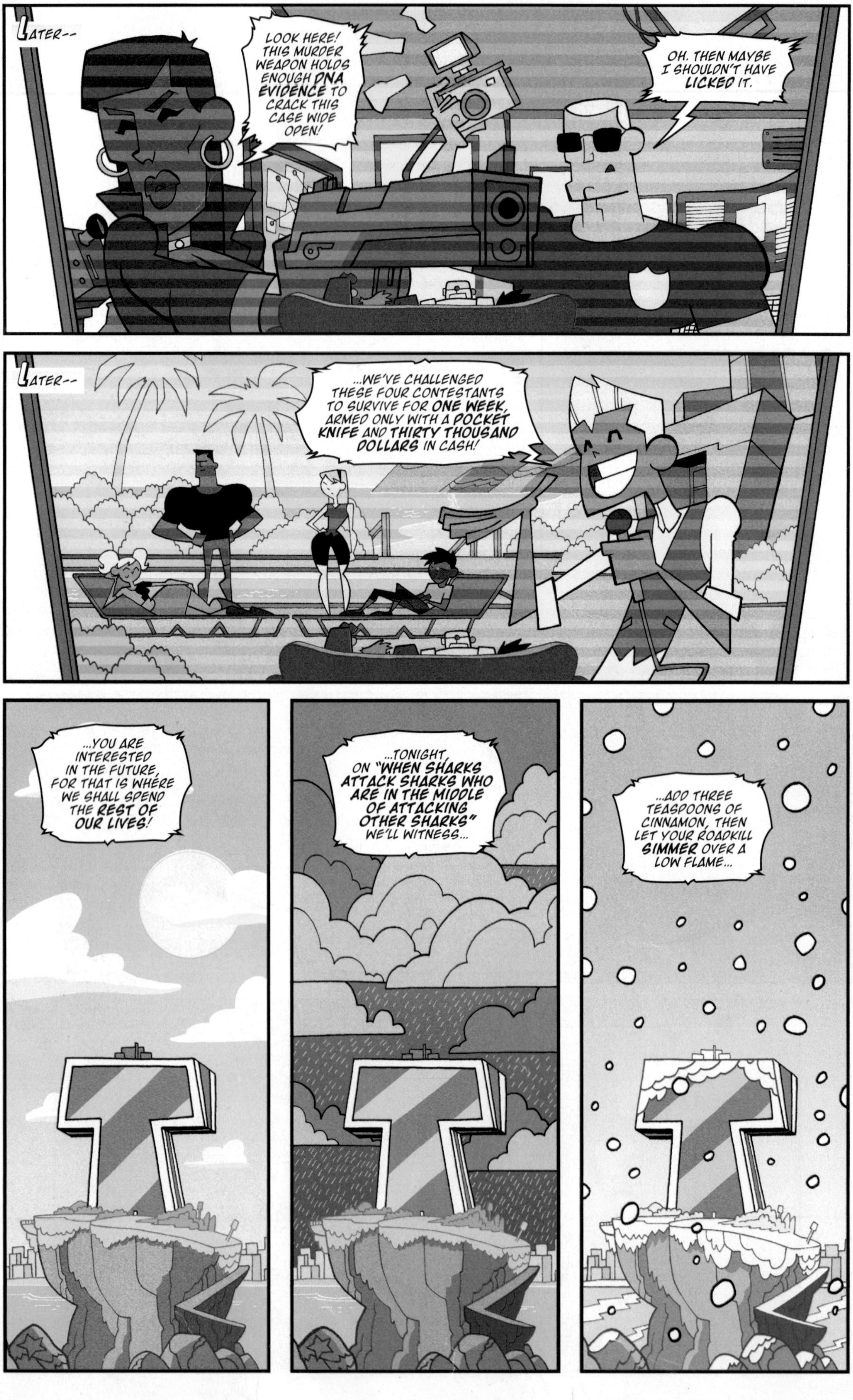
LATER--
LOOK HERE! THIS MURDER WEAPON HOLDS ENOUGH DNA EVIDENCE TO CRACK THIS CASE WIDE OPEN!
OH. THEN MAYBE I SHOULDN'T HAVE LICKED IT.
LATER--
...WE'VE CHALLENGED THESE FOUR CONTESTANTS TO SURVIVE FOR ONE WEEK, ARMED ONLY WITH A POCKET KNIFE AND THIRTY THOUSAND DOLLARS IN CASH!
...YOU ARE INTERESTED IN THE FUTURE, FOR THAT IS WHERE WE SHALL SPEND THE REST OF OUR LIVES!
...TONIGHT, ON "WHEN SHARKS ATTACK SHARKS WHO ARE IN THE MIDDLE OF ATTACKING OTHER SHARKS" WE'LL WITNESS...
...ADD THREE TEASPOONS OF CINNAMON, THEN LET YOUR ROADKILL SIMMER OVER A LOW FLAME...

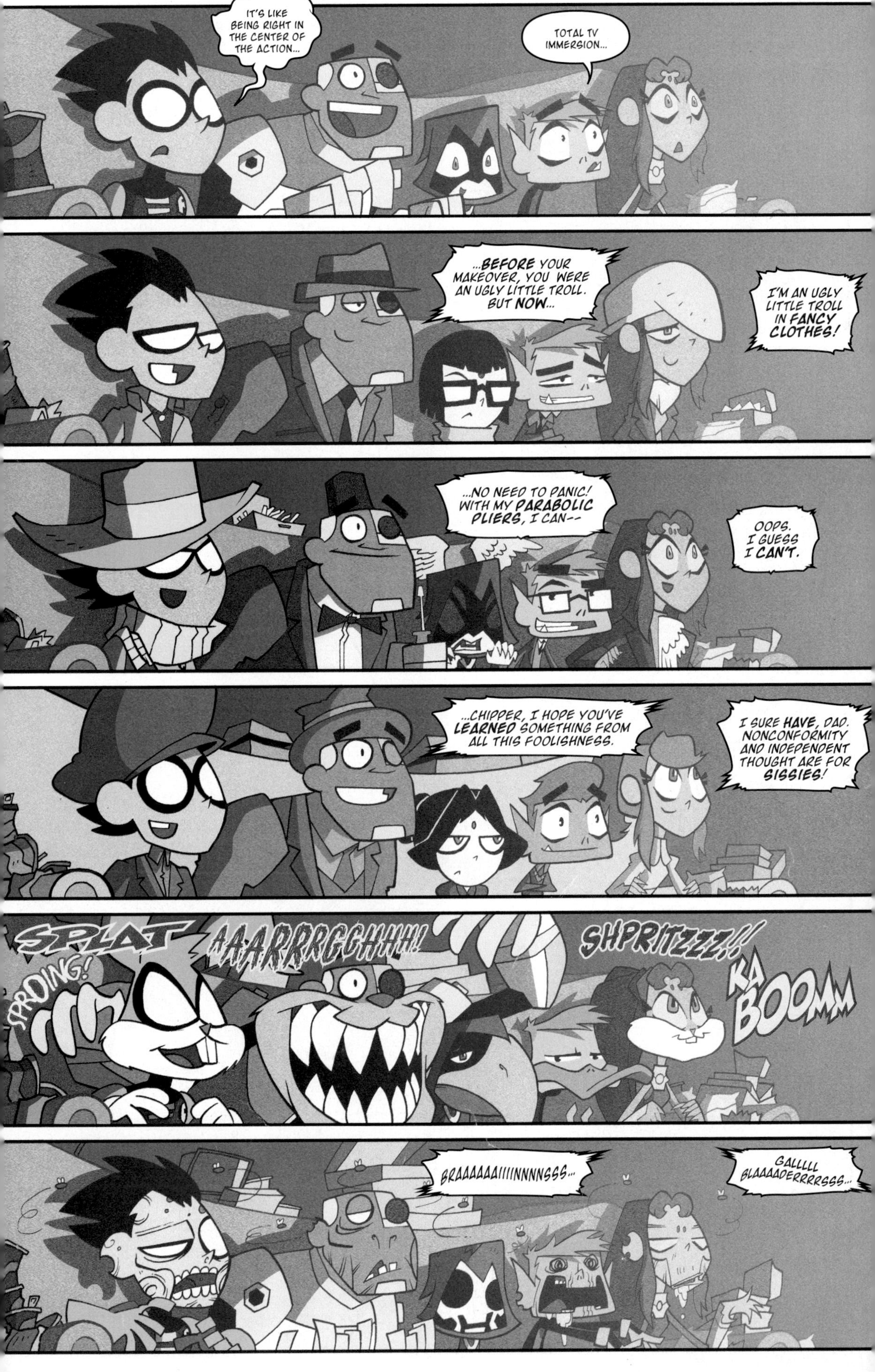
IT'S LIKE BEING RIGHT IN THE CENTER OF THE ACTION...
TOTAL TV IMMERSION...
...BEFORE YOUR MAKEOVER, YOU WERE AN UGLY LITTLE TROLL. BUT NOW...
I'M AN UGLY LITTLE TROLL IN FANCY CLOTHES!
...NO NEED TO PANIC! WITH MY PARABOLIC PLIERS, I CAN--
OOPS. I GUESS I CAN'T.
...CHIPPER, I HOPE YOU'VE LEARNED SOMETHING FROM ALL THIS FOOLISHNESS.
I SURE HAVE, DAD. NONCONFORMITY AND INDEPENDENT THOUGHT ARE FOR SISSIES!
SPLAT
SPROING!
AAARRRGGHHH!
SHPRITZZZ!!
KA BOOMM
BRAAAAAAIIIINNNNSSS...
GALLLLL BLAAAADERRRRSSS...

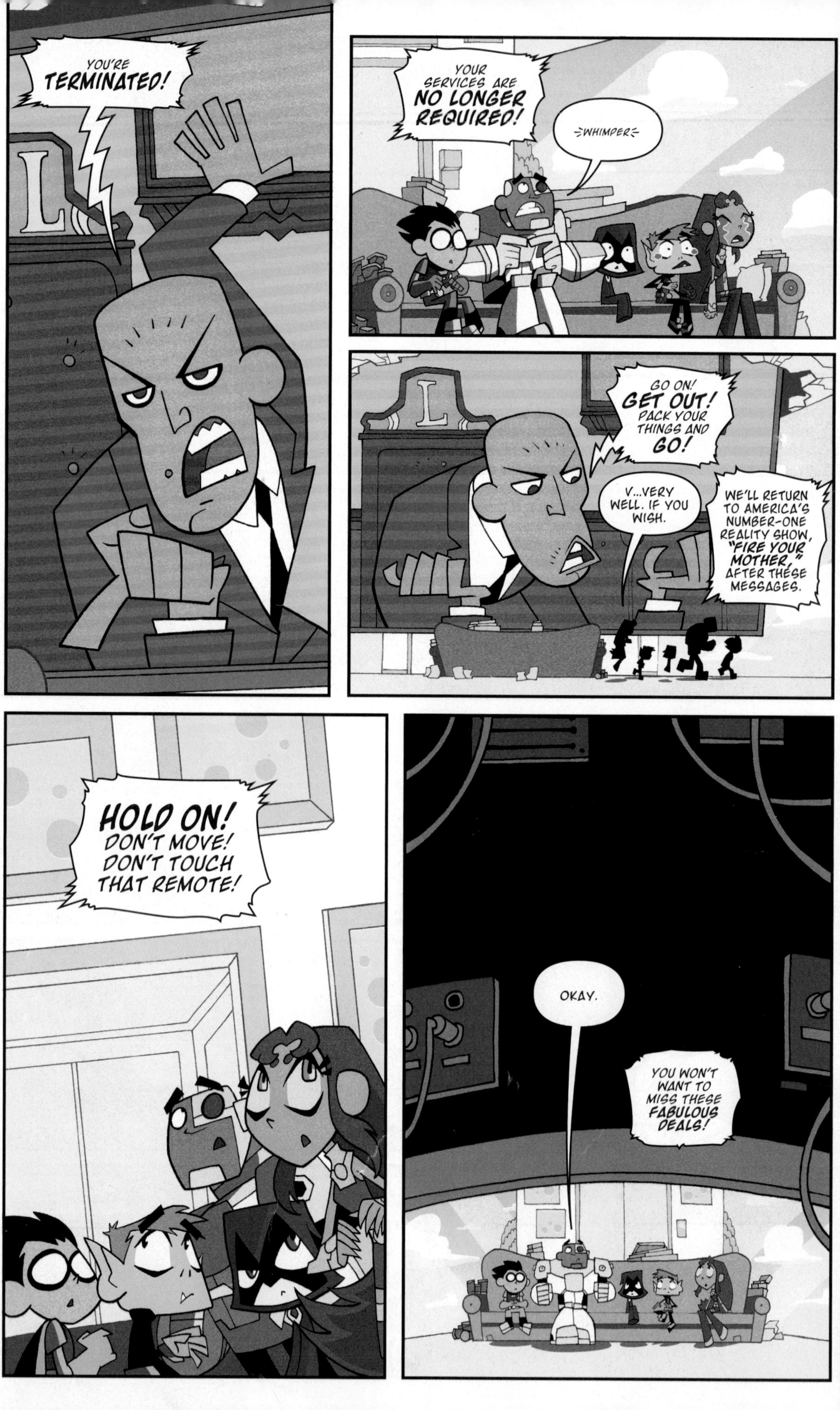

YOU'RE TERMINATED!
YOUR SERVICES ARE NO LONGER REQUIRED!
=WHIMPER=
GO ON! GET OUT! PACK YOUR THINGS AND GO!
V...VERY WELL. IF YOU WISH.
WE'LL RETURN TO AMERICA'S NUMBER-ONE REALITY SHOW, "FIRE YOUR MOTHER," AFTER THESE MESSAGES.
HOLD ON! DON'T MOVE! DON'T TOUCH THAT REMOTE!
OKAY.
YOU WON'T WANT TO MISS THESE FABULOUS DEALS!

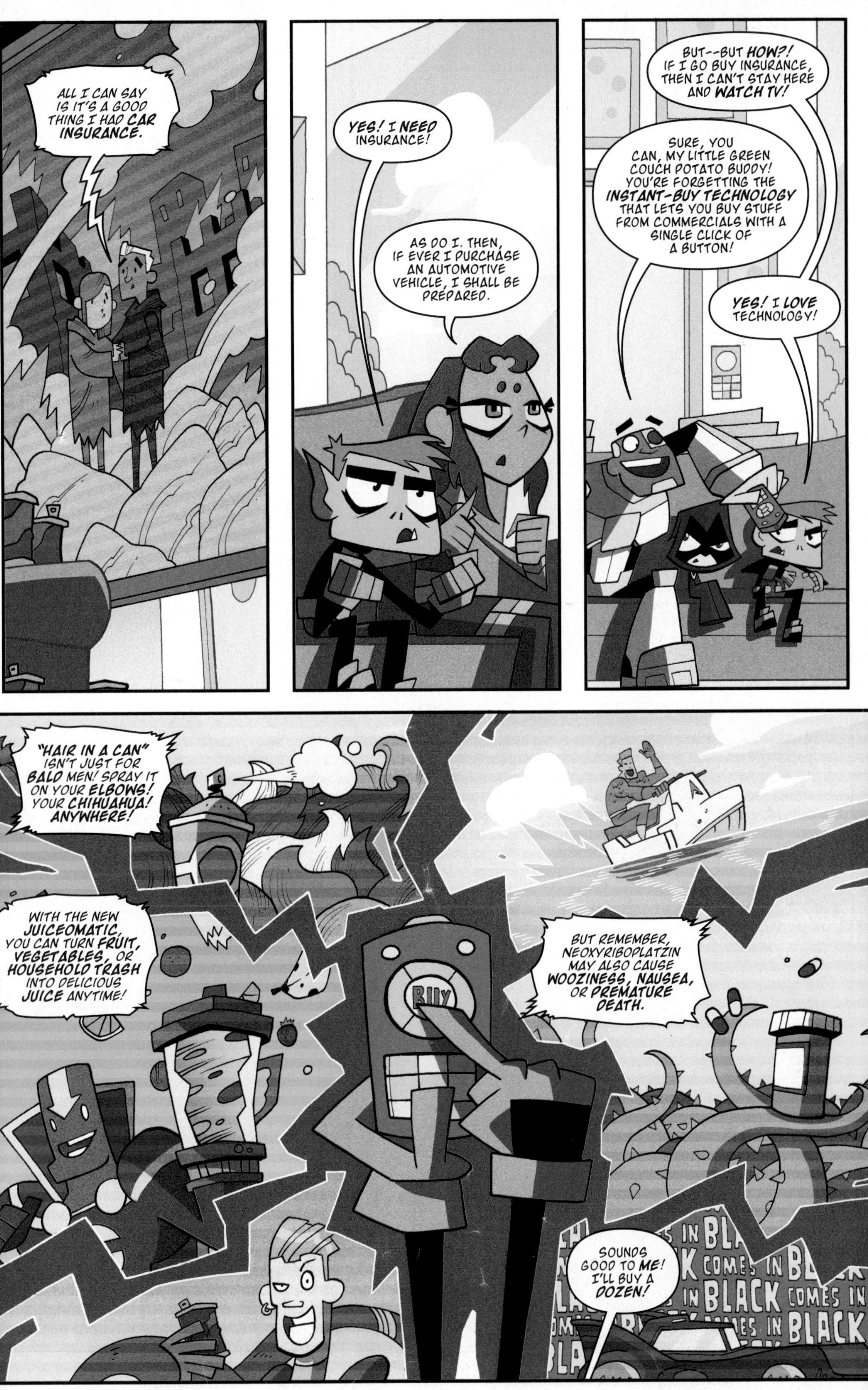
ALL I CAN SAY IS IT'S A GOOD THING I HAD CAR INSURANCE.
YES! I NEED INSURANCE!
AS DO I. THEN, IF EVER I PURCHASE AN AUTOMOTIVE VEHICLE, I SHALL BE PREPARED.
BUT--BUT HOW?! IF I GO BUY INSURANCE, THEN I CAN'T STAY HERE AND WATCH TV!
SURE, YOU CAN, MY LITTLE GREEN COUCH POTATO BUDDY! YOU'RE FORGETTING THE INSTANT-BUY TECHNOLOGY THAT LETS YOU BUY STUFF FROM COMMERCIALS WITH A SINGLE CLICK OF A BUTTON!
YES! I LOVE TECHNOLOGY!
"HAIR IN A CAN" ISN'T JUST FOR BALD MEN! SPRAY IT ON YOUR ELBOWS! YOUR CHIHUAHUA! ANYWHERE!
WITH THE NEW JUICEOMATIC, YOU CAN TURN FRUIT, VEGETABLES, OR HOUSEHOLD TRASH INTO DELICIOUS JUICE ANYTIME!
BUY
BUT REMEMBER, NEOXYRIBOPLATZIN MAY ALSO CAUSE WOOZINESS, NAUSEA, OR PREMATURE DEATH.
SOUNDS GOOD TO ME! I'LL BUY A DOZEN!

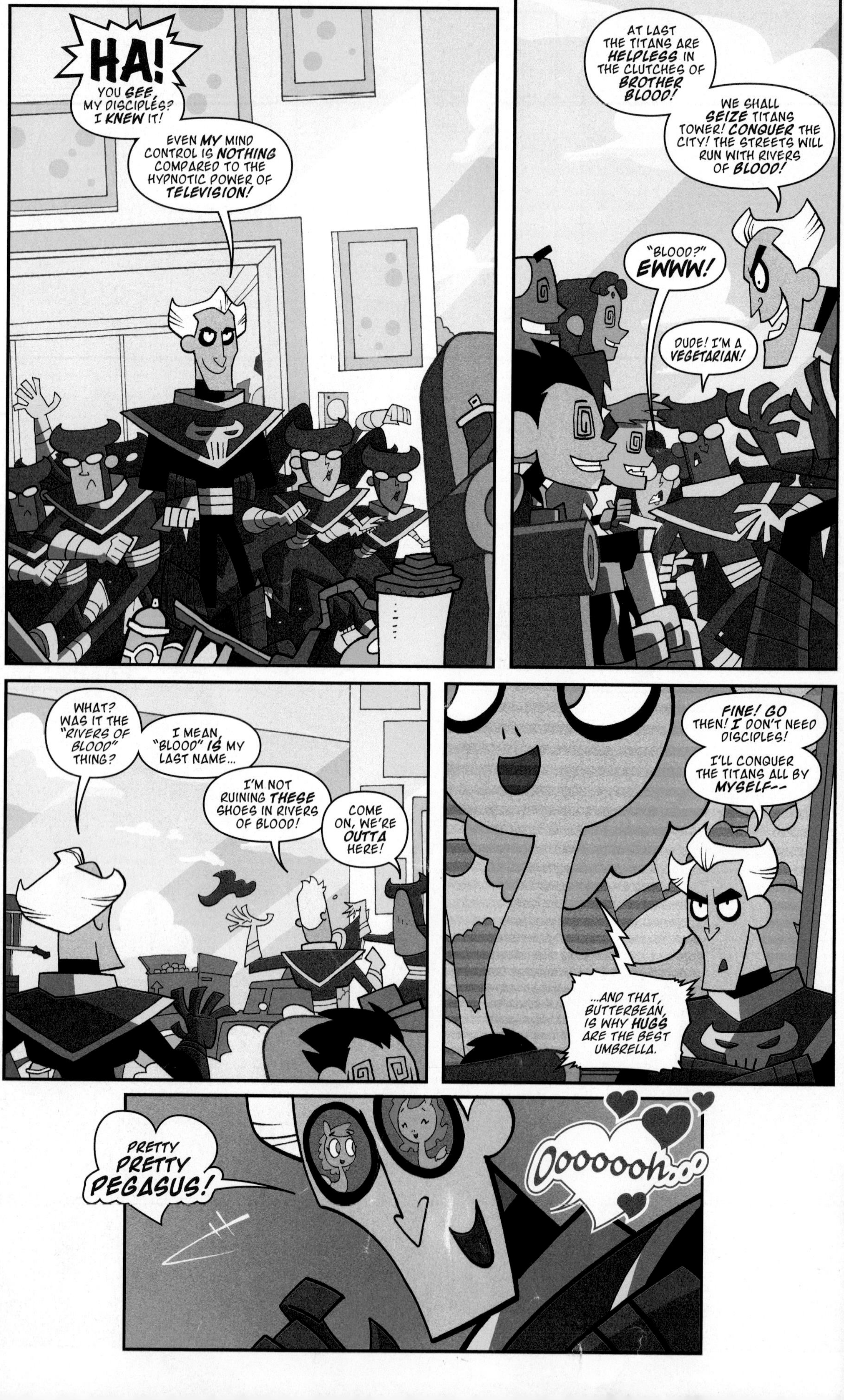
HA!
YOU SEE, MY DISCIPLES? I KNEW IT!
EVEN MY MIND CONTROL IS NOTHING COMPARED TO THE HYPNOTIC POWER OF TELEVISION!
AT LAST THE TITANS ARE HELPLESS IN THE CLUTCHES OF BROTHER BLOOD!
WE SHALL SEIZE TITANS TOWER! CONQUER THE CITY! THE STREETS WILL RUN WITH RIVERS OF BLOOD!
"BLOOD?" EWWW!
DUDE! I'M A VEGETARIAN!
WHAT? WAS IT THE "RIVERS OF BLOOD" THING?
I MEAN, "BLOOD" IS MY LAST NAME...
I'M NOT RUINING THESE SHOES IN RIVERS OF BLOOD!
COME ON, WE'RE OUTTA HERE!
FINE! GO THEN! I DON'T NEED DISCIPLES!
I'LL CONQUER THE TITANS ALL BY MYSELF--
...AND THAT, BUTTERBEAN, IS WHY HUGS ARE THE BEST UMBRELLA.
PRETTY PRETTY PEGASUS!
Ooooooh...

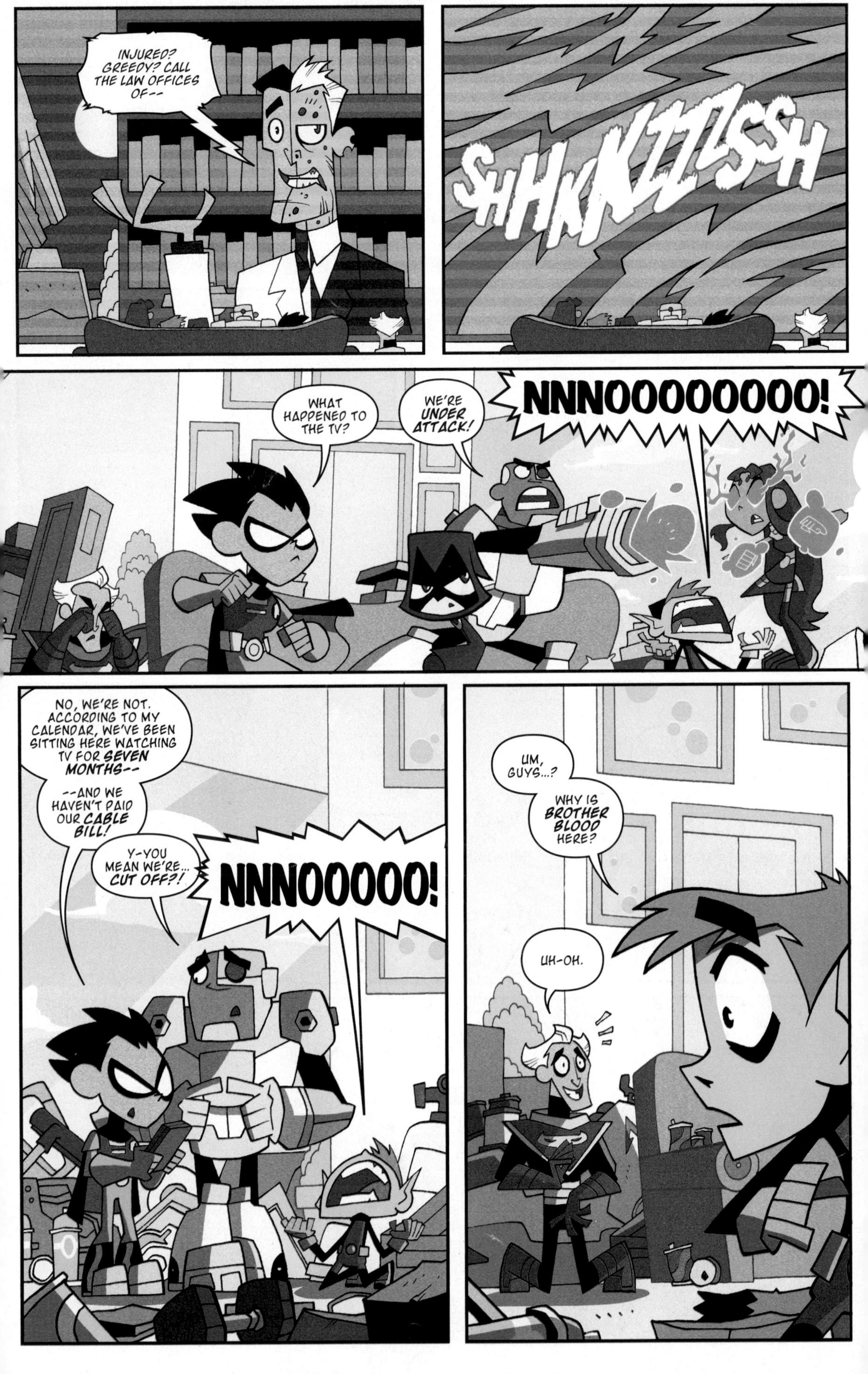
INJURED? GREEDY? CALL THE LAW OFFICES OF--
SHHKKZZZSSH
WHAT HAPPENED TO THE TV?
WE'RE UNDER ATTACK!
NNNOOOOOOOOO!
NO, WE'RE NOT. ACCORDING TO MY CALENDAR, WE'VE BEEN SITTING HERE WATCHING TV FOR SEVEN MONTHS--
--AND WE HAVEN'T PAID OUR CABLE BILL!
Y-YOU MEAN WE'RE... CUT OFF?!
NNNOOOOO!
UM, GUYS...?
WHY IS BROTHER BLOOD HERE?
UH-OH.

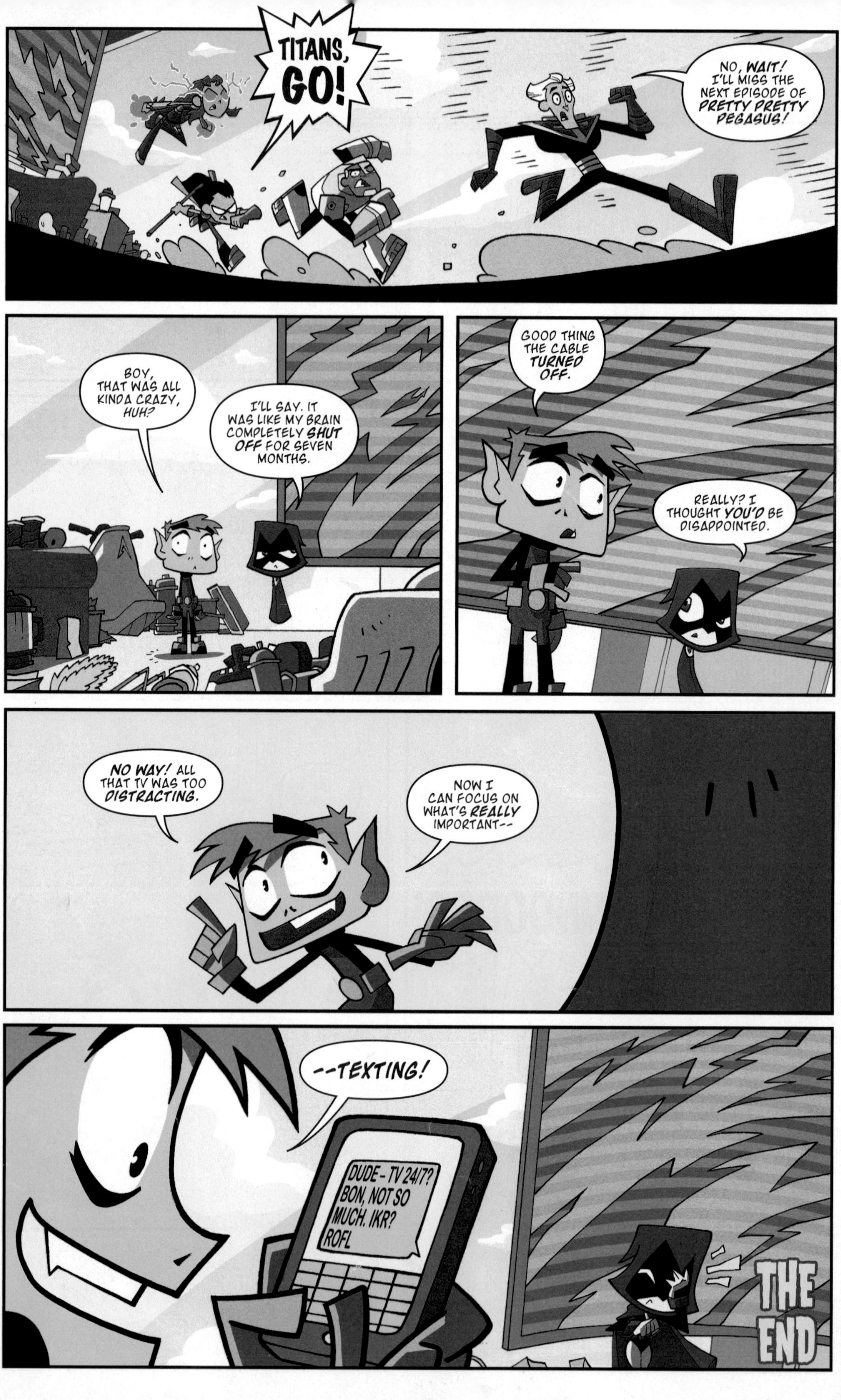
TITANS, GO!
NO, WAIT! I'LL MISS THE NEXT EPISODE OF PRETTY PRETTY PEGASUS!
BOY, THAT WAS ALL KINDA CRAZY, HUH?
I'LL SAY. IT WAS LIKE MY BRAIN COMPLETELY SHUT OFF FOR SEVEN MONTHS.
GOOD THING THE CABLE TURNED OFF.
REALLY? I THOUGHT YOU'D BE DISAPPOINTED.
NO WAY! ALL THAT TV WAS TOO DISTRACTING.
NOW I CAN FOCUS ON WHAT'S REALLY IMPORTANT--
--TEXTING!
DUDE - TV 24/7? BON, NOT SO MUCH. IKR? ROFL
THE END

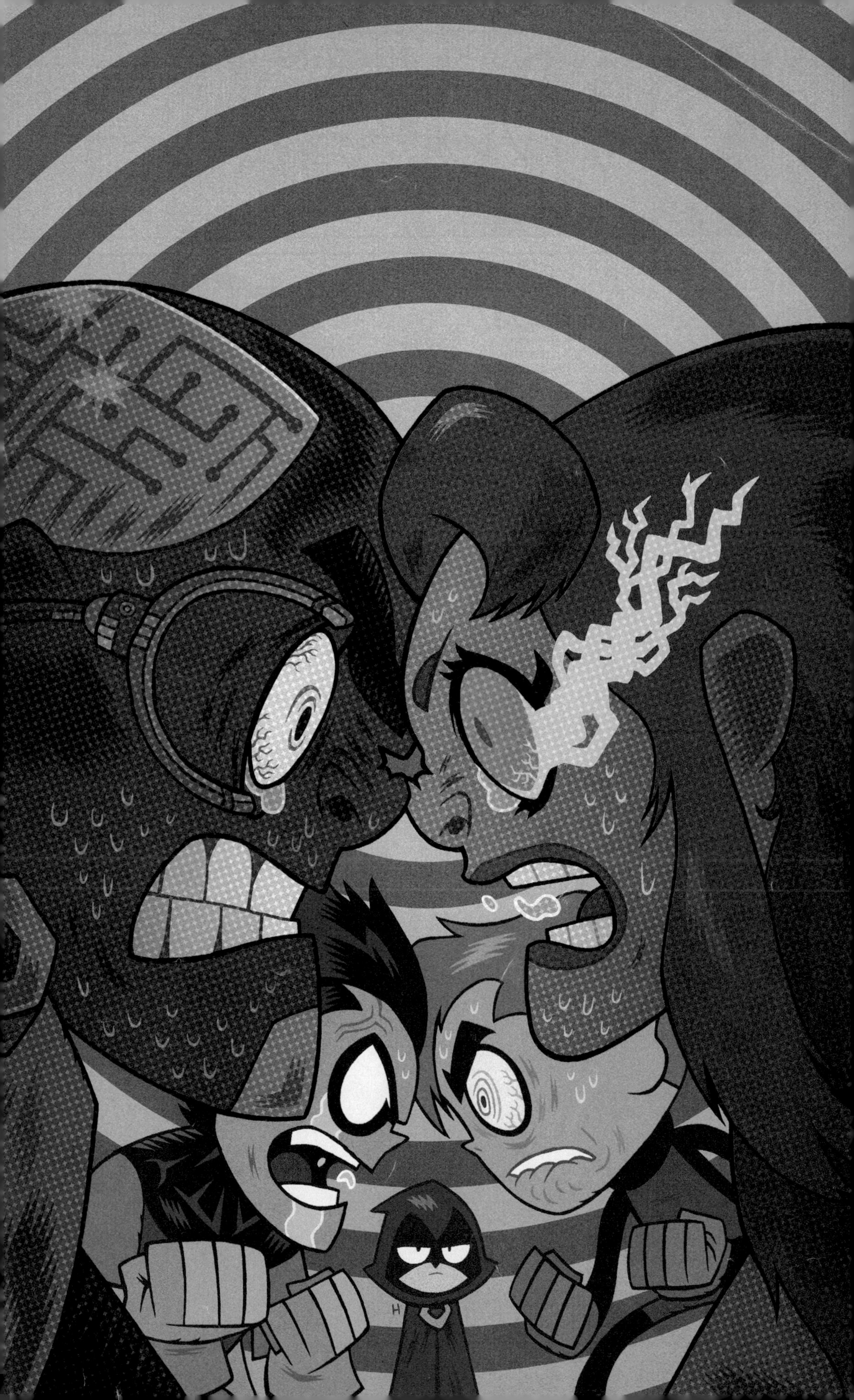

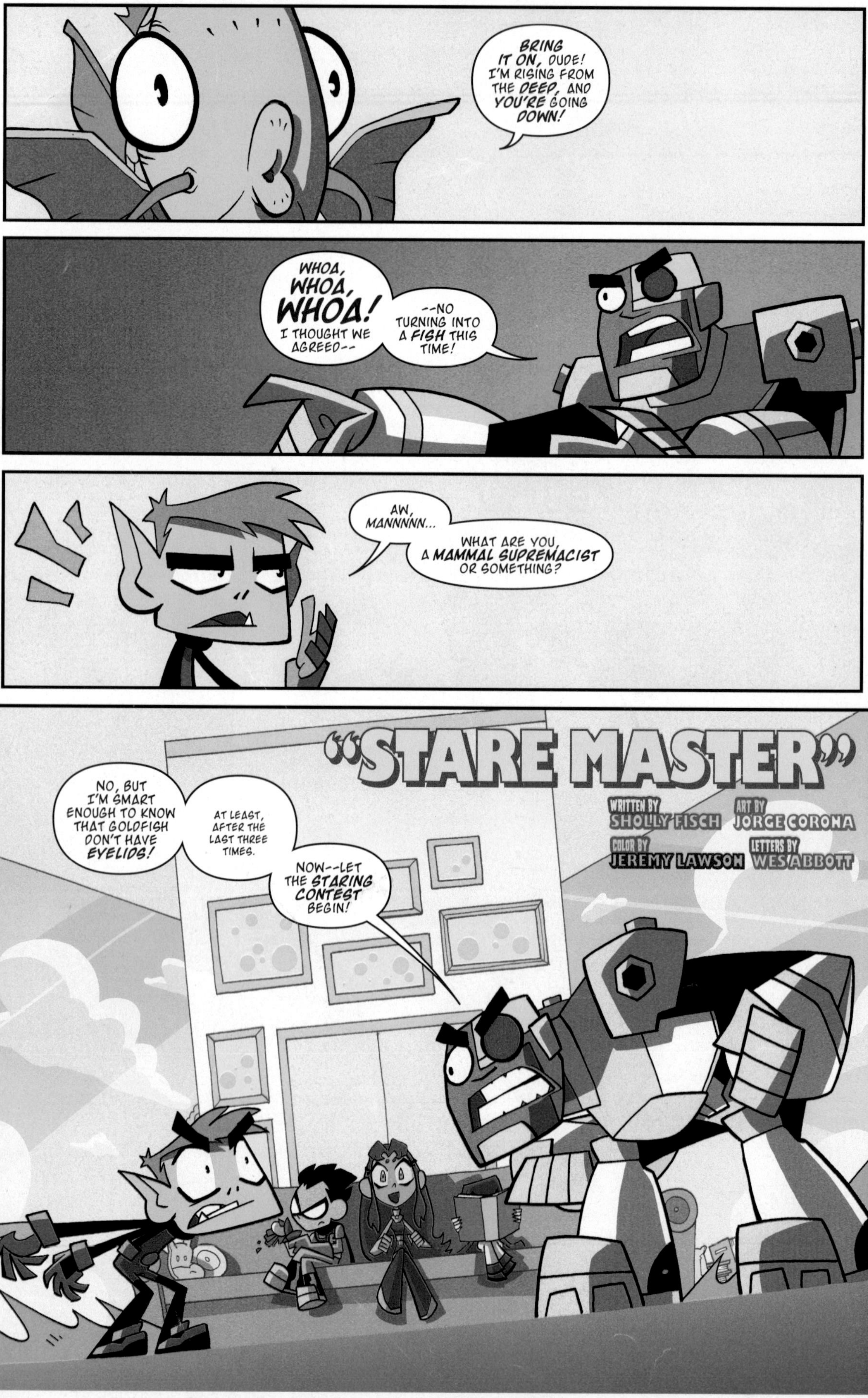
BRING IT ON, DUDE! I'M RISING FROM THE DEEP, AND YOU'RE GOING DOWN!
WHOA, WHOA, WHOA! I THOUGHT WE AGREED--
--NO TURNING INTO A FISH THIS TIME!
AW, MANNNNN...
WHAT ARE YOU, A MAMMAL SUPREMACIST OR SOMETHING?
"STARE MASTER"
WRITTEN BY SHOLLY FISCH
ART BY JORGE CORONA
COLOR BY JEREMY LAWSON
LETTERS BY WES ABBOTT
NO, BUT I'M SMART ENOUGH TO KNOW THAT GOLDFISH DON'T HAVE EYELIDS!
AT LEAST, AFTER THE LAST THREE TIMES.
NOW--LET THE STARING CONTEST BEGIN!

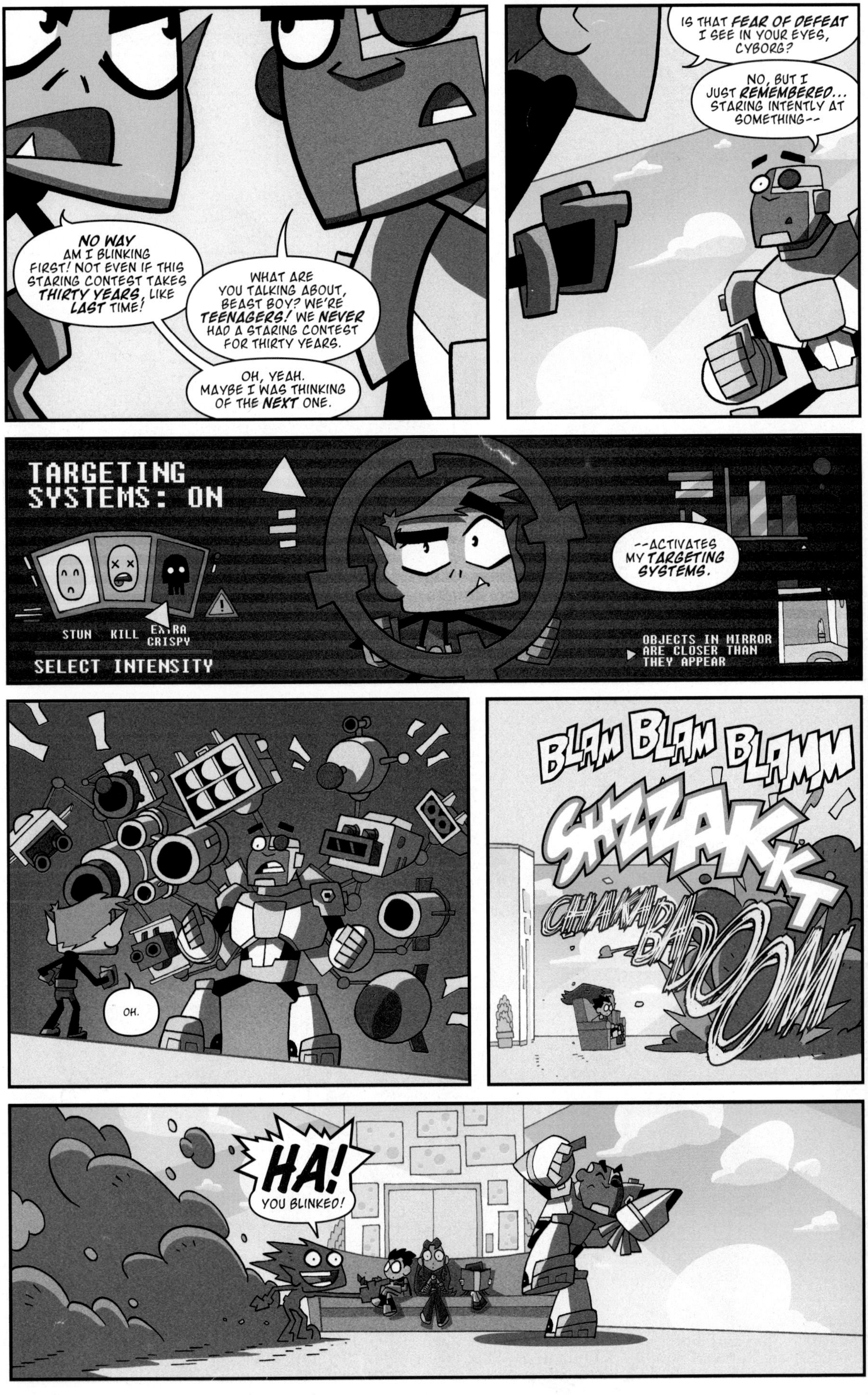
NO WAY AM I BLINKING FIRST! NOT EVEN IF THIS STARING CONTEST TAKES THIRTY YEARS, LIKE LAST TIME!
WHAT ARE YOU TALKING ABOUT, BEAST BOY? WE'RE TEENAGERS! WE NEVER HAD A STARING CONTEST FOR THIRTY YEARS.
OH, YEAH. MAYBE I WAS THINKING OF THE NEXT ONE.
IS THAT FEAR OF DEFEAT I SEE IN YOUR EYES, CYBORG?
NO, BUT I JUST REMEMBERED... STARING INTENTLY AT SOMETHING--
TARGETING SYSTEMS: ON
STUN
KILL
EXTRA CRISPY
SELECT INTENSITY
--ACTIVATES MY TARGETING SYSTEMS.
OBJECTS IN MIRROR ARE CLOSER THAN THEY APPEAR
OH.
BLAM BLAM BLAMM
SHZZAKKT
CHAKADABADOOM
HA! YOU BLINKED!

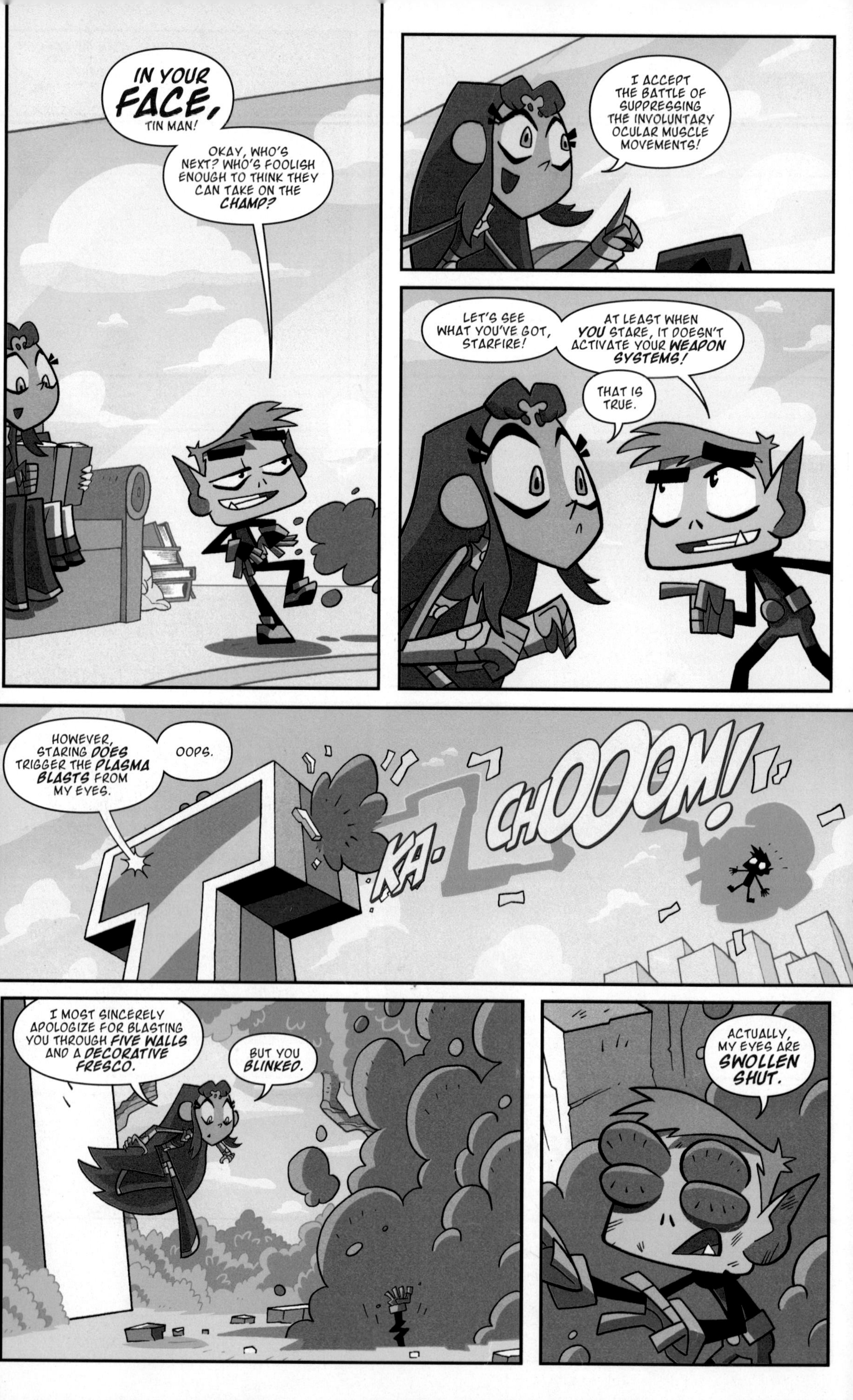

IN YOUR FACE, TIN MAN!
OKAY, WHO'S NEXT? WHO'S FOOLISH ENOUGH TO THINK THEY CAN TAKE ON THE CHAMP?
I ACCEPT THE BATTLE OF SUPPRESSING THE INVOLUNTARY OCULAR MUSCLE MOVEMENTS!
LET'S SEE WHAT YOU'VE GOT, STARFIRE!
AT LEAST WHEN YOU STARE, IT DOESN'T ACTIVATE YOUR WEAPON SYSTEMS!
THAT IS TRUE.
HOWEVER, STARING DOES TRIGGER THE PLASMA BLASTS FROM MY EYES.
OOPS.
KA-CHOOOOM!
I MOST SINCERELY APOLOGIZE FOR BLASTING YOU THROUGH FIVE WALLS AND A DECORATIVE FRESCO.
BUT YOU BLINKED.
ACTUALLY, MY EYES ARE SWOLLEN SHUT.

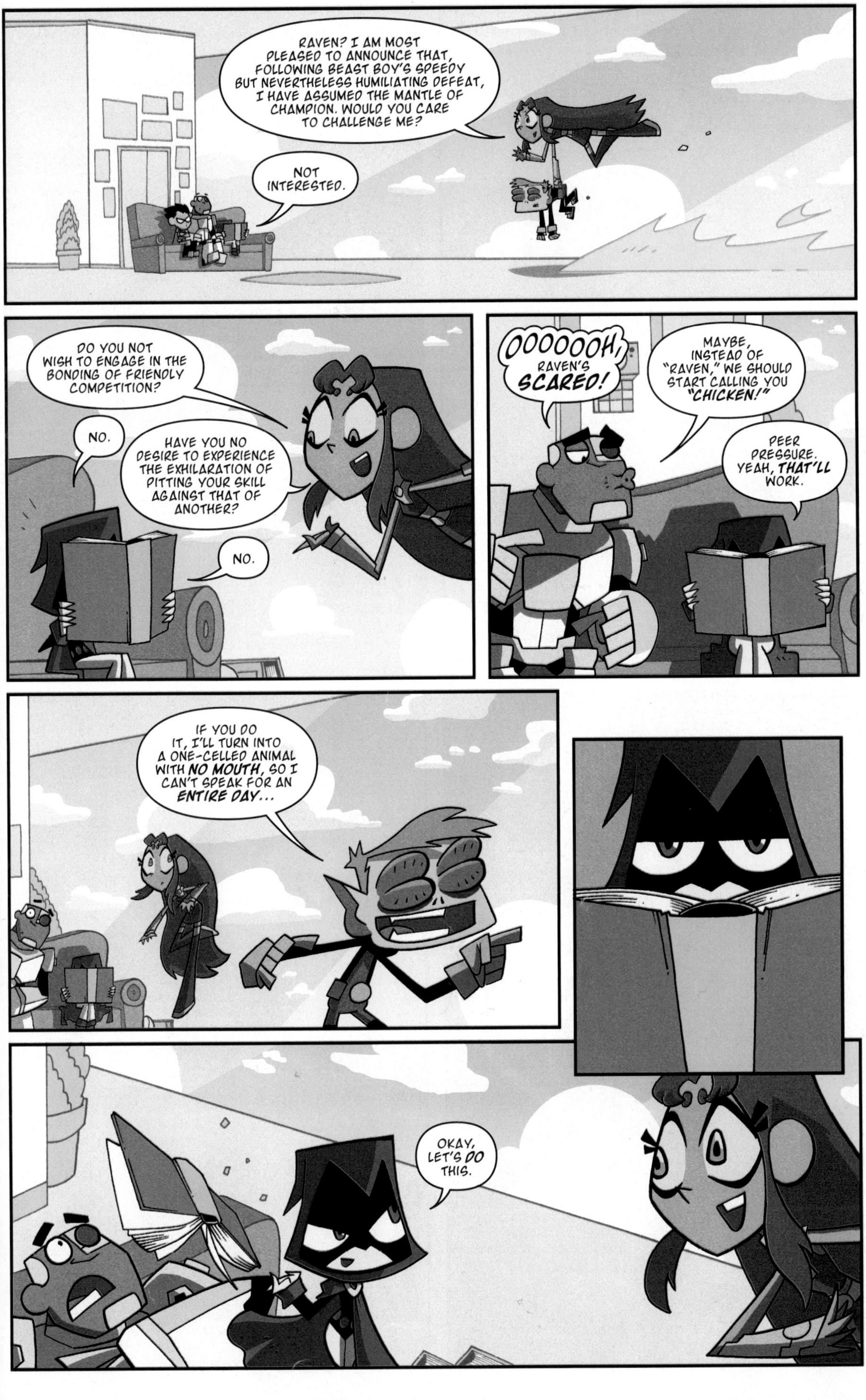
RAVEN? I AM MOST PLEASED TO ANNOUNCE THAT, FOLLOWING BEAST BOY'S SPEEDY BUT NEVERTHELESS HUMILIATING DEFEAT, I HAVE ASSUMED THE MANTLE OF CHAMPION. WOULD YOU CARE TO CHALLENGE ME?
NOT INTERESTED.
DO YOU NOT WISH TO ENGAGE IN THE BONDING OF FRIENDLY COMPETITION?
NO.
HAVE YOU NO DESIRE TO EXPERIENCE THE EXHILARATION OF PITTING YOUR SKILL AGAINST THAT OF ANOTHER?
NO.
OOOOOOH, RAVEN'S SCARED!
MAYBE, INSTEAD OF "RAVEN," WE SHOULD START CALLING YOU "CHICKEN!"
PEER PRESSURE. YEAH, THAT'LL WORK.
IF YOU DO IT, I'LL TURN INTO A ONE-CELLED ANIMAL WITH NO MOUTH, SO I CAN'T SPEAK FOR AN ENTIRE DAY...
OKAY, LET'S DO THIS.

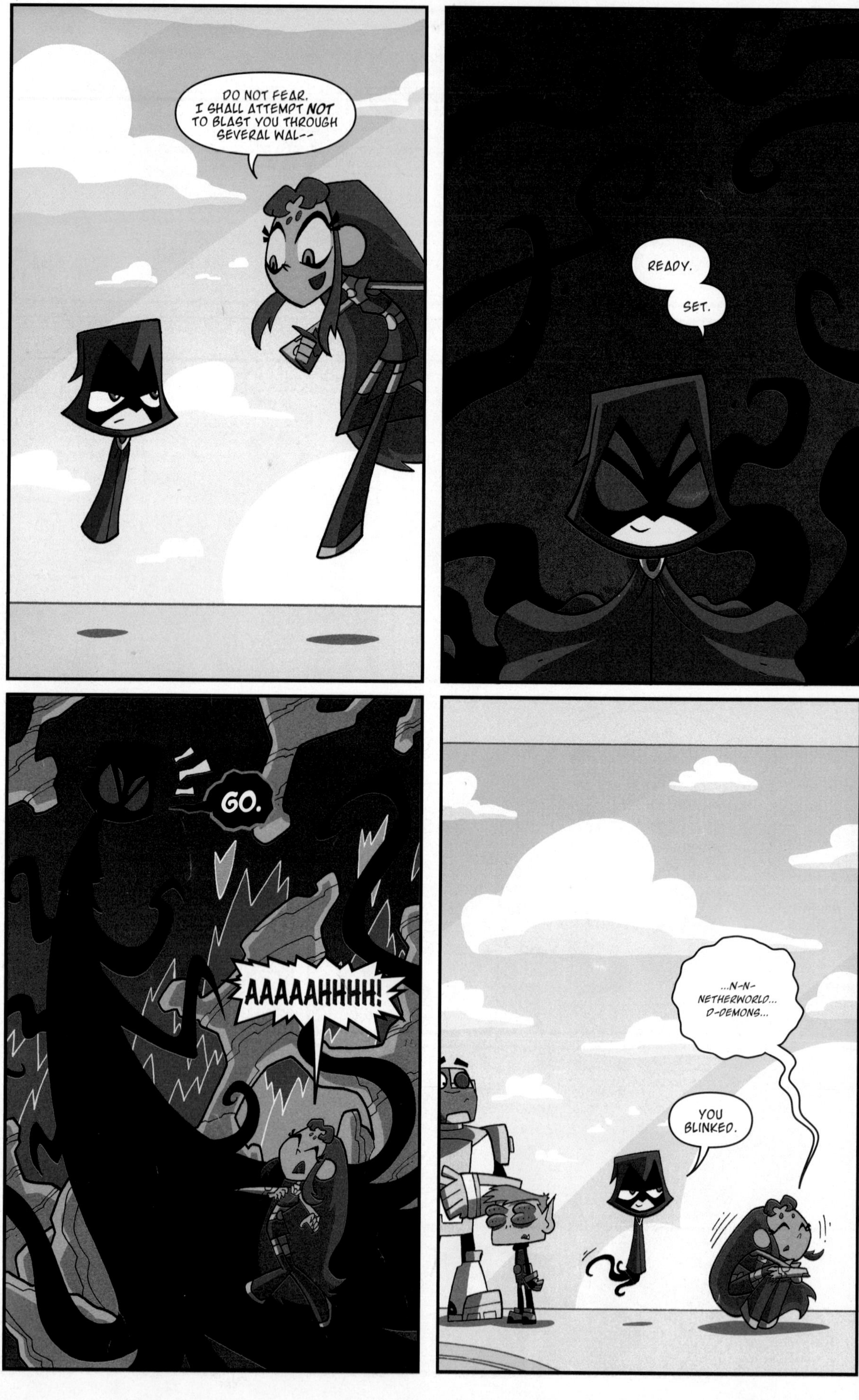
DO NOT FEAR. I SHALL ATTEMPT NOT TO BLAST YOU THROUGH SEVERAL WAL--
READY.
SET.
GO.
AAAAAHHHH!
...N-N- NETHERWORLD... D-DEMONS...
YOU BLINKED.

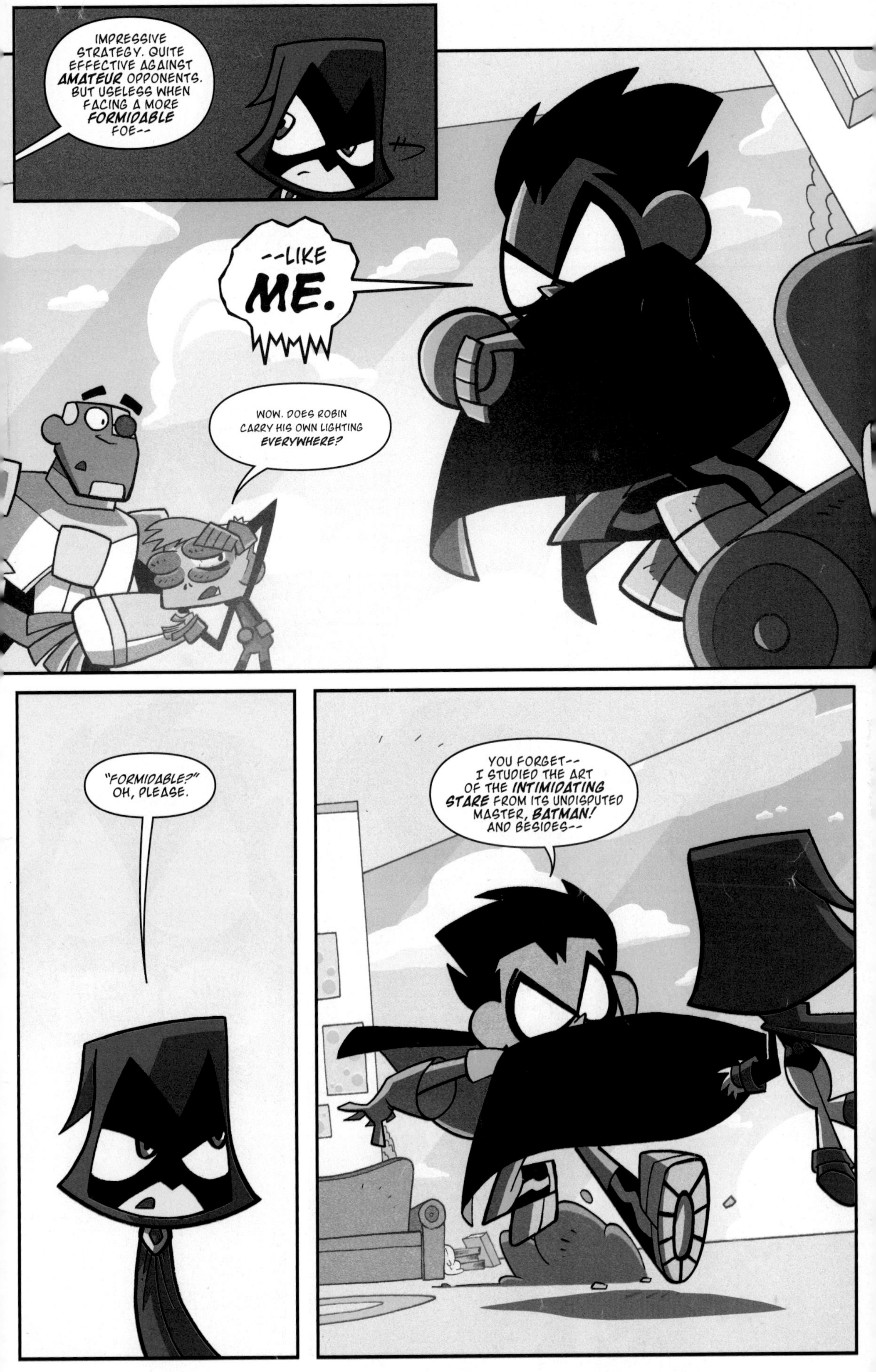

IMPRESSIVE STRATEGY. QUITE EFFECTIVE AGAINST AMATEUR OPPONENTS. BUT USELESS WHEN FACING A MORE FORMIDABLE FOE--
--LIKE ME.
WOW. DOES ROBIN CARRY HIS OWN LIGHTING EVERYWHERE?
"FORMIDABLE?" OH, PLEASE.
YOU FORGET-- I STUDIED THE ART OF THE INTIMIDATING STARE FROM ITS UNDISPUTED MASTER, BATMAN! AND BESIDES--

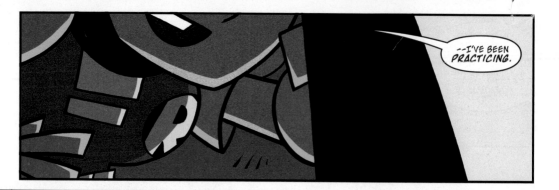

--I'VE BEEN *PRACTICING*.

PRACTICING. RIGHT. WITH *THEM*?

NO...

"...WITH MORE *CHALLENGING* OPPONENTS."

COME ON, *SEE-MORE!* TRY IT! JUST TRY TO STARE ME DOWN! I *DARE* YOU!

DUDE, YOU'RE CREEPING ME OUT!

CAN'T DO IT, CAN YOU, *TEN-EYED MAN?* EVEN THOUGH YOU SEE THROUGH YOUR *FINGERTIPS*, YOU *CRUMBLE* BEFORE MY *WITHERING STARE!*

ARRRGH! FINGERS... CRAMPING...

I'VE GOT *MY* EYE ON *YOU*, *BROTHER EYE!*

HELP! THE HUMAN IS *INSANE!*

HE DOES NOT EVEN *BLINK!*

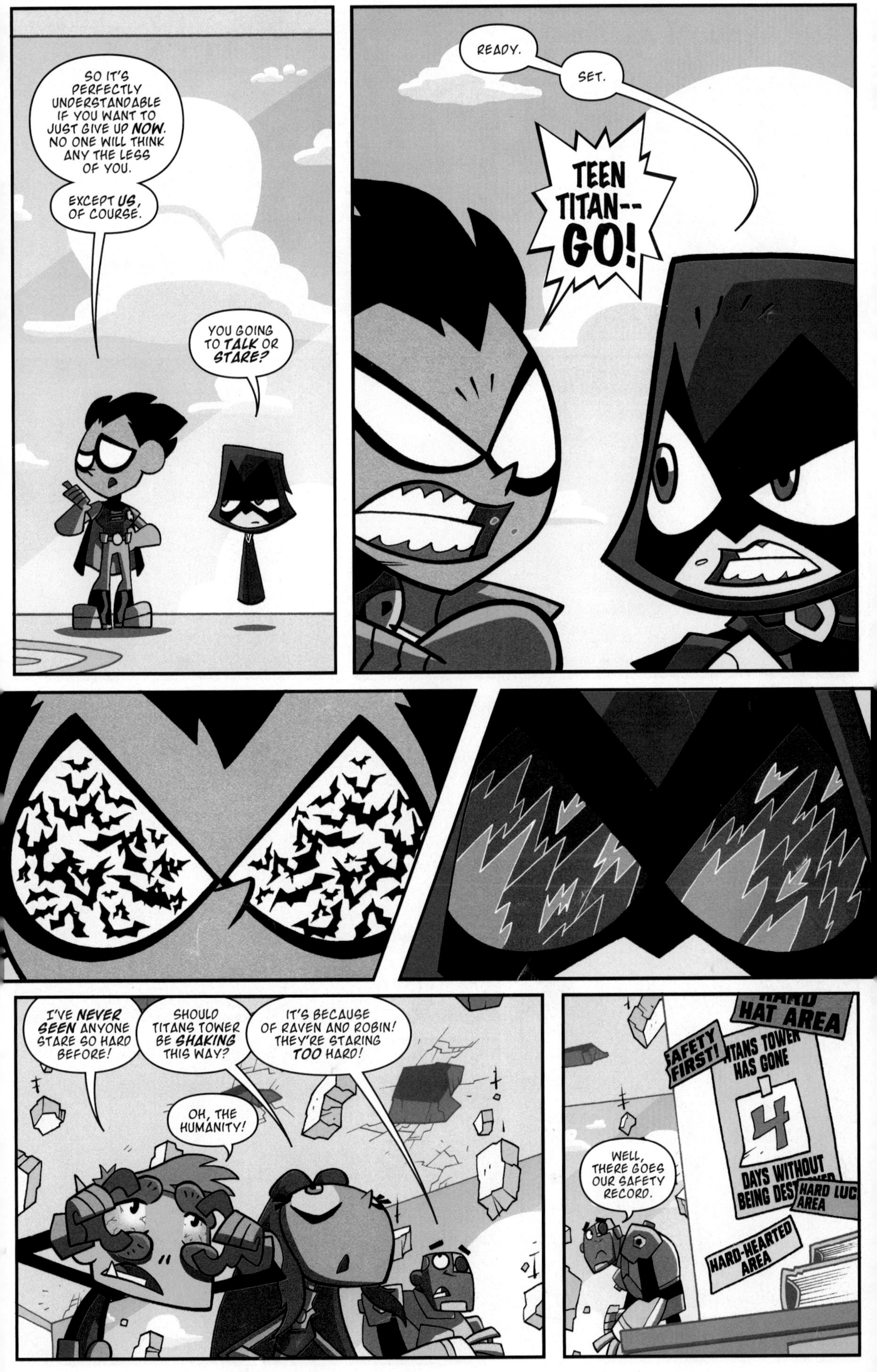
SO IT'S PERFECTLY UNDERSTANDABLE IF YOU WANT TO JUST GIVE UP NOW. NO ONE WILL THINK ANY THE LESS OF YOU.
EXCEPT US, OF COURSE.
YOU GOING TO TALK OR STARE?
READY.
SET.
TEEN TITAN--GO!
I'VE NEVER SEEN ANYONE STARE SO HARD BEFORE!
SHOULD TITANS TOWER BE SHAKING THIS WAY?
IT'S BECAUSE OF RAVEN AND ROBIN! THEY'RE STARING TOO HARD!
OH, THE HUMANITY!
HAT AREA
SAFETY FIRST!
TITANS TOWER HAS GONE
4
DAYS WITHOUT
WELL, THERE GOES OUR SAFETY RECORD.
HARD-HEARTED AREA

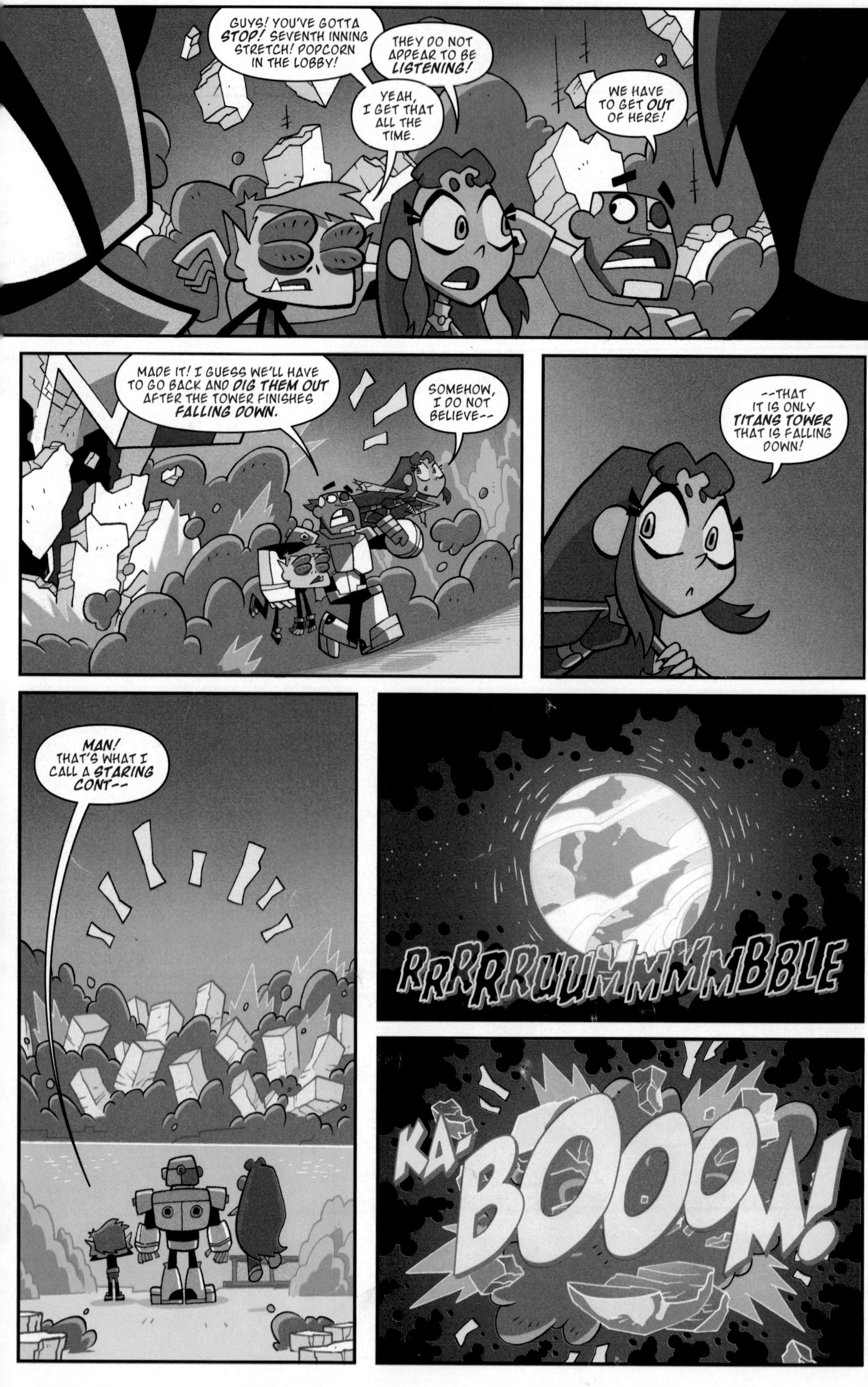
GUYS! YOU'VE GOTTA STOP! SEVENTH INNING STRETCH! POPCORN IN THE LOBBY!
THEY DO NOT APPEAR TO BE LISTENING!
YEAH, I GET THAT ALL THE TIME.
WE HAVE TO GET OUT OF HERE!
MADE IT! I GUESS WE'LL HAVE TO GO BACK AND DIG THEM OUT AFTER THE TOWER FINISHES FALLING DOWN.
SOMEHOW, I DO NOT BELIEVE--
--THAT IT IS ONLY TITANS TOWER THAT IS FALLING DOWN!
MAN! THAT'S WHAT I CALL A STARING CONT--
RRRRRUUMMMMMBBLE
KA-BOOOM!

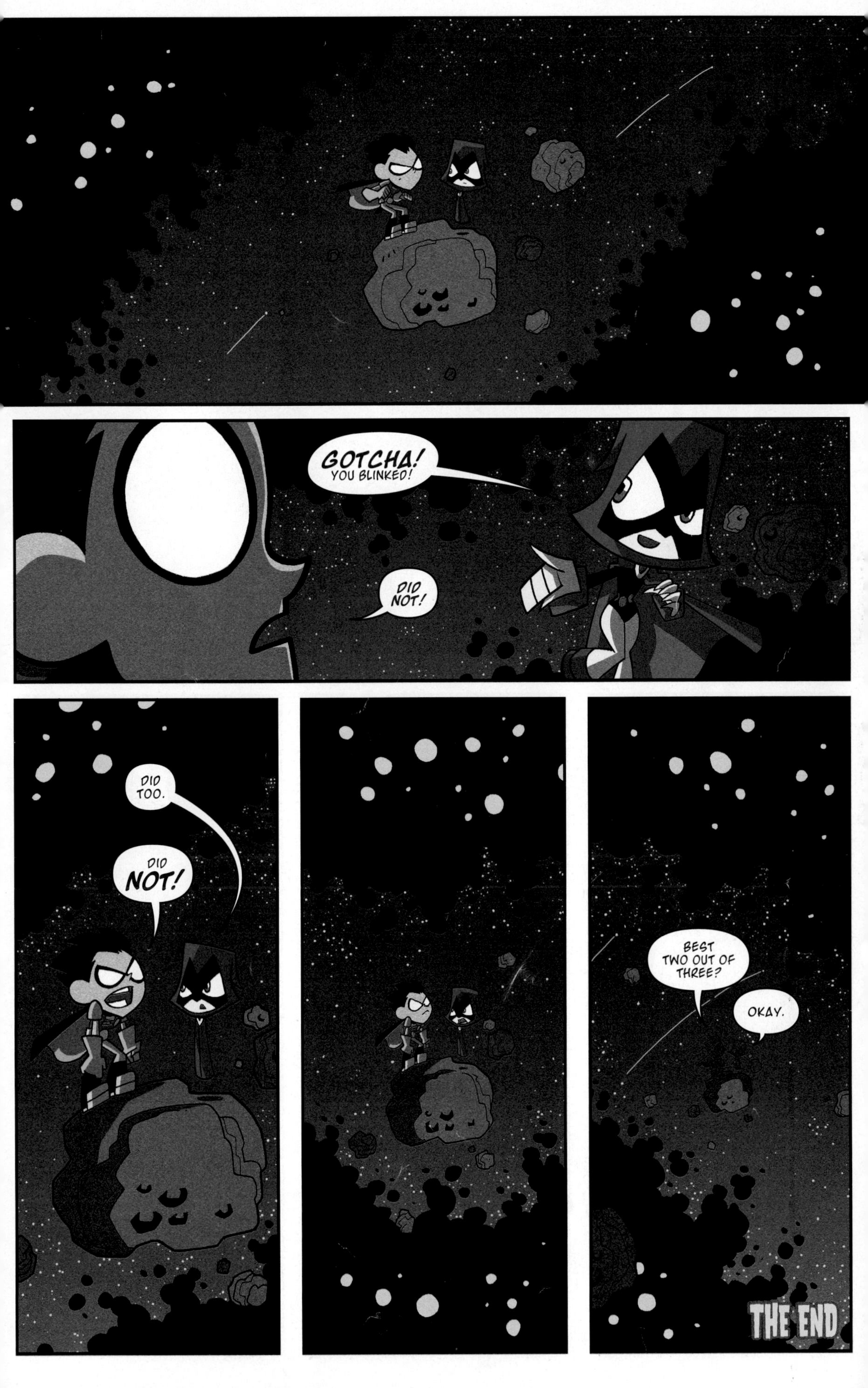
GOTCHA!
YOU BLINKED!
DID NOT!
DID TOO.
DID NOT!
BEST TWO OUT OF THREE?
OKAY.
THE END

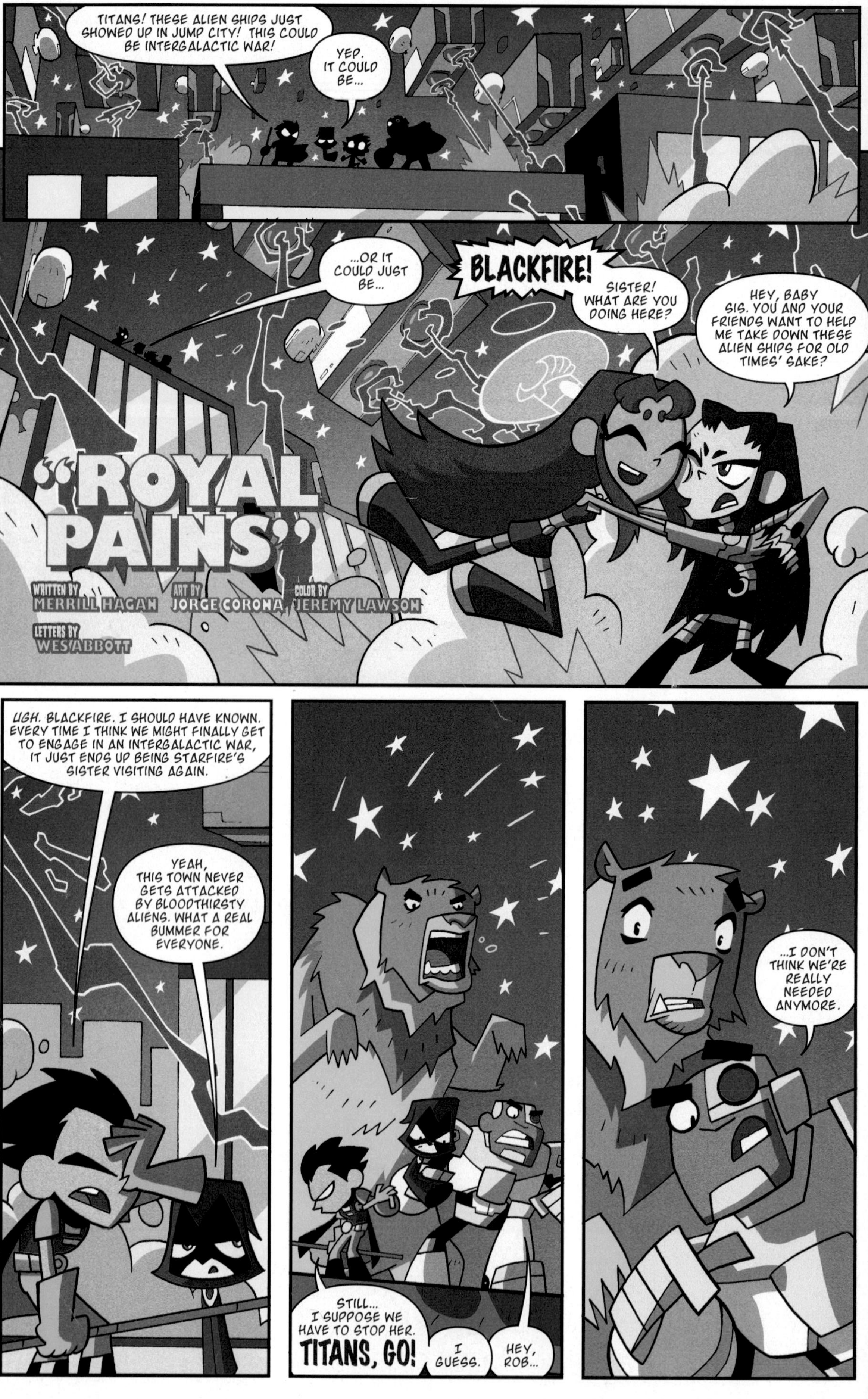

TITANS! THESE ALIEN SHIPS JUST SHOWED UP IN JUMP CITY! THIS COULD BE INTERGALACTIC WAR!
YEP. IT COULD BE...
...OR IT COULD JUST BE...
BLACKFIRE!
SISTER! WHAT ARE YOU DOING HERE?
HEY, BABY SIS. YOU AND YOUR FRIENDS WANT TO HELP ME TAKE DOWN THESE ALIEN SHIPS FOR OLD TIMES' SAKE?
"ROYAL PAINS"
WRITTEN BY MERRILL HAGAN
ART BY JORGE CORONA
COLOR BY JEREMY LAWSON
LETTERS BY WES ABBOTT
UGH. BLACKFIRE. I SHOULD HAVE KNOWN. EVERY TIME I THINK WE MIGHT FINALLY GET TO ENGAGE IN AN INTERGALACTIC WAR, IT JUST ENDS UP BEING STARFIRE'S SISTER VISITING AGAIN.
YEAH, THIS TOWN NEVER GETS ATTACKED BY BLOODTHIRSTY ALIENS. WHAT A REAL BUMMER FOR EVERYONE.
STILL... I SUPPOSE WE HAVE TO STOP HER. TITANS, GO!
I GUESS.
HEY, ROB...
...I DON'T THINK WE'RE REALLY NEEDED ANYMORE.

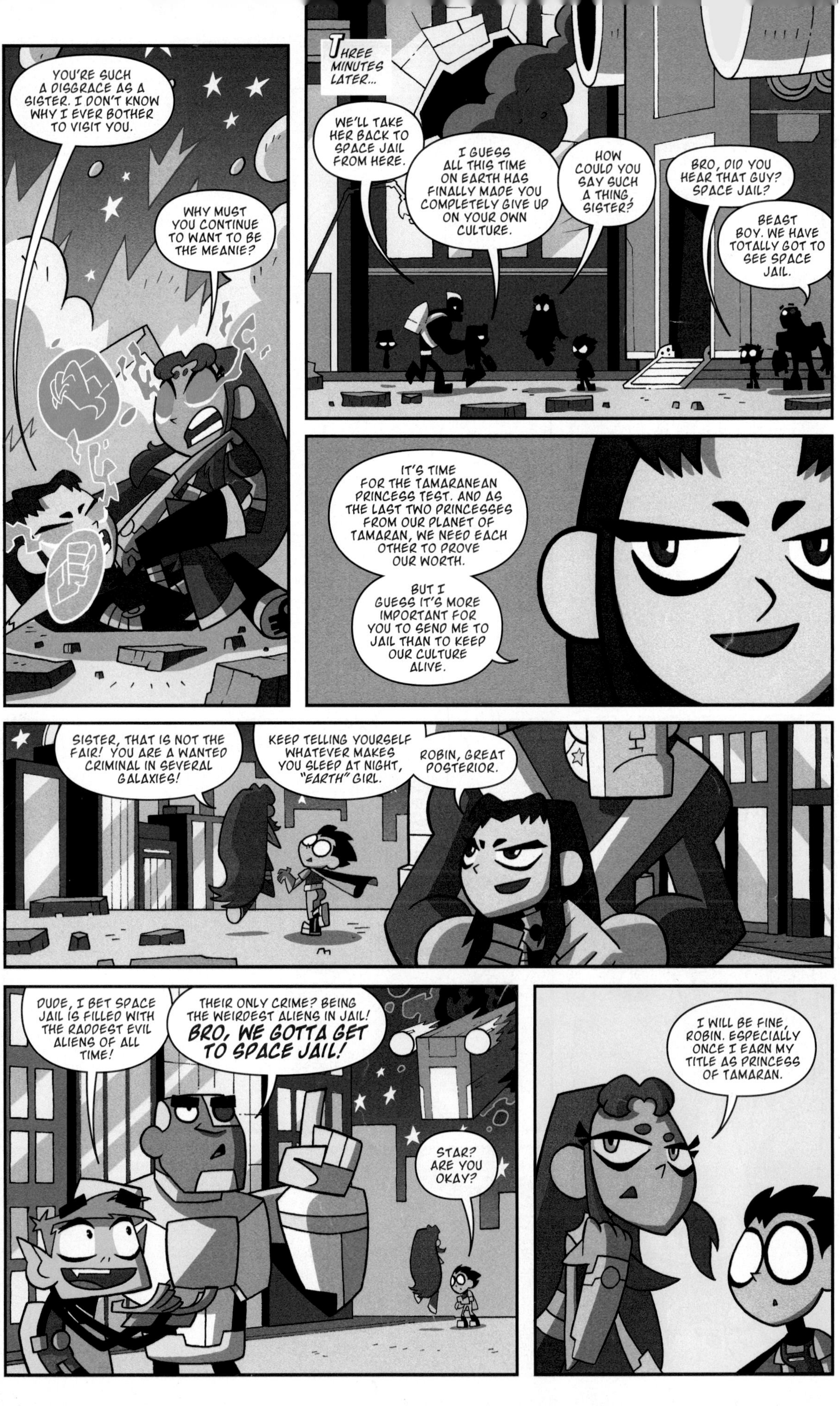
YOU'RE SUCH A DISGRACE AS A SISTER. I DON'T KNOW WHY I EVER BOTHER TO VISIT YOU.
WHY MUST YOU CONTINUE TO WANT TO BE THE MEANIE?
THREE MINUTES LATER...
WE'LL TAKE HER BACK TO SPACE JAIL FROM HERE.
I GUESS ALL THIS TIME ON EARTH HAS FINALLY MADE YOU COMPLETELY GIVE UP ON YOUR OWN CULTURE.
HOW COULD YOU SAY SUCH A THING, SISTER?
BRO, DID YOU HEAR THAT GUY? SPACE JAIL?
BEAST BOY. WE HAVE TOTALLY GOT TO SEE SPACE JAIL.
IT'S TIME FOR THE TAMARANEAN PRINCESS TEST. AND AS THE LAST TWO PRINCESSES FROM OUR PLANET OF TAMARAN, WE NEED EACH OTHER TO PROVE OUR WORTH.
BUT I GUESS IT'S MORE IMPORTANT FOR YOU TO SEND ME TO JAIL THAN TO KEEP OUR CULTURE ALIVE.
SISTER, THAT IS NOT THE FAIR! YOU ARE A WANTED CRIMINAL IN SEVERAL GALAXIES!
KEEP TELLING YOURSELF WHATEVER MAKES YOU SLEEP AT NIGHT, "EARTH" GIRL.
ROBIN, GREAT POSTERIOR.
DUDE, I BET SPACE JAIL IS FILLED WITH THE RADDEST EVIL ALIENS OF ALL TIME!
THEIR ONLY CRIME? BEING THE WEIRDEST ALIENS IN JAIL! BRO, WE GOTTA GET TO SPACE JAIL!
STAR? ARE YOU OKAY?
I WILL BE FINE, ROBIN. ESPECIALLY ONCE I EARN MY TITLE AS PRINCESS OF TAMARAN.

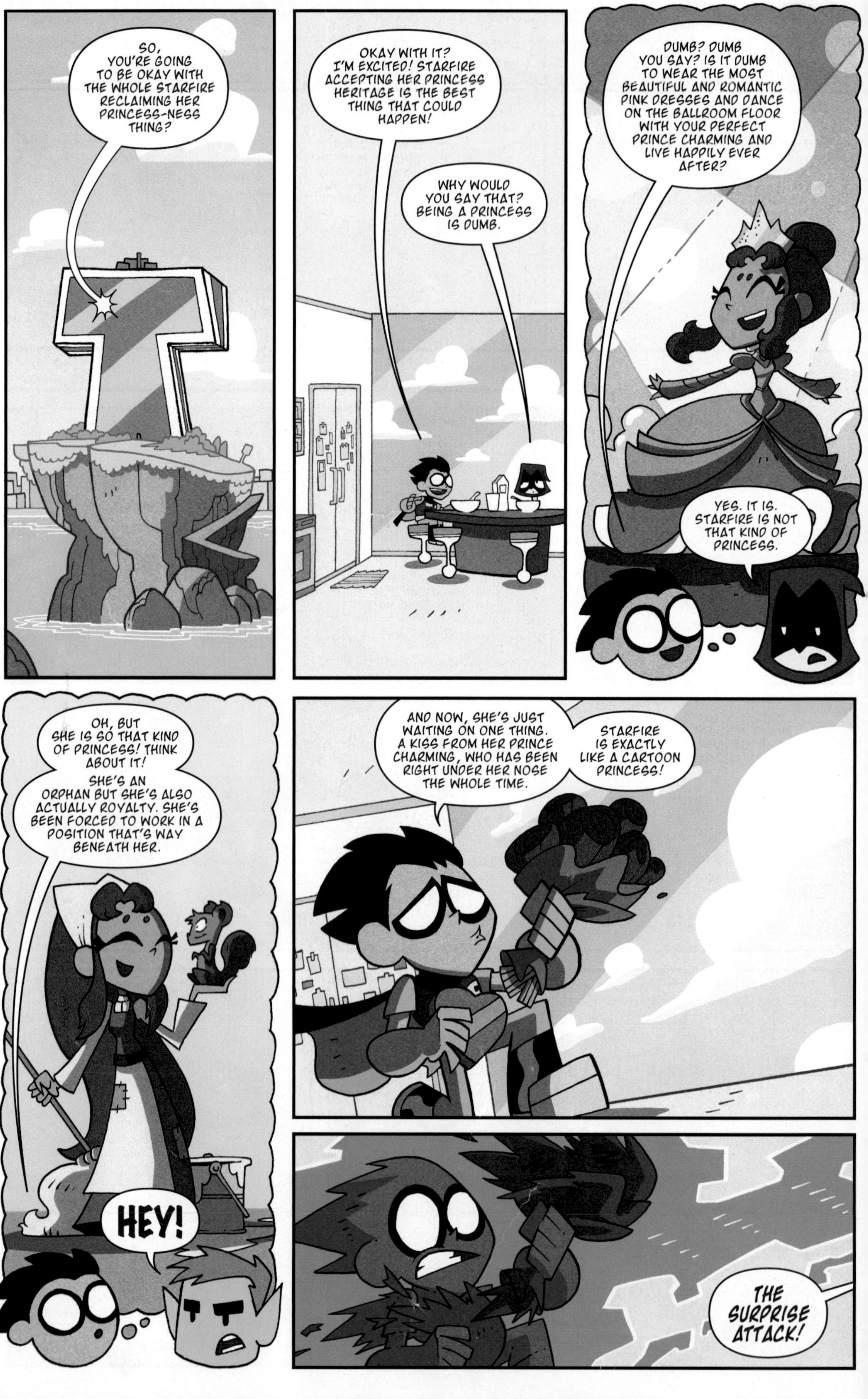
SO, YOU'RE GOING TO BE OKAY WITH THE WHOLE STARFIRE RECLAIMING HER PRINCESS-NESS THING?
OKAY WITH IT? I'M EXCITED! STARFIRE ACCEPTING HER PRINCESS HERITAGE IS THE BEST THING THAT COULD HAPPEN!
WHY WOULD YOU SAY THAT? BEING A PRINCESS IS DUMB.
DUMB? DUMB YOU SAY? IS IT DUMB TO WEAR THE MOST BEAUTIFUL AND ROMANTIC PINK DRESSES AND DANCE ON THE BALLROOM FLOOR WITH YOUR PERFECT PRINCE CHARMING AND LIVE HAPPILY EVER AFTER?
YES. IT IS. STARFIRE IS NOT THAT KIND OF PRINCESS.
OH, BUT SHE IS SO THAT KIND OF PRINCESS! THINK ABOUT IT!
SHE'S AN ORPHAN BUT SHE'S ALSO ACTUALLY ROYALTY. SHE'S BEEN FORCED TO WORK IN A POSITION THAT'S WAY BENEATH HER.
HEY!
STARFIRE IS EXACTLY LIKE A CARTOON PRINCESS!
AND NOW, SHE'S JUST WAITING ON ONE THING. A KISS FROM HER PRINCE CHARMING, WHO HAS BEEN RIGHT UNDER HER NOSE THE WHOLE TIME.
THE SURPRISE ATTACK!

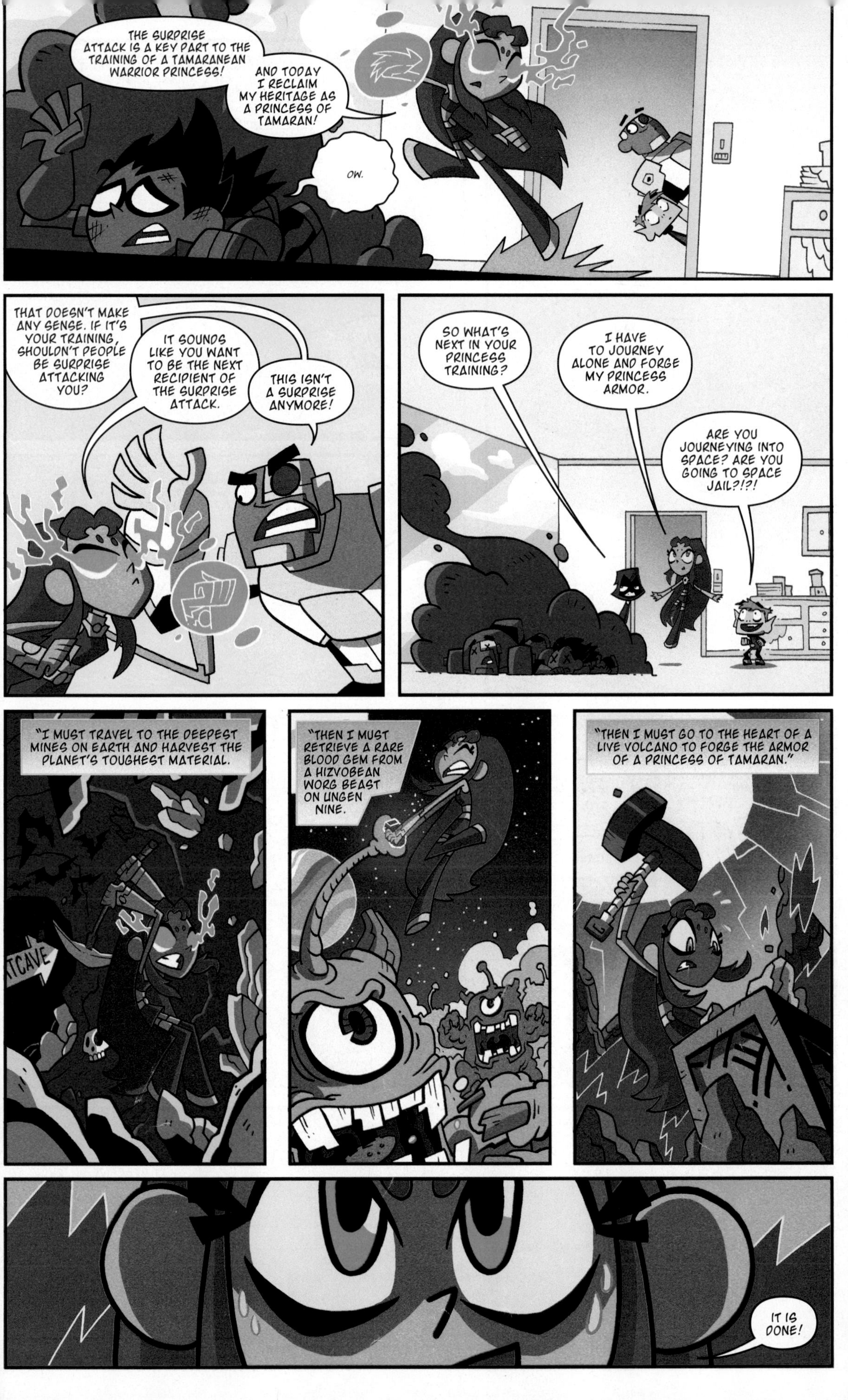
THE SURPRISE ATTACK IS A KEY PART TO THE TRAINING OF A TAMARANEAN WARRIOR PRINCESS!
AND TODAY I RECLAIM MY HERITAGE AS A PRINCESS OF TAMARAN!
OW.
THAT DOESN'T MAKE ANY SENSE. IF IT'S YOUR TRAINING, SHOULDN'T PEOPLE BE SURPRISE ATTACKING YOU?
IT SOUNDS LIKE YOU WANT TO BE THE NEXT RECIPIENT OF THE SURPRISE ATTACK.
THIS ISN'T A SURPRISE ANYMORE!
SO WHAT'S NEXT IN YOUR PRINCESS TRAINING?
I HAVE TO JOURNEY ALONE AND FORGE MY PRINCESS ARMOR.
ARE YOU JOURNEYING INTO SPACE? ARE YOU GOING TO SPACE JAIL?!?!
"I MUST TRAVEL TO THE DEEPEST MINES ON EARTH AND HARVEST THE PLANET'S TOUGHEST MATERIAL.
"THEN I MUST RETRIEVE A RARE BLOOD GEM FROM A HIZVOBEAN WORG BEAST ON UNGEN NINE.
"THEN I MUST GO TO THE HEART OF A LIVE VOLCANO TO FORGE THE ARMOR OF A PRINCESS OF TAMARAN."
IT IS DONE!

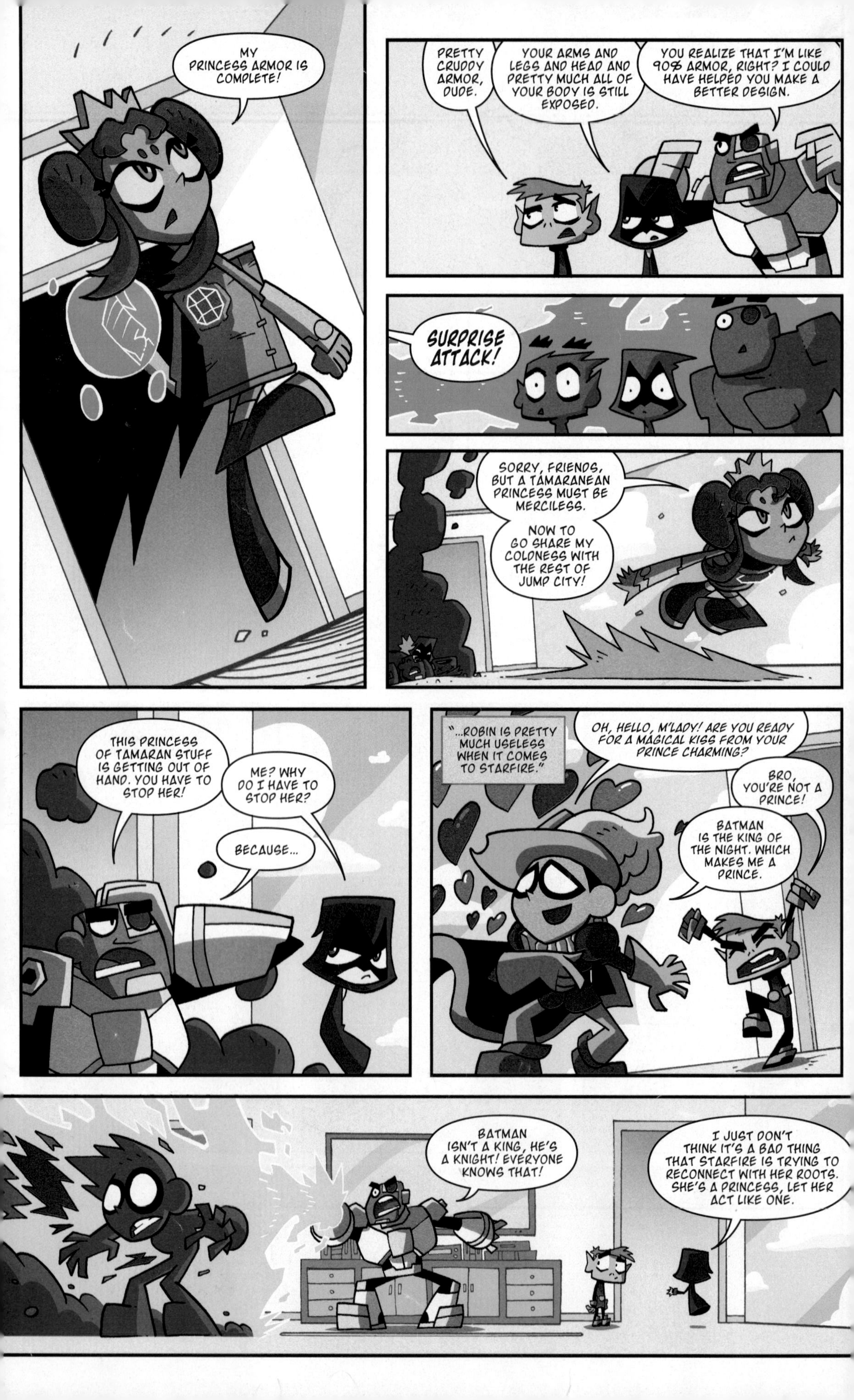
MY PRINCESS ARMOR IS COMPLETE!
PRETTY CRUDDY ARMOR, DUDE.
YOUR ARMS AND LEGS AND HEAD AND PRETTY MUCH ALL OF YOUR BODY IS STILL EXPOSED.
YOU REALIZE THAT I'M LIKE 90% ARMOR, RIGHT? I COULD HAVE HELPED YOU MAKE A BETTER DESIGN.
SURPRISE ATTACK!
SORRY, FRIENDS, BUT A TAMARANEAN PRINCESS MUST BE MERCILESS.
NOW TO GO SHARE MY COLDNESS WITH THE REST OF JUMP CITY!
THIS PRINCESS OF TAMARAN STUFF IS GETTING OUT OF HAND. YOU HAVE TO STOP HER!
ME? WHY DO I HAVE TO STOP HER?
BECAUSE...
"...ROBIN IS PRETTY MUCH USELESS WHEN IT COMES TO STARFIRE."
OH, HELLO, M'LADY! ARE YOU READY FOR A MAGICAL KISS FROM YOUR PRINCE CHARMING?
BRO, YOU'RE NOT A PRINCE!
BATMAN IS THE KING OF THE NIGHT. WHICH MAKES ME A PRINCE.
BATMAN ISN'T A KING, HE'S A KNIGHT! EVERYONE KNOWS THAT!
I JUST DON'T THINK IT'S A BAD THING THAT STARFIRE IS TRYING TO RECONNECT WITH HER ROOTS. SHE'S A PRINCESS, LET HER ACT LIKE ONE.

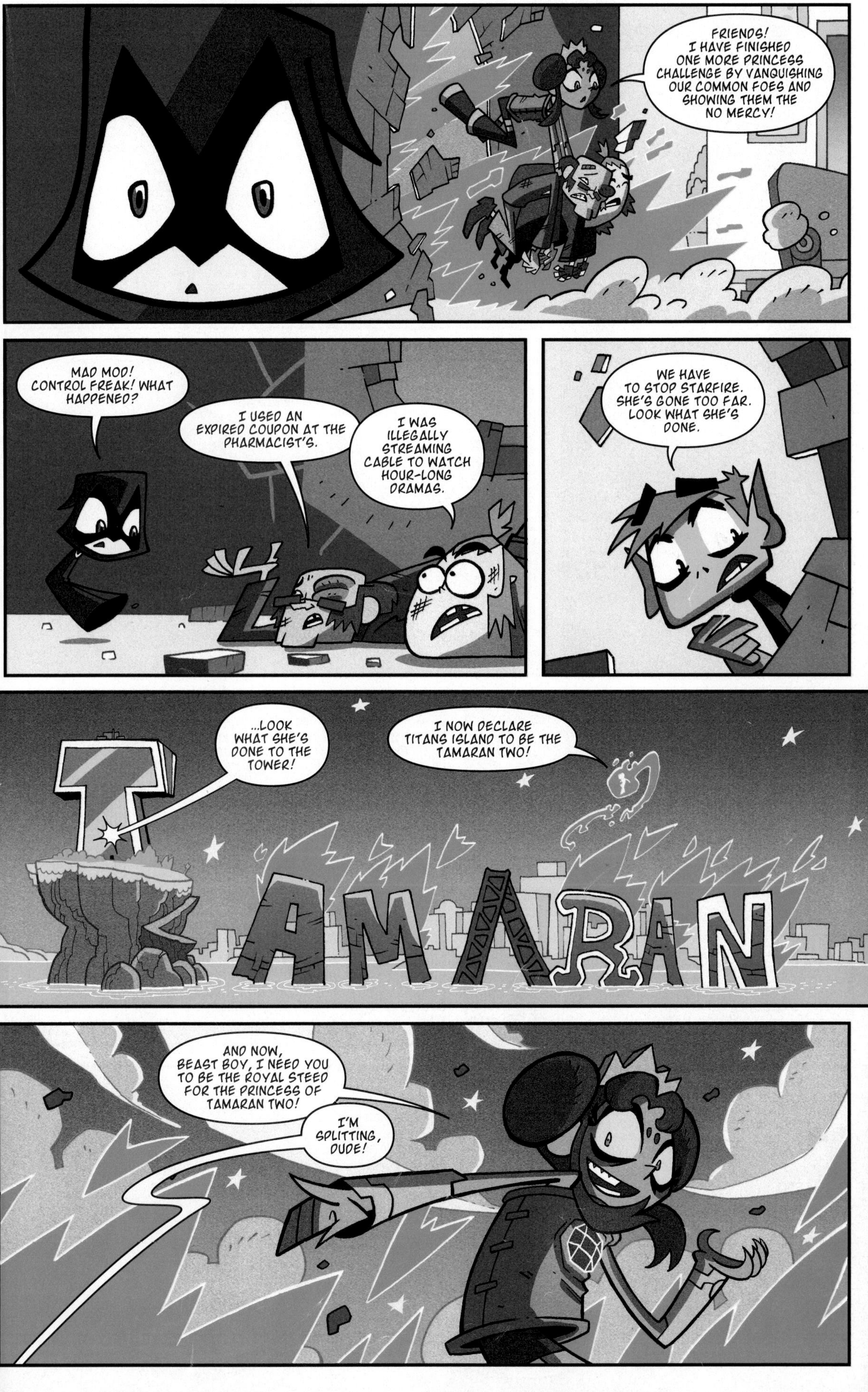
FRIENDS! I HAVE FINISHED ONE MORE PRINCESS CHALLENGE BY VANQUISHING OUR COMMON FOES AND SHOWING THEM THE NO MERCY!
MAD MOD! CONTROL FREAK! WHAT HAPPENED?
I USED AN EXPIRED COUPON AT THE PHARMACIST'S.
I WAS ILLEGALLY STREAMING CABLE TO WATCH HOUR-LONG DRAMAS.
WE HAVE TO STOP STARFIRE. SHE'S GONE TOO FAR. LOOK WHAT SHE'S DONE.
...LOOK WHAT SHE'S DONE TO THE TOWER!
I NOW DECLARE TITANS ISLAND TO BE THE TAMARAN TWO!
TAMARAN
AND NOW, BEAST BOY, I NEED YOU TO BE THE ROYAL STEED FOR THE PRINCESS OF TAMARAN TWO!
I'M SPLITTING, DUDE!

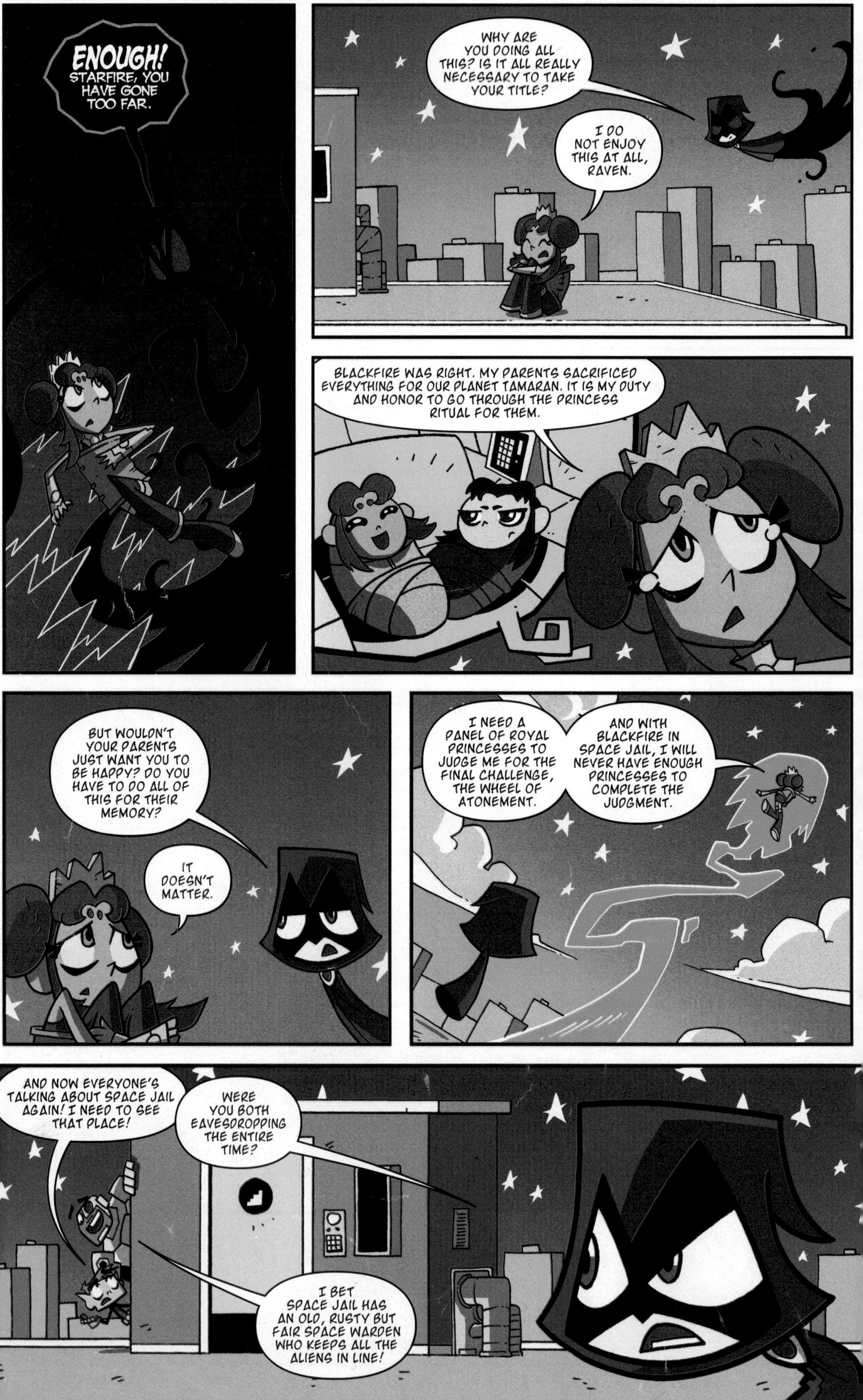
ENOUGH! STARFIRE, YOU HAVE GONE TOO FAR.
WHY ARE YOU DOING ALL THIS? IS IT ALL REALLY NECESSARY TO TAKE YOUR TITLE?
I DO NOT ENJOY THIS AT ALL, RAVEN.
BLACKFIRE WAS RIGHT. MY PARENTS SACRIFICED EVERYTHING FOR OUR PLANET TAMARAN. IT IS MY DUTY AND HONOR TO GO THROUGH THE PRINCESS RITUAL FOR THEM.
BUT WOULDN'T YOUR PARENTS JUST WANT YOU TO BE HAPPY? DO YOU HAVE TO DO ALL OF THIS FOR THEIR MEMORY?
IT DOESN'T MATTER.
I NEED A PANEL OF ROYAL PRINCESSES TO JUDGE ME FOR THE FINAL CHALLENGE, THE WHEEL OF ATONEMENT.
AND WITH BLACKFIRE IN SPACE JAIL, I WILL NEVER HAVE ENOUGH PRINCESSES TO COMPLETE THE JUDGMENT.
AND NOW EVERYONE'S TALKING ABOUT SPACE JAIL AGAIN! I NEED TO SEE THAT PLACE!
WERE YOU BOTH EAVESDROPPING THE ENTIRE TIME?
I BET SPACE JAIL HAS AN OLD, RUSTY BUT FAIR SPACE WARDEN WHO KEEPS ALL THE ALIENS IN LINE!

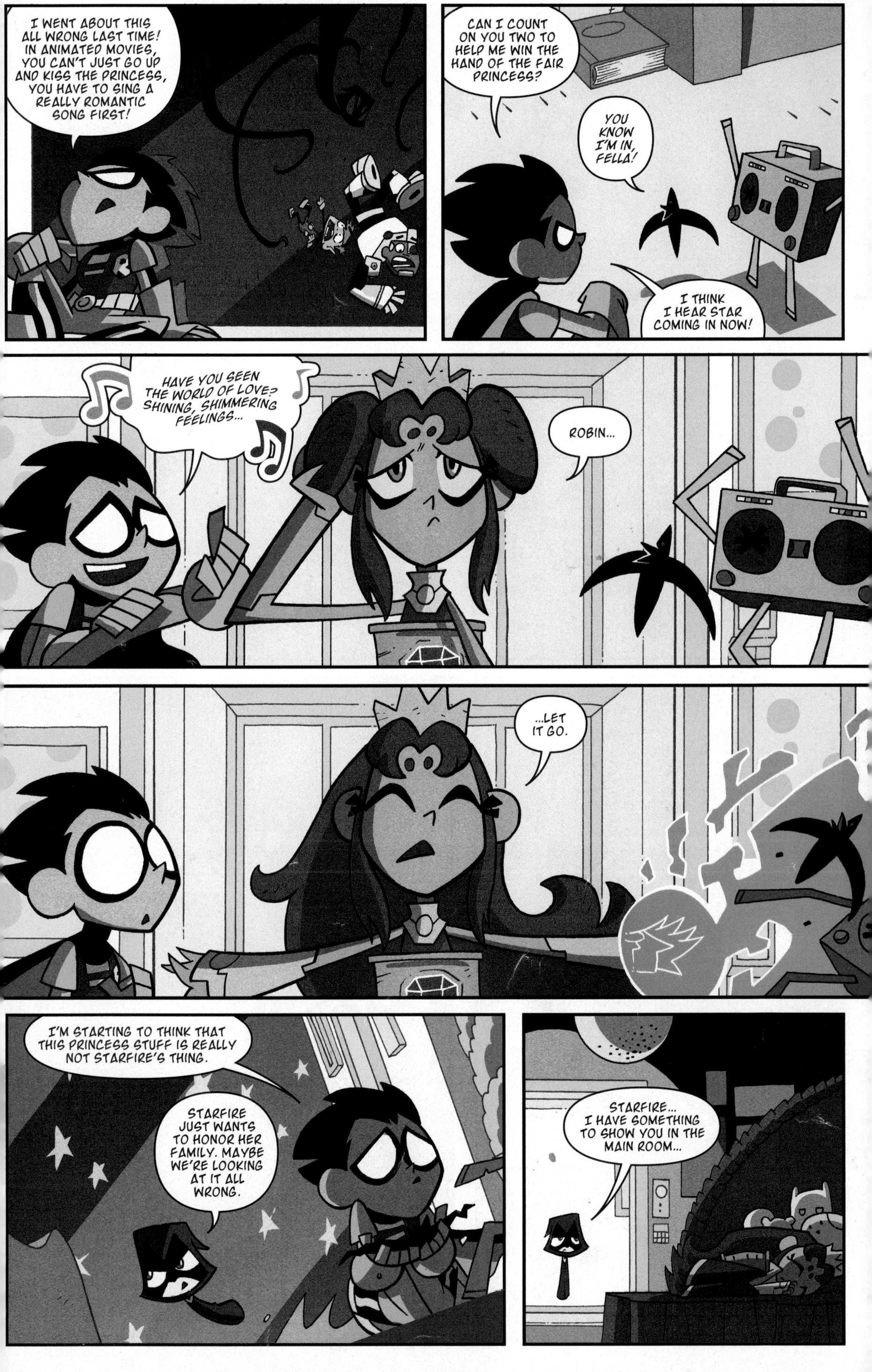
I WENT ABOUT THIS ALL WRONG LAST TIME! IN ANIMATED MOVIES, YOU CAN'T JUST GO UP AND KISS THE PRINCESS, YOU HAVE TO SING A REALLY ROMANTIC SONG FIRST!
CAN I COUNT ON YOU TWO TO HELP ME WIN THE HAND OF THE FAIR PRINCESS?
YOU KNOW I'M IN, FELLA!
I THINK I HEAR STAR COMING IN NOW!
HAVE YOU SEEN THE WORLD OF LOVE? SHINING, SHIMMERING FEELINGS...
ROBIN...
...LET IT GO.
I'M STARTING TO THINK THAT THIS PRINCESS STUFF IS REALLY NOT STARFIRE'S THING.
STARFIRE JUST WANTS TO HONOR HER FAMILY. MAYBE WE'RE LOOKING AT IT ALL WRONG.
STARFIRE... I HAVE SOMETHING TO SHOW YOU IN THE MAIN ROOM...

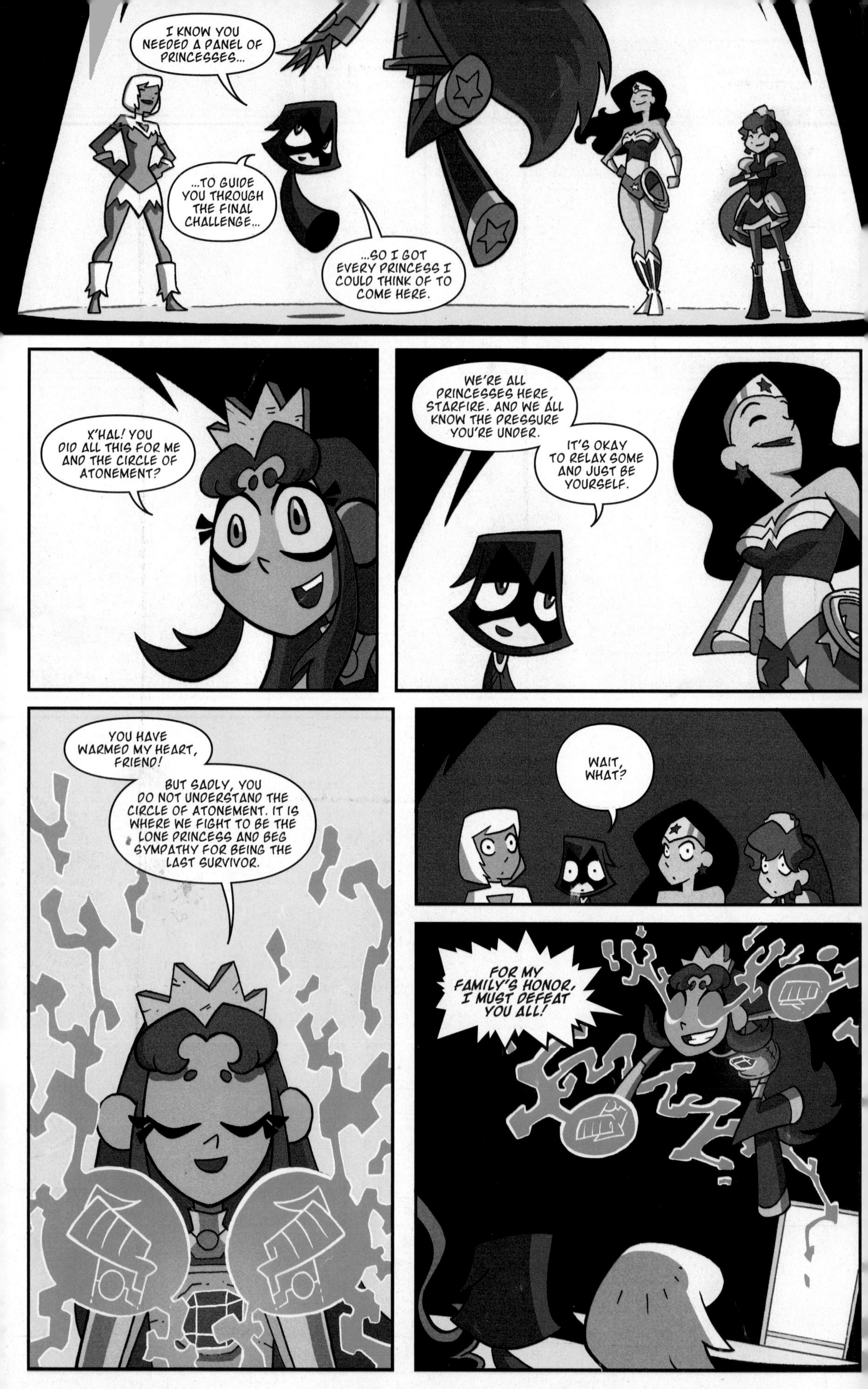
I KNOW YOU NEEDED A PANEL OF PRINCESSES...
...TO GUIDE YOU THROUGH THE FINAL CHALLENGE...
...SO I GOT EVERY PRINCESS I COULD THINK OF TO COME HERE.
X'HAL! YOU DID ALL THIS FOR ME AND THE CIRCLE OF ATONEMENT?
WE'RE ALL PRINCESSES HERE, STARFIRE. AND WE ALL KNOW THE PRESSURE YOU'RE UNDER.
IT'S OKAY TO RELAX SOME AND JUST BE YOURSELF.
YOU HAVE WARMED MY HEART, FRIEND!
BUT SADLY, YOU DO NOT UNDERSTAND THE CIRCLE OF ATONEMENT. IT IS WHERE WE FIGHT TO BE THE LONE PRINCESS AND BEG SYMPATHY FOR BEING THE LAST SURVIVOR.
WAIT, WHAT?
FOR MY FAMILY'S HONOR, I MUST DEFEAT YOU ALL!

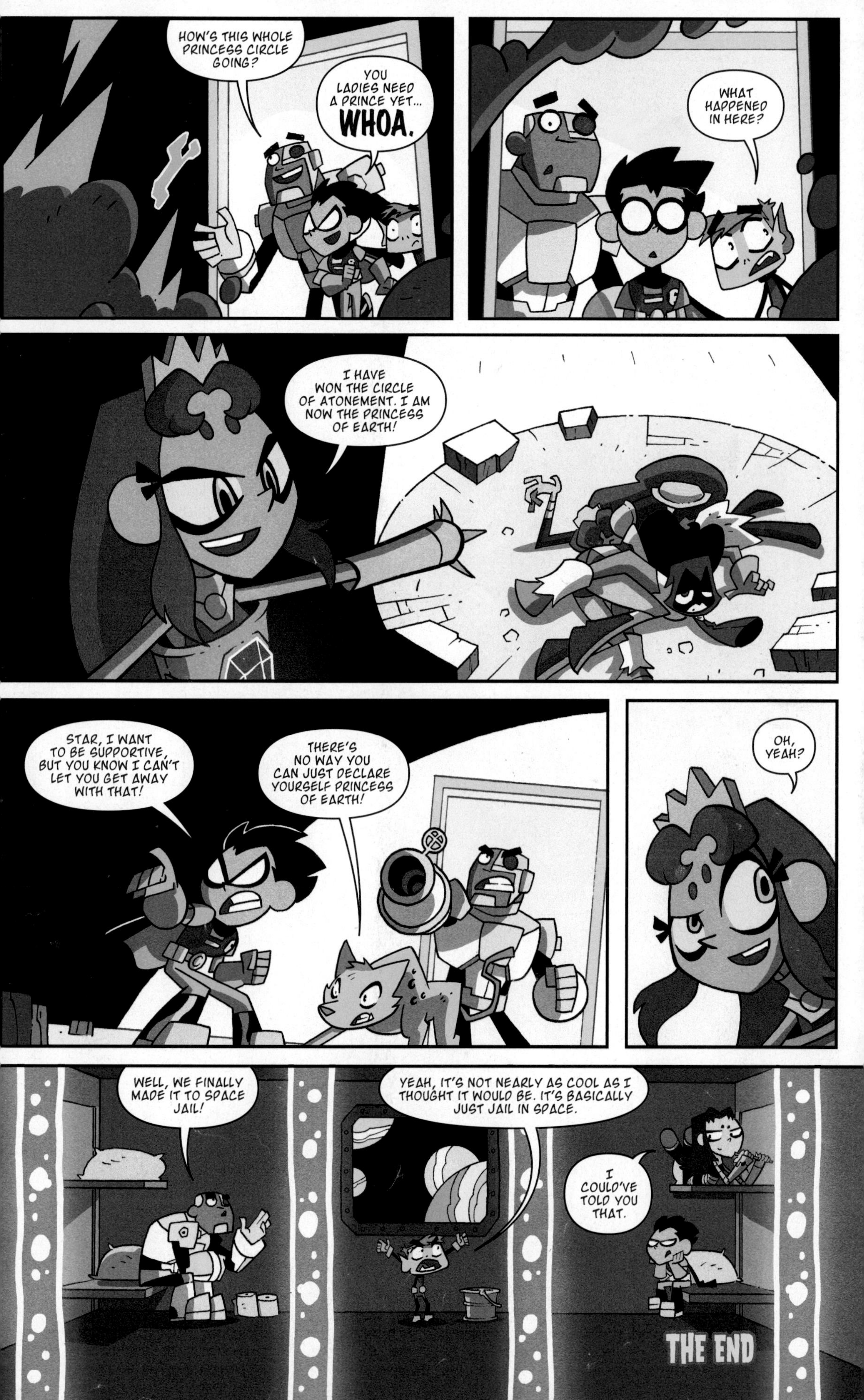
HOW'S THIS WHOLE PRINCESS CIRCLE GOING?
YOU LADIES NEED A PRINCE YET... WHOA.
WHAT HAPPENED IN HERE?
I HAVE WON THE CIRCLE OF ATONEMENT. I AM NOW THE PRINCESS OF EARTH!
STAR, I WANT TO BE SUPPORTIVE, BUT YOU KNOW I CAN'T LET YOU GET AWAY WITH THAT!
THERE'S NO WAY YOU CAN JUST DECLARE YOURSELF PRINCESS OF EARTH!
OH, YEAH?
WELL, WE FINALLY MADE IT TO SPACE JAIL!
YEAH, IT'S NOT NEARLY AS COOL AS I THOUGHT IT WOULD BE. IT'S BASICALLY JUST JAIL IN SPACE.
I COULD'VE TOLD YOU THAT.
THE END

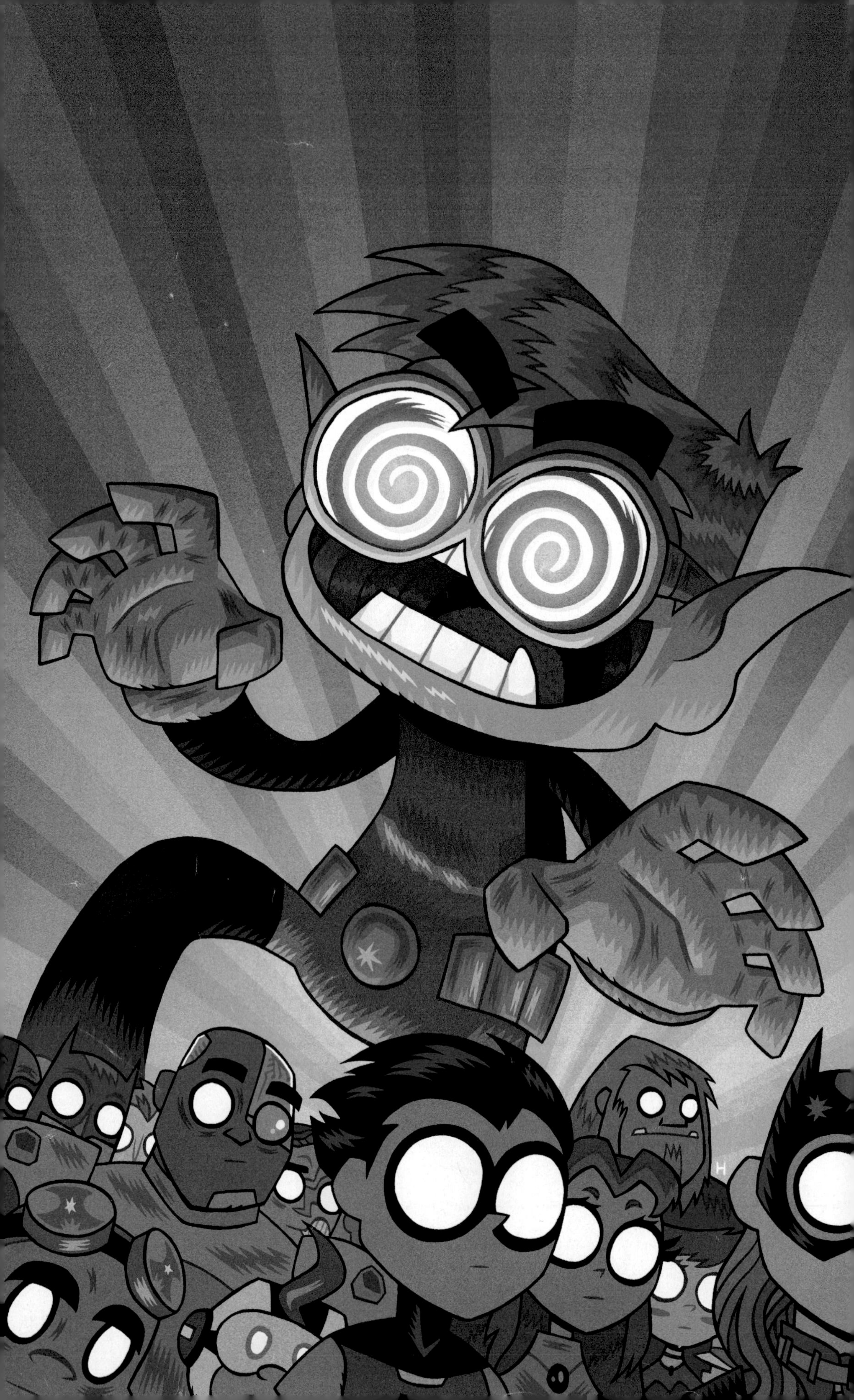

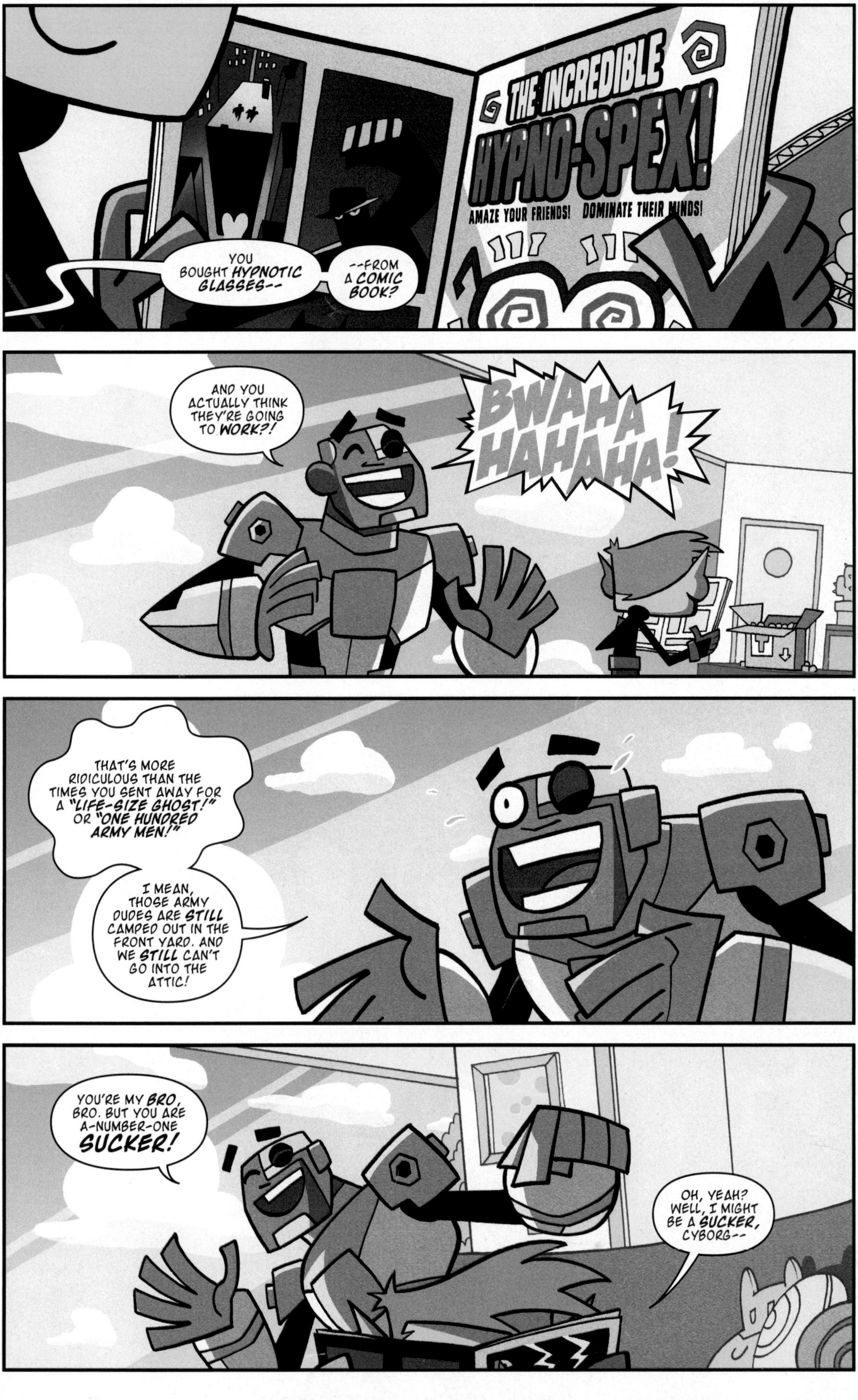
THE INCREDIBLE HYPNO-SPEX!
AMAZE YOUR FRIENDS! DOMINATE THEIR MINDS!
YOU BOUGHT HYPNOTIC GLASSES--
--FROM A COMIC BOOK?
AND YOU ACTUALLY THINK THEY'RE GOING TO WORK?!
BWAHA HAHAHAHA!
THAT'S MORE RIDICULOUS THAN THE TIMES YOU SENT AWAY FOR A "LIFE-SIZE GHOST!" OR "ONE HUNDRED ARMY MEN!"
I MEAN, THOSE ARMY DUDES ARE STILL CAMPED OUT IN THE FRONT YARD. AND WE STILL CAN'T GO INTO THE ATTIC!
YOU'RE MY BRO, BRO. BUT YOU ARE A-NUMBER-ONE SUCKER!
OH, YEAH? WELL, I MIGHT BE A SUCKER, CYBORG--

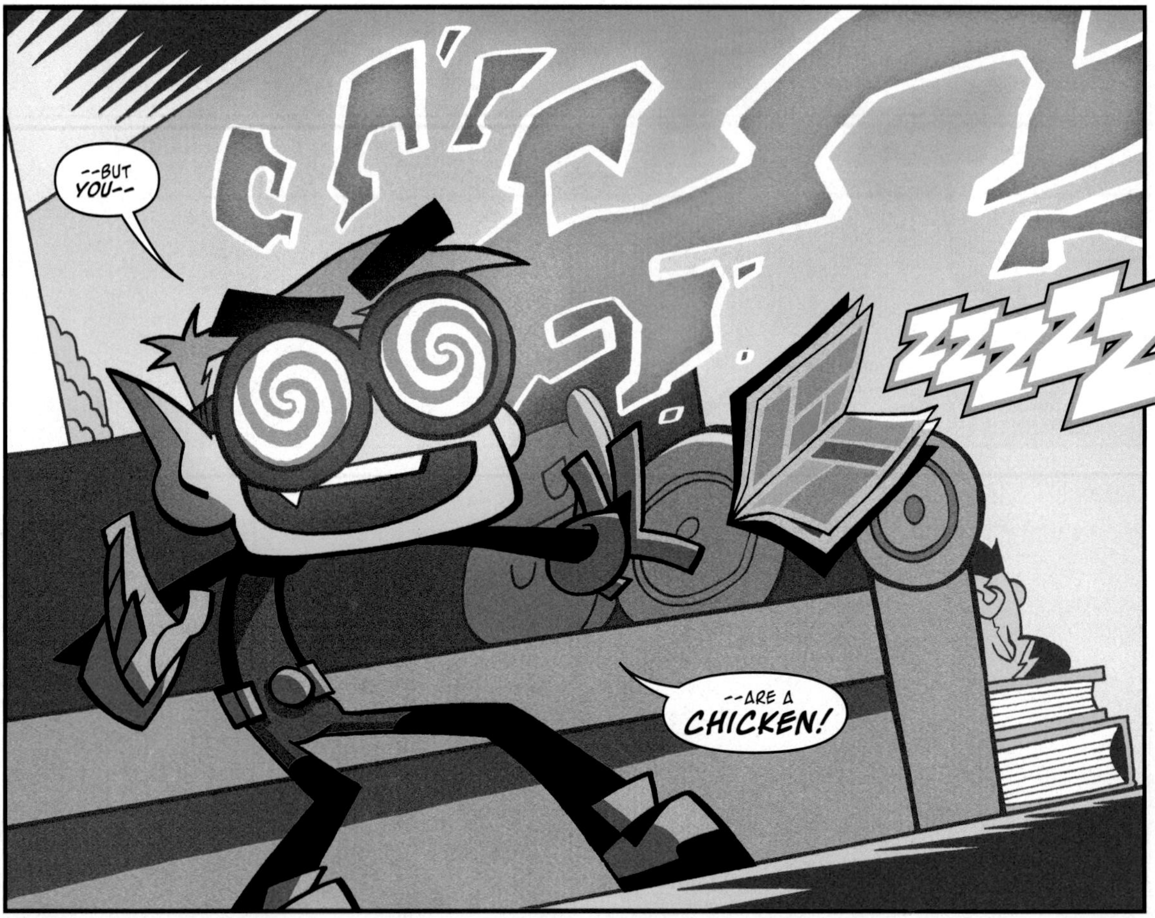

--BUT YOU--
ZZZZZ
--ARE A CHICKEN!

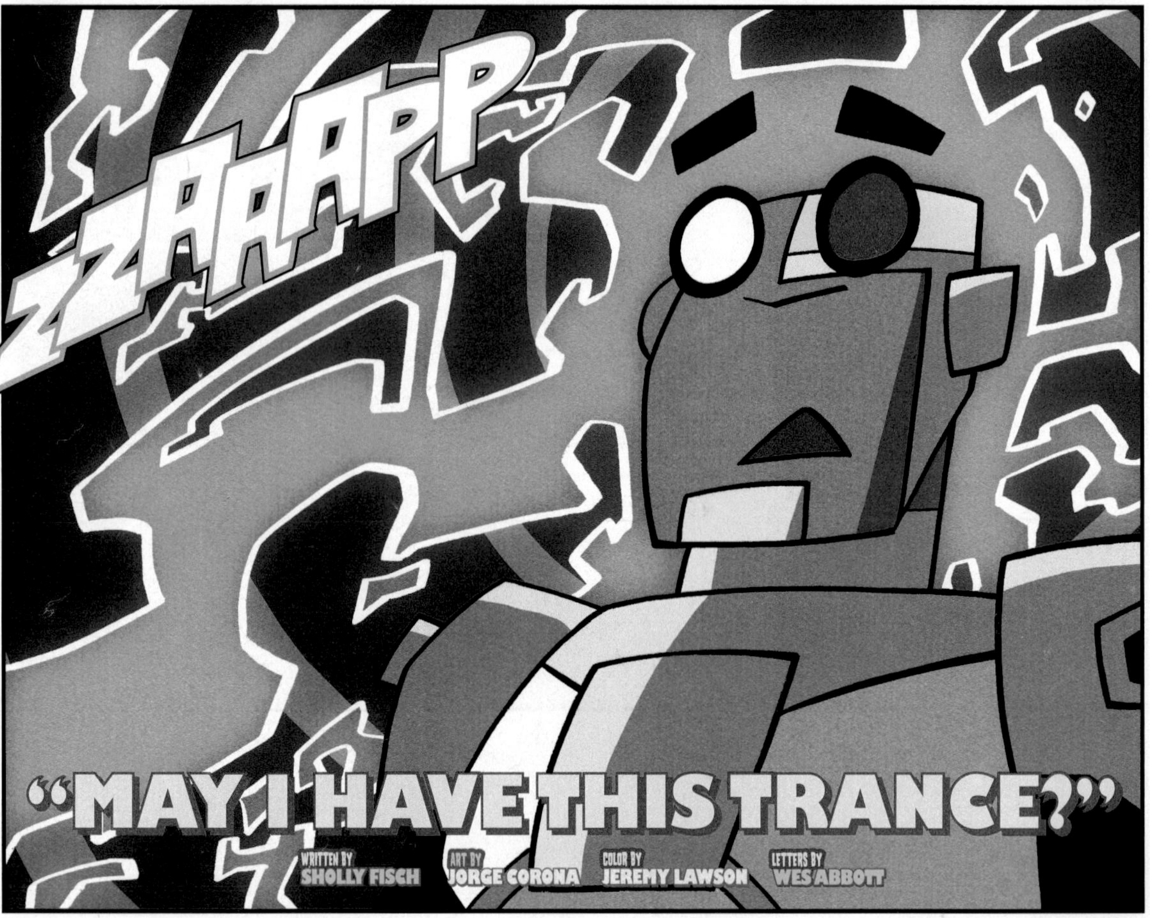

ZZAAAPP
"MAY I HAVE THIS TRANCE?"
WRITTEN BY SHOLLY FISCH
ART BY JORGE CORONA
COLOR BY JEREMY LAWSON
LETTERS BY WES ABBOTT

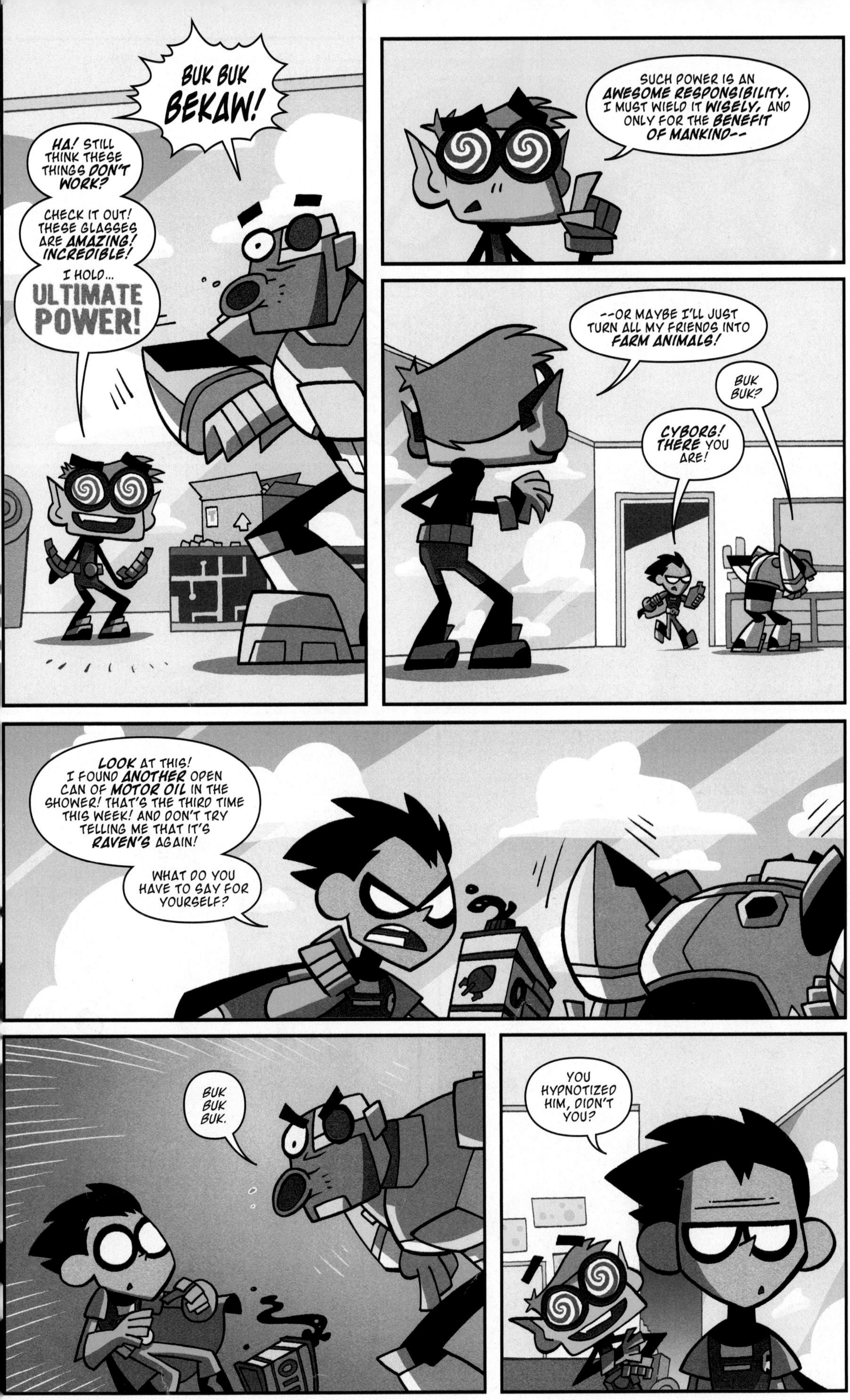
BUK BUK BEKAW!
HA! STILL THINK THESE THINGS DON'T WORK?
CHECK IT OUT! THESE GLASSES ARE AMAZING! INCREDIBLE!
I HOLD... ULTIMATE POWER!
SUCH POWER IS AN AWESOME RESPONSIBILITY. I MUST WIELD IT WISELY, AND ONLY FOR THE BENEFIT OF MANKIND--
--OR MAYBE I'LL JUST TURN ALL MY FRIENDS INTO FARM ANIMALS!
BUK BUK?
CYBORG! THERE YOU ARE!
LOOK AT THIS! I FOUND ANOTHER OPEN CAN OF MOTOR OIL IN THE SHOWER! THAT'S THE THIRD TIME THIS WEEK! AND DON'T TRY TELLING ME THAT IT'S RAVEN'S AGAIN!
WHAT DO YOU HAVE TO SAY FOR YOURSELF?
BUK BUK BUK.
YOU HYPNOTIZED HIM, DIDN'T YOU?

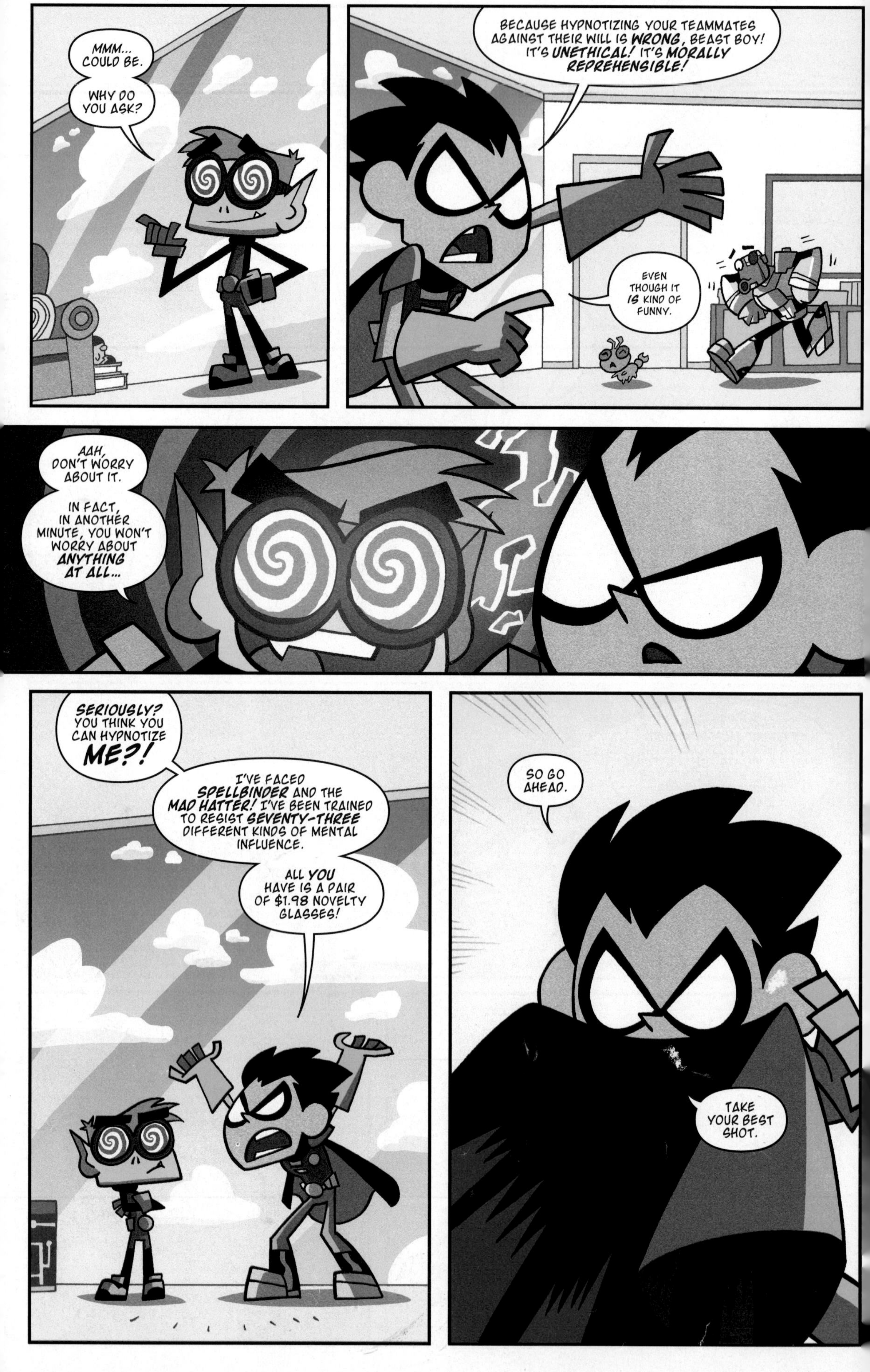
MMM... COULD BE.
WHY DO YOU ASK?
BECAUSE HYPNOTIZING YOUR TEAMMATES AGAINST THEIR WILL IS WRONG, BEAST BOY! IT'S UNETHICAL! IT'S MORALLY REPREHENSIBLE!
EVEN THOUGH IT IS KIND OF FUNNY.
AAH, DON'T WORRY ABOUT IT.
IN FACT, IN ANOTHER MINUTE, YOU WON'T WORRY ABOUT ANYTHING AT ALL...
SERIOUSLY? YOU THINK YOU CAN HYPNOTIZE ME?!
I'VE FACED SPELLBINDER AND THE MAD HATTER! I'VE BEEN TRAINED TO RESIST SEVENTY-THREE DIFFERENT KINDS OF MENTAL INFLUENCE.
ALL YOU HAVE IS A PAIR OF $1.98 NOVELTY GLASSES!
SO GO AHEAD.
TAKE YOUR BEST SHOT.

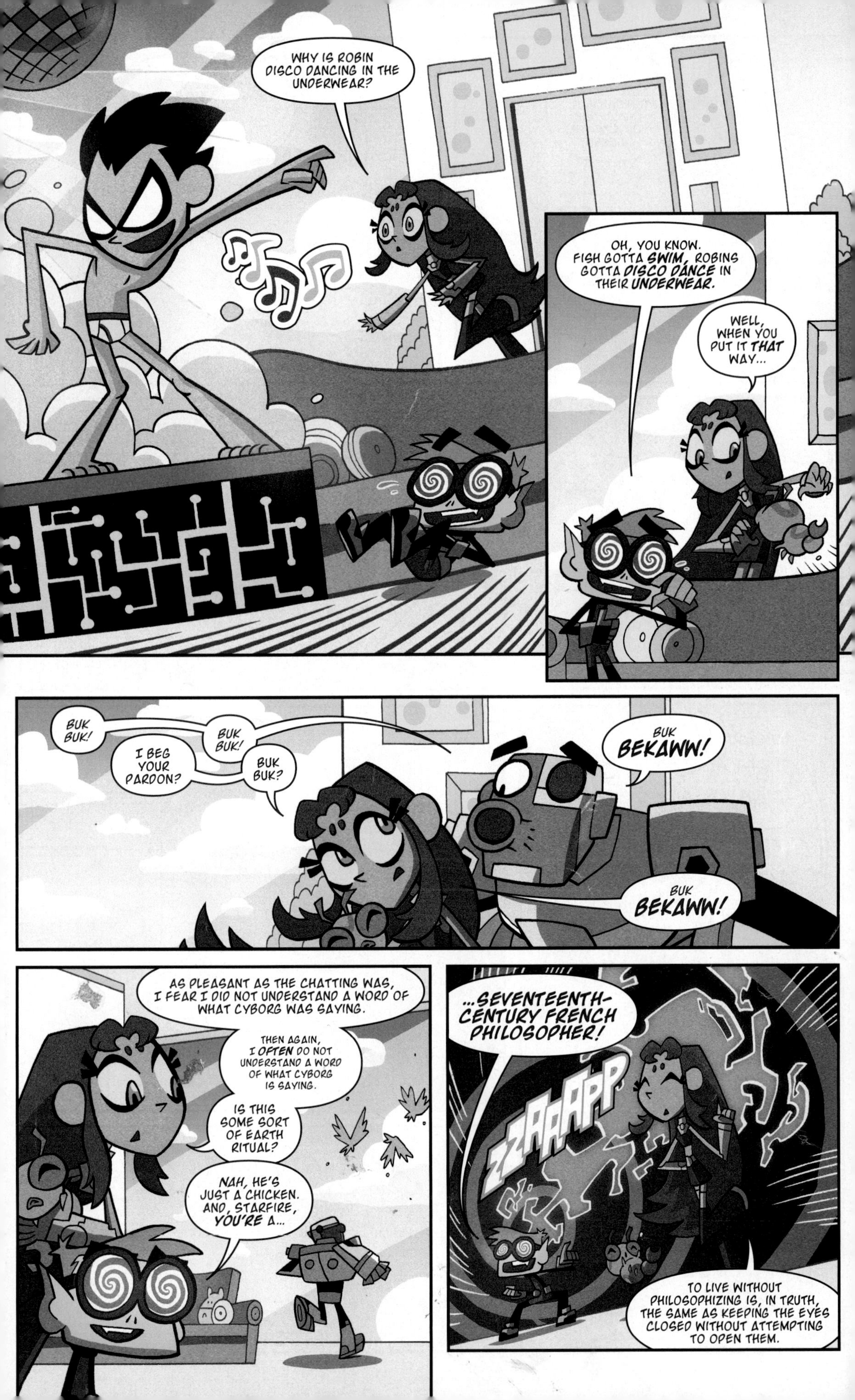
WHY IS ROBIN DISCO DANCING IN THE UNDERWEAR?
OH, YOU KNOW. FISH GOTTA SWIM, ROBINS GOTTA DISCO DANCE IN THEIR UNDERWEAR.
WELL, WHEN YOU PUT IT THAT WAY...
BUK BUK!
BUK BUK!
I BEG YOUR PARDON?
BUK BUK?
BUK BEKAWW!
BUK BEKAWW!
AS PLEASANT AS THE CHATTING WAS, I FEAR I DID NOT UNDERSTAND A WORD OF WHAT CYBORG WAS SAYING.
THEN AGAIN, I OFTEN DO NOT UNDERSTAND A WORD OF WHAT CYBORG IS SAYING.
IS THIS SOME SORT OF EARTH RITUAL?
NAH, HE'S JUST A CHICKEN. AND, STARFIRE, YOU'RE A...
...SEVENTEENTH-CENTURY FRENCH PHILOSOPHER!
ZZAAAPP
TO LIVE WITHOUT PHILOSOPHIZING IS, IN TRUTH, THE SAME AS KEEPING THE EYES CLOSED WITHOUT ATTEMPTING TO OPEN THEM.

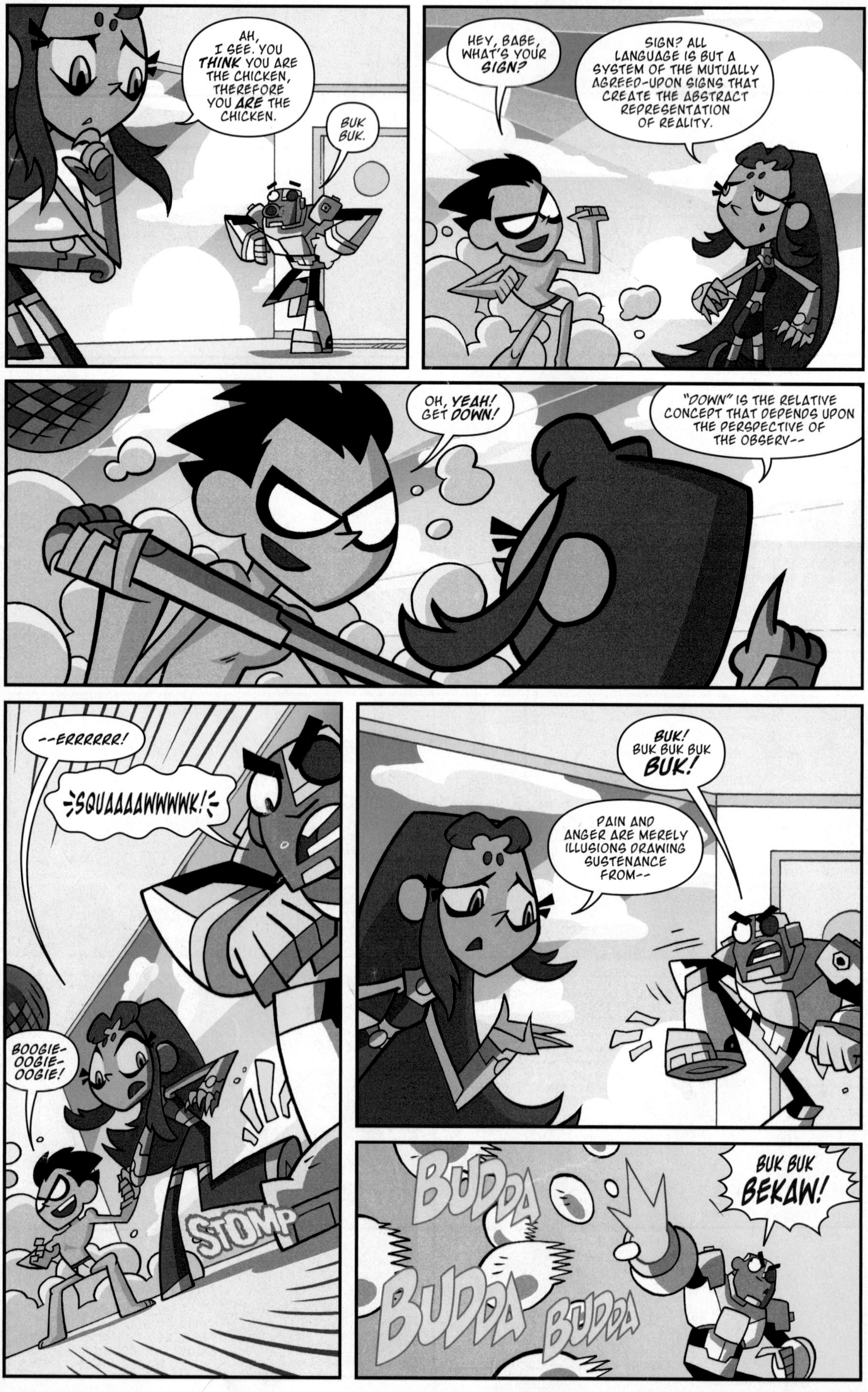
AH, I SEE. YOU THINK YOU ARE THE CHICKEN, THEREFORE YOU ARE THE CHICKEN.
BUK BUK.
HEY, BABE, WHAT'S YOUR SIGN?
SIGN? ALL LANGUAGE IS BUT A SYSTEM OF THE MUTUALLY AGREED-UPON SIGNS THAT CREATE THE ABSTRACT REPRESENTATION OF REALITY.
OH, YEAH! GET DOWN!
"DOWN" IS THE RELATIVE CONCEPT THAT DEPENDS UPON THE PERSPECTIVE OF THE OBSERV--
--ERRRRRR!
SQUAAAAWWWWK!
BOOGIE-OOGIE-OOGIE!
STOMP
BUK! BUK BUK BUK BUK!
PAIN AND ANGER ARE MERELY ILLUSIONS DRAWING SUSTENANCE FROM--
BUK BUK BEKAW!
BUDDA
BUDDA
BUDDA

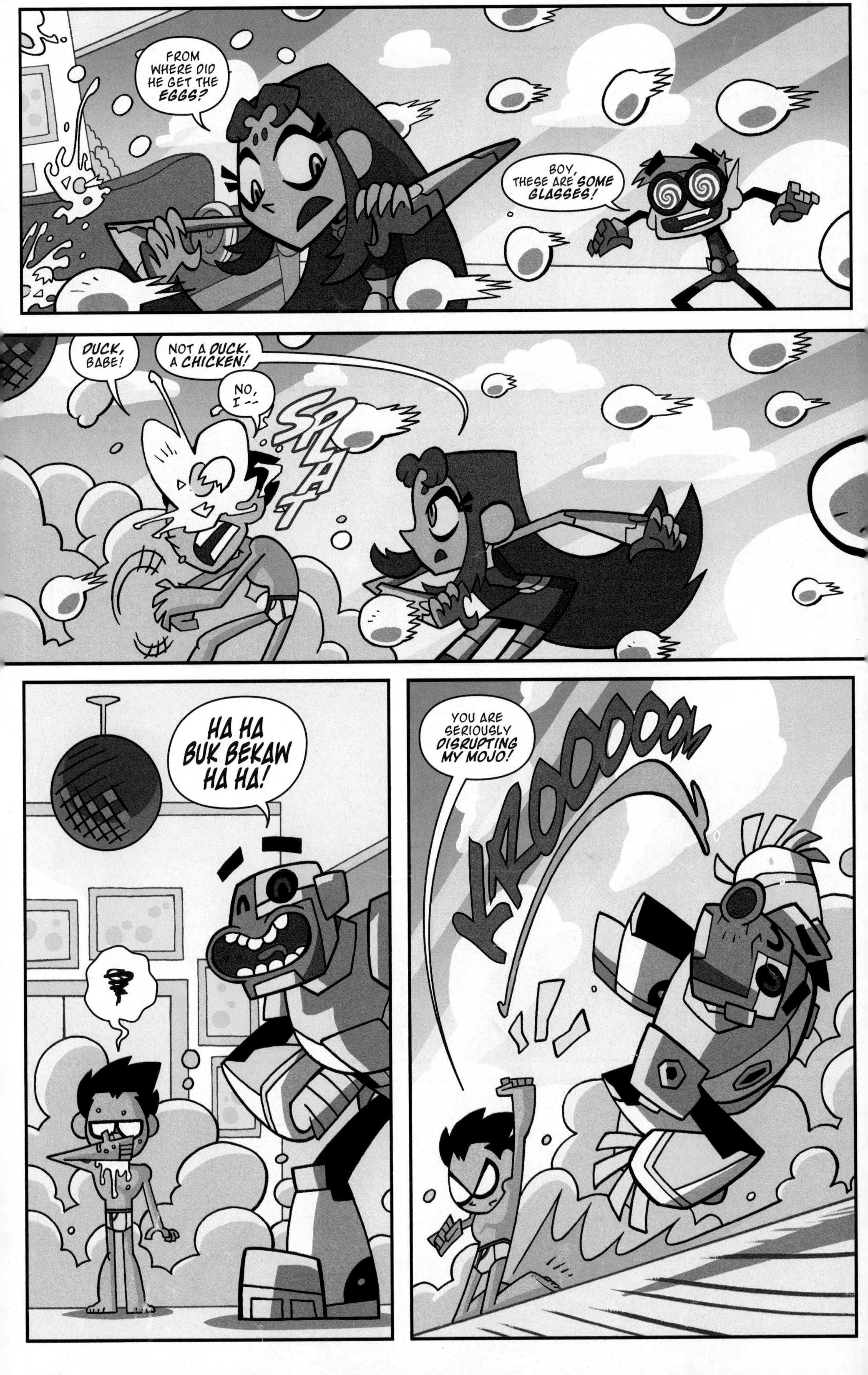
FROM WHERE DID HE GET THE EGGS?
BOY, THESE ARE SOME GLASSES!
DUCK, BABE!
NOT A DUCK. A CHICKEN!
NO, I --
SPLAT
HA HA BUK BEKAW HA HA!
YOU ARE SERIOUSLY DISRUPTING MY MOJO!
KROOOOOM

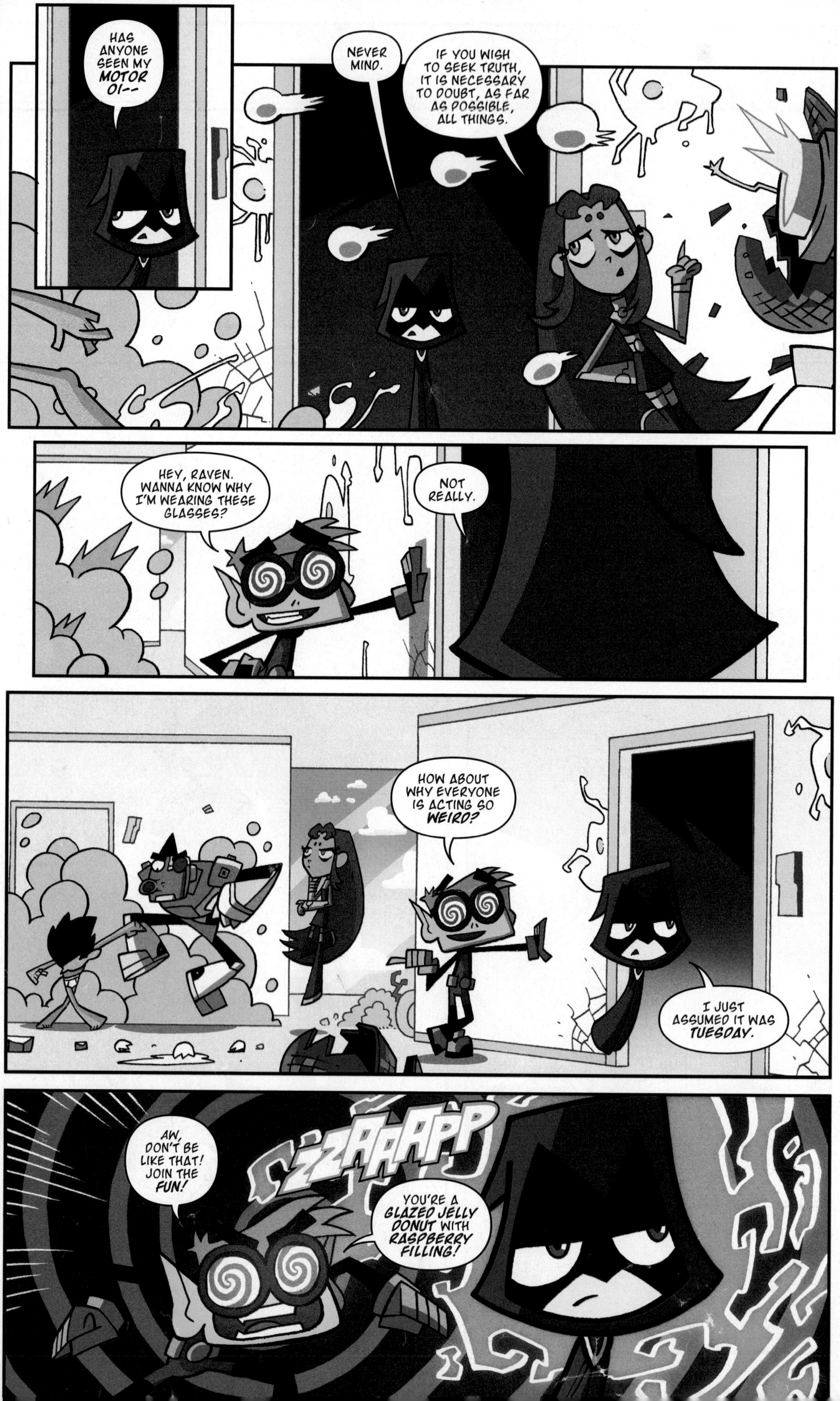
HAS ANYONE SEEN MY MOTOR OI--
NEVER MIND.
IF YOU WISH TO SEEK TRUTH, IT IS NECESSARY TO DOUBT, AS FAR AS POSSIBLE, ALL THINGS.
HEY, RAVEN. WANNA KNOW WHY I'M WEARING THESE GLASSES?
NOT REALLY.
HOW ABOUT WHY EVERYONE IS ACTING SO WEIRD?
I JUST ASSUMED IT WAS TUESDAY.
AW, DON'T BE LIKE THAT! JOIN THE FUN!
ZZRRAAPP
YOU'RE A GLAZED JELLY DONUT WITH RASPBERRY FILLING!

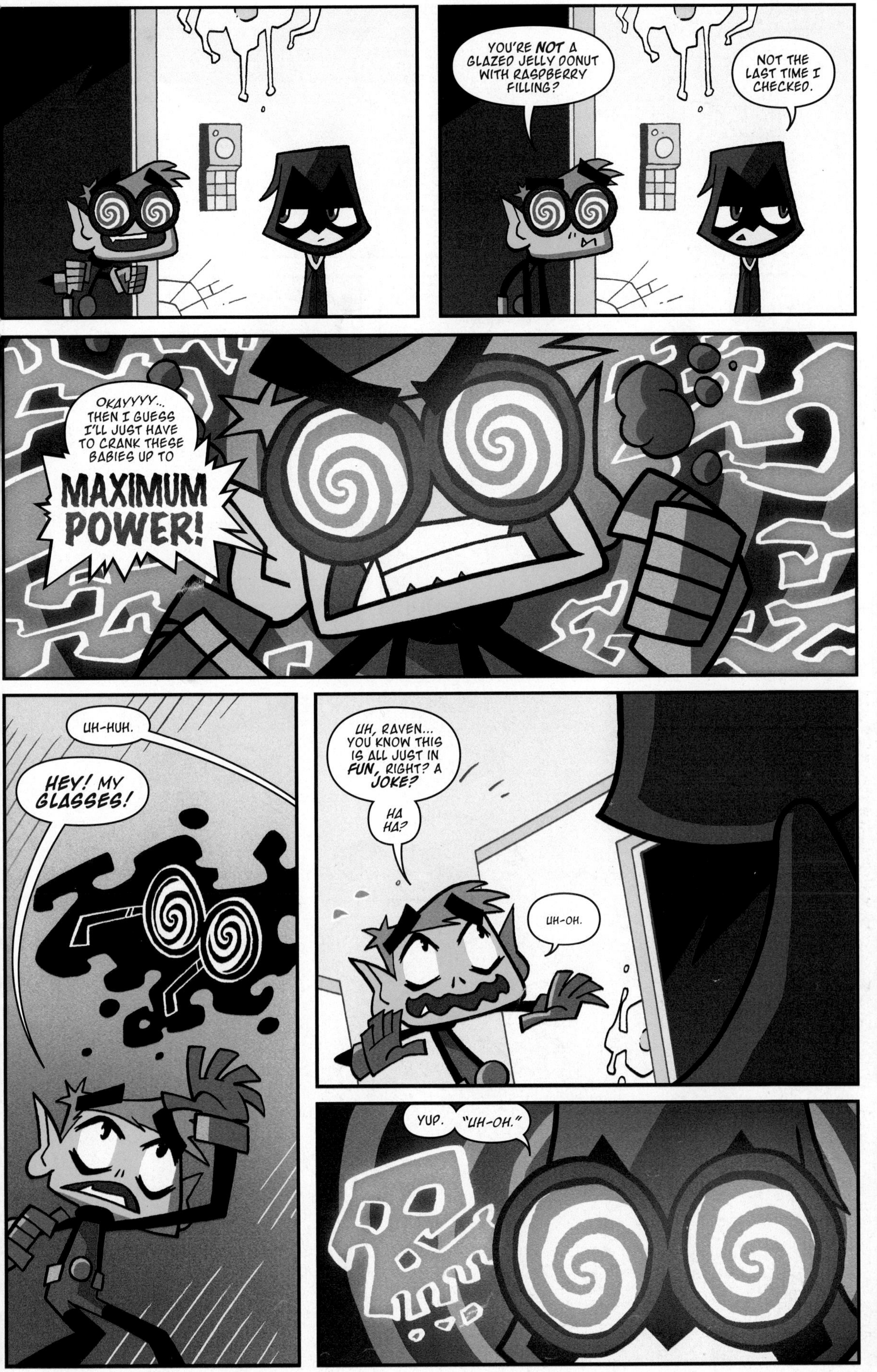
YOU'RE NOT A GLAZED JELLY DONUT WITH RASPBERRY FILLING?
NOT THE LAST TIME I CHECKED.
OKAYYYY... THEN I GUESS I'LL JUST HAVE TO CRANK THESE BABIES UP TO
MAXIMUM POWER!
UH-HUH.
HEY! MY GLASSES!
UH, RAVEN... YOU KNOW THIS IS ALL JUST IN FUN, RIGHT? A JOKE?
HA HA?
UH-OH.
YUP.
"UH-OH."

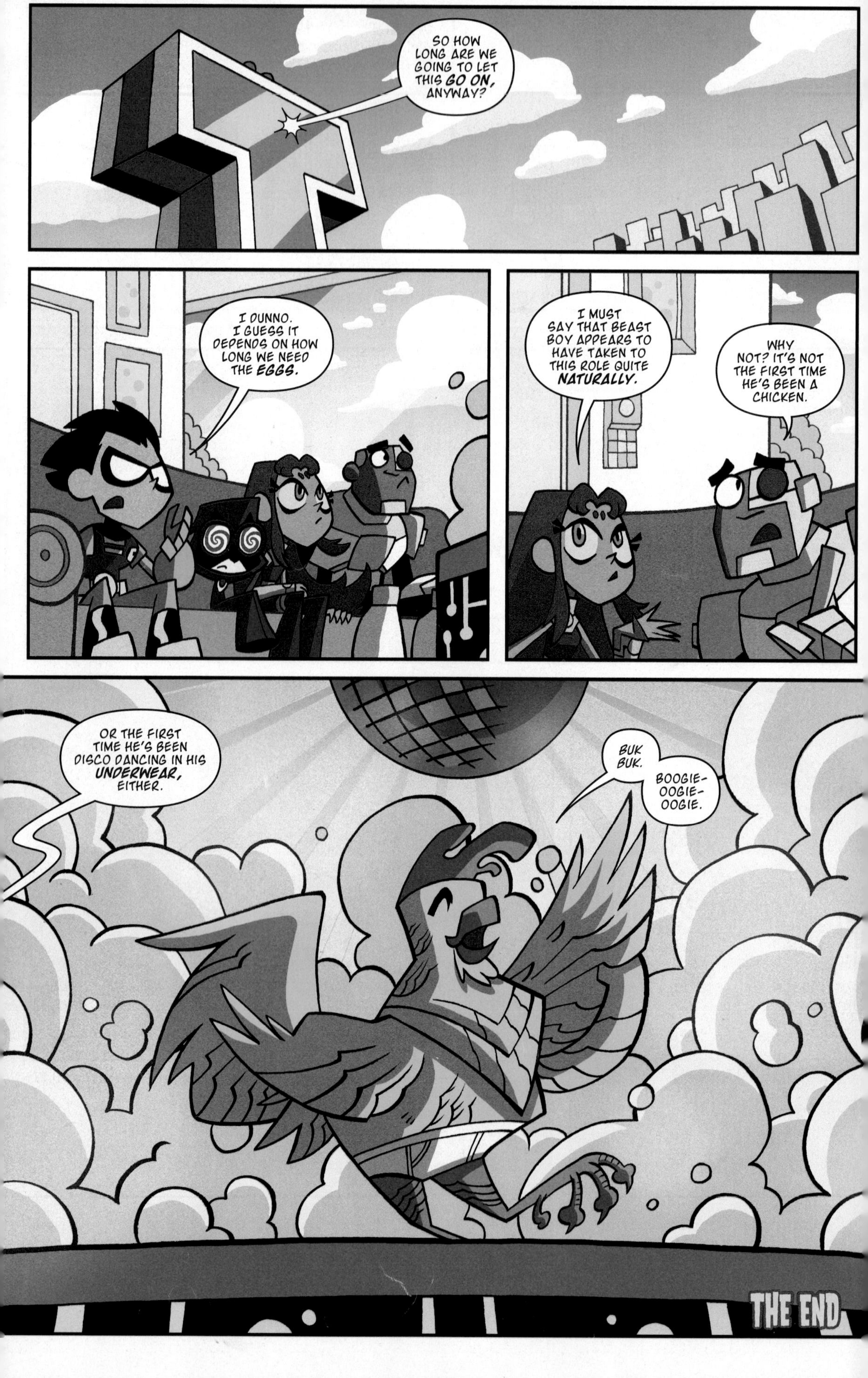
SO HOW LONG ARE WE GOING TO LET THIS GO ON, ANYWAY?
I DUNNO. I GUESS IT DEPENDS ON HOW LONG WE NEED THE EGGS.
I MUST SAY THAT BEAST BOY APPEARS TO HAVE TAKEN TO THIS ROLE QUITE NATURALLY.
WHY NOT? IT'S NOT THE FIRST TIME HE'S BEEN A CHICKEN.
OR THE FIRST TIME HE'S BEEN DISCO DANCING IN HIS UNDERWEAR, EITHER.
BUK BUK.
BOOGIE-OOGIE-OOGIE.
THE END

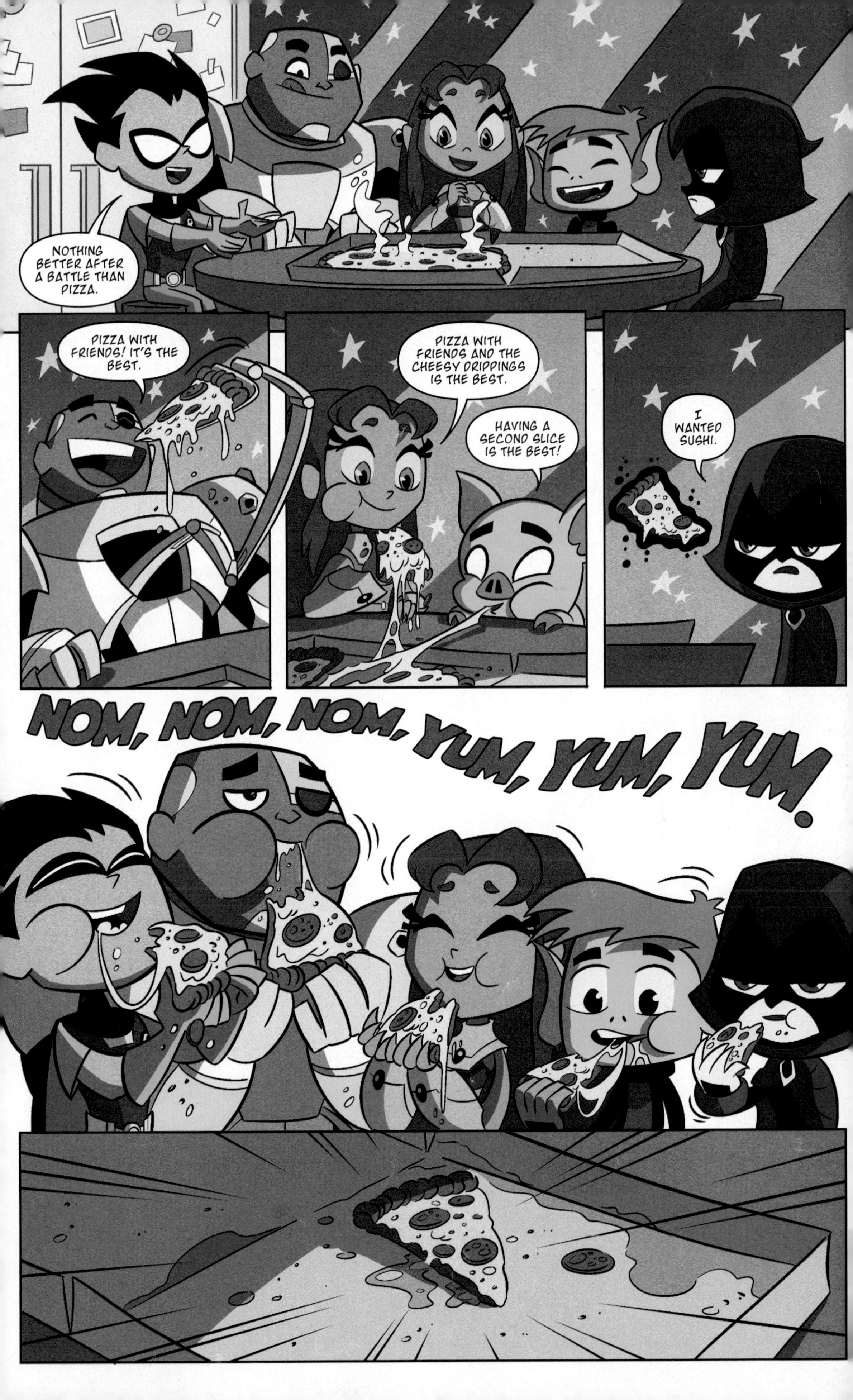
NOTHING BETTER AFTER A BATTLE THAN PIZZA.
PIZZA WITH FRIENDS! IT'S THE BEST.
PIZZA WITH FRIENDS AND THE CHEESY DRIPPINGS IS THE BEST.
HAVING A SECOND SLICE IS THE BEST!
I WANTED SUSHI.
NOM, NOM, NOM, YUM, YUM, YUM.

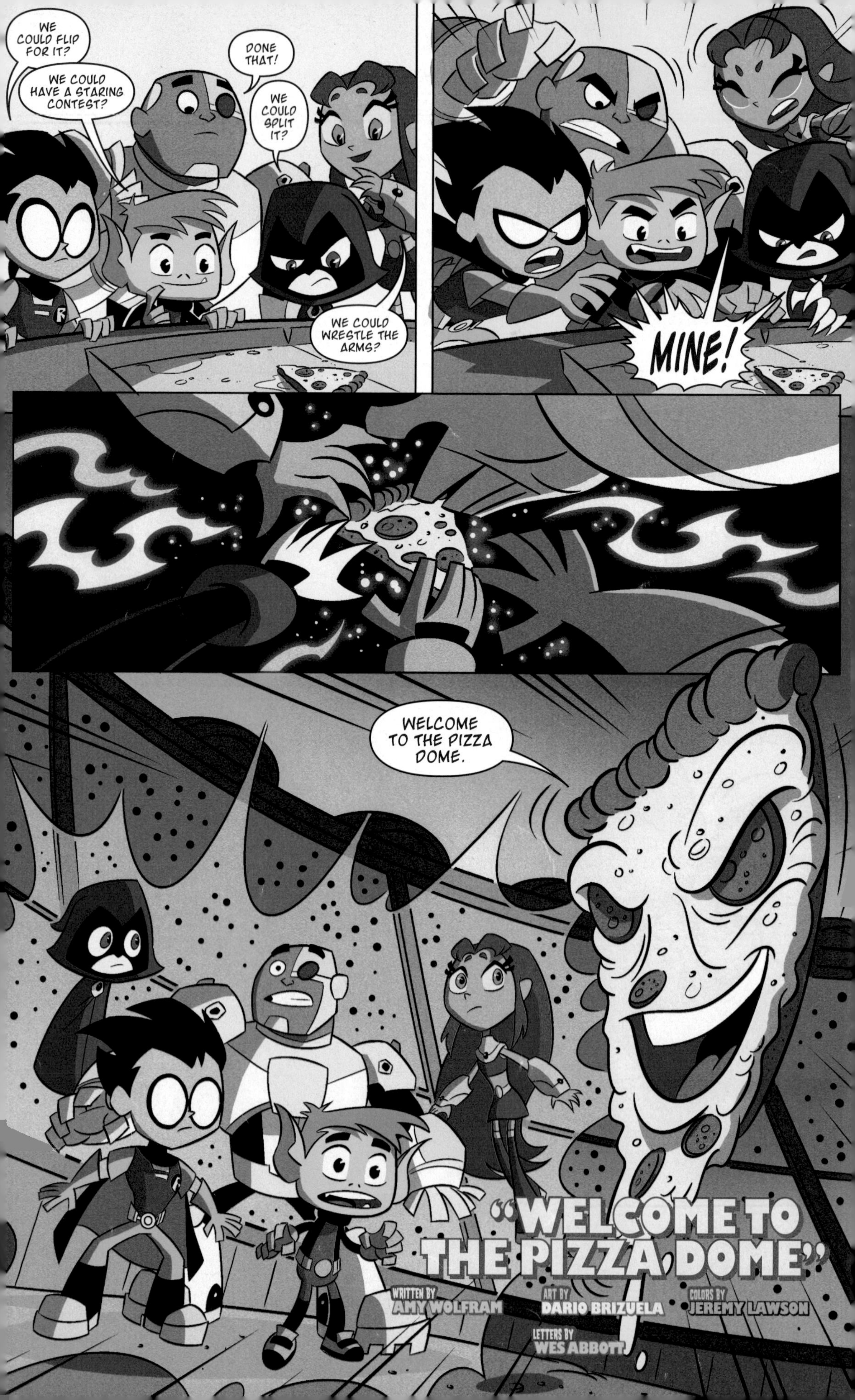
WE COULD FLIP FOR IT?
WE COULD HAVE A STARING CONTEST?
DONE THAT!
WE COULD SPLIT IT?
WE COULD WRESTLE THE ARMS?
MINE!
WELCOME TO THE PIZZA DOME.
"WELCOME TO THE PIZZA DOME"
WRITTEN BY AMY WOLFRAM
ART BY DARIO BRIZUELA
COLORS BY JEREMY LAWSON
LETTERS BY WES ABBOTT

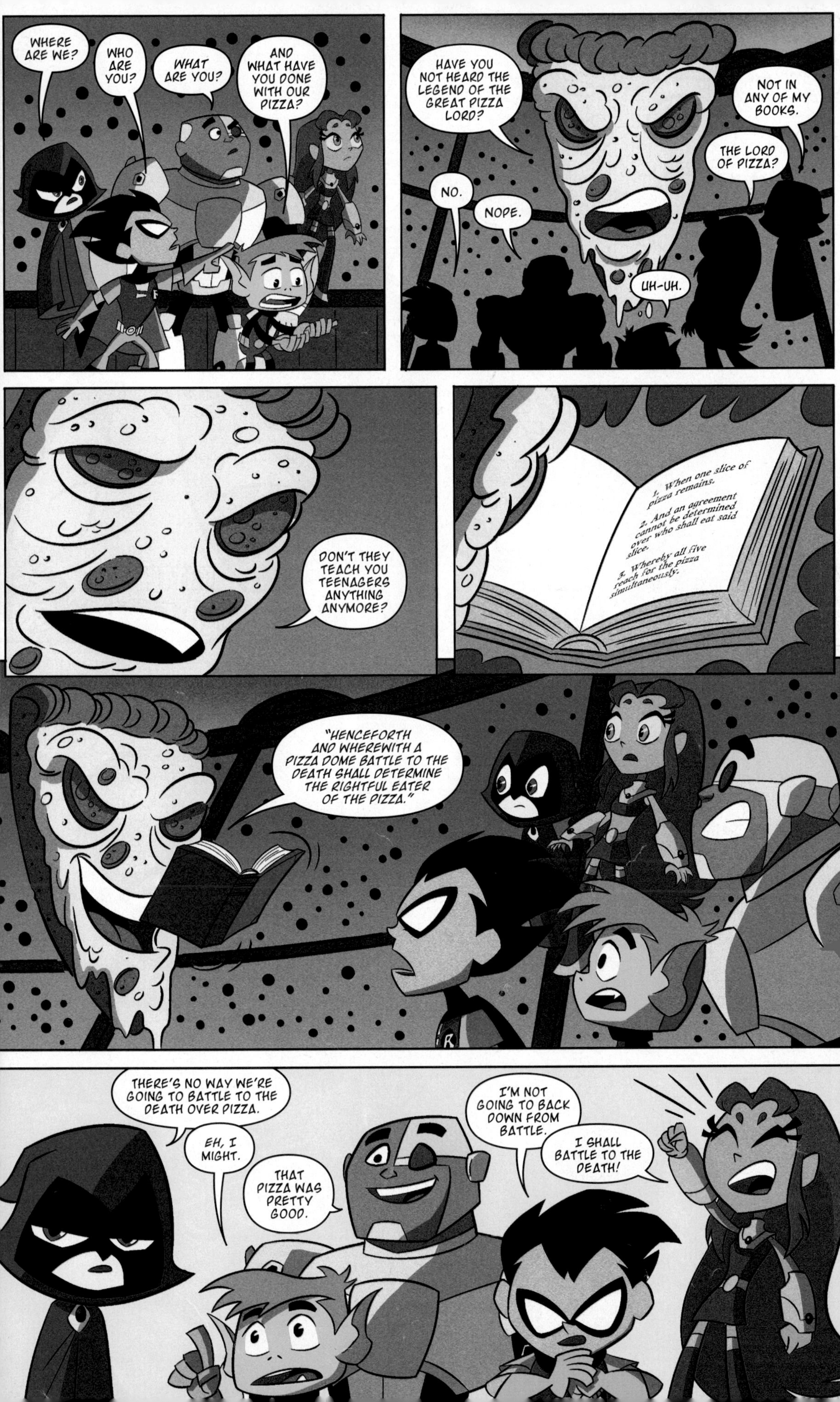
WHERE ARE WE?
WHO ARE YOU?
WHAT ARE YOU?
AND WHAT HAVE YOU DONE WITH OUR PIZZA?
HAVE YOU NOT HEARD THE LEGEND OF THE GREAT PIZZA LORD?
NO.
NOPE.
NOT IN ANY OF MY BOOKS.
THE LORD OF PIZZA?
UH-UH.
DON'T THEY TEACH YOU TEENAGERS ANYTHING ANYMORE?
1. When one slice of pizza remains.
2. And an agreement cannot be determined over who shall eat said slice.
3. Whereby all five reach for the pizza simultaneously.
"HENCEFORTH AND WHEREWITH A PIZZA DOME BATTLE TO THE DEATH SHALL DETERMINE THE RIGHTFUL EATER OF THE PIZZA."
THERE'S NO WAY WE'RE GOING TO BATTLE TO THE DEATH OVER PIZZA.
EH, I MIGHT.
THAT PIZZA WAS PRETTY GOOD.
I'M NOT GOING TO BACK DOWN FROM BATTLE.
I SHALL BATTLE TO THE DEATH!

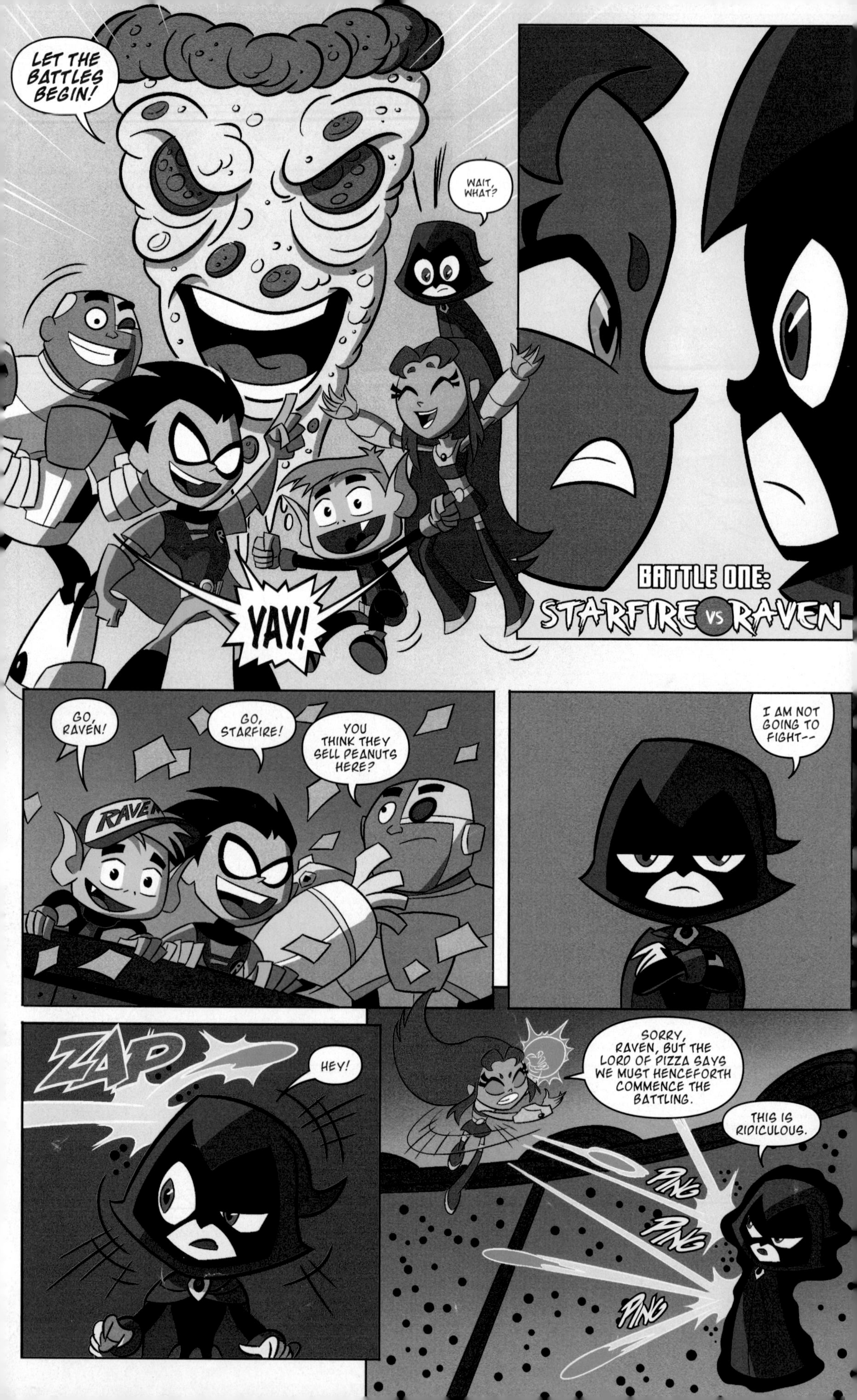
LET THE BATTLES BEGIN!
WAIT, WHAT?
YAY!
BATTLE ONE:
STARFIRE VS RAVEN
GO, RAVEN!
GO, STARFIRE!
YOU THINK THEY SELL PEANUTS HERE?
RAVEN
I AM NOT GOING TO FIGHT--
ZAP
HEY!
SORRY, RAVEN, BUT THE LORD OF PIZZA SAYS WE MUST HENCEFORTH COMMENCE THE BATTLING.
THIS IS RIDICULOUS.
PING
PING
PING

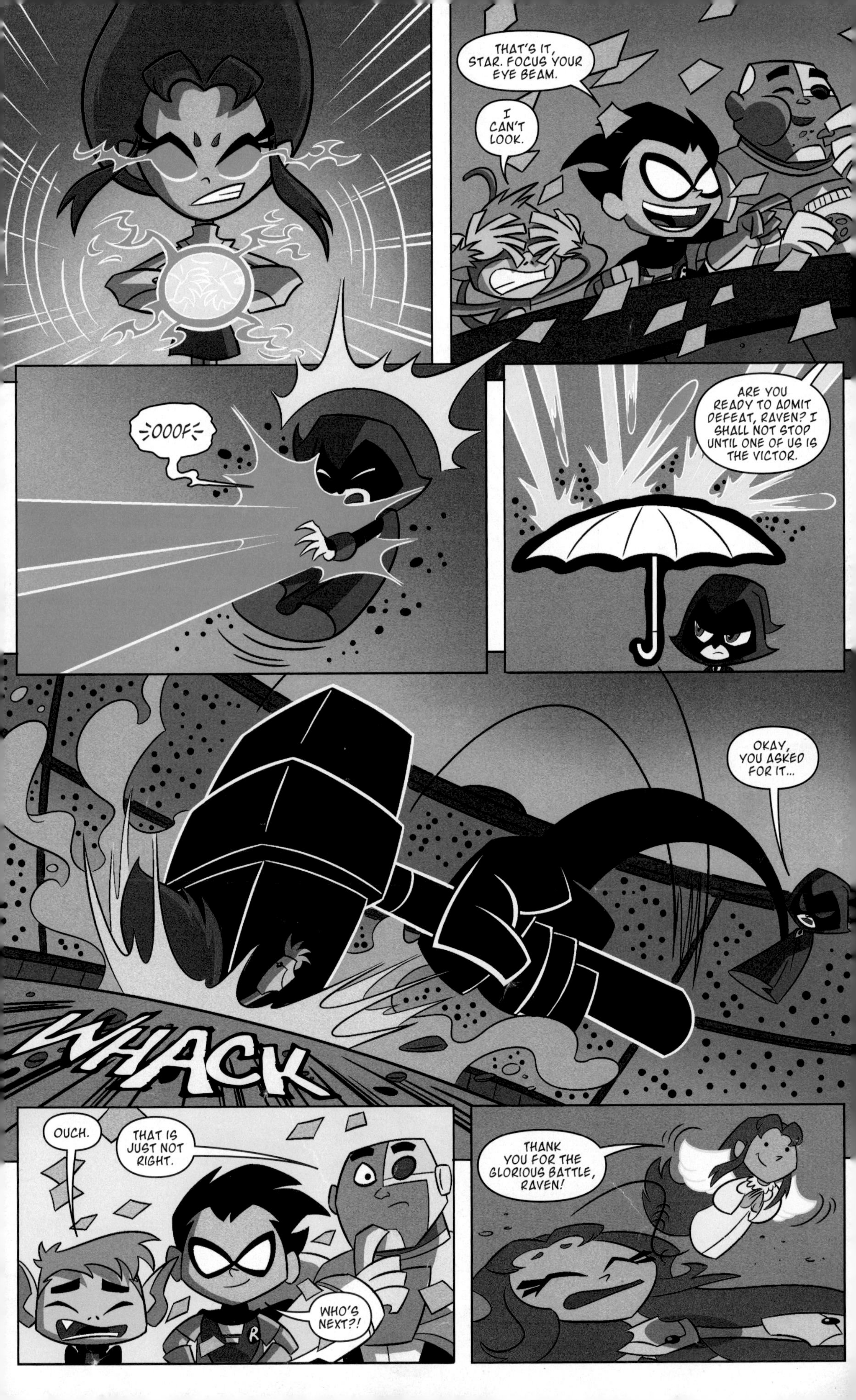
THAT'S IT, STAR. FOCUS YOUR EYE BEAM.
I CAN'T LOOK.
OOOF
ARE YOU READY TO ADMIT DEFEAT, RAVEN? I SHALL NOT STOP UNTIL ONE OF US IS THE VICTOR.
OKAY, YOU ASKED FOR IT...
WHACK
OUCH.
THAT IS JUST NOT RIGHT.
WHO'S NEXT?!
THANK YOU FOR THE GLORIOUS BATTLE, RAVEN!

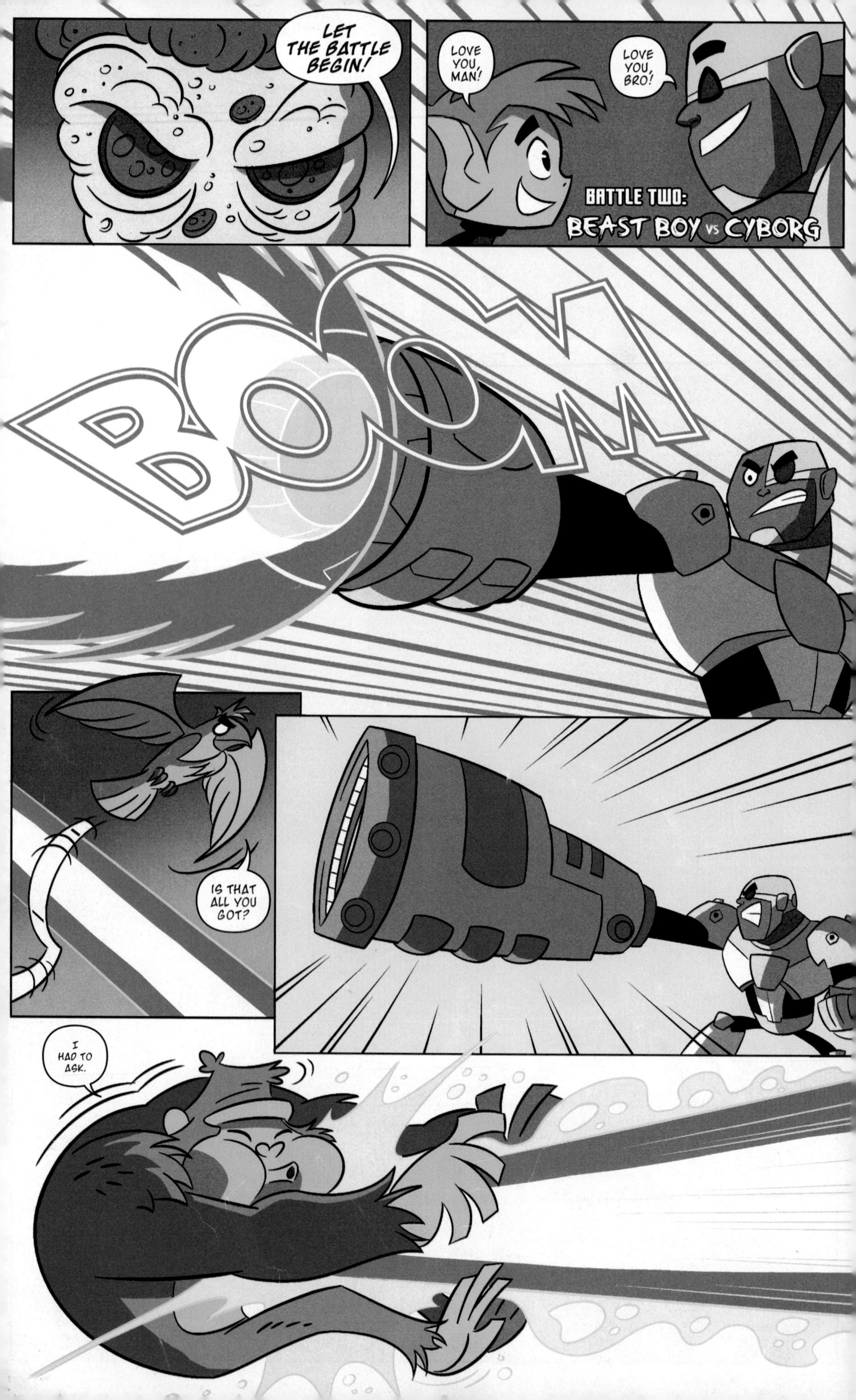

LET THE BATTLE BEGIN!
LOVE YOU, MAN!
LOVE YOU, BRO!
BATTLE TWO:
BEAST BOY VS CYBORG
BOOM
IS THAT ALL YOU GOT?
I HAD TO ASK.

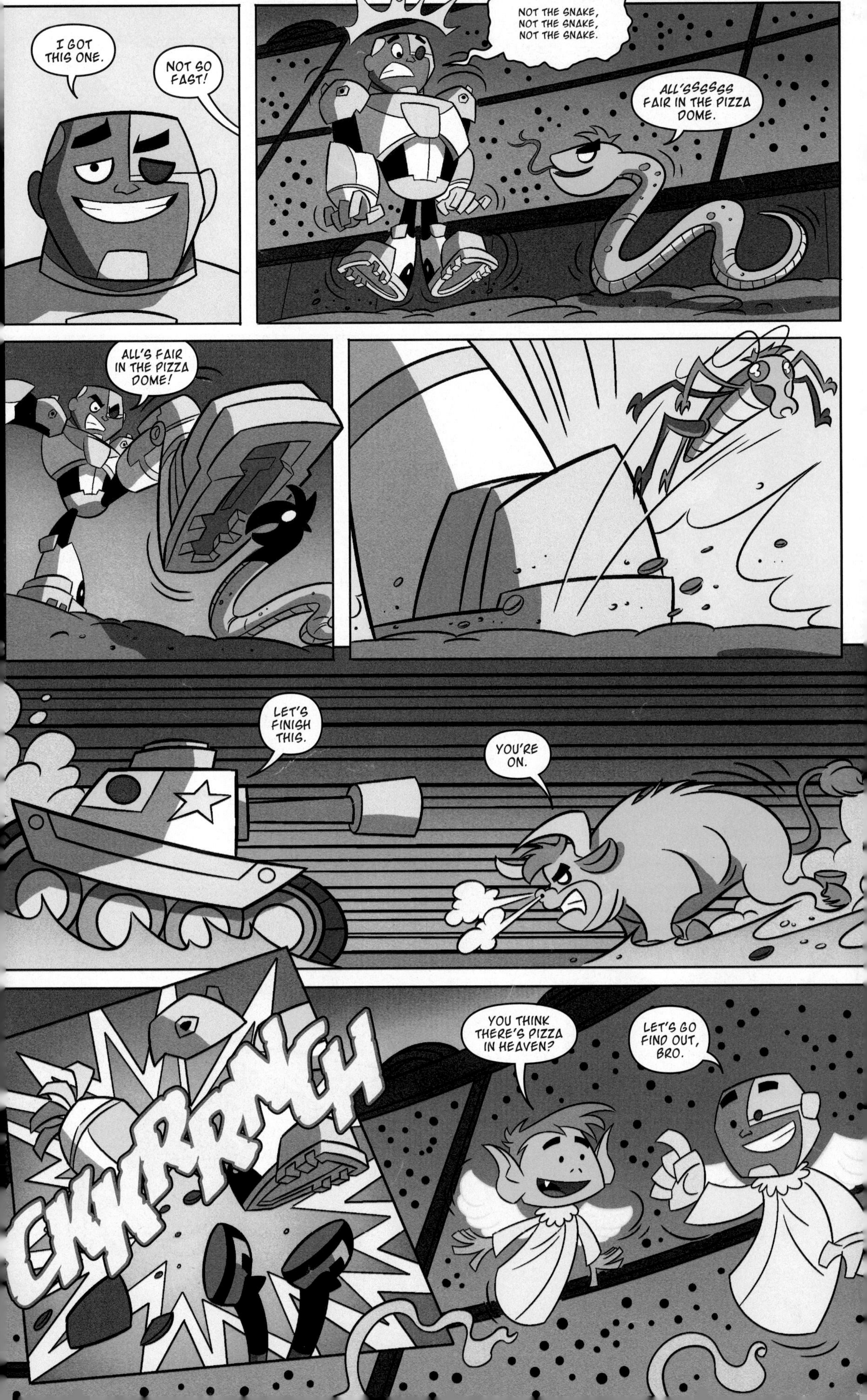
I GOT THIS ONE.
NOT SO FAST!
NOT THE SNAKE, NOT THE SNAKE, NOT THE SNAKE.
ALL'SSSSSS FAIR IN THE PIZZA DOME.
ALL'S FAIR IN THE PIZZA DOME!
LET'S FINISH THIS.
YOU'RE ON.
CHKRRRNCH
YOU THINK THERE'S PIZZA IN HEAVEN?
LET'S GO FIND OUT, BRO.

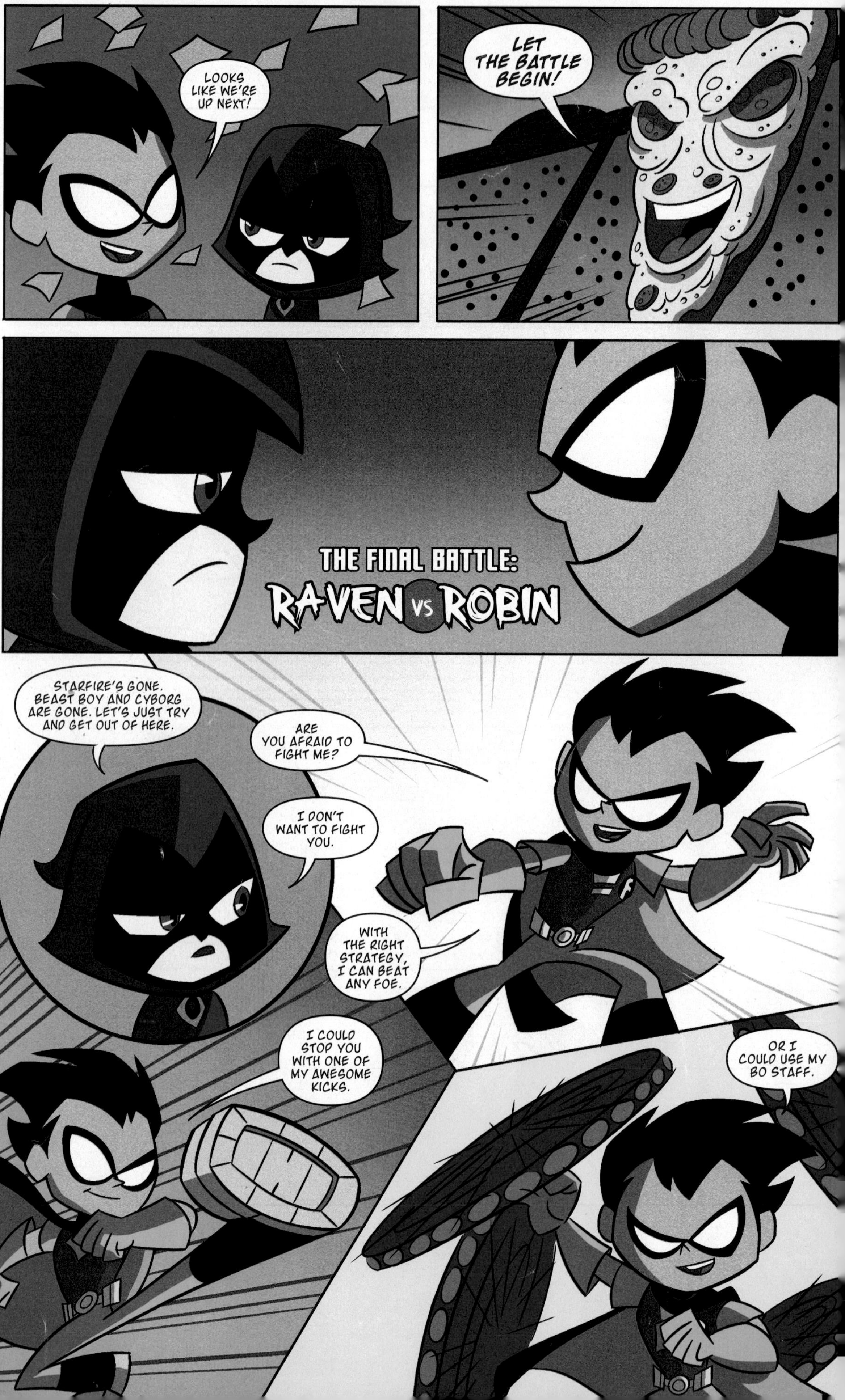
LOOKS LIKE WE'RE UP NEXT!
LET THE BATTLE BEGIN!
THE FINAL BATTLE:
RAVEN VS ROBIN
STARFIRE'S GONE. BEAST BOY AND CYBORG ARE GONE. LET'S JUST TRY AND GET OUT OF HERE.
ARE YOU AFRAID TO FIGHT ME?
I DON'T WANT TO FIGHT YOU.
WITH THE RIGHT STRATEGY, I CAN BEAT ANY FOE.
I COULD STOP YOU WITH ONE OF MY AWESOME KICKS.
OR I COULD USE MY BO STAFF.

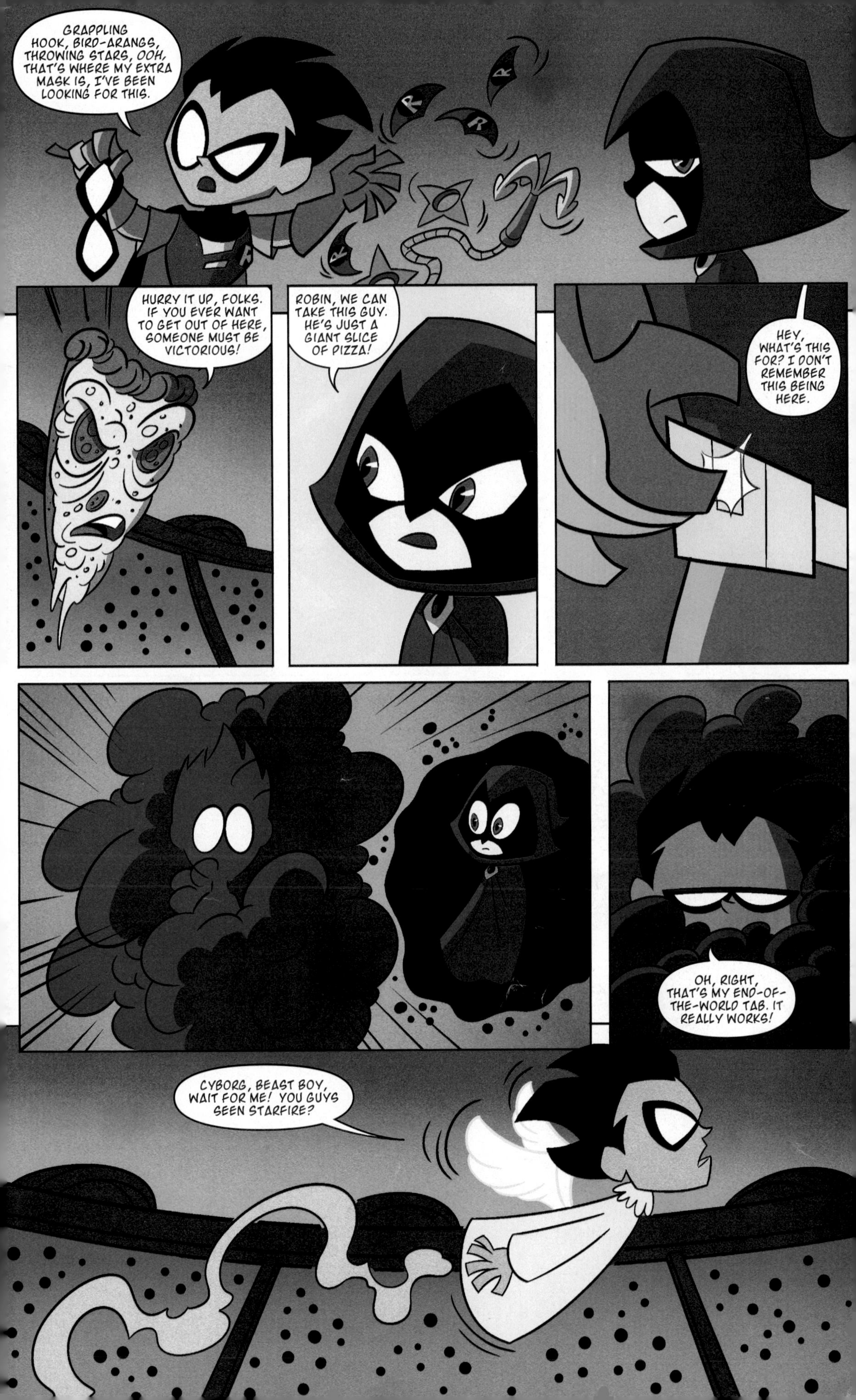
GRAPPLING HOOK, BIRD-ARANGS, THROWING STARS, OOH, THAT'S WHERE MY EXTRA MASK IS, I'VE BEEN LOOKING FOR THIS.
HURRY IT UP, FOLKS. IF YOU EVER WANT TO GET OUT OF HERE, SOMEONE MUST BE VICTORIOUS!
ROBIN, WE CAN TAKE THIS GUY. HE'S JUST A GIANT SLICE OF PIZZA!
HEY, WHAT'S THIS FOR? I DON'T REMEMBER THIS BEING HERE.
OH, RIGHT, THAT'S MY END-OF-THE-WORLD TAB. IT REALLY WORKS!
CYBORG, BEAST BOY, WAIT FOR ME! YOU GUYS SEEN STARFIRE?

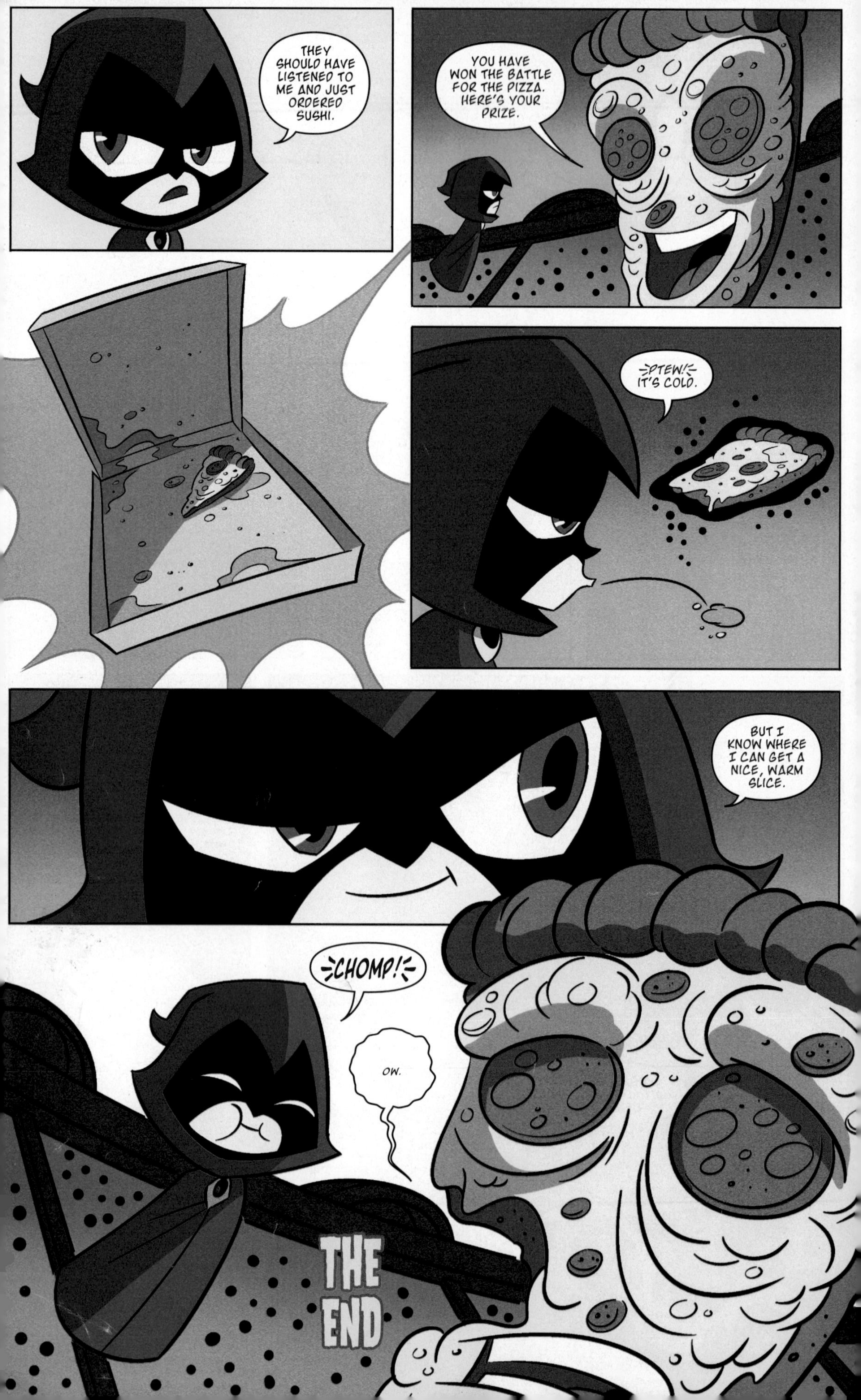
THEY SHOULD HAVE LISTENED TO ME AND JUST ORDERED SUSHI.
YOU HAVE WON THE BATTLE FOR THE PIZZA. HERE'S YOUR PRIZE.
PTEW! IT'S COLD.
BUT I KNOW WHERE I CAN GET A NICE, WARM SLICE.
CHOMP!
OW.
THE END

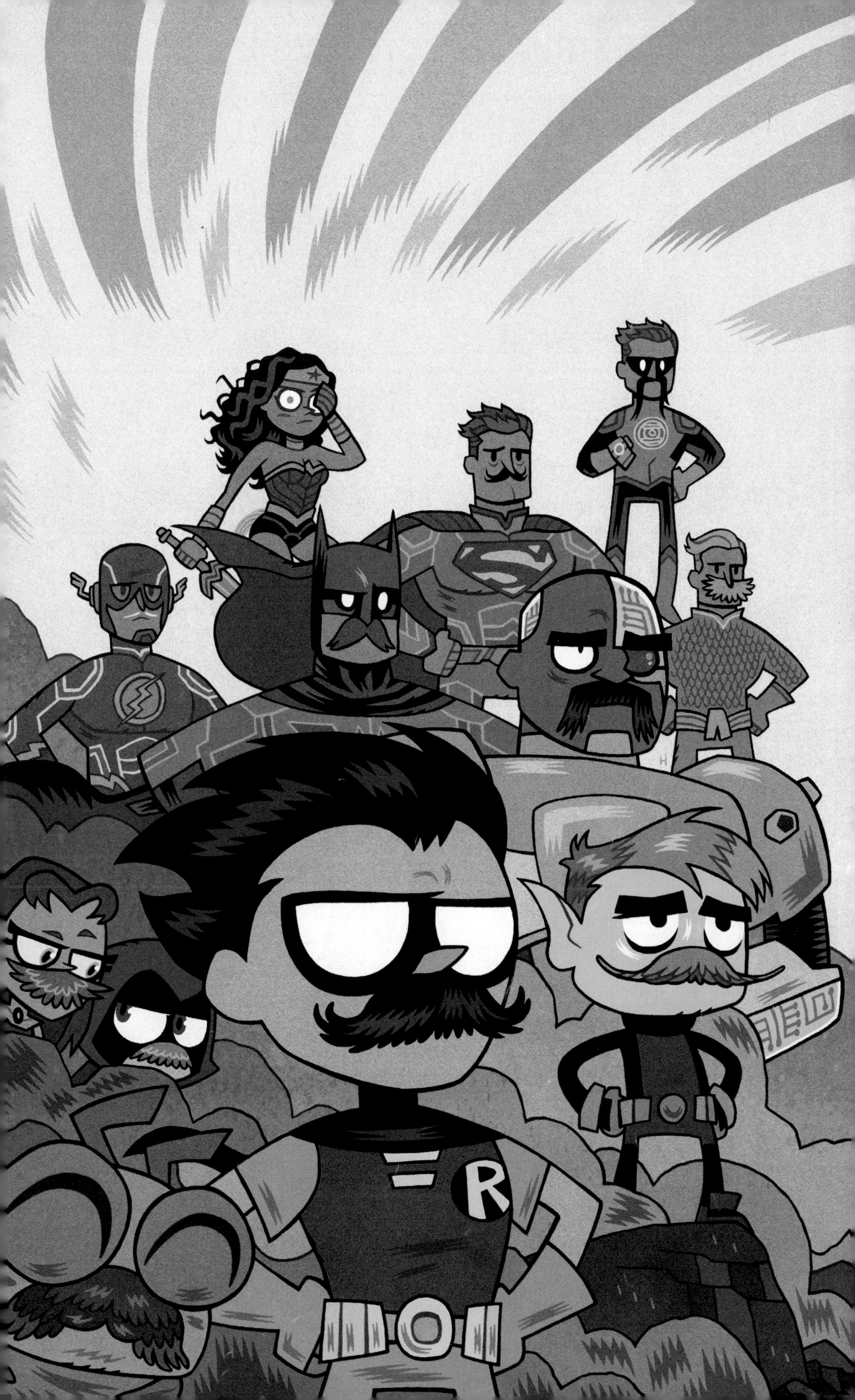

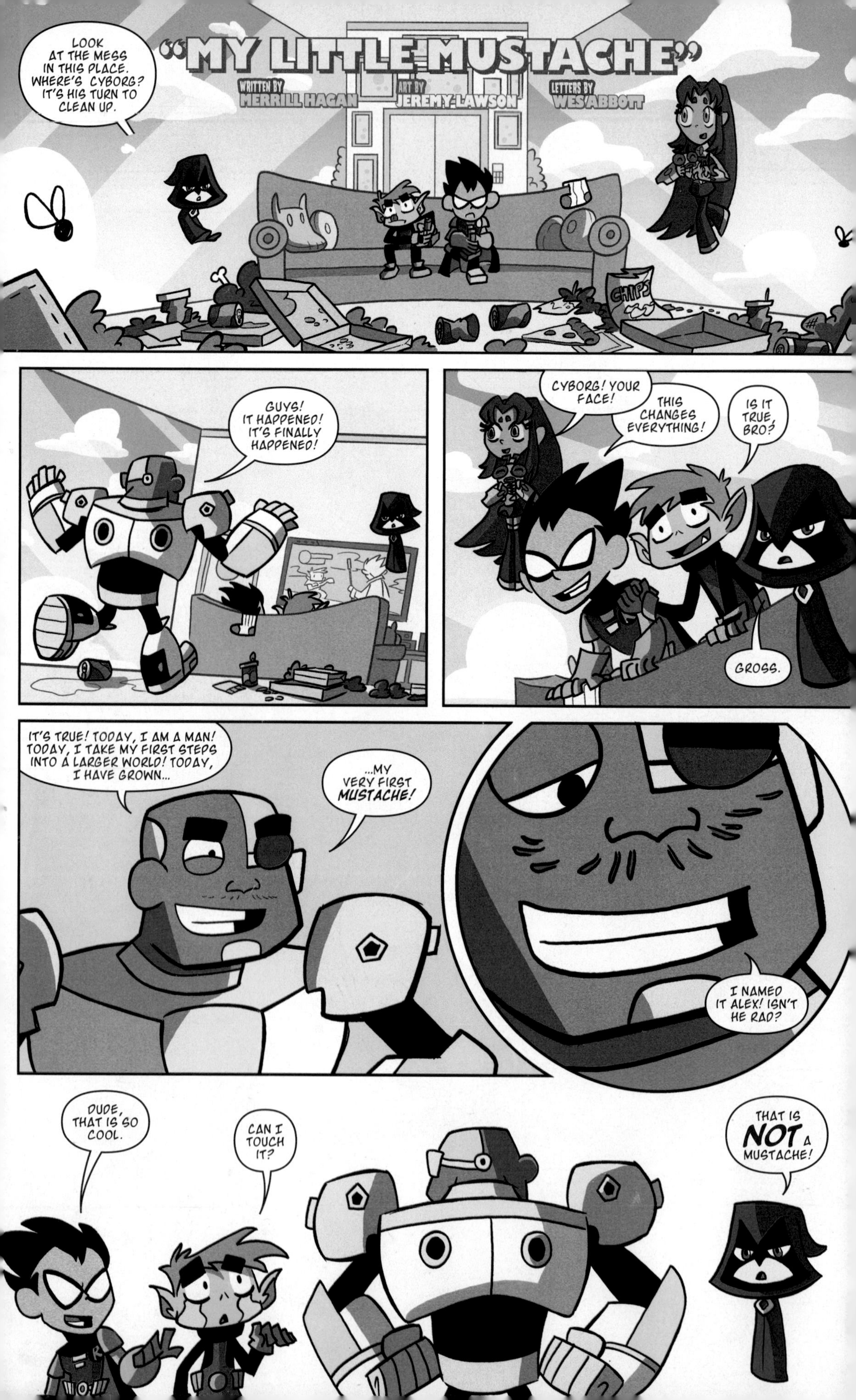
"MY LITTLE MUSTACHE"
WRITTEN BY MERRILL HAGAN
ART BY JEREMY LAWSON
LETTERS BY WES ABBOTT
LOOK AT THE MESS IN THIS PLACE. WHERE'S CYBORG? IT'S HIS TURN TO CLEAN UP.
CHIPS
GUYS! IT HAPPENED! IT'S FINALLY HAPPENED!
CYBORG! YOUR FACE!
THIS CHANGES EVERYTHING!
IS IT TRUE, BRO?
GROSS.
IT'S TRUE! TODAY, I AM A MAN! TODAY, I TAKE MY FIRST STEPS INTO A LARGER WORLD! TODAY, I HAVE GROWN...
...MY VERY FIRST MUSTACHE!
I NAMED IT ALEX! ISN'T HE RAD?
DUDE, THAT IS SO COOL.
CAN I TOUCH IT?
THAT IS NOT A MUSTACHE!

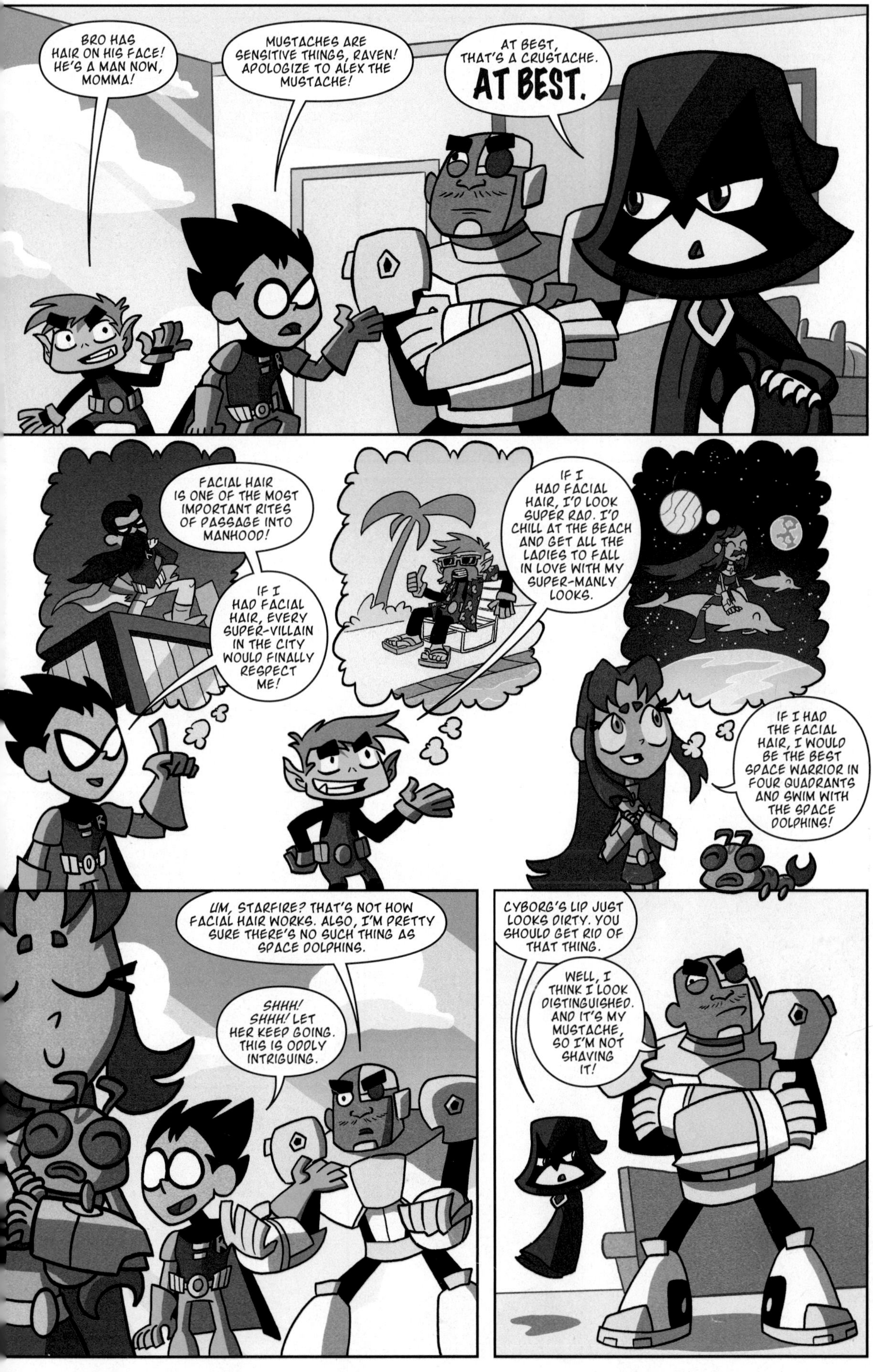
BRO HAS HAIR ON HIS FACE! HE'S A MAN NOW, MOMMA!
MUSTACHES ARE SENSITIVE THINGS, RAVEN! APOLOGIZE TO ALEX THE MUSTACHE!
AT BEST, THAT'S A CRUSTACHE. AT BEST.
FACIAL HAIR IS ONE OF THE MOST IMPORTANT RITES OF PASSAGE INTO MANHOOD!
IF I HAD FACIAL HAIR, EVERY SUPER-VILLAIN IN THE CITY WOULD FINALLY RESPECT ME!
IF I HAD FACIAL HAIR, I'D LOOK SUPER RAD. I'D CHILL AT THE BEACH AND GET ALL THE LADIES TO FALL IN LOVE WITH MY SUPER-MANLY LOOKS.
IF I HAD THE FACIAL HAIR, I WOULD BE THE BEST SPACE WARRIOR IN FOUR QUADRANTS AND SWIM WITH THE SPACE DOLPHINS!
UM, STARFIRE? THAT'S NOT HOW FACIAL HAIR WORKS. ALSO, I'M PRETTY SURE THERE'S NO SUCH THING AS SPACE DOLPHINS.
SHHH! SHHH! LET HER KEEP GOING. THIS IS ODDLY INTRIGUING.
CYBORG'S LIP JUST LOOKS DIRTY. YOU SHOULD GET RID OF THAT THING.
WELL, I THINK I LOOK DISTINGUISHED. AND IT'S MY MUSTACHE, SO I'M NOT SHAVING IT!

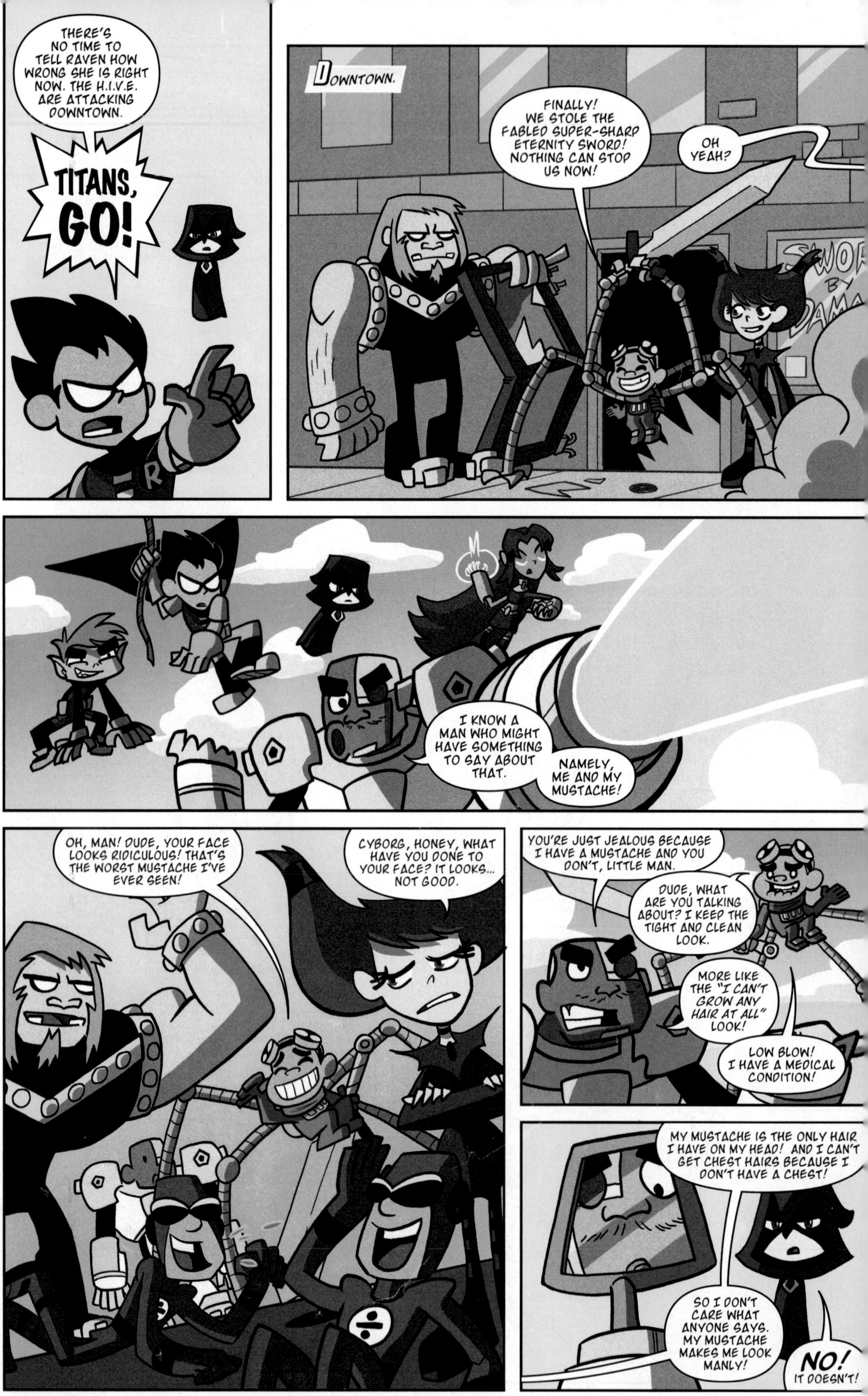
THERE'S NO TIME TO TELL RAVEN HOW WRONG SHE IS RIGHT NOW. THE H.I.V.E. ARE ATTACKING DOWNTOWN.
TITANS, GO!
DOWNTOWN.
FINALLY! WE STOLE THE FABLED SUPER-SHARP ETERNITY SWORD! NOTHING CAN STOP US NOW!
OH YEAH?
I KNOW A MAN WHO MIGHT HAVE SOMETHING TO SAY ABOUT THAT.
NAMELY, ME AND MY MUSTACHE!
OH, MAN! DUDE, YOUR FACE LOOKS RIDICULOUS! THAT'S THE WORST MUSTACHE I'VE EVER SEEN!
CYBORG, HONEY, WHAT HAVE YOU DONE TO YOUR FACE? IT LOOKS... NOT GOOD.
YOU'RE JUST JEALOUS BECAUSE I HAVE A MUSTACHE AND YOU DON'T, LITTLE MAN.
DUDE, WHAT ARE YOU TALKING ABOUT? I KEEP THE TIGHT AND CLEAN LOOK.
MORE LIKE THE "I CAN'T GROW ANY HAIR AT ALL" LOOK!
LOW BLOW! I HAVE A MEDICAL CONDITION!
MY MUSTACHE IS THE ONLY HAIR I HAVE ON MY HEAD! AND I CAN'T GET CHEST HAIRS BECAUSE I DON'T HAVE A CHEST!
SO I DON'T CARE WHAT ANYONE SAYS. MY MUSTACHE MAKES ME LOOK MANLY!
NO! IT DOESN'T!

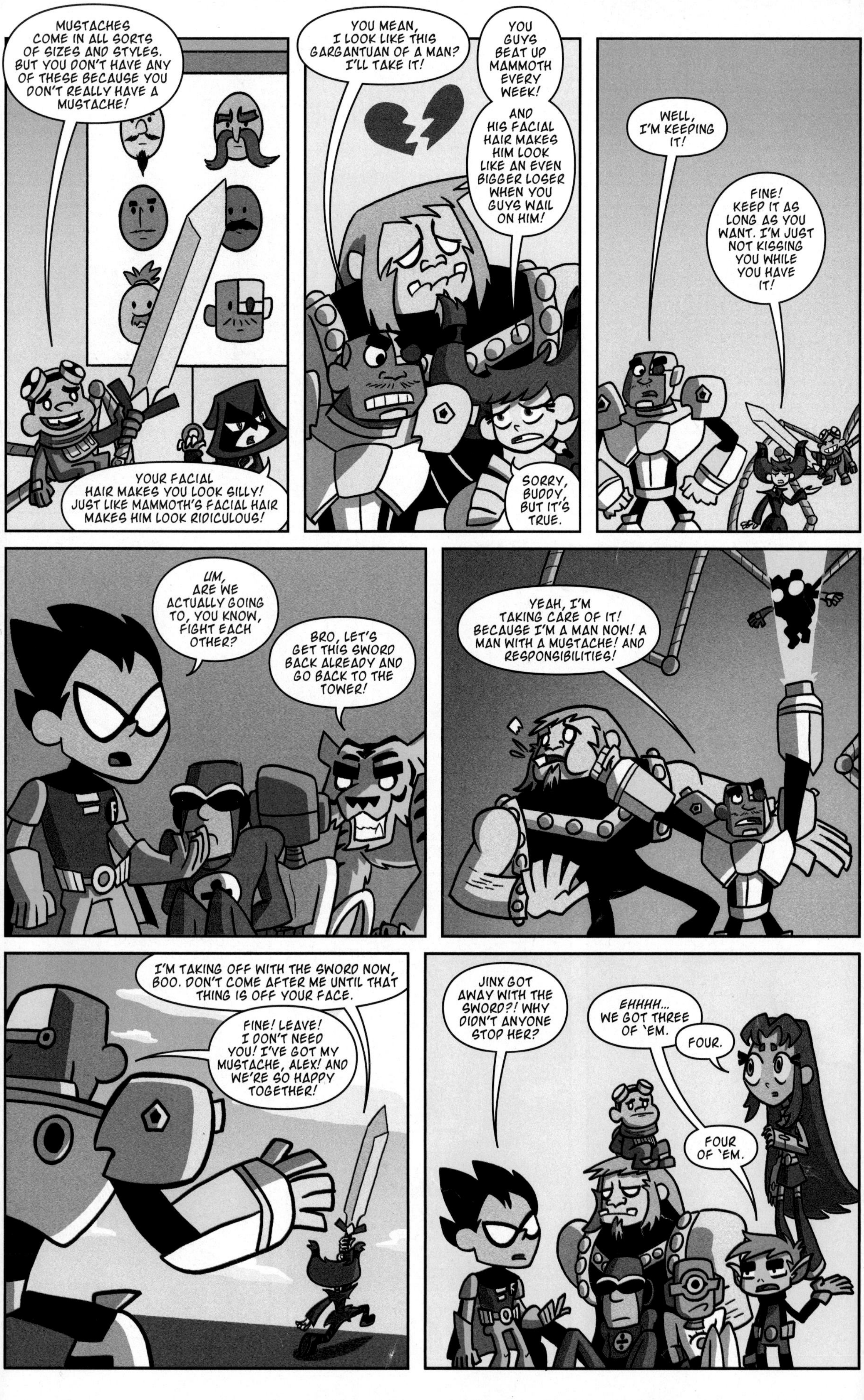
MUSTACHES COME IN ALL SORTS OF SIZES AND STYLES. BUT YOU DON'T HAVE ANY OF THESE BECAUSE YOU DON'T REALLY HAVE A MUSTACHE!
YOUR FACIAL HAIR MAKES YOU LOOK SILLY! JUST LIKE MAMMOTH'S FACIAL HAIR MAKES HIM LOOK RIDICULOUS!
YOU MEAN, I LOOK LIKE THIS GARGANTUAN OF A MAN? I'LL TAKE IT!
YOU GUYS BEAT UP MAMMOTH EVERY WEEK!
AND HIS FACIAL HAIR MAKES HIM LOOK LIKE AN EVEN BIGGER LOSER WHEN YOU GUYS WAIL ON HIM!
SORRY, BUDDY, BUT IT'S TRUE.
WELL, I'M KEEPING IT!
FINE! KEEP IT AS LONG AS YOU WANT. I'M JUST NOT KISSING YOU WHILE YOU HAVE IT!
UM, ARE WE ACTUALLY GOING TO, YOU KNOW, FIGHT EACH OTHER?
BRO, LET'S GET THIS SWORD BACK ALREADY AND GO BACK TO THE TOWER!
YEAH, I'M TAKING CARE OF IT! BECAUSE I'M A MAN NOW! A MAN WITH A MUSTACHE! AND RESPONSIBILITIES!
I'M TAKING OFF WITH THE SWORD NOW, BOO. DON'T COME AFTER ME UNTIL THAT THING IS OFF YOUR FACE.
FINE! LEAVE! I DON'T NEED YOU! I'VE GOT MY MUSTACHE, ALEX! AND WE'RE SO HAPPY TOGETHER!
JINX GOT AWAY WITH THE SWORD?! WHY DIDN'T ANYONE STOP HER?
EHHHH... WE GOT THREE OF 'EM.
FOUR.
FOUR OF 'EM.

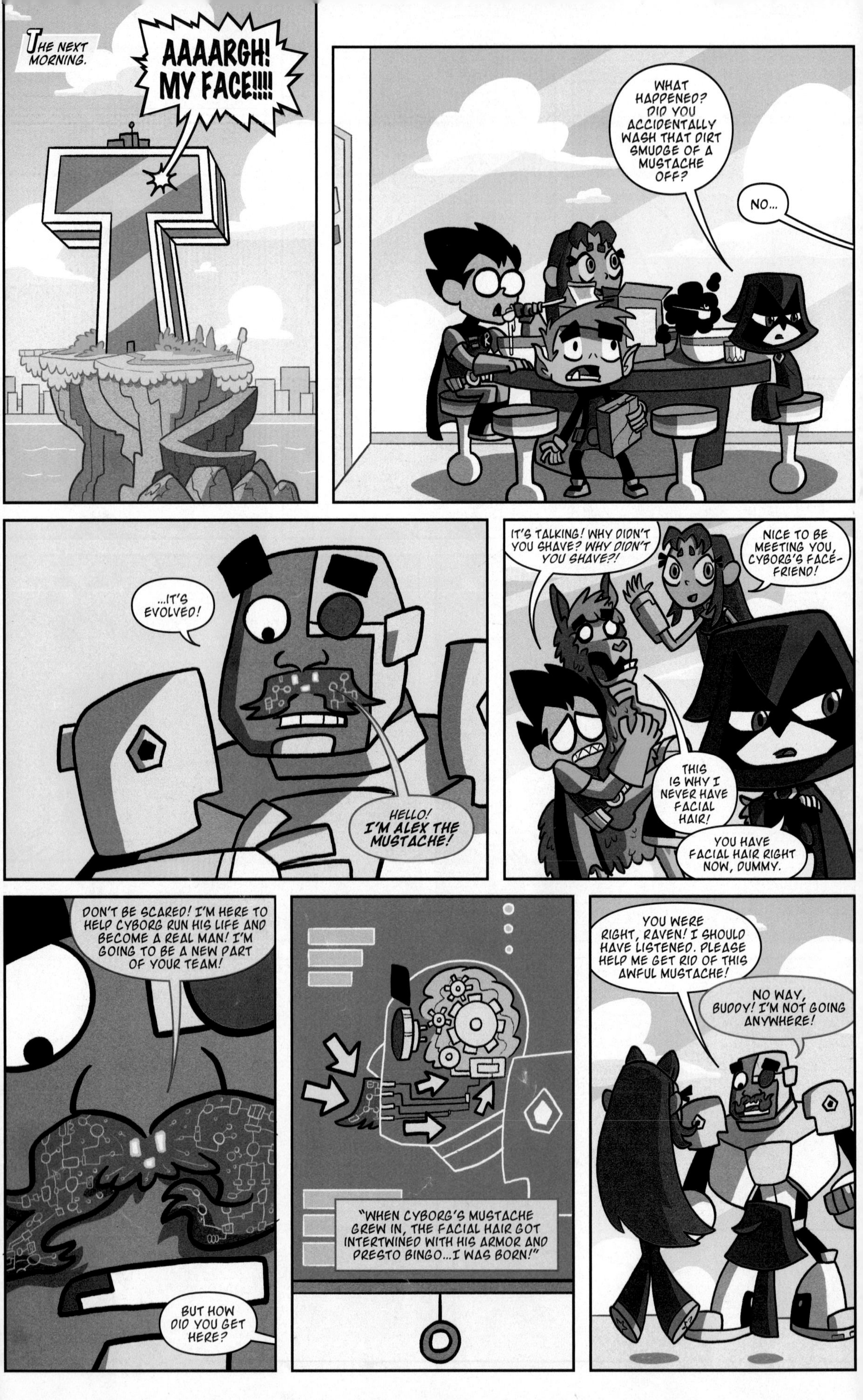
THE NEXT MORNING.
AAAARGH! MY FACE!!!!
WHAT HAPPENED? DID YOU ACCIDENTALLY WASH THAT DIRT SMUDGE OF A MUSTACHE OFF?
NO...
...IT'S EVOLVED!
HELLO! I'M ALEX THE MUSTACHE!
IT'S TALKING! WHY DIDN'T YOU SHAVE? WHY DIDN'T YOU SHAVE?!
NICE TO BE MEETING YOU, CYBORG'S FACE-FRIEND!
THIS IS WHY I NEVER HAVE FACIAL HAIR!
YOU HAVE FACIAL HAIR RIGHT NOW, DUMMY.
DON'T BE SCARED! I'M HERE TO HELP CYBORG RUN HIS LIFE AND BECOME A REAL MAN! I'M GOING TO BE A NEW PART OF YOUR TEAM!
BUT HOW DID YOU GET HERE?
"WHEN CYBORG'S MUSTACHE GREW IN, THE FACIAL HAIR GOT INTERTWINED WITH HIS ARMOR AND PRESTO BINGO...I WAS BORN!"
YOU WERE RIGHT, RAVEN! I SHOULD HAVE LISTENED. PLEASE HELP ME GET RID OF THIS AWFUL MUSTACHE!
NO WAY, BUDDY! I'M NOT GOING ANYWHERE!

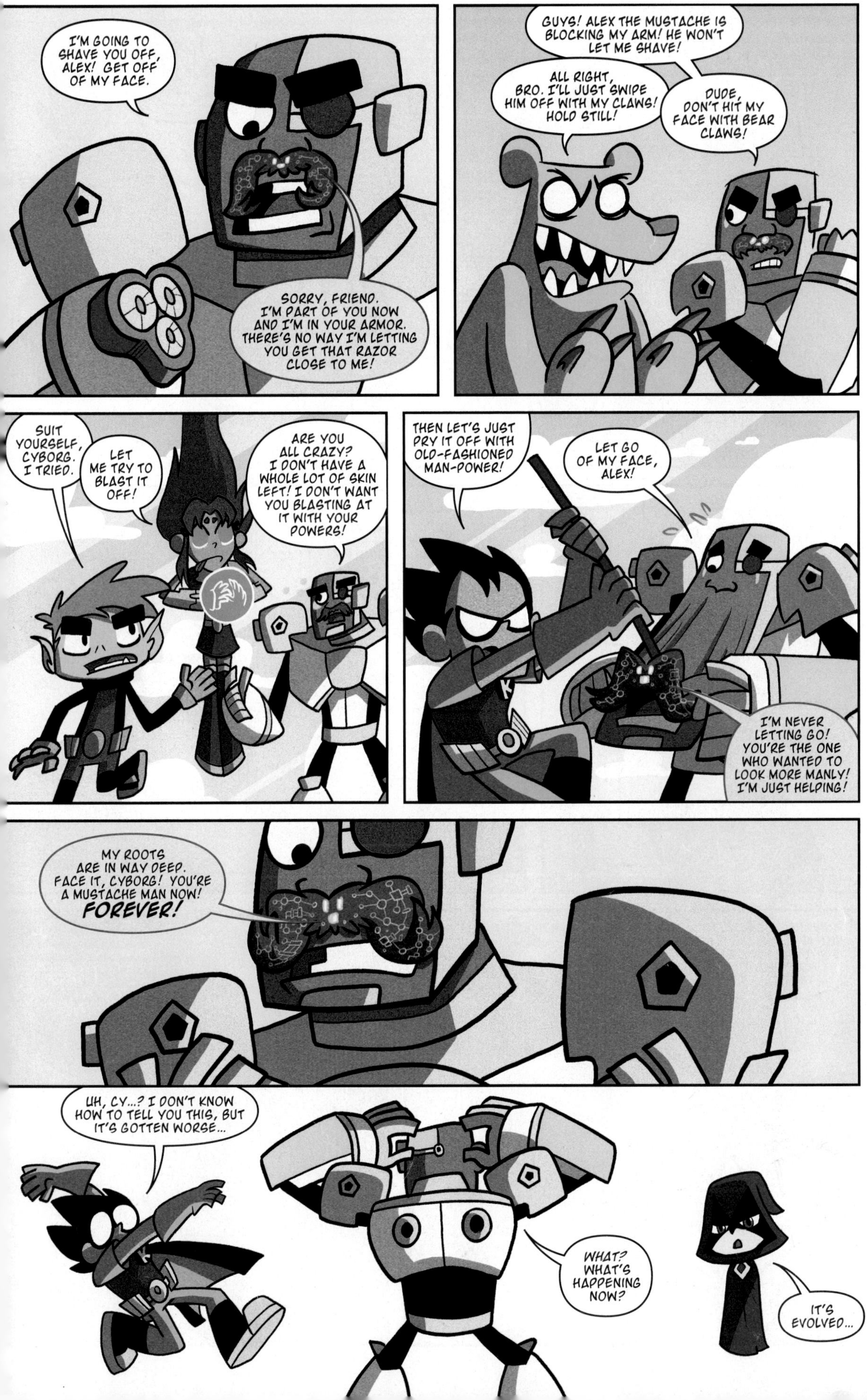

I'M GOING TO SHAVE YOU OFF, ALEX! GET OFF OF MY FACE.
SORRY, FRIEND. I'M PART OF YOU NOW AND I'M IN YOUR ARMOR. THERE'S NO WAY I'M LETTING YOU GET THAT RAZOR CLOSE TO ME!
GUYS! ALEX THE MUSTACHE IS BLOCKING MY ARM! HE WON'T LET ME SHAVE!
ALL RIGHT, BRO. I'LL JUST SWIPE HIM OFF WITH MY CLAWS! HOLD STILL!
DUDE, DON'T HIT MY FACE WITH BEAR CLAWS!
SUIT YOURSELF, CYBORG. I TRIED.
LET ME TRY TO BLAST IT OFF!
ARE YOU ALL CRAZY? I DON'T HAVE A WHOLE LOT OF SKIN LEFT! I DON'T WANT YOU BLASTING AT IT WITH YOUR POWERS!
THEN LET'S JUST PRY IT OFF WITH OLD-FASHIONED MAN-POWER!
LET GO OF MY FACE, ALEX!
I'M NEVER LETTING GO! YOU'RE THE ONE WHO WANTED TO LOOK MORE MANLY! I'M JUST HELPING!
MY ROOTS ARE IN WAY DEEP. FACE IT, CYBORG! YOU'RE A MUSTACHE MAN NOW! FOREVER!
UH, CY...? I DON'T KNOW HOW TO TELL YOU THIS, BUT IT'S GOTTEN WORSE...
WHAT? WHAT'S HAPPENING NOW?
IT'S EVOLVED...

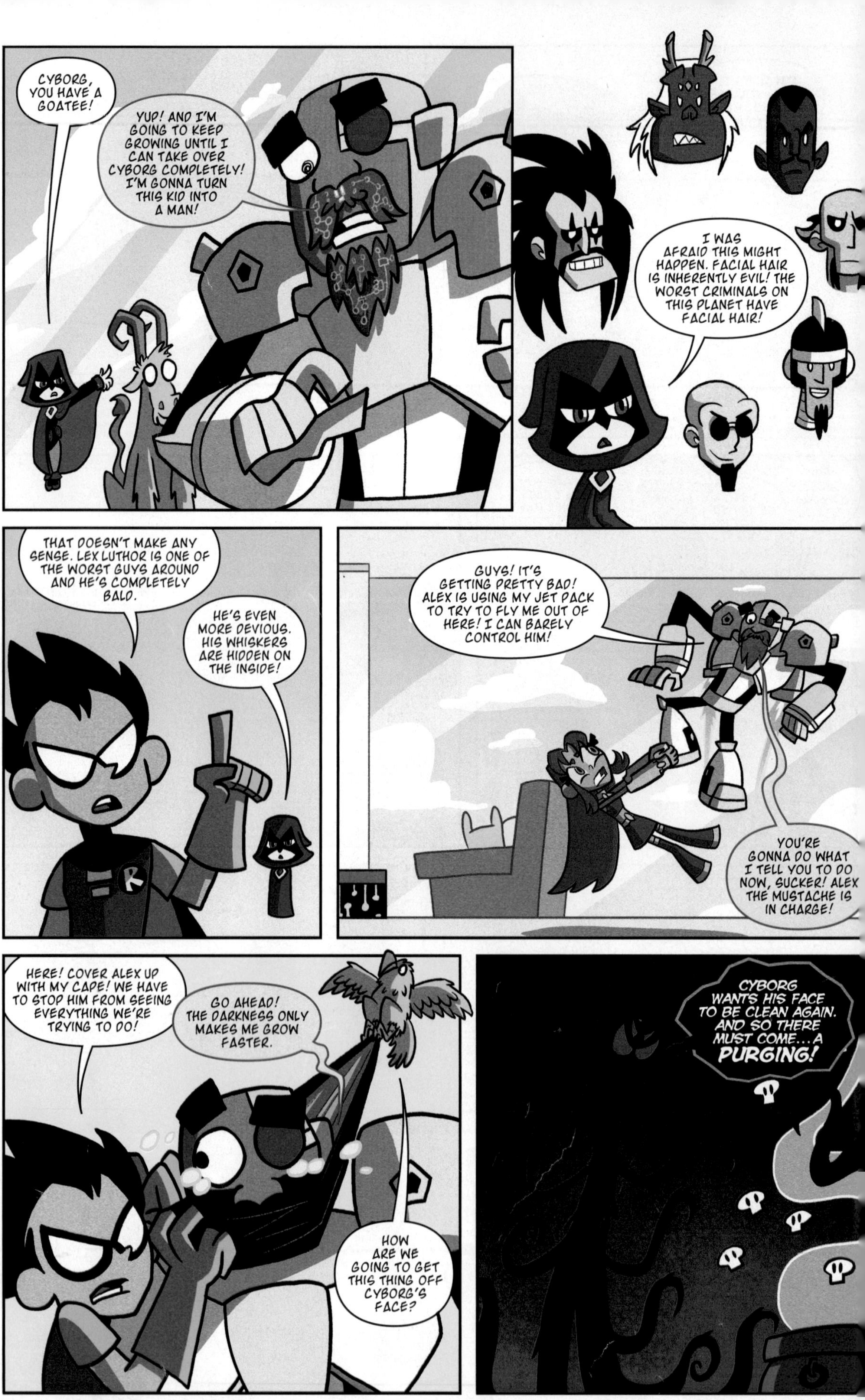
CYBORG, YOU HAVE A GOATEE!
YUP! AND I'M GOING TO KEEP GROWING UNTIL I CAN TAKE OVER CYBORG COMPLETELY! I'M GONNA TURN THIS KID INTO A MAN!
I WAS AFRAID THIS MIGHT HAPPEN. FACIAL HAIR IS INHERENTLY EVIL! THE WORST CRIMINALS ON THIS PLANET HAVE FACIAL HAIR!
THAT DOESN'T MAKE ANY SENSE. LEX LUTHOR IS ONE OF THE WORST GUYS AROUND AND HE'S COMPLETELY BALD.
HE'S EVEN MORE DEVIOUS. HIS WHISKERS ARE HIDDEN ON THE INSIDE!
GUYS! IT'S GETTING PRETTY BAD! ALEX IS USING MY JET PACK TO TRY TO FLY ME OUT OF HERE! I CAN BARELY CONTROL HIM!
YOU'RE GONNA DO WHAT I TELL YOU TO DO NOW, SUCKER! ALEX THE MUSTACHE IS IN CHARGE!
HERE! COVER ALEX UP WITH MY CAPE! WE HAVE TO STOP HIM FROM SEEING EVERYTHING WE'RE TRYING TO DO!
GO AHEAD! THE DARKNESS ONLY MAKES ME GROW FASTER.
HOW ARE WE GOING TO GET THIS THING OFF CYBORG'S FACE?
CYBORG WANTS HIS FACE TO BE CLEAN AGAIN. AND SO THERE MUST COME... A PURGING!

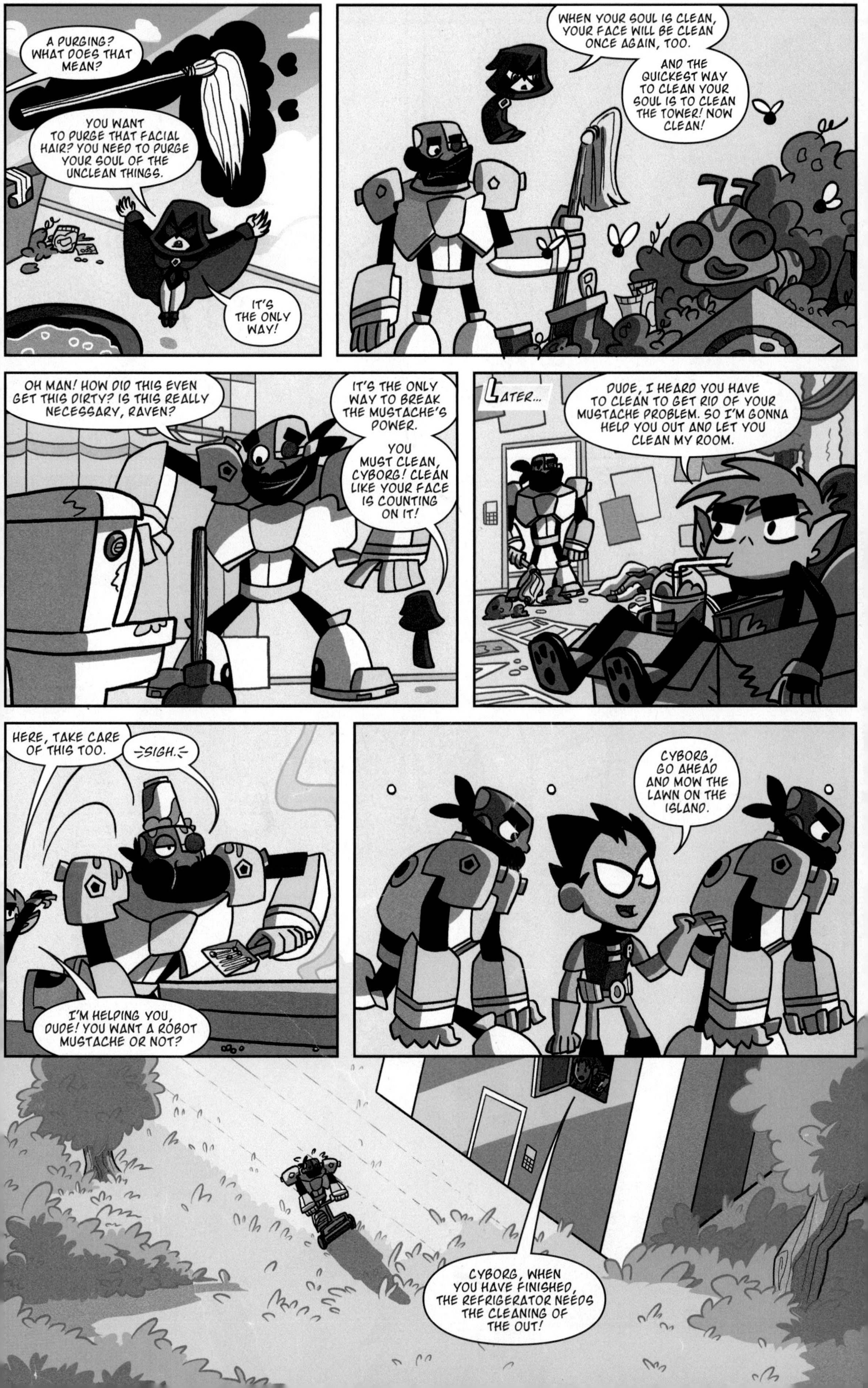
A PURGING? WHAT DOES THAT MEAN?
YOU WANT TO PURGE THAT FACIAL HAIR? YOU NEED TO PURGE YOUR SOUL OF THE UNCLEAN THINGS.
IT'S THE ONLY WAY!
WHEN YOUR SOUL IS CLEAN, YOUR FACE WILL BE CLEAN ONCE AGAIN, TOO.
AND THE QUICKEST WAY TO CLEAN YOUR SOUL IS TO CLEAN THE TOWER! NOW CLEAN!
OH MAN! HOW DID THIS EVEN GET THIS DIRTY? IS THIS REALLY NECESSARY, RAVEN?
IT'S THE ONLY WAY TO BREAK THE MUSTACHE'S POWER.
YOU MUST CLEAN, CYBORG! CLEAN LIKE YOUR FACE IS COUNTING ON IT!
LATER...
DUDE, I HEARD YOU HAVE TO CLEAN TO GET RID OF YOUR MUSTACHE PROBLEM. SO I'M GONNA HELP YOU OUT AND LET YOU CLEAN MY ROOM.
HERE, TAKE CARE OF THIS TOO.
SIGH.
I'M HELPING YOU, DUDE! YOU WANT A ROBOT MUSTACHE OR NOT?
CYBORG, GO AHEAD AND MOW THE LAWN ON THE ISLAND.
CYBORG, WHEN YOU HAVE FINISHED, THE REFRIGERATOR NEEDS THE CLEANING OF THE OUT!

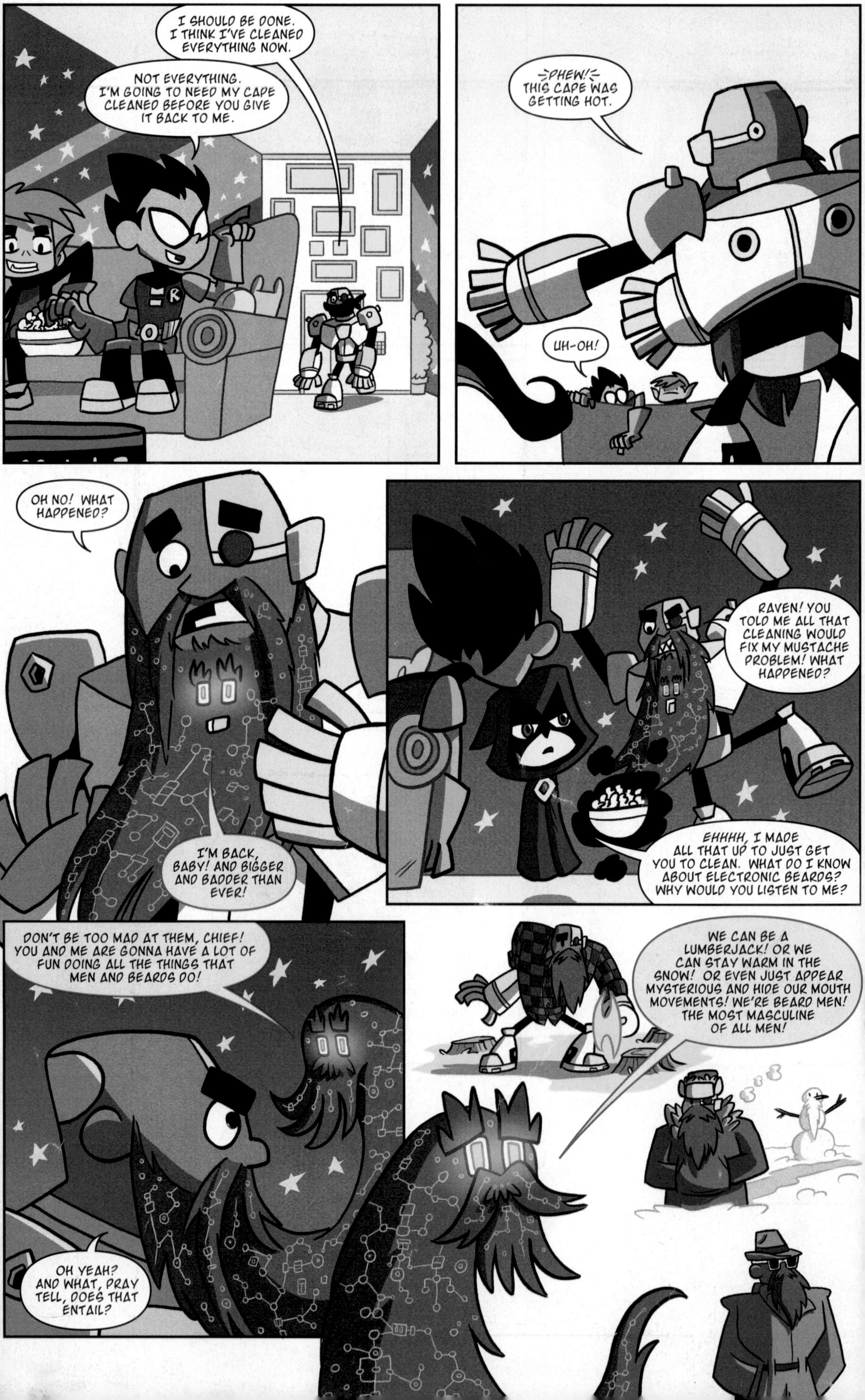
I SHOULD BE DONE. I THINK I'VE CLEANED EVERYTHING NOW.
NOT EVERYTHING. I'M GOING TO NEED MY CAPE CLEANED BEFORE YOU GIVE IT BACK TO ME.
PHEW! THIS CAPE WAS GETTING HOT.
UH-OH!
OH NO! WHAT HAPPENED?
I'M BACK, BABY! AND BIGGER AND BADDER THAN EVER!
RAVEN! YOU TOLD ME ALL THAT CLEANING WOULD FIX MY MUSTACHE PROBLEM! WHAT HAPPENED?
EHHHH, I MADE ALL THAT UP TO JUST GET YOU TO CLEAN. WHAT DO I KNOW ABOUT ELECTRONIC BEARDS? WHY WOULD YOU LISTEN TO ME?
DON'T BE TOO MAD AT THEM, CHIEF! YOU AND ME ARE GONNA HAVE A LOT OF FUN DOING ALL THE THINGS THAT MEN AND BEARDS DO!
OH YEAH? AND WHAT, PRAY TELL, DOES THAT ENTAIL?
WE CAN BE A LUMBERJACK! OR WE CAN STAY WARM IN THE SNOW! OR EVEN JUST APPEAR MYSTERIOUS AND HIDE OUR MOUTH MOVEMENTS! WE'RE BEARD MEN! THE MOST MASCULINE OF ALL MEN!

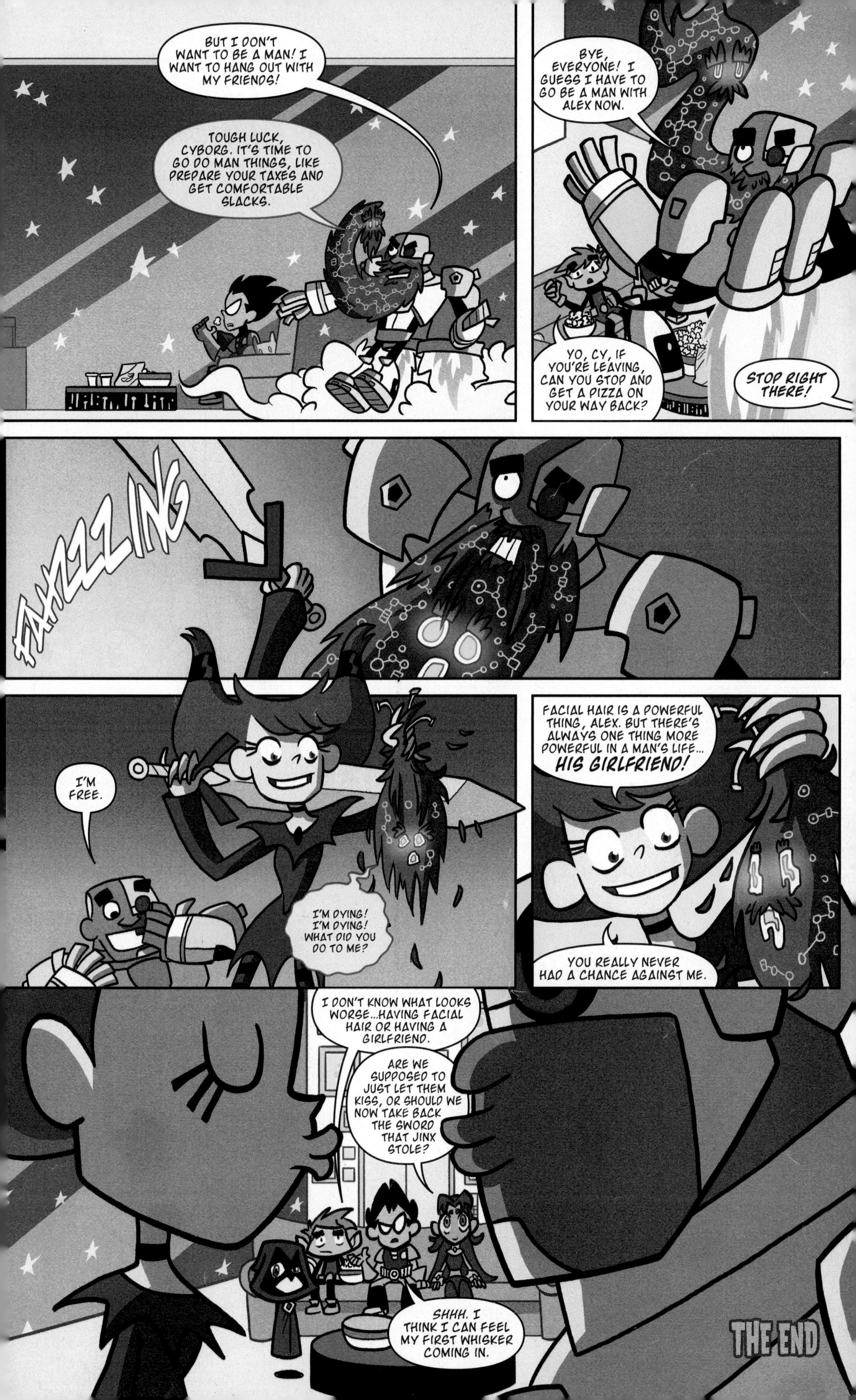

BUT I DON'T WANT TO BE A MAN! I WANT TO HANG OUT WITH MY FRIENDS!
TOUGH LUCK, CYBORG. IT'S TIME TO GO DO MAN THINGS, LIKE PREPARE YOUR TAXES AND GET COMFORTABLE SLACKS.
BYE, EVERYONE! I GUESS I HAVE TO GO BE A MAN WITH ALEX NOW.
YO, CY, IF YOU'RE LEAVING, CAN YOU STOP AND GET A PIZZA ON YOUR WAY BACK?
STOP RIGHT THERE!
FAHZZZLING
I'M FREE.
I'M DYING! I'M DYING! WHAT DID YOU DO TO ME?
FACIAL HAIR IS A POWERFUL THING, ALEX. BUT THERE'S ALWAYS ONE THING MORE POWERFUL IN A MAN'S LIFE... HIS GIRLFRIEND!
YOU REALLY NEVER HAD A CHANCE AGAINST ME.
I DON'T KNOW WHAT LOOKS WORSE...HAVING FACIAL HAIR OR HAVING A GIRLFRIEND.
ARE WE SUPPOSED TO JUST LET THEM KISS, OR SHOULD WE NOW TAKE BACK THE SWORD THAT JINX STOLE?
SHHH. I THINK I CAN FEEL MY FIRST WHISKER COMING IN.
THE END

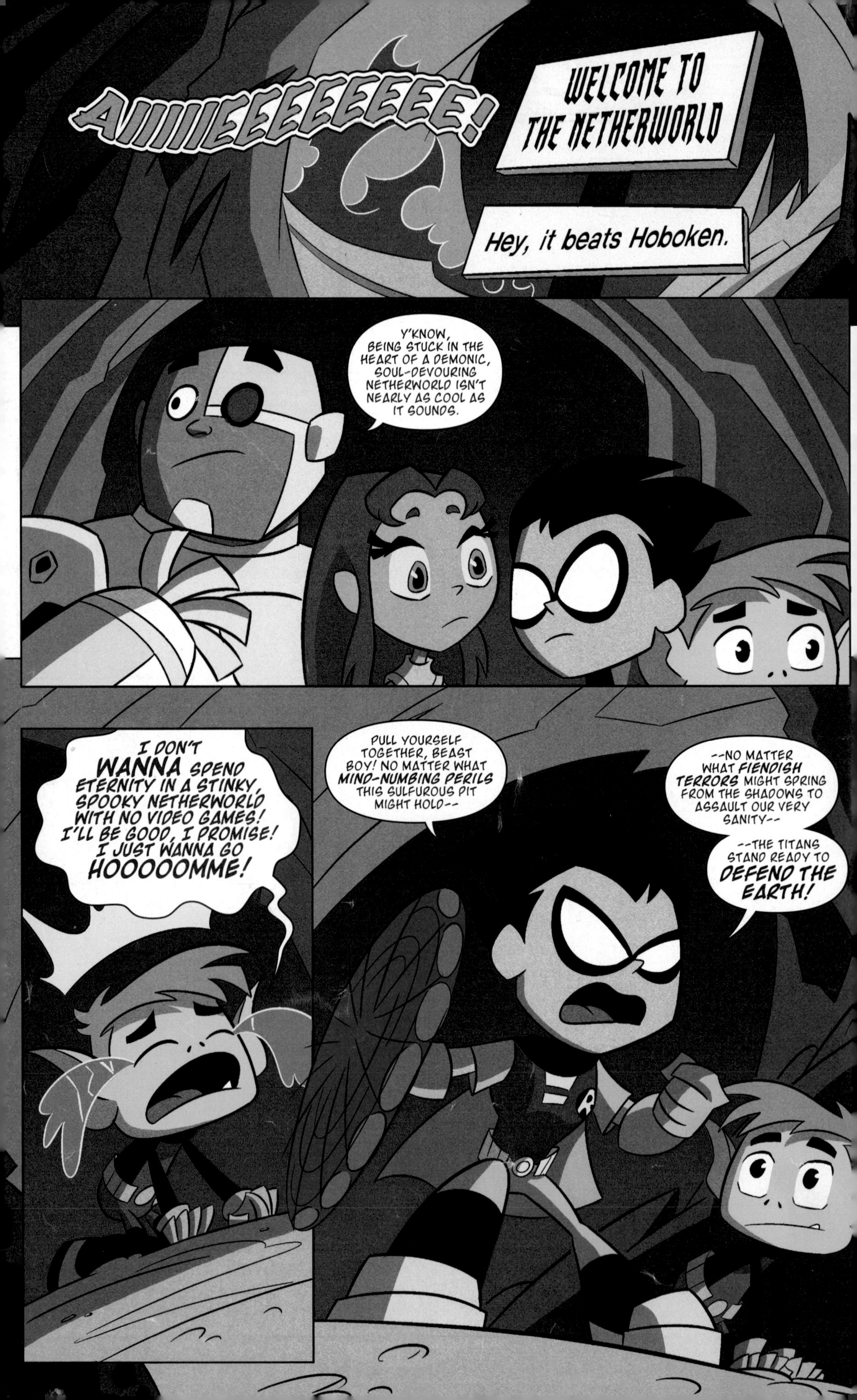

AIIIIIEEEEEEEEE!
WELCOME TO THE NETHERWORLD
Hey, it beats Hoboken.
Y'KNOW, BEING STUCK IN THE HEART OF A DEMONIC, SOUL-DEVOURING NETHERWORLD ISN'T NEARLY AS COOL AS IT SOUNDS.
I DON'T WANNA SPEND ETERNITY IN A STINKY, SPOOKY NETHERWORLD WITH NO VIDEO GAMES! I'LL BE GOOD, I PROMISE! I JUST WANNA GO HOOOOOMME!
PULL YOURSELF TOGETHER, BEAST BOY! NO MATTER WHAT MIND-NUMBING PERILS THIS SULFUROUS PIT MIGHT HOLD--
--NO MATTER WHAT FIENDISH TERRORS MIGHT SPRING FROM THE SHADOWS TO ASSAULT OUR VERY SANITY--
--THE TITANS STAND READY TO DEFEND THE EARTH!

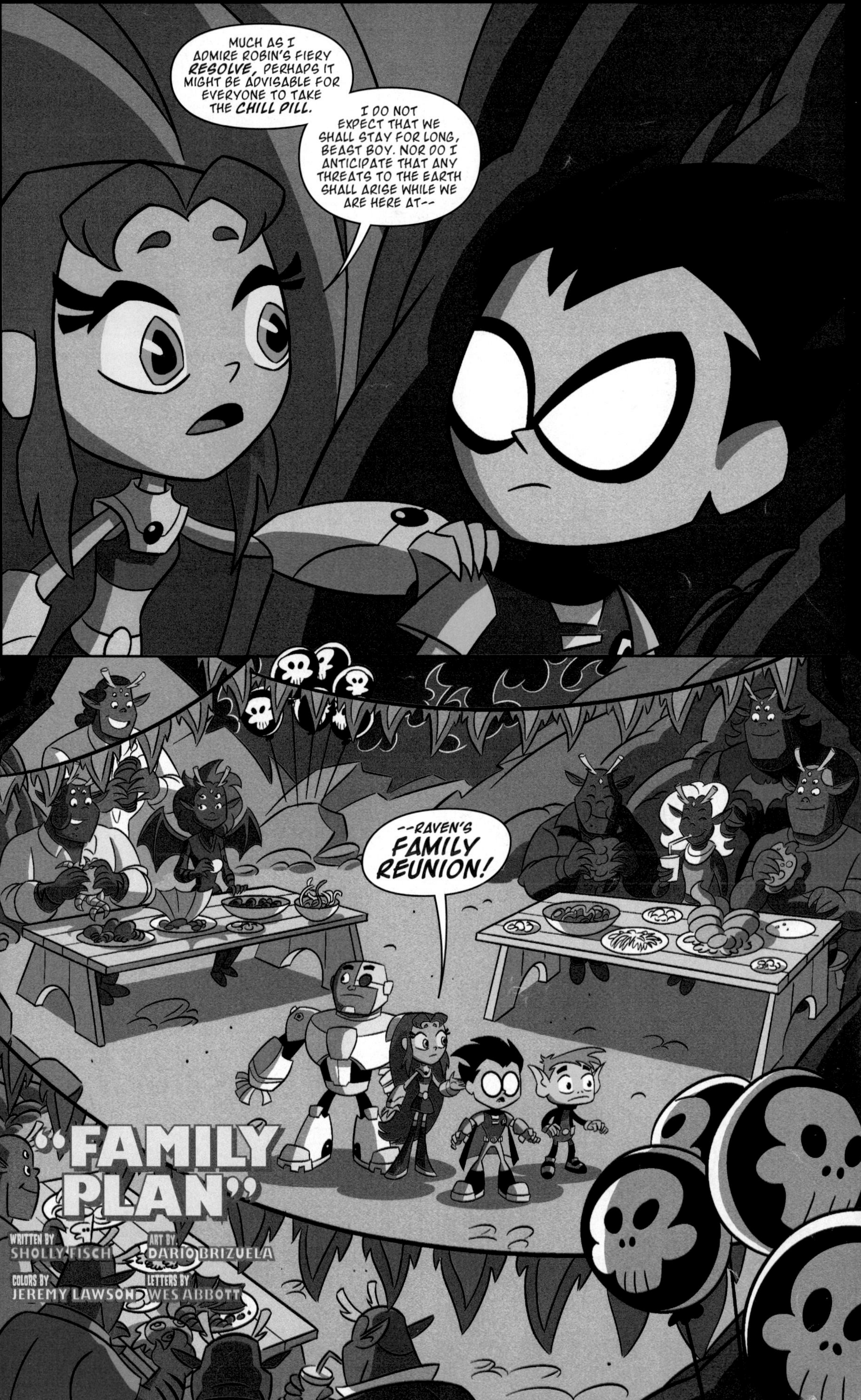
MUCH AS I ADMIRE ROBIN'S FIERY RESOLVE, PERHAPS IT MIGHT BE ADVISABLE FOR EVERYONE TO TAKE THE CHILL PILL.
I DO NOT EXPECT THAT WE SHALL STAY FOR LONG, BEAST BOY. NOR DO I ANTICIPATE THAT ANY THREATS TO THE EARTH SHALL ARISE WHILE WE ARE HERE AT--
--RAVEN'S FAMILY REUNION!
"FAMILY PLAN"
WRITTEN BY SHOLLY FISCH
ART BY DARIO BRIZUELA
COLORS BY JEREMY LAWSON
LETTERS BY WES ABBOTT

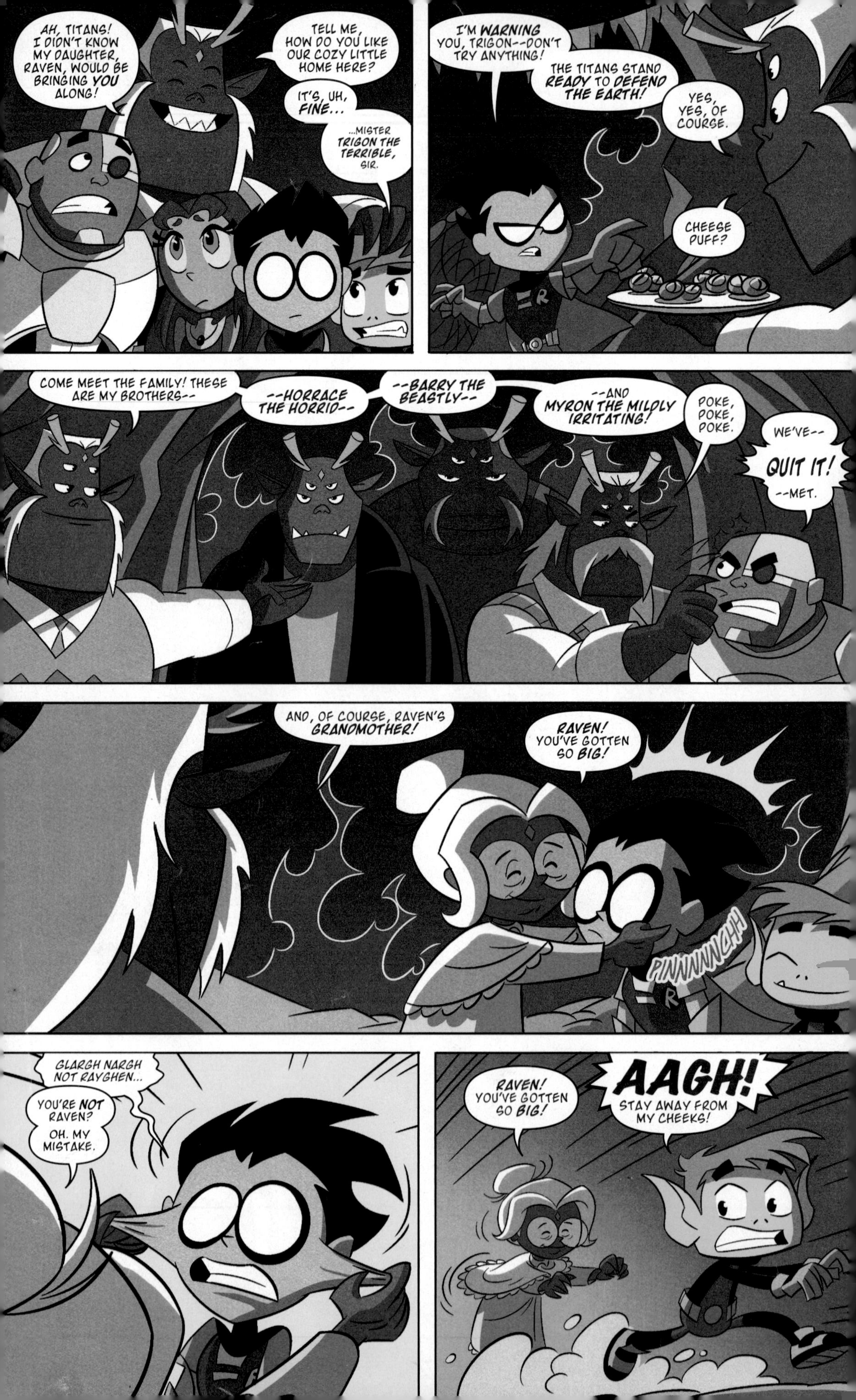
AH, TITANS! I DIDN'T KNOW MY DAUGHTER, RAVEN, WOULD BE BRINGING YOU ALONG!
TELL ME, HOW DO YOU LIKE OUR COZY LITTLE HOME HERE?
IT'S, UH, FINE...
...MISTER TRIGON THE TERRIBLE, SIR.
I'M WARNING YOU, TRIGON--DON'T TRY ANYTHING!
THE TITANS STAND READY TO DEFEND THE EARTH!
YES, YES, OF COURSE.
CHEESE PUFF?
COME MEET THE FAMILY! THESE ARE MY BROTHERS--
--HORRACE THE HORRID--
--BARRY THE BEASTLY--
--AND MYRON THE MILDLY IRRITATING!
POKE, POKE, POKE.
WE'VE--
QUIT IT!
--MET.
AND, OF COURSE, RAVEN'S GRANDMOTHER!
RAVEN! YOU'VE GOTTEN SO BIG!
PINNNNNCHH
GLARGH NARGH NOT RAYGHEN...
YOU'RE NOT RAVEN?
OH. MY MISTAKE.
RAVEN! YOU'VE GOTTEN SO BIG!
AAGH!
STAY AWAY FROM MY CHEEKS!

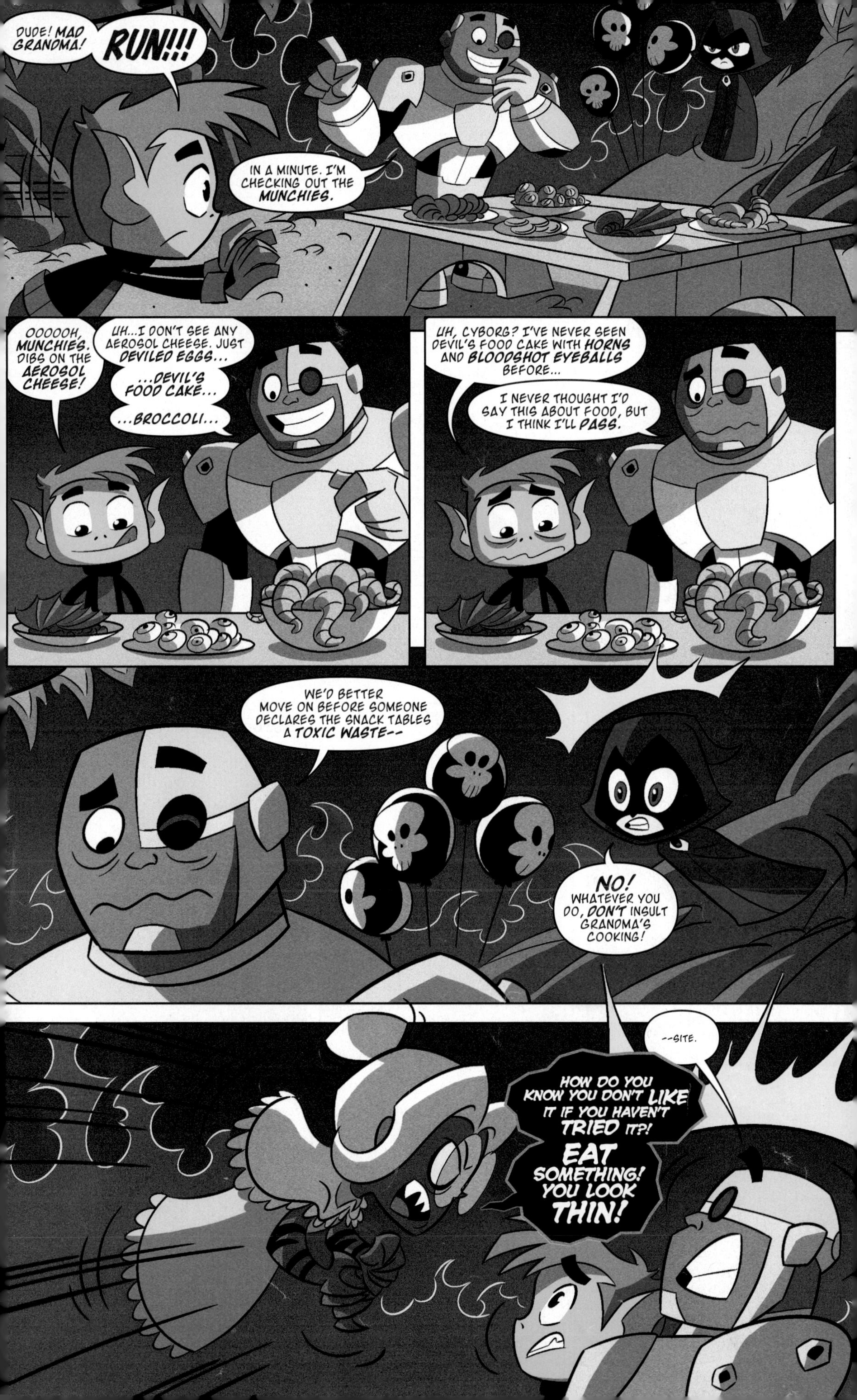
DUDE! MAD GRANDMA!
RUN!!!
IN A MINUTE. I'M CHECKING OUT THE MUNCHIES.
OOOOOH, MUNCHIES. DIBS ON THE AEROSOL CHEESE!
UH...I DON'T SEE ANY AEROSOL CHEESE. JUST DEVILED EGGS...
...DEVIL'S FOOD CAKE...
...BROCCOLI...
UH, CYBORG? I'VE NEVER SEEN DEVIL'S FOOD CAKE WITH HORNS AND BLOODSHOT EYEBALLS BEFORE...
I NEVER THOUGHT I'D SAY THIS ABOUT FOOD, BUT I THINK I'LL PASS.
WE'D BETTER MOVE ON BEFORE SOMEONE DECLARES THE SNACK TABLES A TOXIC WASTE--
NO! WHATEVER YOU DO, DON'T INSULT GRANDMA'S COOKING!
--SITE.
HOW DO YOU KNOW YOU DON'T LIKE IT IF YOU HAVEN'T TRIED IT?! EAT SOMETHING! YOU LOOK THIN!

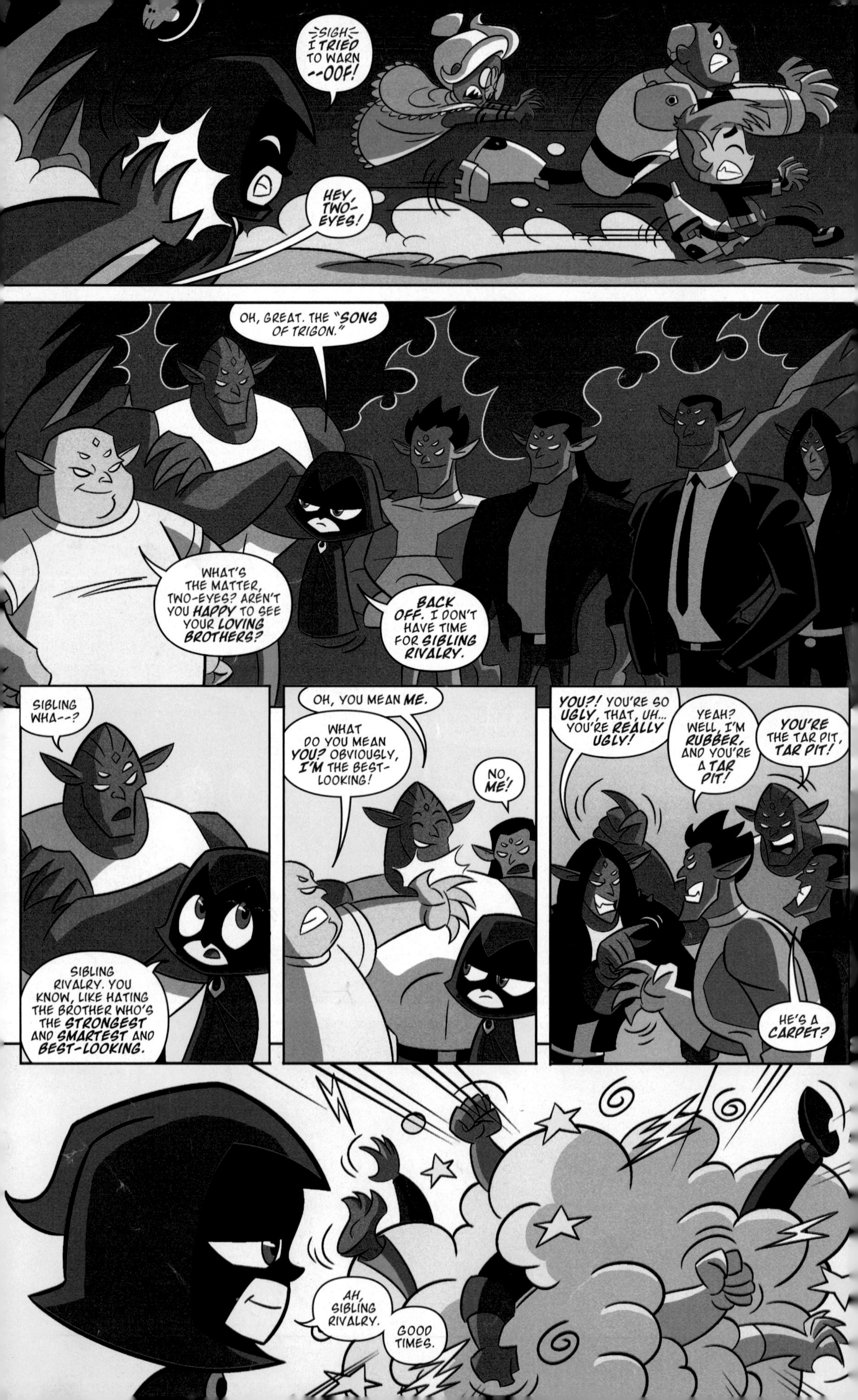

SIGH I TRIED TO WARN --OOF!
HEY, TWO-EYES!
OH, GREAT. THE "SONS OF TRIGON."
WHAT'S THE MATTER, TWO-EYES? AREN'T YOU HAPPY TO SEE YOUR LOVING BROTHERS?
BACK OFF. I DON'T HAVE TIME FOR SIBLING RIVALRY.
SIBLING WHA--?
SIBLING RIVALRY. YOU KNOW, LIKE HATING THE BROTHER WHO'S THE STRONGEST AND SMARTEST AND BEST-LOOKING.
OH, YOU MEAN ME.
WHAT DO YOU MEAN YOU? OBVIOUSLY, I'M THE BEST-LOOKING!
NO, ME!
YOU?! YOU'RE SO UGLY, THAT, UH... YOU'RE REALLY UGLY!
YEAH? WELL, I'M RUBBER, AND YOU'RE A TAR PIT!
YOU'RE THE TAR PIT, TAR PIT!
HE'S A CARPET?
AH, SIBLING RIVALRY.
GOOD TIMES.

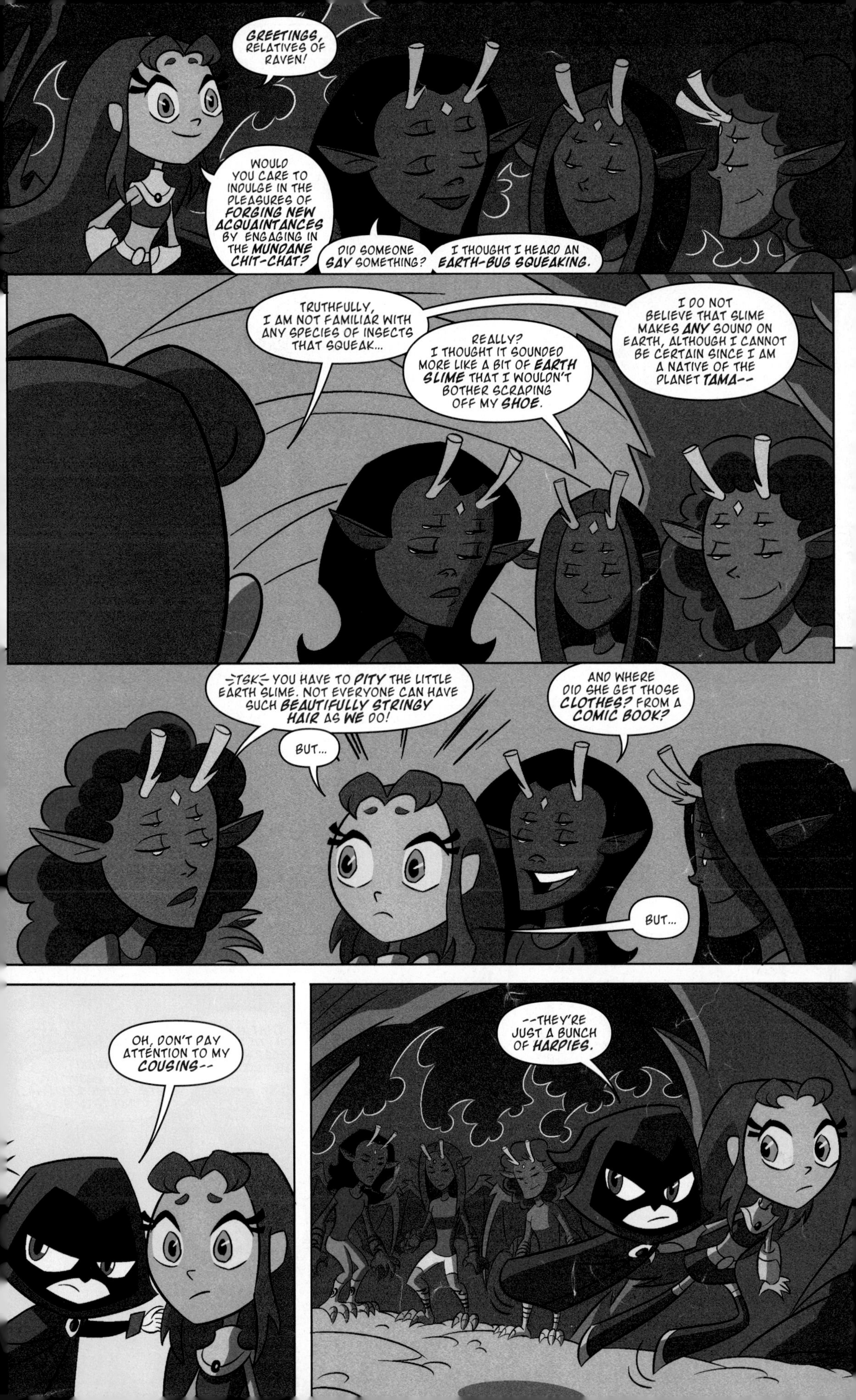
GREETINGS, RELATIVES OF RAVEN!
WOULD YOU CARE TO INDULGE IN THE PLEASURES OF FORGING NEW ACQUAINTANCES BY ENGAGING IN THE MUNDANE CHIT-CHAT?
DID SOMEONE SAY SOMETHING?
I THOUGHT I HEARD AN EARTH-BUG SQUEAKING.
TRUTHFULLY, I AM NOT FAMILIAR WITH ANY SPECIES OF INSECTS THAT SQUEAK...
REALLY? I THOUGHT IT SOUNDED MORE LIKE A BIT OF EARTH SLIME THAT I WOULDN'T BOTHER SCRAPING OFF MY SHOE.
I DO NOT BELIEVE THAT SLIME MAKES ANY SOUND ON EARTH, ALTHOUGH I CANNOT BE CERTAIN SINCE I AM A NATIVE OF THE PLANET TAMA--
=TSK= YOU HAVE TO PITY THE LITTLE EARTH SLIME. NOT EVERYONE CAN HAVE SUCH BEAUTIFULLY STRINGY HAIR AS WE DO!
BUT...
AND WHERE DID SHE GET THOSE CLOTHES? FROM A COMIC BOOK?
BUT...
OH, DON'T PAY ATTENTION TO MY COUSINS--
--THEY'RE JUST A BUNCH OF HARPIES.

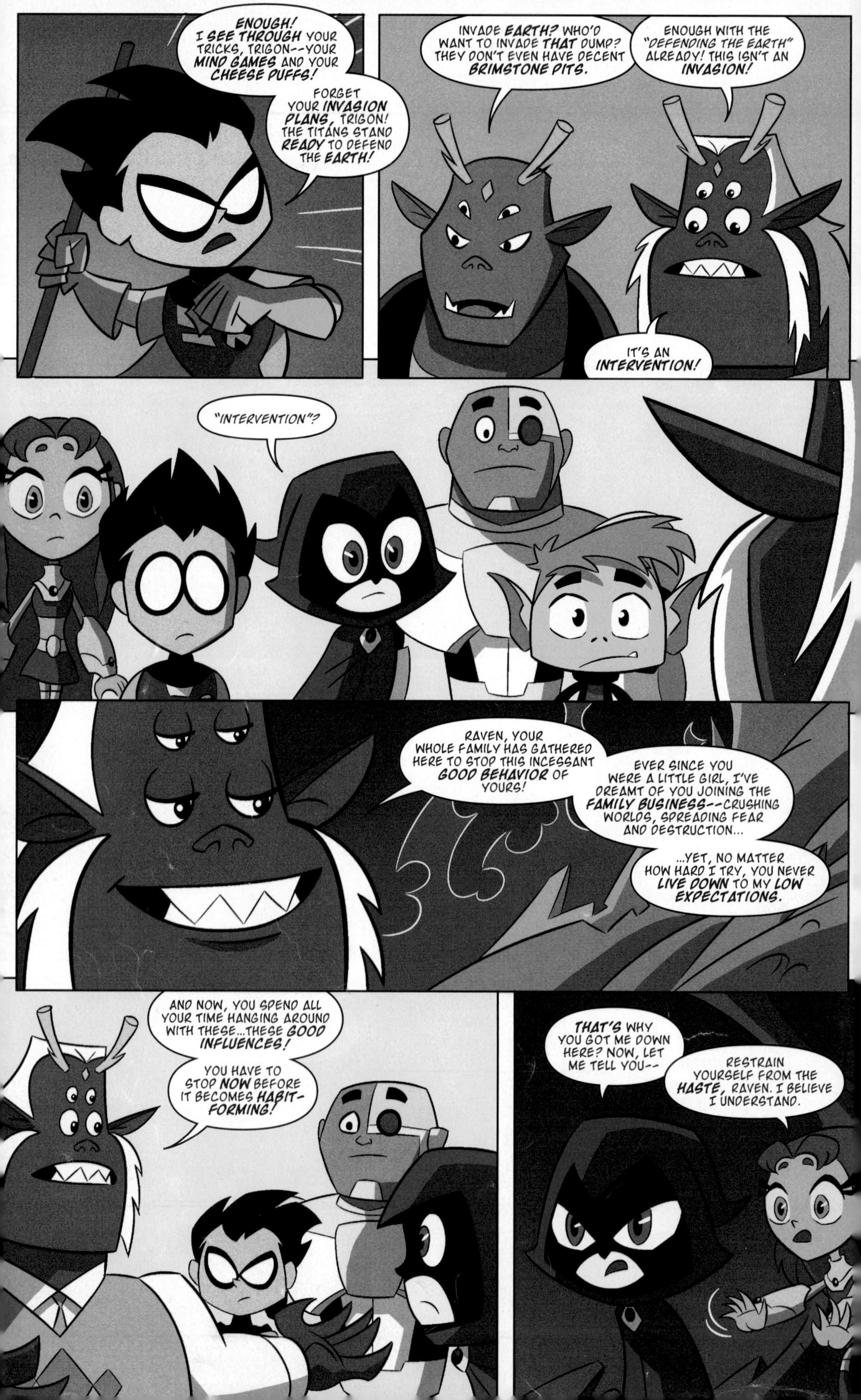
ENOUGH! I SEE THROUGH YOUR TRICKS, TRIGON--YOUR MIND GAMES AND YOUR CHEESE PUFFS!
FORGET YOUR INVASION PLANS, TRIGON! THE TITANS STAND READY TO DEFEND THE EARTH!
INVADE EARTH? WHO'D WANT TO INVADE THAT DUMP? THEY DON'T EVEN HAVE DECENT BRIMSTONE PITS.
ENOUGH WITH THE "DEFENDING THE EARTH" ALREADY! THIS ISN'T AN INVASION!
IT'S AN INTERVENTION!
"INTERVENTION"?
RAVEN, YOUR WHOLE FAMILY HAS GATHERED HERE TO STOP THIS INCESSANT GOOD BEHAVIOR OF YOURS!
EVER SINCE YOU WERE A LITTLE GIRL, I'VE DREAMT OF YOU JOINING THE FAMILY BUSINESS--CRUSHING WORLDS, SPREADING FEAR AND DESTRUCTION...
...YET, NO MATTER HOW HARD I TRY, YOU NEVER LIVE DOWN TO MY LOW EXPECTATIONS.
AND NOW, YOU SPEND ALL YOUR TIME HANGING AROUND WITH THESE...THESE GOOD INFLUENCES!
YOU HAVE TO STOP NOW BEFORE IT BECOMES HABIT-FORMING!
THAT'S WHY YOU GOT ME DOWN HERE? NOW, LET ME TELL YOU--
RESTRAIN YOURSELF FROM THE HASTE, RAVEN. I BELIEVE I UNDERSTAND.

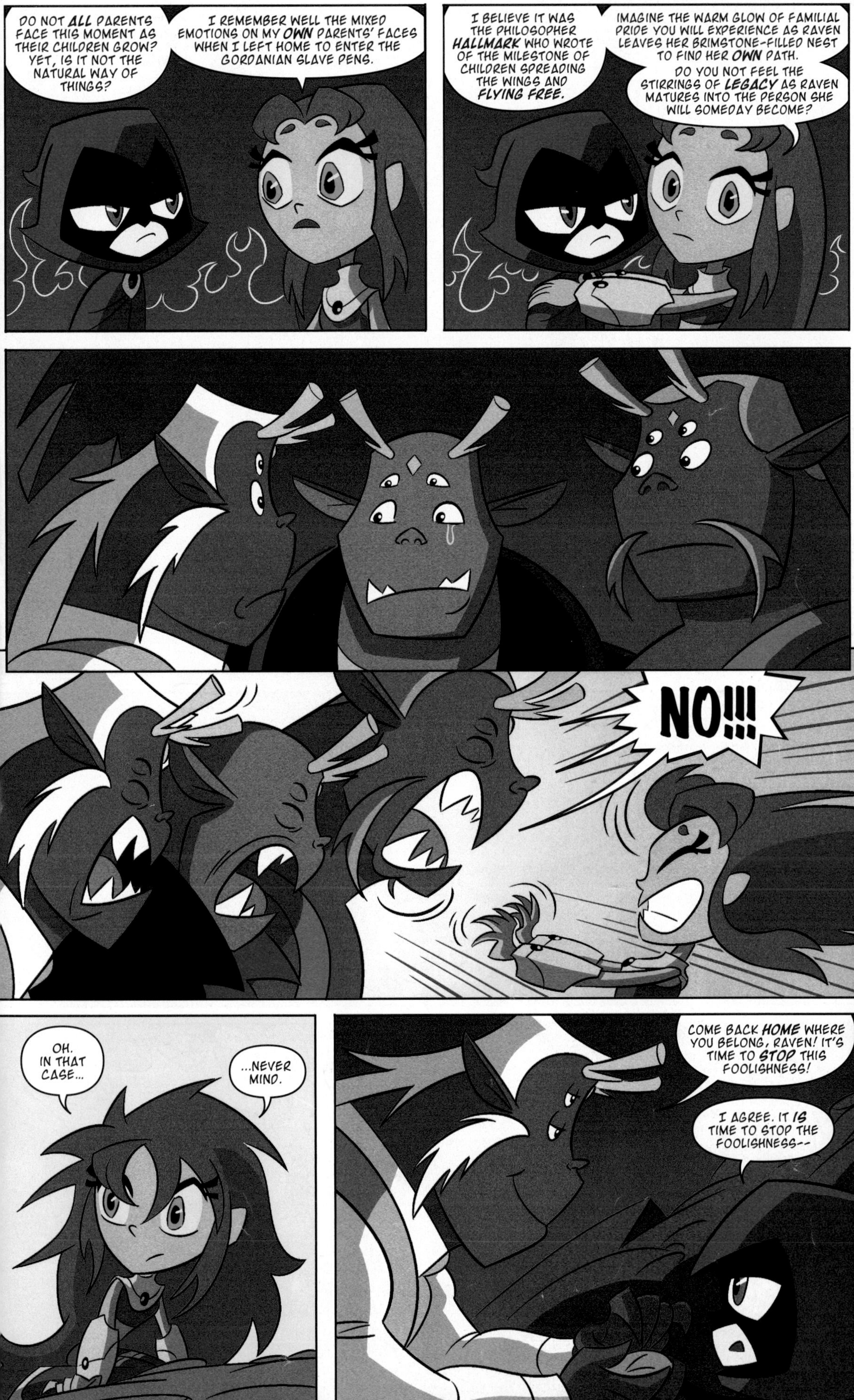
DO NOT ALL PARENTS FACE THIS MOMENT AS THEIR CHILDREN GROW? YET, IS IT NOT THE NATURAL WAY OF THINGS?
I REMEMBER WELL THE MIXED EMOTIONS ON MY OWN PARENTS' FACES WHEN I LEFT HOME TO ENTER THE GORDANIAN SLAVE PENS.
I BELIEVE IT WAS THE PHILOSOPHER HALLMARK WHO WROTE OF THE MILESTONE OF CHILDREN SPREADING THE WINGS AND FLYING FREE.
IMAGINE THE WARM GLOW OF FAMILIAL PRIDE YOU WILL EXPERIENCE AS RAVEN LEAVES HER BRIMSTONE-FILLED NEST TO FIND HER OWN PATH.
DO YOU NOT FEEL THE STIRRINGS OF LEGACY AS RAVEN MATURES INTO THE PERSON SHE WILL SOMEDAY BECOME?
NO!!!
OH. IN THAT CASE...
...NEVER MIND.
COME BACK HOME WHERE YOU BELONG, RAVEN! IT'S TIME TO STOP THIS FOOLISHNESS!
I AGREE. IT IS TIME TO STOP THE FOOLISHNESS--

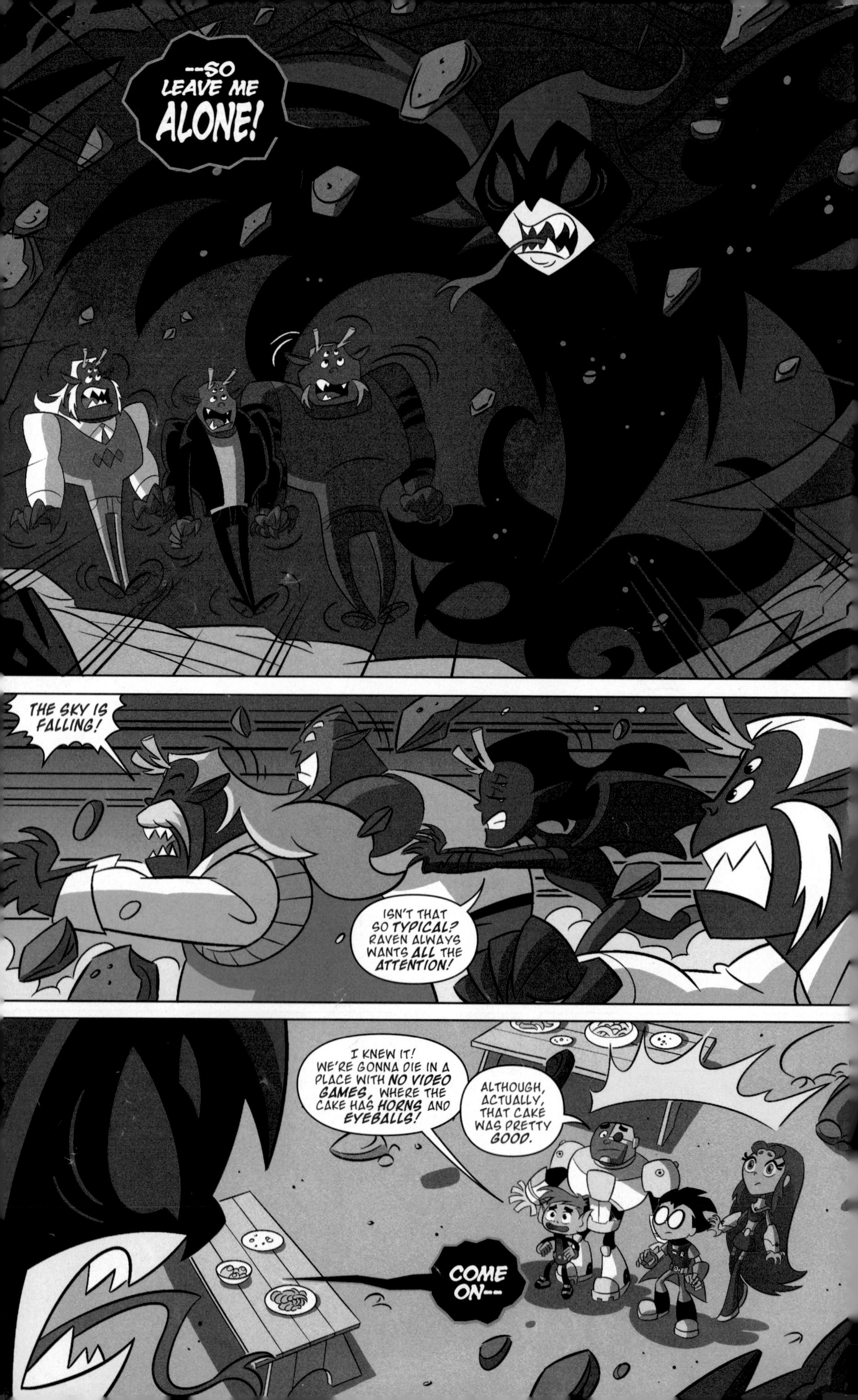
--SO LEAVE ME ALONE!
THE SKY IS FALLING!
ISN'T THAT SO TYPICAL? RAVEN ALWAYS WANTS ALL THE ATTENTION!
I KNEW IT! WE'RE GONNA DIE IN A PLACE WITH NO VIDEO GAMES, WHERE THE CAKE HAS HORNS AND EYEBALLS!
ALTHOUGH, ACTUALLY, THAT CAKE WAS PRETTY GOOD.
COME ON--

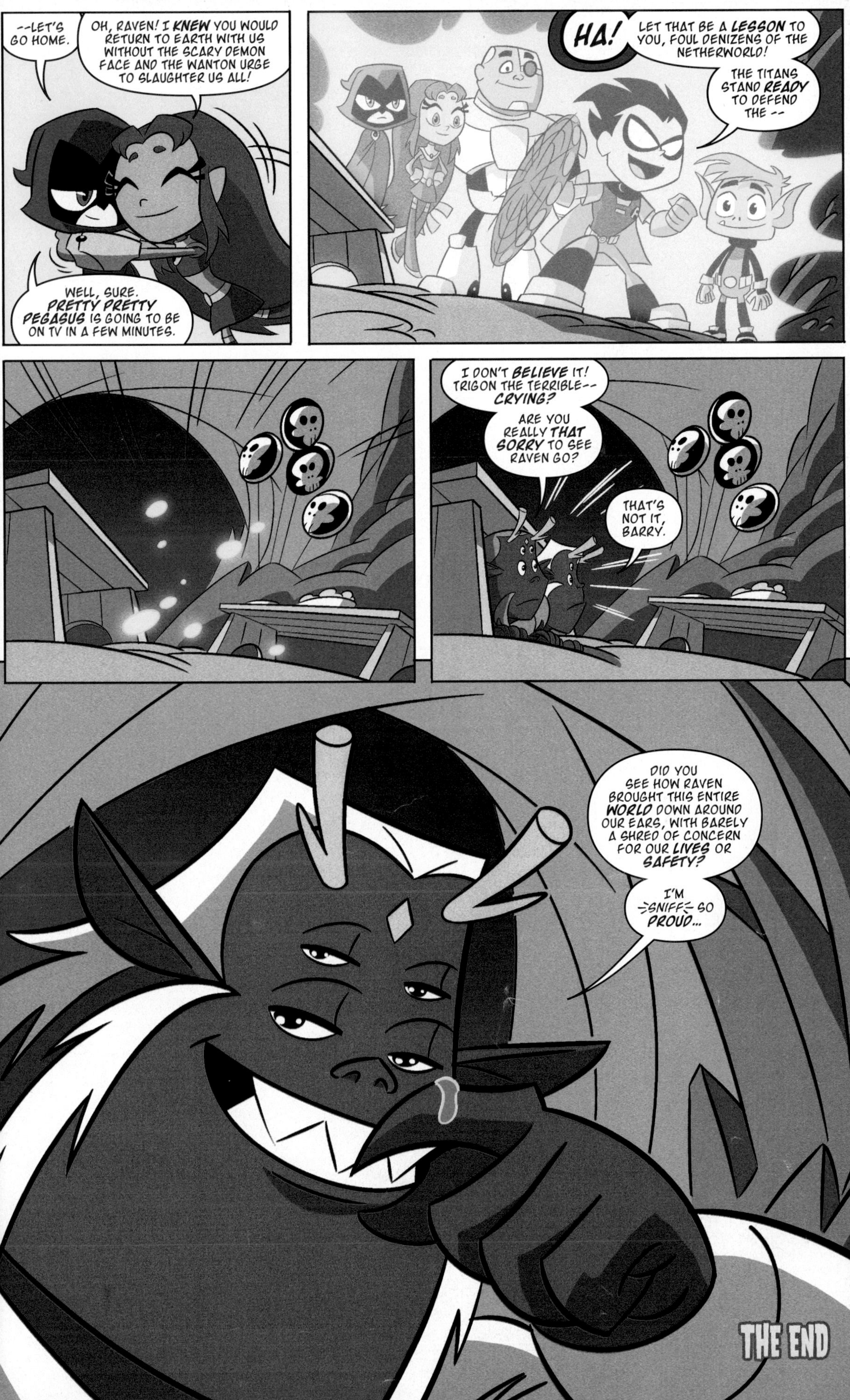
--LET'S GO HOME.
OH, RAVEN! I KNEW YOU WOULD RETURN TO EARTH WITH US WITHOUT THE SCARY DEMON FACE AND THE WANTON URGE TO SLAUGHTER US ALL!
WELL, SURE. PRETTY PRETTY PEGASUS IS GOING TO BE ON TV IN A FEW MINUTES.
HA!
LET THAT BE A LESSON TO YOU, FOUL DENIZENS OF THE NETHERWORLD!
THE TITANS STAND READY TO DEFEND THE --
I DON'T BELIEVE IT! TRIGON THE TERRIBLE-- CRYING?
ARE YOU REALLY THAT SORRY TO SEE RAVEN GO?
THAT'S NOT IT, BARRY.
DID YOU SEE HOW RAVEN BROUGHT THIS ENTIRE WORLD DOWN AROUND OUR EARS, WITH BARELY A SHRED OF CONCERN FOR OUR LIVES OR SAFETY?
I'M =SNIFF= SO PROUD...
THE END

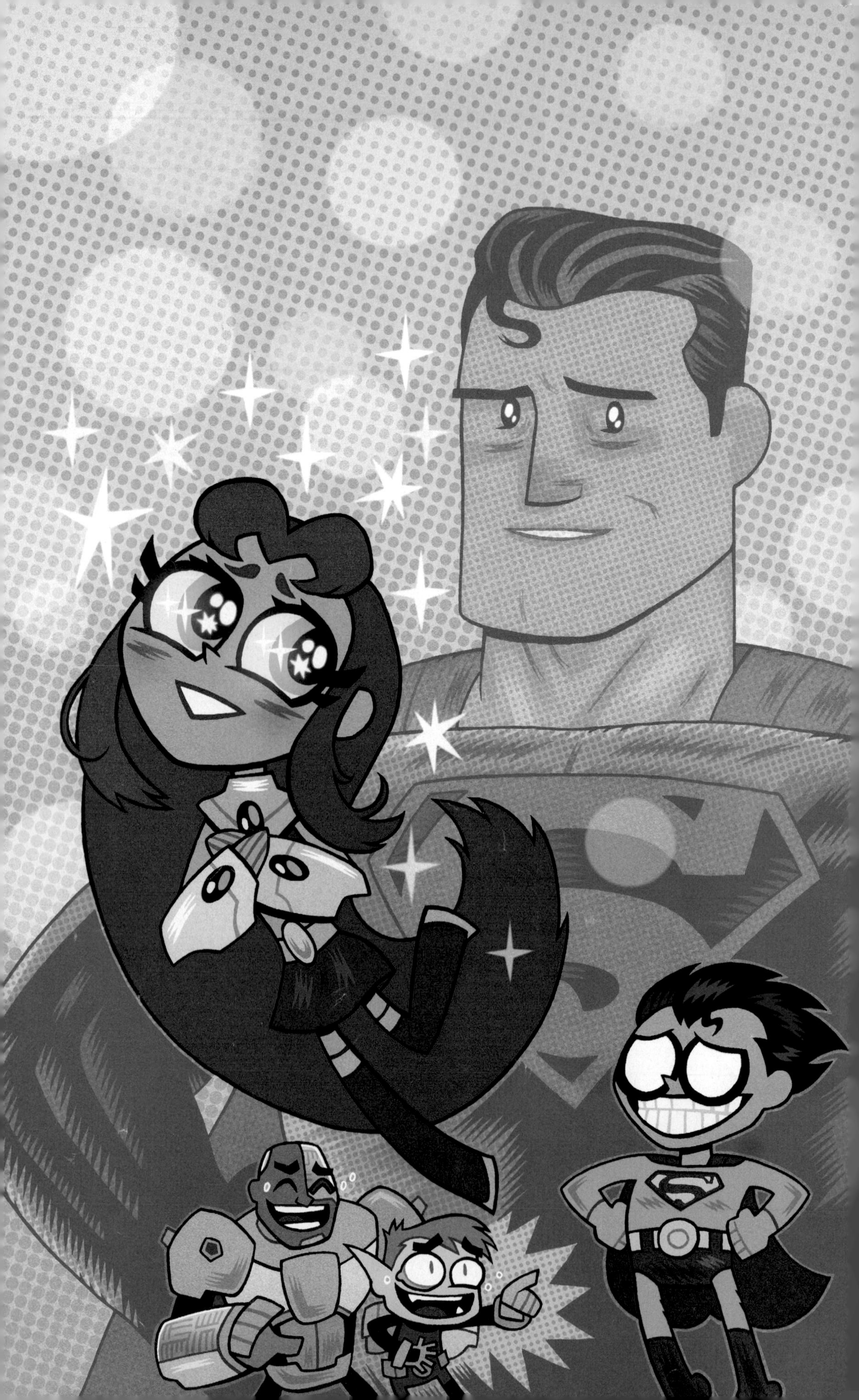

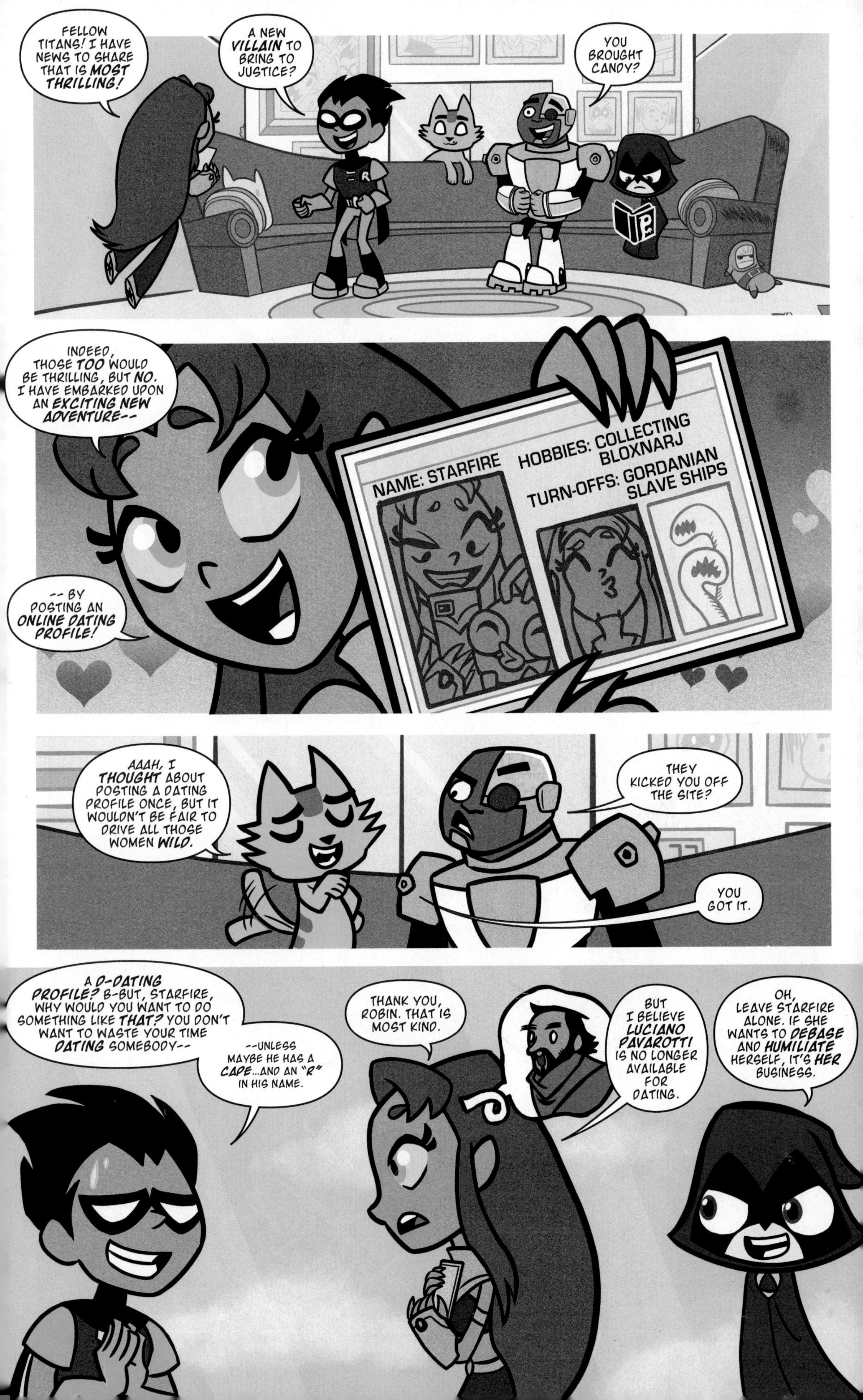
FELLOW TITANS! I HAVE NEWS TO SHARE THAT IS MOST THRILLING!
A NEW VILLAIN TO BRING TO JUSTICE?
YOU BROUGHT CANDY?
INDEED, THOSE TOO WOULD BE THRILLING, BUT NO. I HAVE EMBARKED UPON AN EXCITING NEW ADVENTURE--
NAME: STARFIRE
HOBBIES: COLLECTING BLOXNARJ
TURN-OFFS: GORDANIAN SLAVE SHIPS
-- BY POSTING AN ONLINE DATING PROFILE!
AAAH, I THOUGHT ABOUT POSTING A DATING PROFILE ONCE, BUT IT WOULDN'T BE FAIR TO DRIVE ALL THOSE WOMEN WILD.
THEY KICKED YOU OFF THE SITE?
YOU GOT IT.
A D-DATING PROFILE? B-BUT, STARFIRE, WHY WOULD YOU WANT TO DO SOMETHING LIKE THAT? YOU DON'T WANT TO WASTE YOUR TIME DATING SOMEBODY--
--UNLESS MAYBE HE HAS A CAPE...AND AN "R" IN HIS NAME.
THANK YOU, ROBIN. THAT IS MOST KIND.
BUT I BELIEVE LUCIANO PAVAROTTI IS NO LONGER AVAILABLE FOR DATING.
OH, LEAVE STARFIRE ALONE. IF SHE WANTS TO DEBASE AND HUMILIATE HERSELF, IT'S HER BUSINESS.

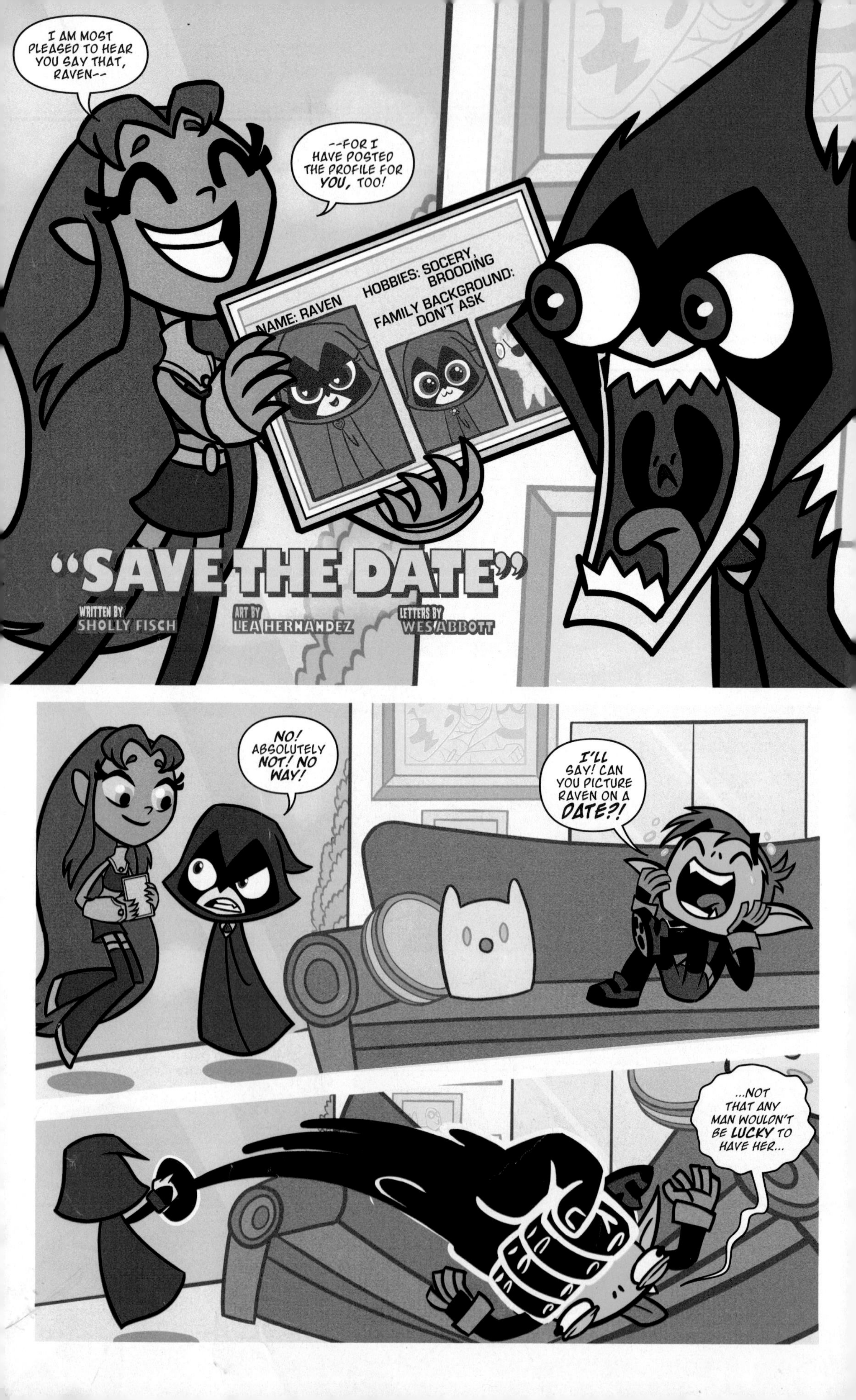
I AM MOST PLEASED TO HEAR YOU SAY THAT, RAVEN--
--FOR I HAVE POSTED THE PROFILE FOR YOU, TOO!
NAME: RAVEN
HOBBIES: SOCERY, BROODING
FAMILY BACKGROUND: DON'T ASK
"SAVE THE DATE"
WRITTEN BY SHOLLY FISCH
ART BY LEA HERNANDEZ
LETTERS BY WES ABBOTT
NO! ABSOLUTELY NOT! NO WAY!
I'LL SAY! CAN YOU PICTURE RAVEN ON A DATE?!
...NOT THAT ANY MAN WOULDN'T BE LUCKY TO HAVE HER...

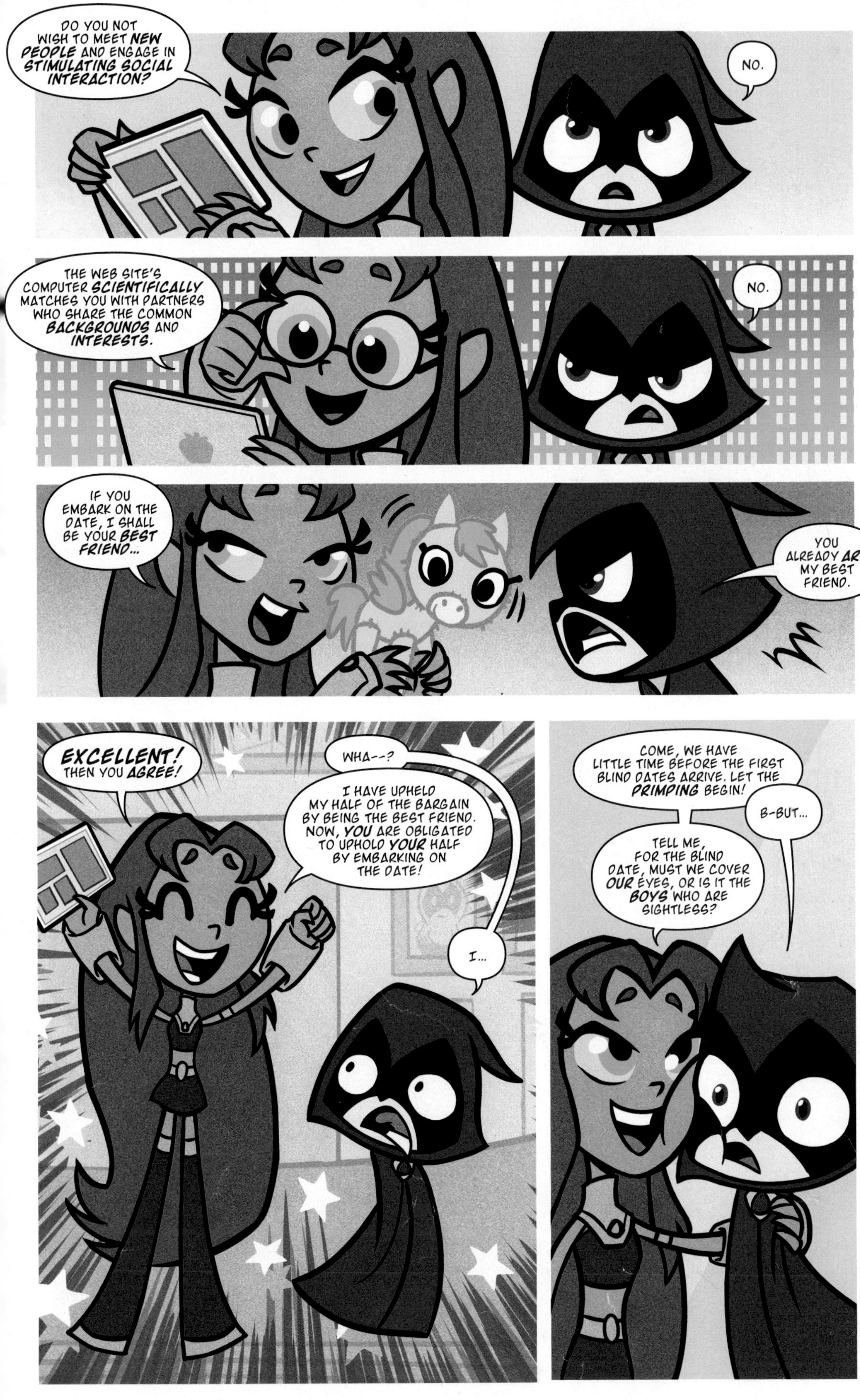
DO YOU NOT WISH TO MEET NEW PEOPLE AND ENGAGE IN STIMULATING SOCIAL INTERACTION?
NO.
THE WEB SITE'S COMPUTER SCIENTIFICALLY MATCHES YOU WITH PARTNERS WHO SHARE THE COMMON BACKGROUNDS AND INTERESTS.
NO.
IF YOU EMBARK ON THE DATE, I SHALL BE YOUR BEST FRIEND...
YOU ALREADY ARE MY BEST FRIEND.
EXCELLENT! THEN YOU AGREE!
WHA--?
I HAVE UPHELD MY HALF OF THE BARGAIN BY BEING THE BEST FRIEND. NOW, YOU ARE OBLIGATED TO UPHOLD YOUR HALF BY EMBARKING ON THE DATE!
I...
COME, WE HAVE LITTLE TIME BEFORE THE FIRST BLIND DATES ARRIVE. LET THE PRIMPING BEGIN!
B-BUT...
TELL ME, FOR THE BLIND DATE, MUST WE COVER OUR EYES, OR IS IT THE BOYS WHO ARE SIGHTLESS?

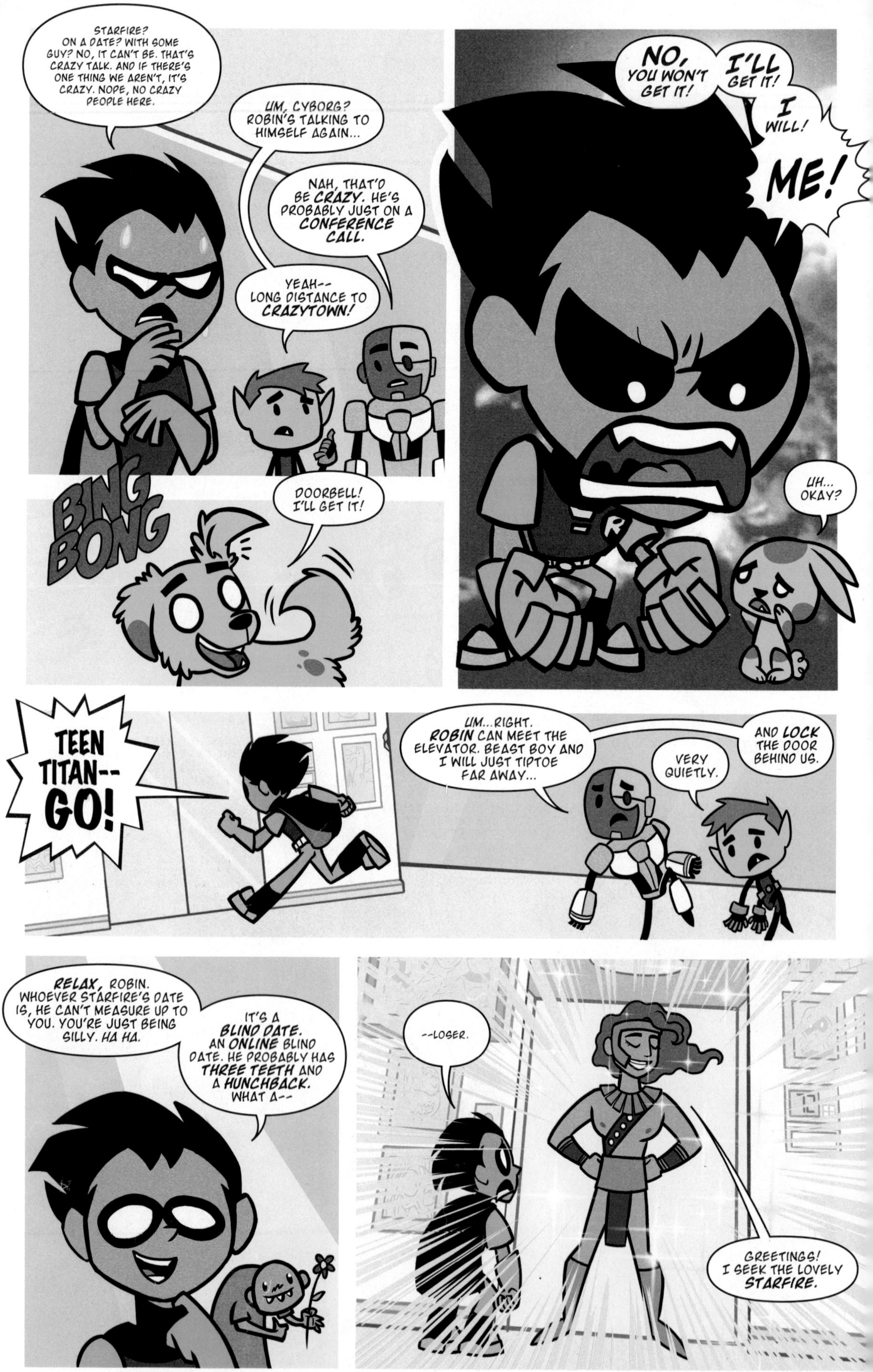
STARFIRE? ON A DATE? WITH SOME GUY? NO, IT CAN'T BE. THAT'S CRAZY TALK. AND IF THERE'S ONE THING WE AREN'T, IT'S CRAZY. NOPE, NO CRAZY PEOPLE HERE.
UM, CYBORG? ROBIN'S TALKING TO HIMSELF AGAIN...
NAH, THAT'D BE CRAZY. HE'S PROBABLY JUST ON A CONFERENCE CALL.
YEAH-- LONG DISTANCE TO CRAZYTOWN!
BING BONG
DOORBELL! I'LL GET IT!
NO, YOU WON'T GET IT!
I'LL GET IT!
I WILL!
ME!
UH... OKAY?
TEEN TITAN-- GO!
UM... RIGHT. ROBIN CAN MEET THE ELEVATOR. BEAST BOY AND I WILL JUST TIPTOE FAR AWAY...
VERY QUIETLY.
AND LOCK THE DOOR BEHIND US.
RELAX, ROBIN. WHOEVER STARFIRE'S DATE IS, HE CAN'T MEASURE UP TO YOU. YOU'RE JUST BEING SILLY. HA HA.
IT'S A BLIND DATE. AN ONLINE BLIND DATE. HE PROBABLY HAS THREE TEETH AND A HUNCHBACK. WHAT A--
--LOSER.
GREETINGS! I SEEK THE LOVELY STARFIRE.

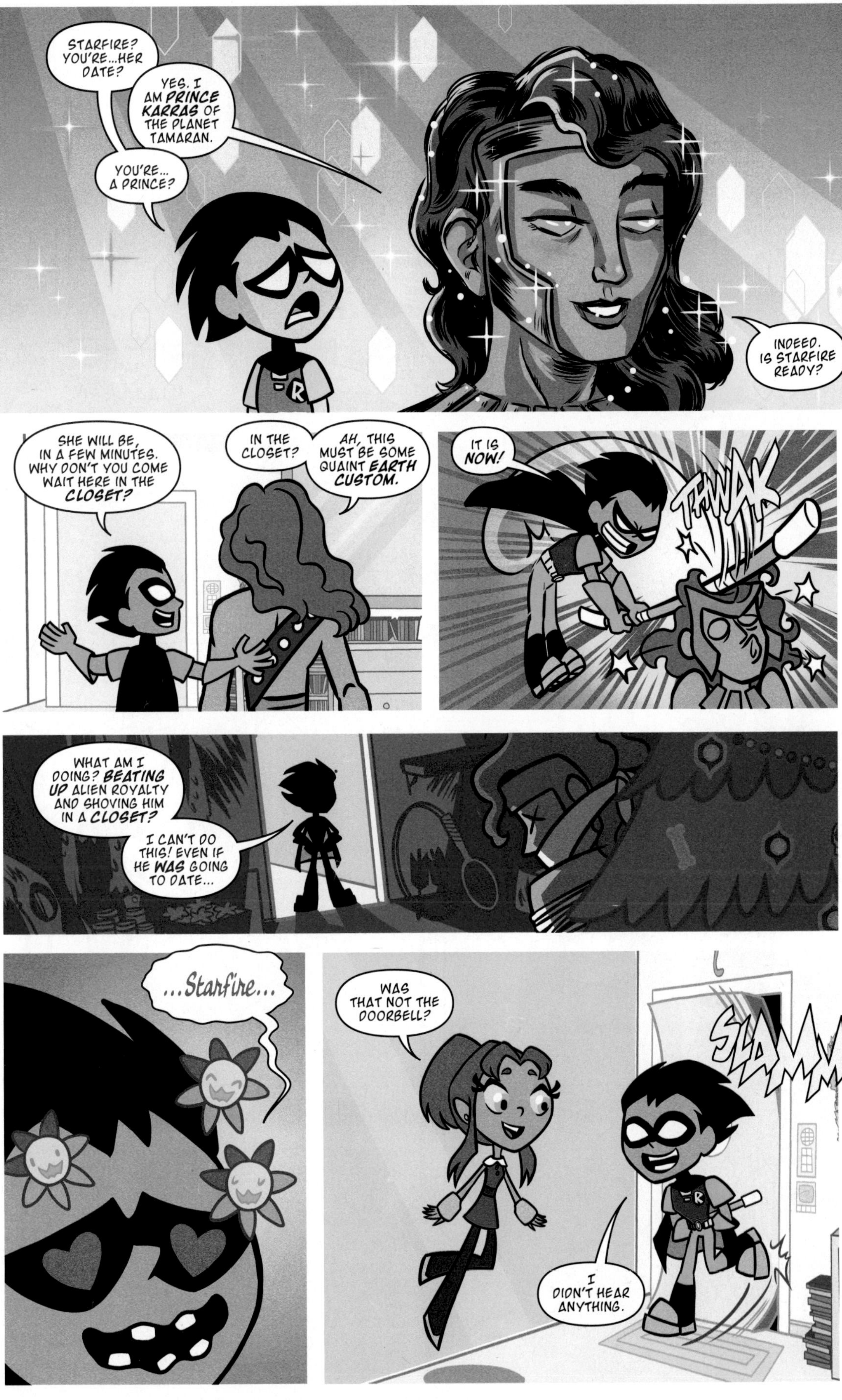

STARFIRE? YOU'RE...HER DATE?
YES. I AM PRINCE KARRAS OF THE PLANET TAMARAN.
YOU'RE... A PRINCE?
INDEED. IS STARFIRE READY?
SHE WILL BE, IN A FEW MINUTES. WHY DON'T YOU COME WAIT HERE IN THE CLOSET?
IN THE CLOSET?
AH, THIS MUST BE SOME QUAINT EARTH CUSTOM.
IT IS NOW!
THWAK
WHAT AM I DOING? BEATING UP ALIEN ROYALTY AND SHOVING HIM IN A CLOSET?
I CAN'T DO THIS! EVEN IF HE WAS GOING TO DATE...
...Starfire...
WAS THAT NOT THE DOORBELL?
SLAMM
I DIDN'T HEAR ANYTHING.

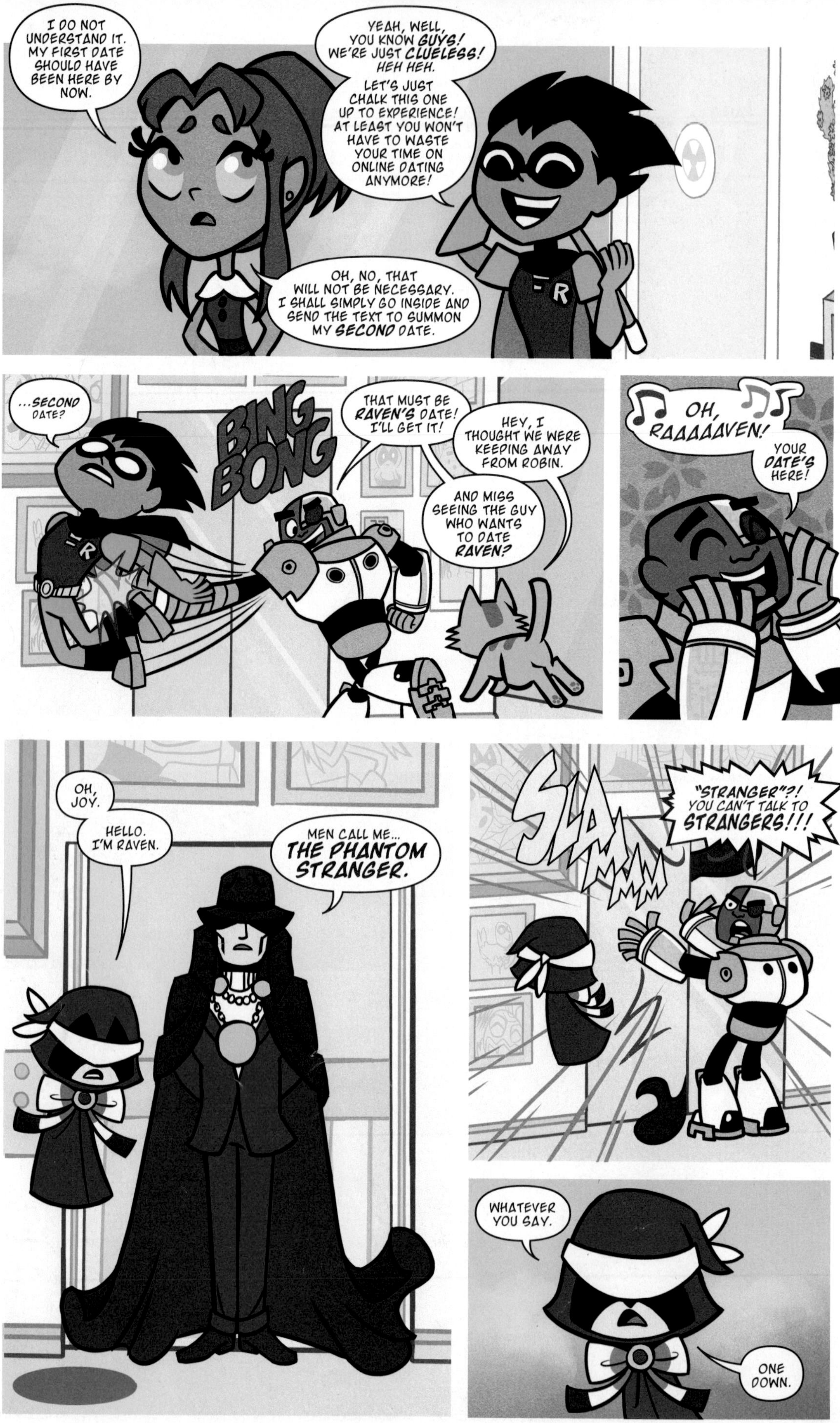

I DO NOT UNDERSTAND IT. MY FIRST DATE SHOULD HAVE BEEN HERE BY NOW.
YEAH, WELL, YOU KNOW GUYS! WE'RE JUST CLUELESS! HEH HEH.
LET'S JUST CHALK THIS ONE UP TO EXPERIENCE! AT LEAST YOU WON'T HAVE TO WASTE YOUR TIME ON ONLINE DATING ANYMORE!
OH, NO, THAT WILL NOT BE NECESSARY. I SHALL SIMPLY GO INSIDE AND SEND THE TEXT TO SUMMON MY SECOND DATE.
...SECOND DATE?
BING BONG
THAT MUST BE RAVEN'S DATE! I'LL GET IT!
HEY, I THOUGHT WE WERE KEEPING AWAY FROM ROBIN.
AND MISS SEEING THE GUY WHO WANTS TO DATE RAVEN?
OH, RAAAAAVEN!
YOUR DATE'S HERE!
OH, JOY.
HELLO. I'M RAVEN.
MEN CALL ME... THE PHANTOM STRANGER.
SLAMMM
"STRANGER"?! YOU CAN'T TALK TO STRANGERS!!!
WHATEVER YOU SAY.
ONE DOWN.

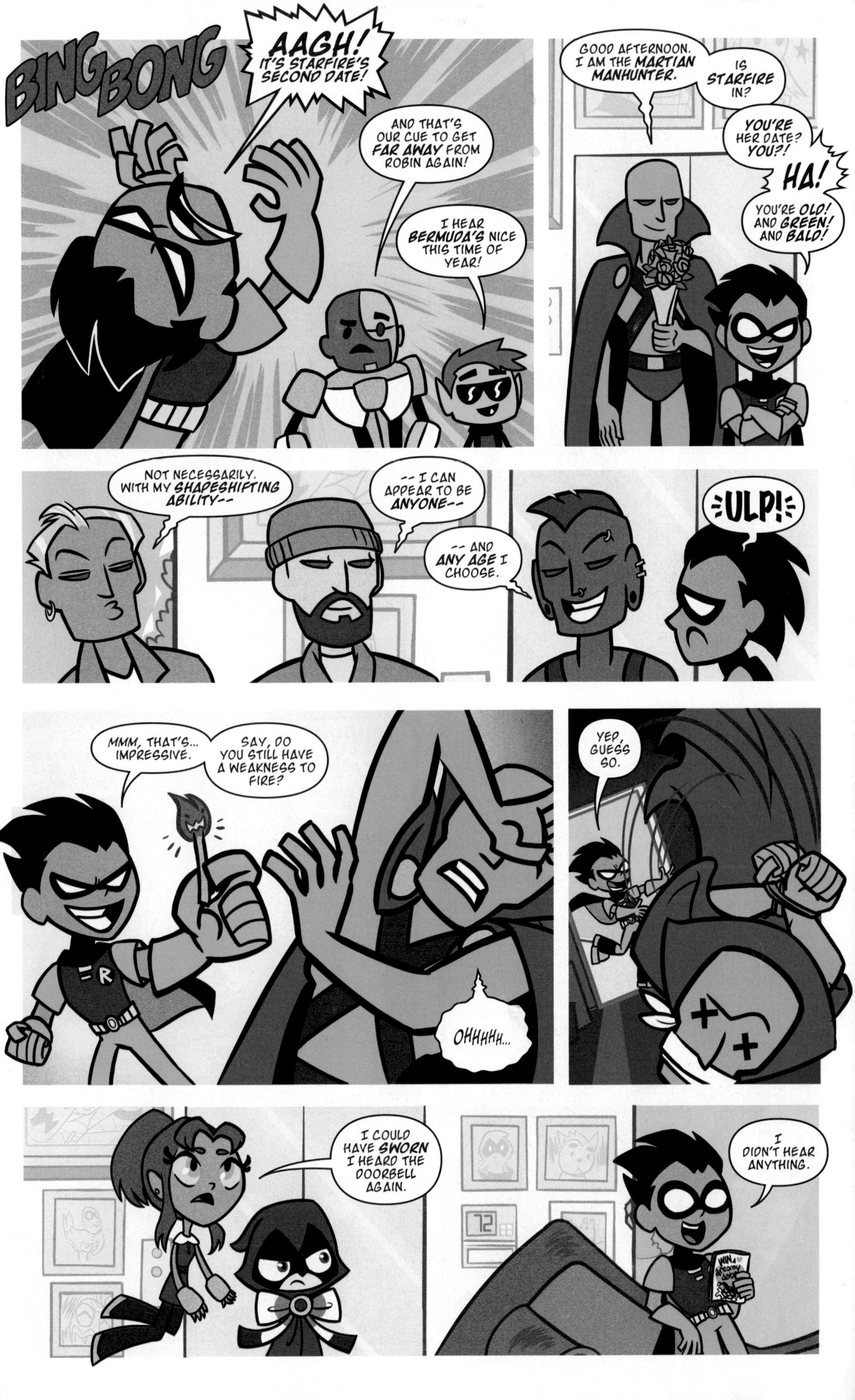
BING BONG
AAGH! IT'S STARFIRE'S SECOND DATE!
AND THAT'S OUR CUE TO GET FAR AWAY FROM ROBIN AGAIN!
I HEAR BERMUDA'S NICE THIS TIME OF YEAR!
GOOD AFTERNOON. I AM THE MARTIAN MANHUNTER.
IS STARFIRE IN?
YOU'RE HER DATE? YOU?!
HA!
YOU'RE OLD! AND GREEN! AND BALD!
NOT NECESSARILY. WITH MY SHAPESHIFTING ABILITY--
-- I CAN APPEAR TO BE ANYONE--
-- AND ANY AGE I CHOOSE.
ULP!
MMM, THAT'S... IMPRESSIVE.
SAY, DO YOU STILL HAVE A WEAKNESS TO FIRE?
OHHHHH...
YEP, GUESS SO.
I COULD HAVE SWORN I HEARD THE DOORBELL AGAIN.
I DIDN'T HEAR ANYTHING.

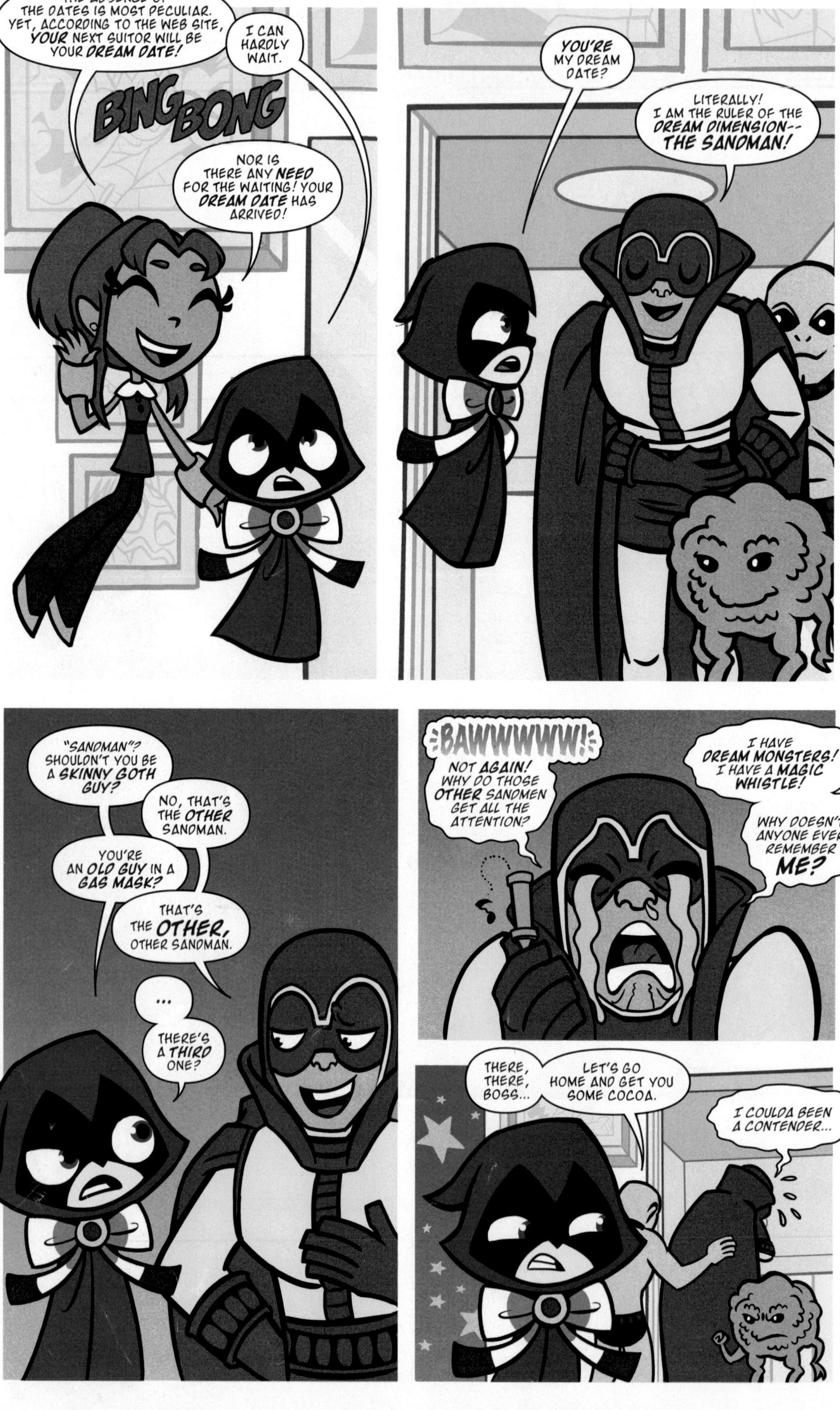
THE ABSENCE OF THE DATES IS MOST PECULIAR. YET, ACCORDING TO THE WEB SITE, YOUR NEXT SUITOR WILL BE YOUR DREAM DATE!
I CAN HARDLY WAIT.
BING BONG
NOR IS THERE ANY NEED FOR THE WAITING! YOUR DREAM DATE HAS ARRIVED!
YOU'RE MY DREAM DATE?
LITERALLY! I AM THE RULER OF THE DREAM DIMENSION-- THE SANDMAN!
"SANDMAN"? SHOULDN'T YOU BE A SKINNY GOTH GUY?
NO, THAT'S THE OTHER SANDMAN.
YOU'RE AN OLD GUY IN A GAS MASK?
THAT'S THE OTHER, OTHER SANDMAN.
...
THERE'S A THIRD ONE?
BAWWWWW!
NOT AGAIN! WHY DO THOSE OTHER SANDMEN GET ALL THE ATTENTION?
I HAVE DREAM MONSTERS! I HAVE A MAGIC WHISTLE!
WHY DOESN'T ANYONE EVER REMEMBER ME?
THERE, THERE, BOSS...
LET'S GO HOME AND GET YOU SOME COCOA.
I COULDA BEEN A CONTENDER...

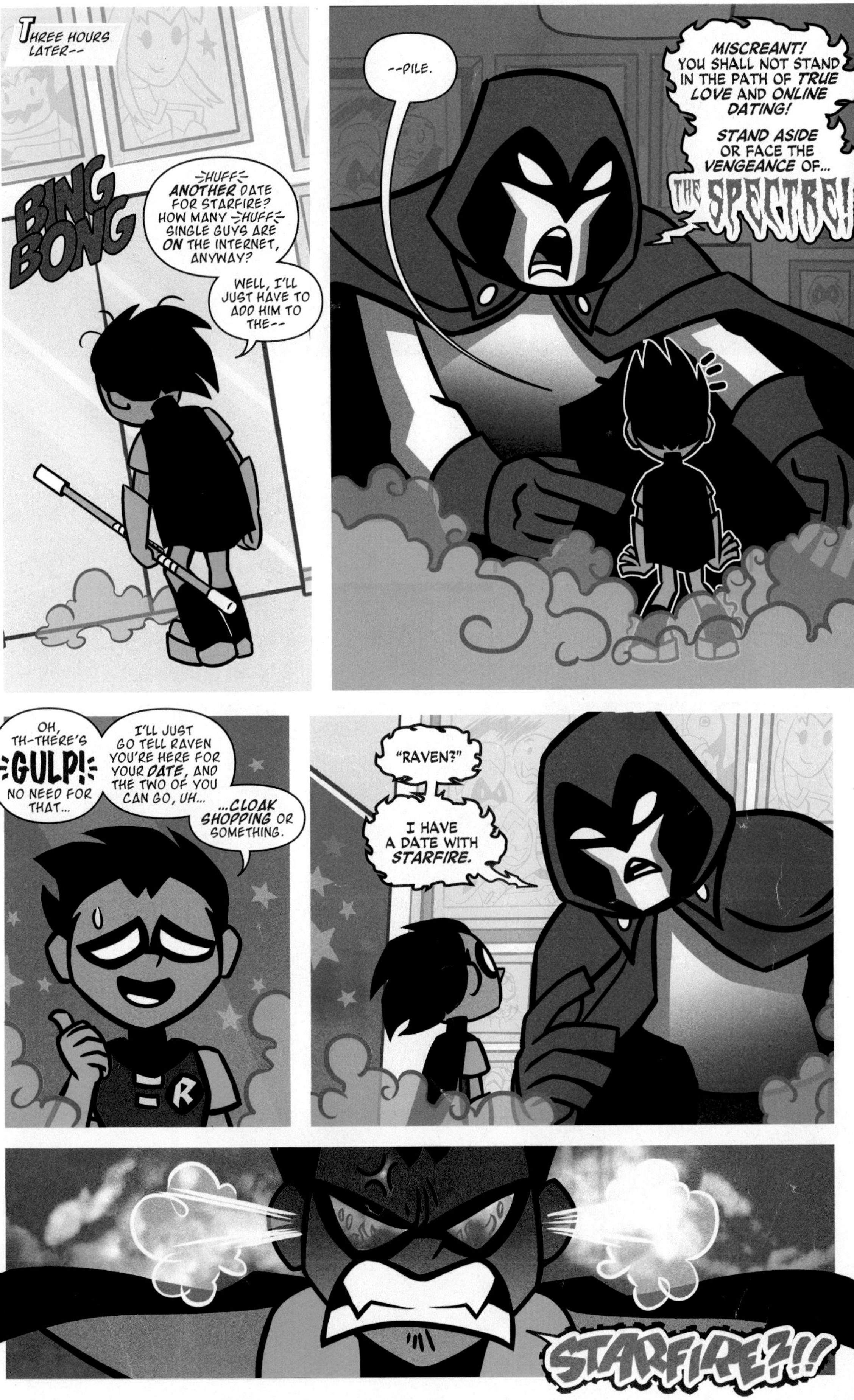
THREE HOURS LATER--
BING BONG
HUFF ANOTHER DATE FOR STARFIRE? HOW MANY HUFF SINGLE GUYS ARE ON THE INTERNET, ANYWAY?
WELL, I'LL JUST HAVE TO ADD HIM TO THE--
--PILE.
MISCREANT! YOU SHALL NOT STAND IN THE PATH OF TRUE LOVE AND ONLINE DATING!
STAND ASIDE OR FACE THE VENGEANCE OF... THE SPECTRE!
OH, TH-THERE'S GULP! NO NEED FOR THAT...
I'LL JUST GO TELL RAVEN YOU'RE HERE FOR YOUR DATE, AND THE TWO OF YOU CAN GO, UH...
...CLOAK SHOPPING OR SOMETHING.
"RAVEN?"
I HAVE A DATE WITH STARFIRE.
STARFIRE?!!

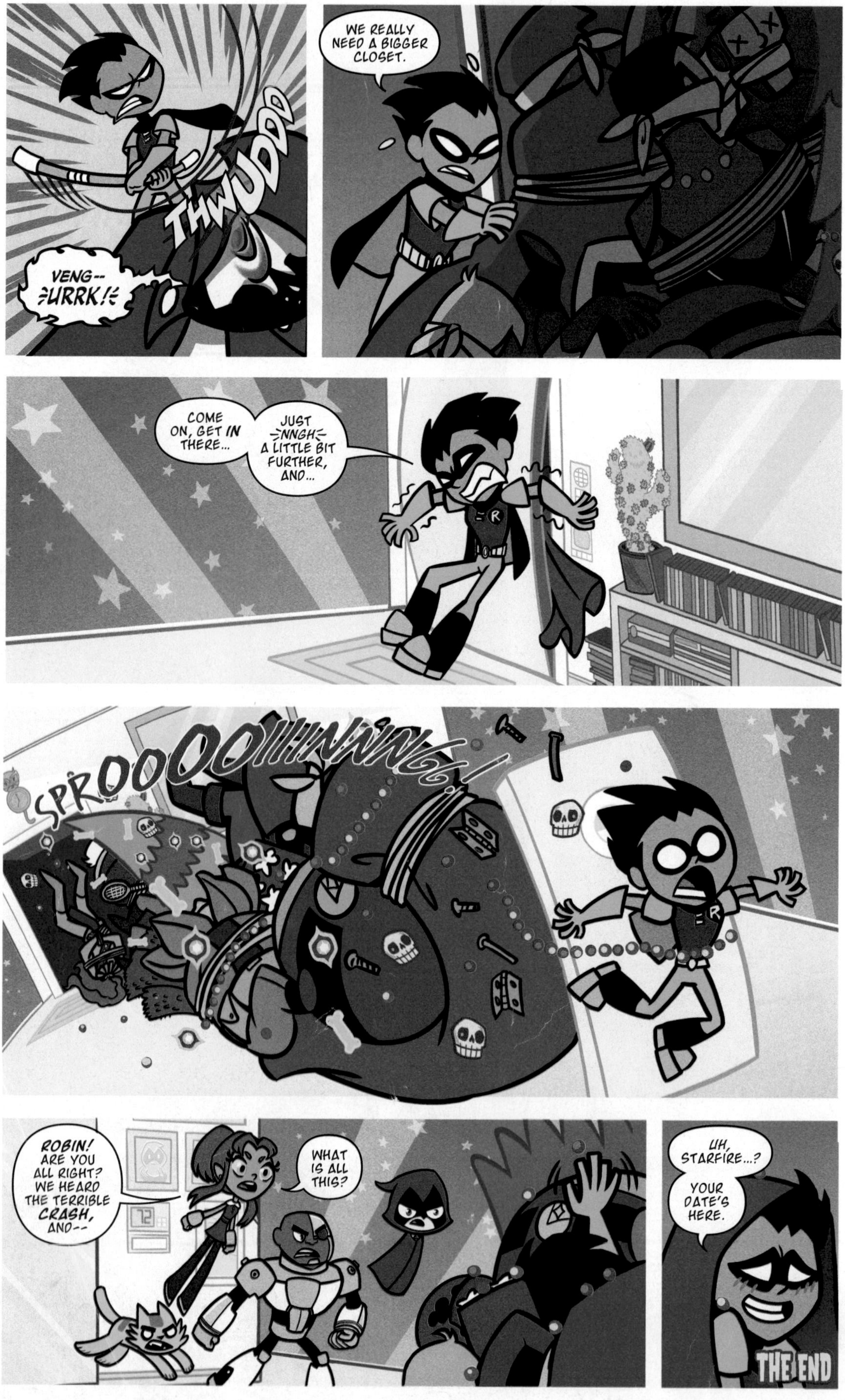
THWUDD
VENG--
URRK!
WE REALLY NEED A BIGGER CLOSET.
COME ON, GET IN THERE...
JUST NNGH A LITTLE BIT FURTHER, AND...
SPROOOOIIIINNNGG!
ROBIN! ARE YOU ALL RIGHT? WE HEARD THE TERRIBLE CRASH, AND--
WHAT IS ALL THIS?
UH, STARFIRE...?
YOUR DATE'S HERE.
THE END

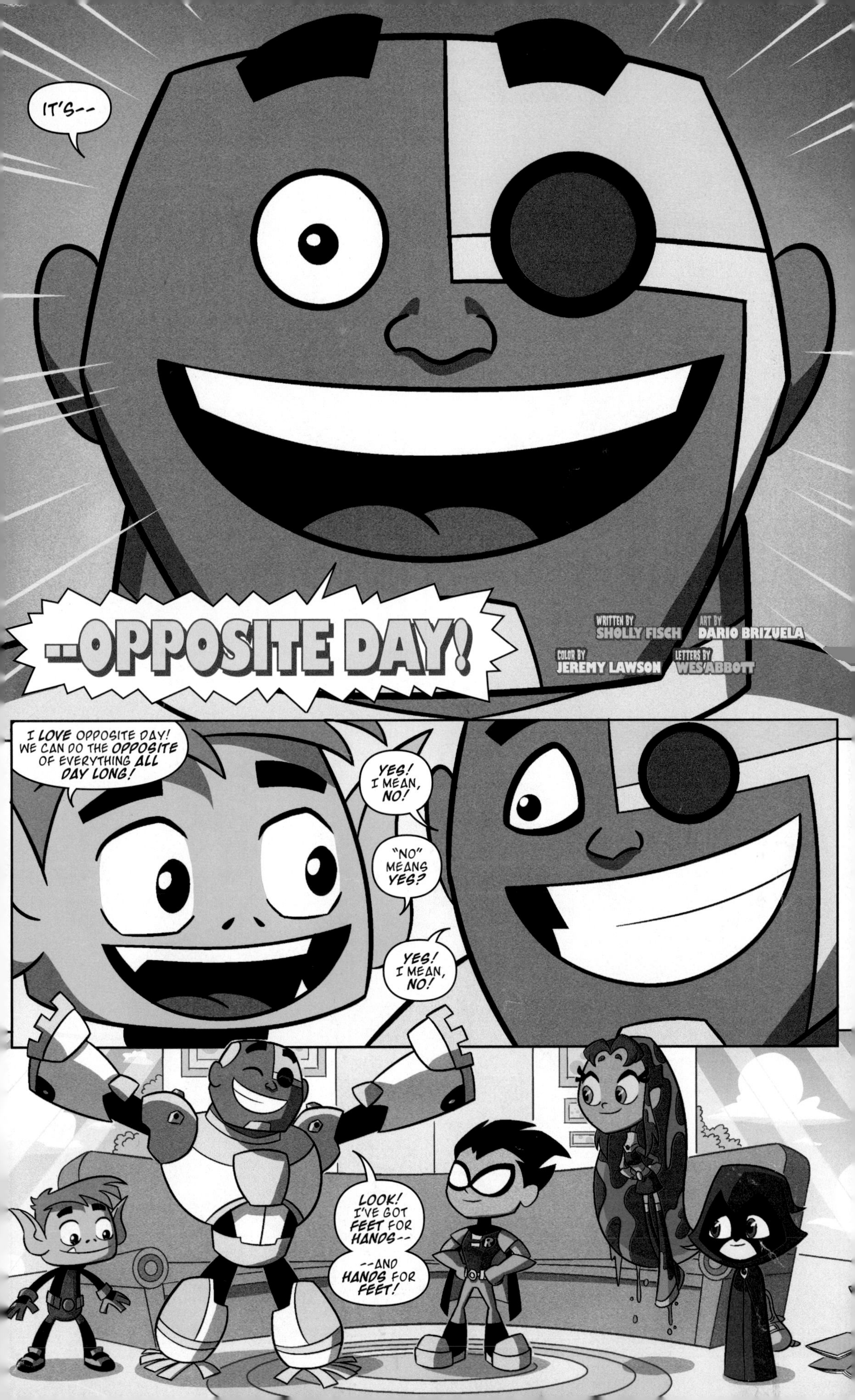
IT'S--
--OPPOSITE DAY!
WRITTEN BY SHOLLY FISCH
ART BY DARIO BRIZUELA
COLOR BY JEREMY LAWSON
LETTERS BY WES ABBOTT
I LOVE OPPOSITE DAY! WE CAN DO THE OPPOSITE OF EVERYTHING ALL DAY LONG!
YES! I MEAN, NO!
"NO" MEANS YES?
YES! I MEAN, NO!
LOOK! I'VE GOT FEET FOR HANDS--
--AND HANDS FOR FEET!

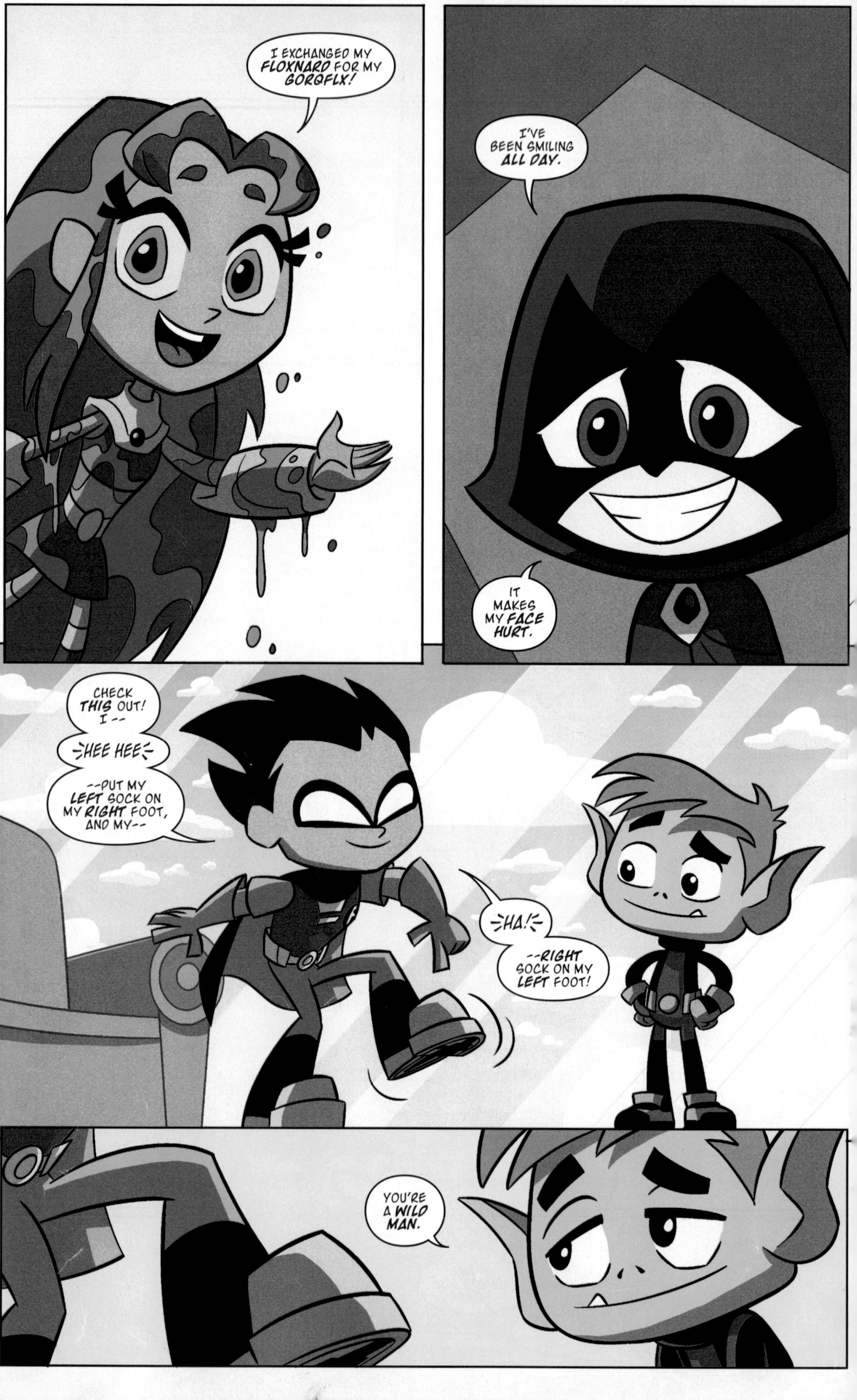
I EXCHANGED MY FLOXNARD FOR MY GORQFLX!
I'VE BEEN SMILING ALL DAY.
IT MAKES MY FACE HURT.
CHECK THIS OUT! I --
HEE HEE
--PUT MY LEFT SOCK ON MY RIGHT FOOT, AND MY--
HA!
--RIGHT SOCK ON MY LEFT FOOT!
YOU'RE A WILD MAN.

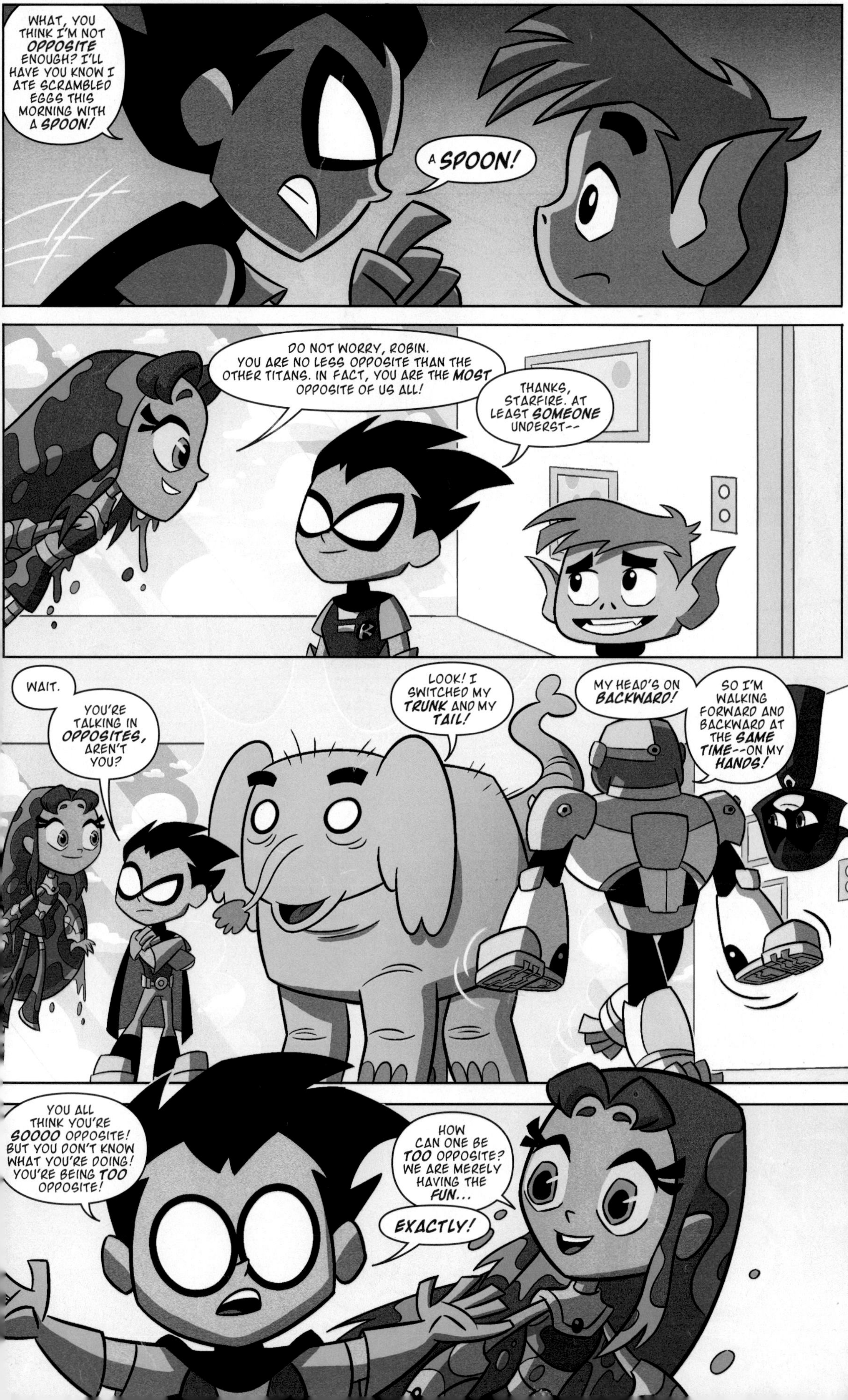
WHAT, YOU THINK I'M NOT OPPOSITE ENOUGH? I'LL HAVE YOU KNOW I ATE SCRAMBLED EGGS THIS MORNING WITH A SPOON!
A SPOON!
DO NOT WORRY, ROBIN. YOU ARE NO LESS OPPOSITE THAN THE OTHER TITANS. IN FACT, YOU ARE THE MOST OPPOSITE OF US ALL!
THANKS, STARFIRE. AT LEAST SOMEONE UNDERST--
WAIT.
YOU'RE TALKING IN OPPOSITES, AREN'T YOU?
LOOK! I SWITCHED MY TRUNK AND MY TAIL!
MY HEAD'S ON BACKWARD!
SO I'M WALKING FORWARD AND BACKWARD AT THE SAME TIME--ON MY HANDS!
YOU ALL THINK YOU'RE SOOOO OPPOSITE! BUT YOU DON'T KNOW WHAT YOU'RE DOING! YOU'RE BEING TOO OPPOSITE!
HOW CAN ONE BE TOO OPPOSITE? WE ARE MERELY HAVING THE FUN...
EXACTLY!

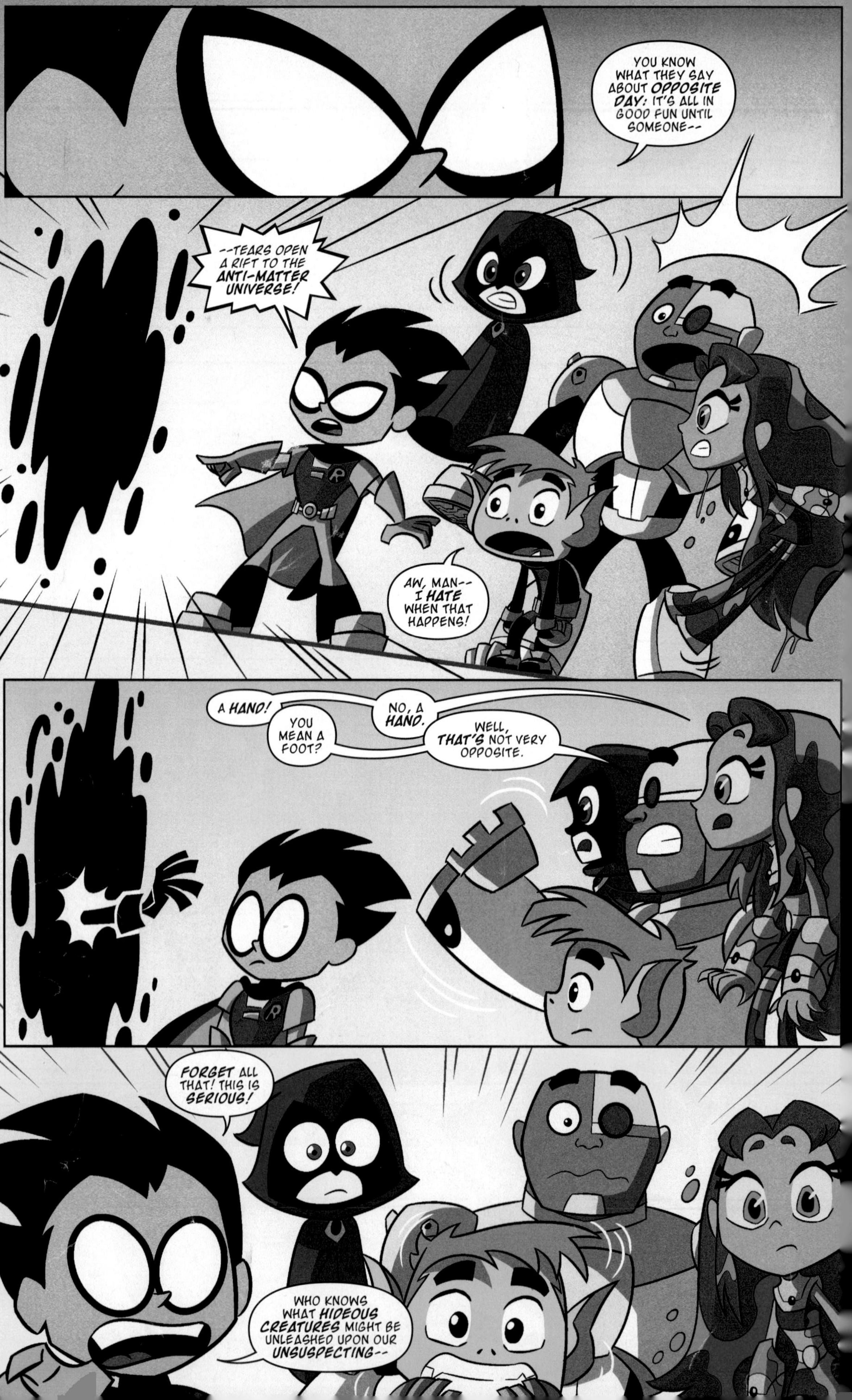
YOU KNOW WHAT THEY SAY ABOUT OPPOSITE DAY: IT'S ALL IN GOOD FUN UNTIL SOMEONE--
--TEARS OPEN A RIFT TO THE ANTI-MATTER UNIVERSE!
AW, MAN-- I HATE WHEN THAT HAPPENS!
A HAND!
YOU MEAN A FOOT?
NO, A HAND.
WELL, THAT'S NOT VERY OPPOSITE.
FORGET ALL THAT! THIS IS SERIOUS!
WHO KNOWS WHAT HIDEOUS CREATURES MIGHT BE UNLEASHED UPON OUR UNSUSPECTING--

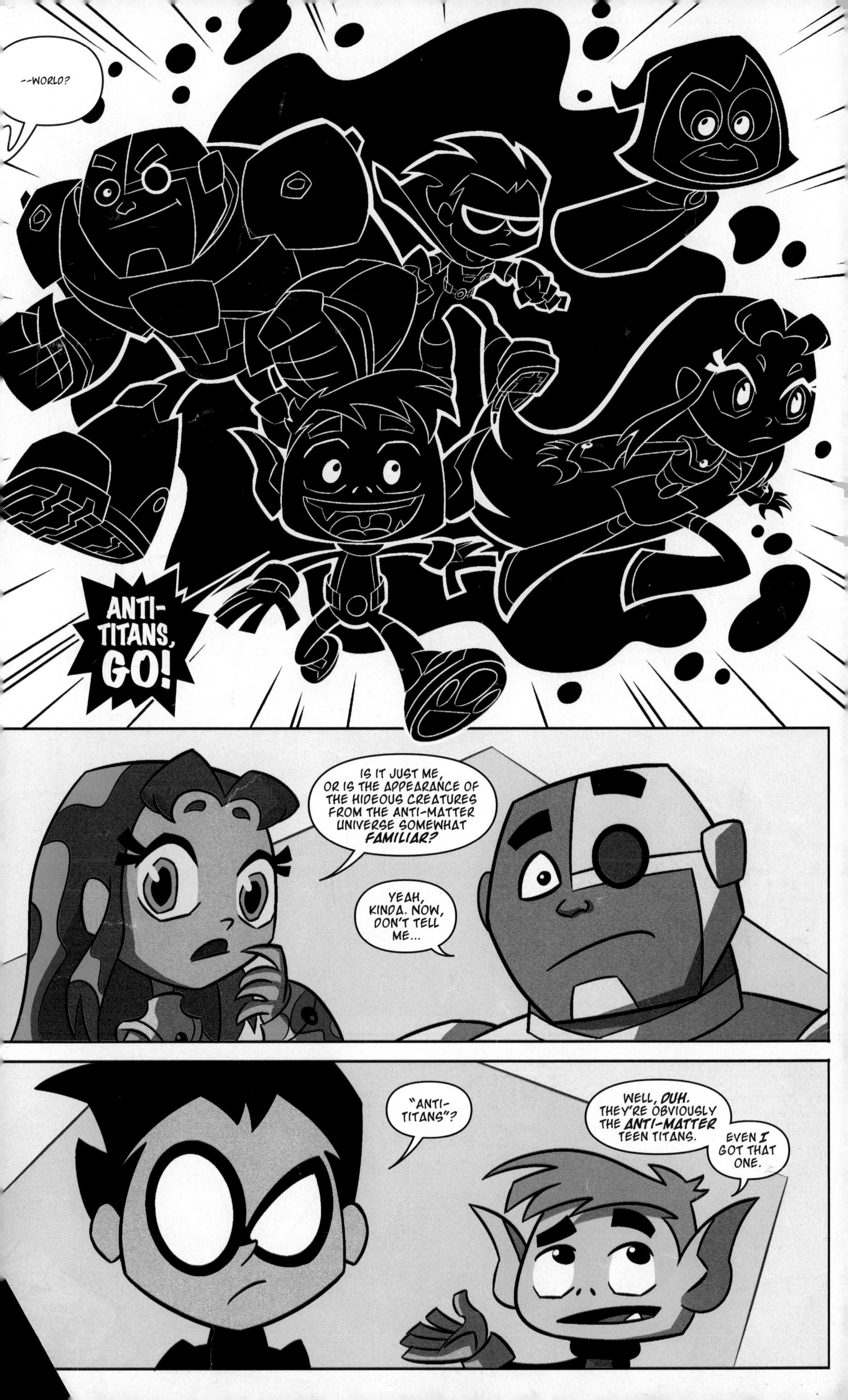
--WORLD?
ANTI-TITANS, GO!
IS IT JUST ME, OR IS THE APPEARANCE OF THE HIDEOUS CREATURES FROM THE ANTI-MATTER UNIVERSE SOMEWHAT FAMILIAR?
YEAH, KINDA. NOW, DON'T TELL ME...
"ANTI-TITANS"?
WELL, DUH. THEY'RE OBVIOUSLY THE ANTI-MATTER TEEN TITANS.
EVEN I GOT THAT ONE.

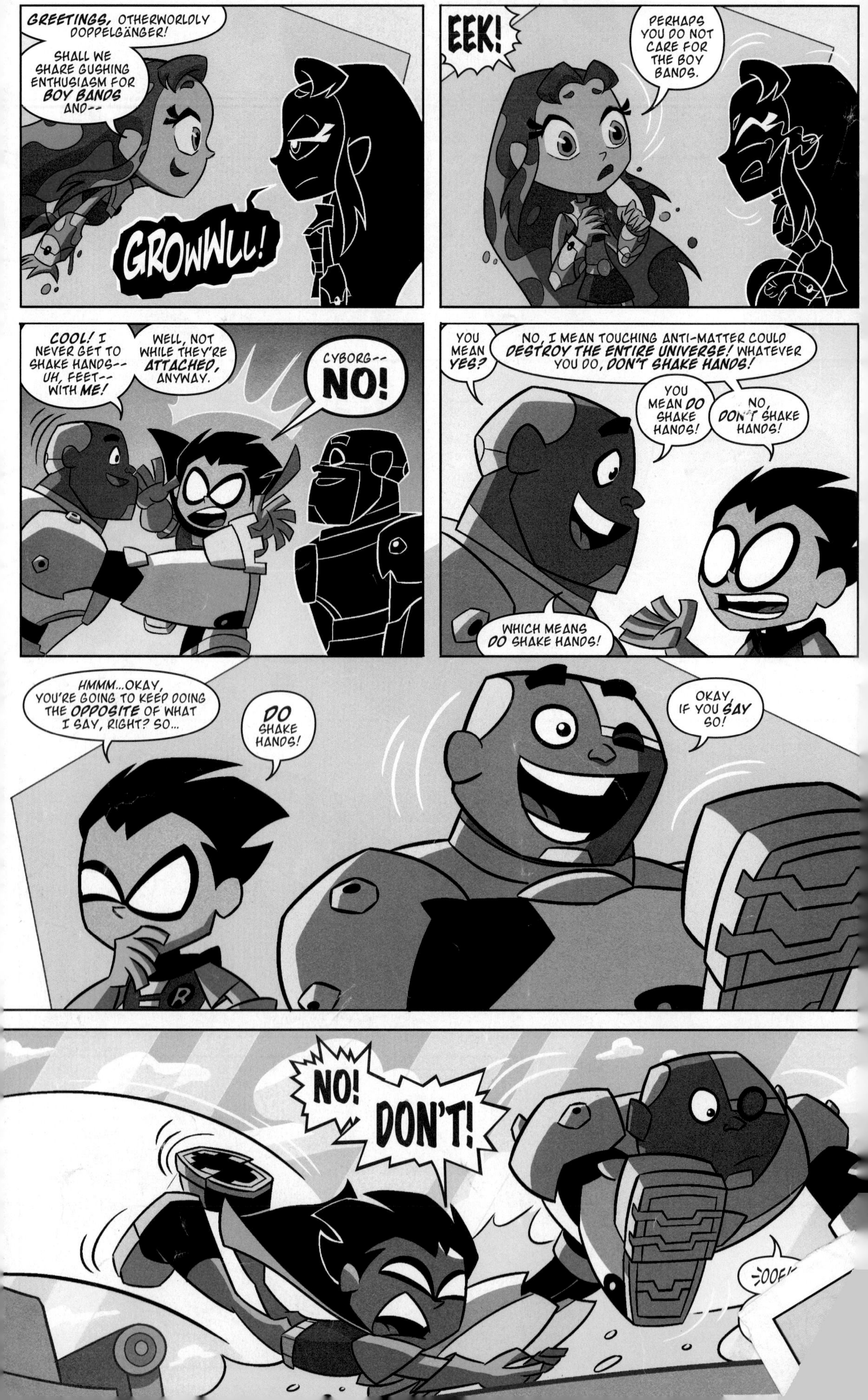
GREETINGS, OTHERWORLDLY DOPPELGÄNGER!
SHALL WE SHARE GUSHING ENTHUSIASM FOR BOY BANDS AND--
GROWLL!
EEK!
PERHAPS YOU DO NOT CARE FOR THE BOY BANDS.
COOL! I NEVER GET TO SHAKE HANDS-- UH, FEET-- WITH ME!
WELL, NOT WHILE THEY'RE ATTACHED, ANYWAY.
CYBORG-- NO!
YOU MEAN YES?
NO, I MEAN TOUCHING ANTI-MATTER COULD DESTROY THE ENTIRE UNIVERSE! WHATEVER YOU DO, DON'T SHAKE HANDS!
YOU MEAN DO SHAKE HANDS!
NO, DON'T SHAKE HANDS!
WHICH MEANS DO SHAKE HANDS!
HMMM...OKAY, YOU'RE GOING TO KEEP DOING THE OPPOSITE OF WHAT I SAY, RIGHT? SO...
DO SHAKE HANDS!
OKAY, IF YOU SAY SO!
NO! DON'T!

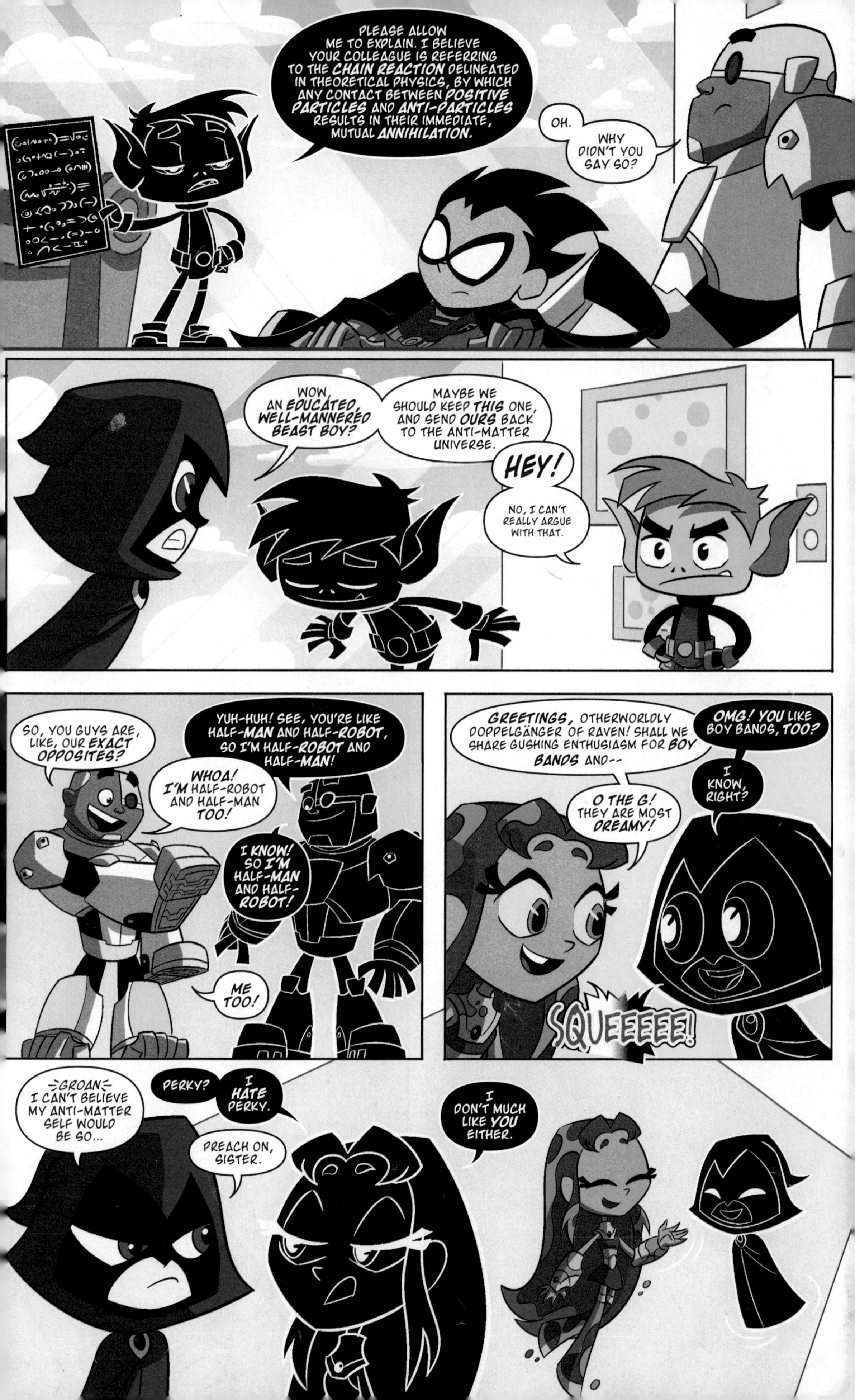
PLEASE ALLOW ME TO EXPLAIN. I BELIEVE YOUR COLLEAGUE IS REFERRING TO THE CHAIN REACTION DELINEATED IN THEORETICAL PHYSICS, BY WHICH ANY CONTACT BETWEEN POSITIVE PARTICLES AND ANTI-PARTICLES RESULTS IN THEIR IMMEDIATE, MUTUAL ANNIHILATION.
OH.
WHY DIDN'T YOU SAY SO?
WOW, AN EDUCATED, WELL-MANNERED BEAST BOY?
MAYBE WE SHOULD KEEP THIS ONE, AND SEND OURS BACK TO THE ANTI-MATTER UNIVERSE.
HEY!
NO, I CAN'T REALLY ARGUE WITH THAT.
SO, YOU GUYS ARE, LIKE, OUR EXACT OPPOSITES?
YUH-HUH! SEE, YOU'RE LIKE HALF-MAN AND HALF-ROBOT, SO I'M HALF-ROBOT AND HALF-MAN!
WHOA! I'M HALF-ROBOT AND HALF-MAN TOO!
I KNOW! SO I'M HALF-MAN AND HALF-ROBOT!
ME TOO!
GREETINGS, OTHERWORLDLY DOPPELGÄNGER OF RAVEN! SHALL WE SHARE GUSHING ENTHUSIASM FOR BOY BANDS AND--
OMG! YOU LIKE BOY BANDS, TOO?
I KNOW, RIGHT?
O THE G! THEY ARE MOST DREAMY!
SQUEEEEEE!
=GROAN= I CAN'T BELIEVE MY ANTI-MATTER SELF WOULD BE SO...
PERKY?
I HATE PERKY.
PREACH ON, SISTER.
I DON'T MUCH LIKE YOU EITHER.

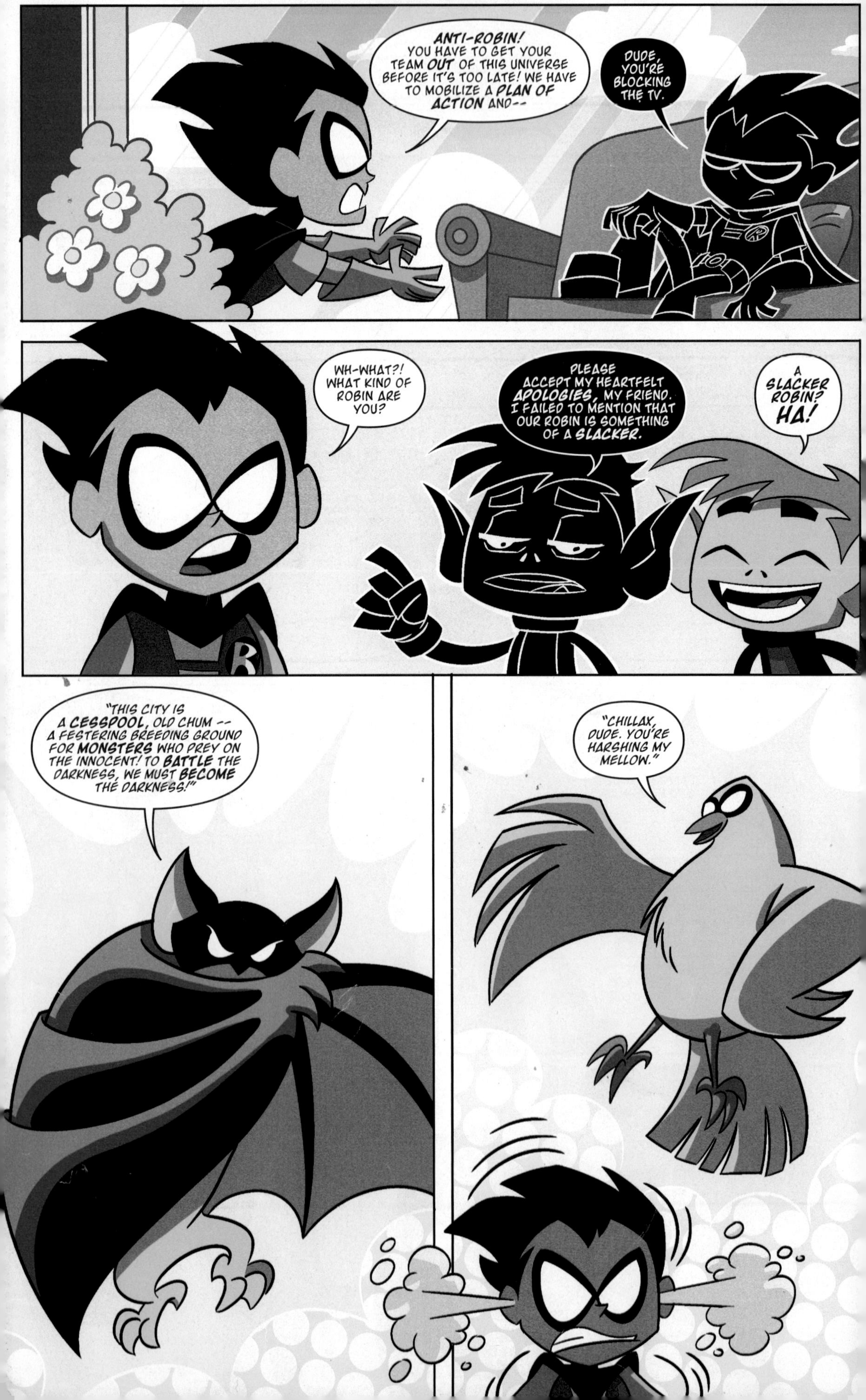
ANTI-ROBIN! YOU HAVE TO GET YOUR TEAM OUT OF THIS UNIVERSE BEFORE IT'S TOO LATE! WE HAVE TO MOBILIZE A PLAN OF ACTION AND--
DUDE, YOU'RE BLOCKING THE TV.
WH-WHAT?! WHAT KIND OF ROBIN ARE YOU?
PLEASE ACCEPT MY HEARTFELT APOLOGIES, MY FRIEND. I FAILED TO MENTION THAT OUR ROBIN IS SOMETHING OF A SLACKER.
A SLACKER ROBIN? HA!
"THIS CITY IS A CESSPOOL, OLD CHUM -- A FESTERING BREEDING GROUND FOR MONSTERS WHO PREY ON THE INNOCENT! TO BATTLE THE DARKNESS, WE MUST BECOME THE DARKNESS!"
"CHILLAX, DUDE. YOU'RE HARSHING MY MELLOW."

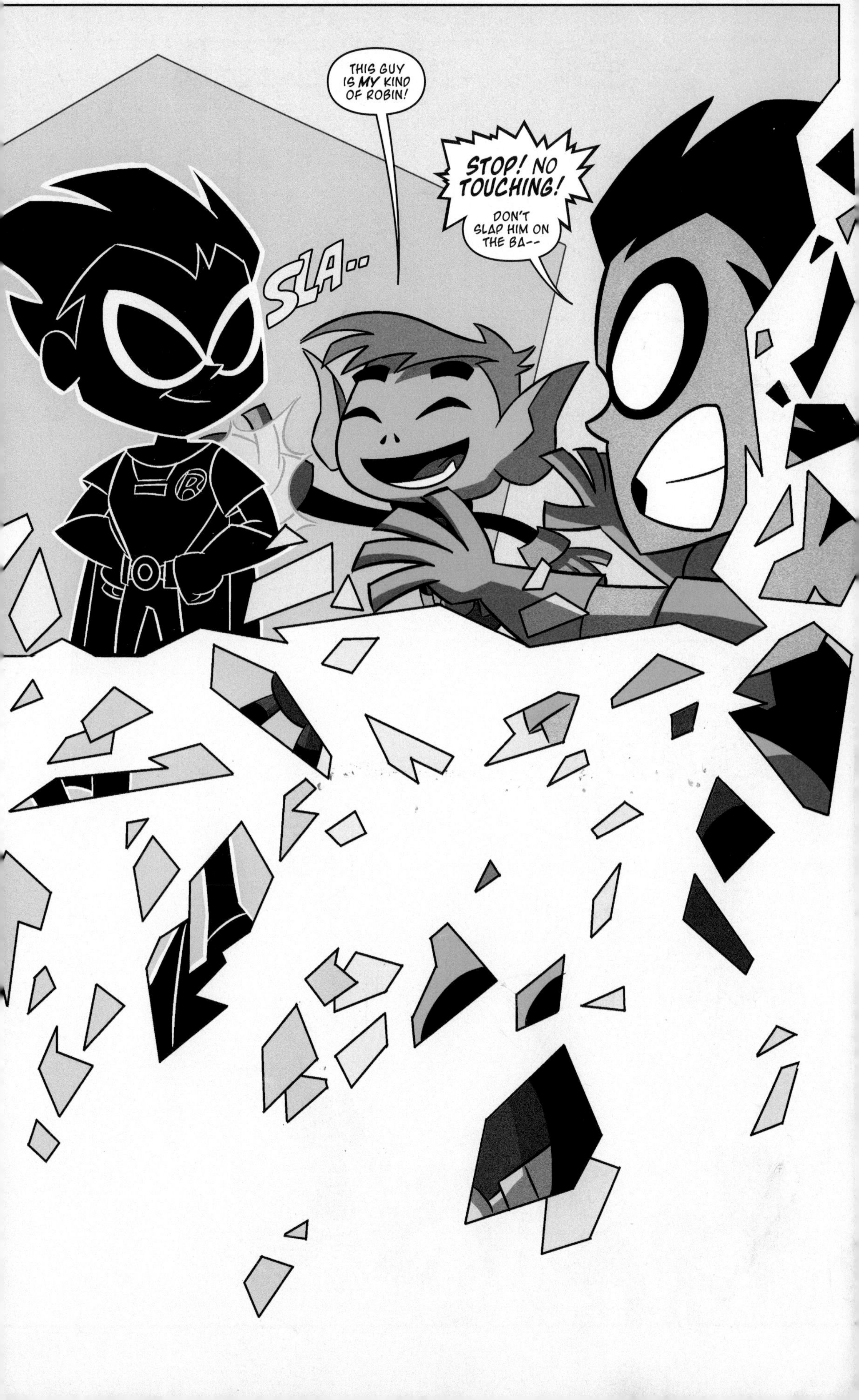
THIS GUY IS MY KIND OF ROBIN!
STOP! NO TOUCHING!
DON'T SLAP HIM ON THE BA--
SLA..

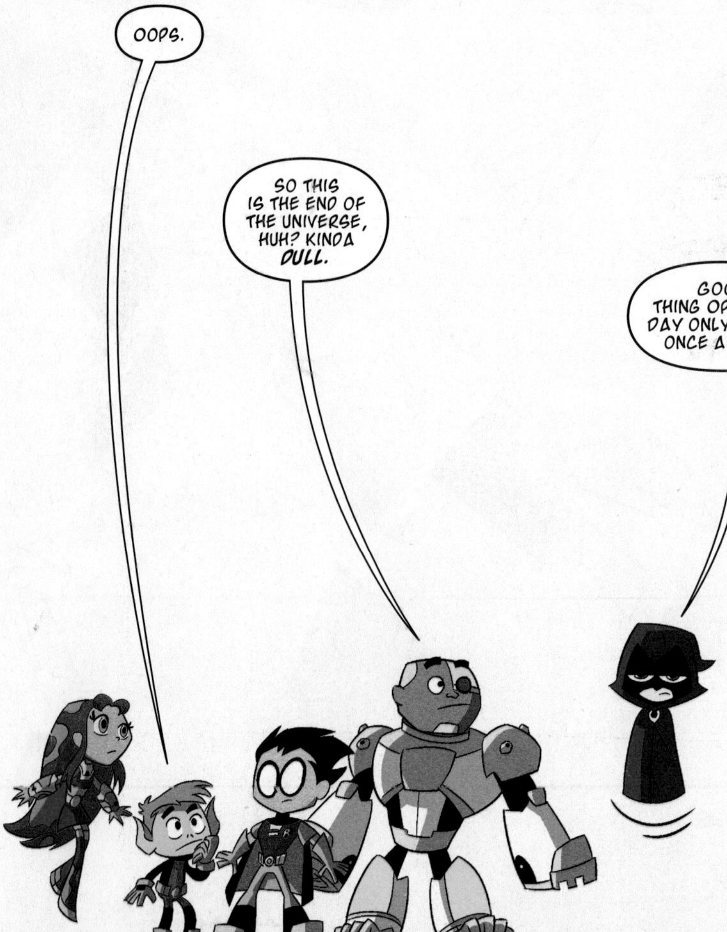
OOPS.
SO THIS IS THE END OF THE UNIVERSE, HUH? KINDA DULL.
GOOD THING OPPOSITE DAY ONLY COMES ONCE A YEAR.

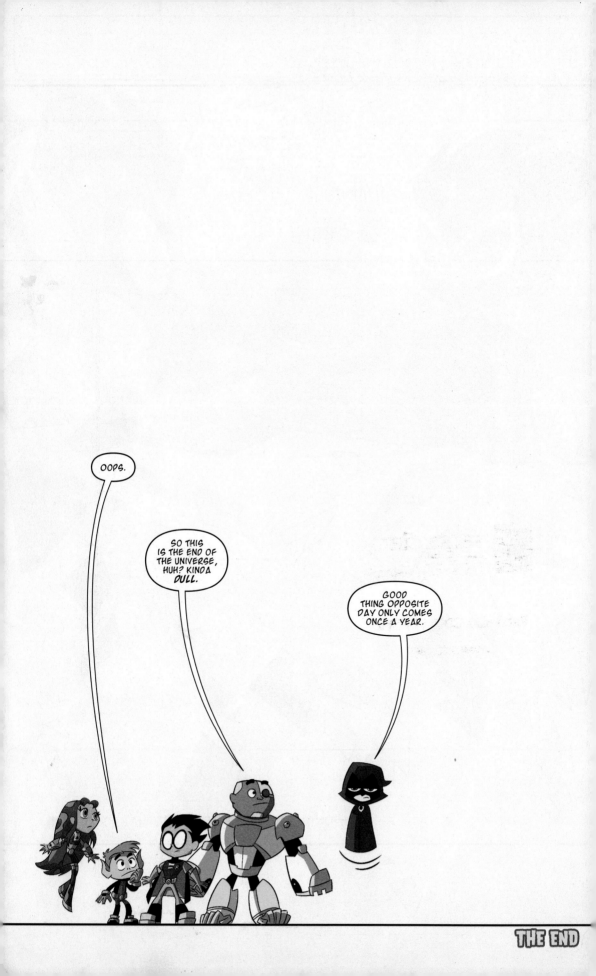

THE END